PUCCINI'S BUTTERFLY

SUE HOWARD

First print edition: Sydney, 2024.
First ebook edition: Sydney, 2024.
Publisher: Sydney School of Arts & Humanities
Paddington NSW 2021 Australia.
www.ssoa.com.au

Puccini's Butterfly
ISBN:
978-0-6487505-4-3- (print book)
978-0-6487505-3-6- (ebook)
Copyright ©Sue Howard, 2024.

Cover design & formatting: Ferdinando Manzo
Typeset Times New Roman
Printed and bound by Lightning Source, 2024.

National Library of Australia Cataloguing-in-Publication data:
Sue Howard, author, 2024.
Puccini's Butterfly /Howard, Sue

ISBN:
978-0-6487505-4-3- (print book)
978-0-6487505-3-6- (ebook)

DEDICATION

For Pier Luigi Braccini, and to the memory of Stefano.

ACKNOWLEDGEMENTS

This novel, wholly the work of the author Sue Howard, now deceased, is being published in acknowledgement of her talent as a writer and her wish for the story to see the light of day. Her first book, a love story titled *Leaning Towards Pisa*, was published by Bantam Random House in 2005.

Thanks go to Sue's daughter, Sam, and son, Matthew, and to her close friends Dee and Andrew Hilton for carrying the publishing project through to completion. Thanks also to Deb Brown and Christine Williams for their editorial assistance.

AUTHOR'S NOTES

The fictional characters in this novel are broadly based on historical figures with some names modified to avoid confusion and/or protect identities.

It is understood that Elvira Gemignani left her husband, Narciso Gemignani, for Puccini in 1886 (when she could no longer hide her pregnancy), taking Fosca with her but leaving her son, Renato, behind. Despite entreaties from Elvira, her husband refused to have their marriage annulled, obliging her to live in a de facto relationship with Puccini for nearly twenty years.

In 1900, Puccini began an affair with a young woman identified recently as Maria Coriasco. Little is known of her full life because all correspondence and references to their liaison are reported to have been destroyed as part of a legal settlement brokered by Giulio Ricordi. It has been suggested, however, that she was a student of jurisprudence at the University of Torino, and that she met Puccini on a train. The affair lasted a number of years and Elvira, who is thought to have known about it as early as 1901, is said to have considered it a serious threat to her relationship with Puccini.

A motorcar accident described in this fictional work is reported as having occurred, although the driver was a village man, believed to be Guido Barsuglia. Elvira's husband was reported to have died the following day from injuries received in a fist fight.

Doria Manfredi is recorded as having gone to work at Puccini's villa in March 1903.

Following the success of Madama Butterfly, Puccini went on to write The Girl of the Golden West (1910), La Rondine (1917), Il Trittico (1918) and Turandot (with its famous Nessun Dorma aria), which he was working on around the time of his death in November 1924, while undergoing treatment for throat cancer in Brussels. Elvira died in 1930 and Antonio in 1946. They, along with Antonio's wife, Rita, are interred in the chapel of Villa Puccini at Torre del Lago.

I am indebted to Angela Carpos, Janet Masini and Sam Howard for their comments, to Lucia Viegi for botanical information, to Paola Foà for sharing her extensive knowledge of social history in Tuscany and to the following print sources:

Julian Budden, Puccini: his life and works. OUP, 2002 Claudio Casini, Giacomo Puccini. Torino: UTET, 1978 De Ranieri & Lubrani, Giacomo Puccini, luoghi e sentimenti. Firenze: Edizioni Polistampa, 2004 Mosco Garner, Puccini. 3rd edn. London: Duckworth, 1992 Howard Greenfeld, Puccini, a biography. London: Robert Hale, 1981 George R Marek, Puccini. London: Cassell & Co. Ltd, 1952 Pagano, ed. Puccini: lettere & rime (1884–1924). Napoli: Tolmino, 1999 Giampaolo Rugarli, La Divina Elvira, Pavia: Almilcare Pizzi, 1998.

Contents

Siamo vittime dei nostri temperamenti …
We are victims of our temperaments …
— *Giacomo Puccini*

Chapter 1
ELVIRA SEEKS OUT HER SON

Our tale begins one still afternoon in the summer of 1900 when the air lies over the Tuscan town of Lucca like a thick blanket, and even the sparrows are hiding under the eaves of the terracotta-tiled roofs to avoid the scorching rays of the sun. The lanes and alleyways are deserted as residents snooze or while away the slow hours until five o'clock. Then their front doors will open, spilling out shopkeepers off to their stores to scoop olives from a barrel or slice thin strips of prosciutto onto brown paper, mothers taking small children in sun bonnets out for a stroll, and elderly ladies, arm in arm, hobbling towards the benches in the cool shade of the lime trees, up on the ramparts of the medieval walls. Deserted, that is, except for a figure standing outside the jewellery shop in Piazza Bernardini, her gloved hands moving nervously between the strap of her bag and the handle of her parasol.

A housemaid busy hanging curtains in the room above the shop glances through the window and sees a tall woman of around forty, statuesque and beautiful, with strong eyebrows, a straight nose and lips that are tinged red – a striking woman. Her ample figure is pulled into shape by a corset overlaid with a rough textured chemise that is well covered by a soft bone-coloured muslin dress. She is wearing a hat with a wide brim that sweeps around her face, hiding most of her hair, which is thick and dark, twisted into a French knot, while her eyes – as black as any gypsy's – have that wistful look of a woman who yearns for her youth when she was innocent, and life was carefree and full of hope. Or perhaps this is just a trick of the light. In any case, from her dress and bearing she is clearly a lady, although the maid, on hearing her name, would surely gasp and drop the curtain stick, or even lose her footing on the stepladder. For although nearly two decades have passed, Elvira Gemignani is still remembered as that disgraceful *mignotta* who scandalised the town by deserting her husband and small son to elope – pregnant, if you please! – with the penniless composer, Giacomo Puccini.

The jeweller has his wares prettily displayed on velvet stands, but Elvira is paying no attention to the filigree earrings, the amethyst brooches and garnet dress rings, the seed-pearl chokers or the fine gold chains that glitter like waterfalls. Instead, she is watching the doorway behind her which is mirrored in the glass, hoping to see Renato, the son she abandoned eleven years before. Today is his eighteenth birthday, and despite the court order that forbids her from seeing him, Elvira is determined to meet him face to face, to speak to him, to touch him, to feel the flesh that she herself created, and which has been so cruelly denied her all these years.

Elvira shifts her thumb under the strap of her handbag. Inside the silk lining is a gift for Renato: a photograph of a chubby four-year-old, dressed in a sailor suit, sitting beside his older sister, Fosca. It was taken the month before she and Fosca left home. Not a week has gone by when Elvira hasn't taken it from the drawer of her dressing table and gazed intently at the chocolate depths of Renato's dark eyes, at the gorgeous thick eyelashes that any woman would be glad to have. Memories from that far-off time squeeze inside Elvira's chest, making her breathless and giddy. She leans against the shop window, pulls a handkerchief from her cuff and holds it to her mouth, breathing in a reviving whiff of eau de cologne. Just then there is a click, a door opens, and a youth appears on the threshold of the house where Elvira spent seven difficult years as the wife of Narciso Gemignani, captive to him and his peevish old mother. The youth is her height, more or less, with slender shoulders and narrow limbs, as if he hasn't quite grown into himself; he has a small moustache trimmed into a rectangle, and her own thick hair, well oiled and combed into place. Whistling to himself, he pulls the door to and ambles down the front steps.

Not wasting a moment, Elvira rushes towards him holding out her arms. 'Renato!' she cries, 'Oh my dear boy!' She knows it is him, for what mother wouldn't recognise her own son?

The young man pauses, his expression slipping from cheerfulness to disbelief. 'Mother! Is that you? What are you doing here?' The words are uttered in a voice that is deep, like his father's, which surprises her. How often has Elvira dreamed of this moment and rehearsed what she will say, imagining folding her son in an embrace so warm it would melt away the years. Now, stung by his tone, all she can do is fumble in her bag and bring out the package. 'I've brought you this ... for your birthday ...'

He barely glances at her outstretched hand. 'Really?' he says, his mouth twisting into a sneer. 'How very thoughtful of you!' Then he turns his back and starts to walk away.

Elvira, though, is too quick for him. Grabbing his arm, she locks it in her grip. 'No ... please, Renato,' she begs, pulling him towards her. 'Listen to me! It's not what you think. I never wanted to leave you. They tricked me ...'

The young man turns his head and fixes her with a stare that makes her shrink back and release her hold. 'How would you know what I think?' he says, angry now. 'Go away and leave me alone! I'm not interested in your lies!'

'Lies? What have they told you? Oh Renato, don't you see, they've poisoned you against me!'

He gives a bitter laugh, a sound that would curdle milk. 'Poisoned me? Why would they bother when you've done such a good job yourself? Or have you forgotten humiliating our family and making us the centre of the most vile gossip?'

'Oh, my dear,' she pleads. 'It wasn't like that at all ...'

He doesn't let her finish. 'More of your lies! They call you Puccini's whore,' he says, loading each word with his hate. 'Did you know that? *Puccini's whore!*'

Elvira reels back. 'Stop it! Stop it! You don't know what you're saying! Your father and I didn't get on. He couldn't have cared less whether I stayed or not. It's your grandmother's doing, all this spite and revenge, the court order against me ...'

She sees him stiffen.

'How dare you speak against Grandma!' he hisses. 'You're unbelievable, you are, coming here and saying such things after all these years. Go away! I never want to see you again!' And with a final glare, he turns and strides over the cobblestones towards the lane that leads to the cathedral. Elvira, unable to move, watches him go and as she stands there a cloud, light as whipped cream, floats above her, casting her into shadow. She takes a breath, but the air seems as thick as glue and cannot pass down her throat. She coughs, and then again. The square has begun to shift, the tall buildings with their shuttered windows trembling as they work loose from their foundations and start to spin around her ...

She grips the handle of her parasol, only for it to slide away from her and clatter to the ground. Clutching the air in a desperate bid to save herself, she lets out a whimper, then with a cry, crumples onto the steps and slides into darkness.

Chapter 2
CORINNA TRAVELS TO THE SEASIDE

That same afternoon, a train is puffing its way through the vine-covered hills between Turin and Genoa, and from there across the plains on the southern edge of the Apuan Alps. These grey-veined mountains with marble innards were hacked out by the Romans to build triumphal arches, temples, impluvia and fountains that played through the mouths of their gods. Midway along the train, in an airless carriage that smells of leather and tobacco, is a slim young woman with pale skin, eyes shaped like almonds and black hair pulled back under a ribbonless bonnet. She is wearing a plain white blouse, a yellow skirt that reaches her ankles and shoes with a sensible Louis heel, an outfit that suggests origins in a middle-class family of modest means, one where the teachings of the church determine the tone of everyday life, and where any hint of flash or show is deemed an offence against common decency. For all that, there is something about this young woman that makes men stop and take a second look. Their gaze is drawn, not so much to the fine-boned delicacy of her frame, but to her unusual eyes, intelligent eyes that gleam with the pent-up energy of someone who wants to live life to the full but cannot. They *are* the determined eyes of a young woman prepared to crack open the carapace of her existence like the shell of a freshly boiled egg.

Corinna, for that is her name, lowers her book, yawns and stretches back into her seat, feeling the damp slither of her camisole against her skin. If only she could take off her bonnet, or better still, tear off all her clothes and throw herself into the icy cool shallows of a lake! The thought brings an amused smile to her lips which instantly fades when she remembers the purpose of her journey, to spend the summer holidays – all of them! – with her spinster great aunt, sitting beside her, and her grandmother waiting at her home, a woman who lives life as one long penance that allows for no fun, no laughter and no joy. *Especially no joy.* Brushing away the fly that has settled on her arm, Corinna watches it spin towards the man sitting opposite her, then buzz off towards the window in a futile attempt to escape his cigarette smoke. Five hours! It has been five interminable hours, with nothing to do but read or watch the countryside slide past, with at least thirty minutes still to go. Now that she is nearly twenty, Corinna cannot believe that as a child she had looked forward to this journey, the black tunnels that snaked mysteriously through the mountains, the villages that clung to the slopes like monkeys on sticks, the blocks of marble scattered at the foot of the quarries containing luminous figures waiting to be chipped free. And then images of the holiday. Sharp-scented pine trees, scorching sand that bit into the soles of her feet, cooling waves, the gelato topped with a fan-shaped wafer, eaten slowly, as if each lick of the spoon would be her last. Now, the thought of two months in the company of her elderly relatives presses on her like a grinding stone.

Sunlight, the colour of lemons, is beaming in through the dusty window, making flickering patterns on Aunt Adelaide's coat, slumped back as she is in her seat like a loosely folded eiderdown. The old lady has nodded off, her bonnet skewed sideways against the antimacassar, her mouth hinged open revealing large yellow teeth. Sounds rumble and gurgle in her throat, and a thread of spittle slides down her chin where it hangs like a caterpillar in search of a leaf. Corinna, fighting back the impulse to laugh, raises her book and tries to read, only to find that the words are swimming about in a film of watery mirth. And so she peeks over the top at the gentleman in the far corner, who is hiding behind a newspaper she recognises as La Stampa from her home town of Turin.

The headline spans the image of an elderly figure in full military regalia, standing stiffly to attention, a man with white hair, a handlebar moustache and the staring eyes of the slightly mad. This is King Umberto, monarch for more than twenty years, who the previous day was assassinated by an anarchist's gun. Not that Corinna approved of the royal personage. Far from it: a puffed-up little man who strutted about like a peacock on a lawn. Her friend Aurelia, who knew about such things, was quite certain that he was dangerous, what with his arch conservative views and pretensions to an empire in Africa! Aurelia, she knew, went even further with her conclusions, but to Corinna's mind, shooting him in cold blood would do nothing to calm the unrest that was already undermining the country's precarious social order.

Her thoughts on the matter exhausted, Corinna turns to gaze through the window, relieved to see that at last they have reached the *pianura*, an expanse of flat, patchwork land shimmering to the horizon. Peasants are working in the fields, the men bent over scythes slicing down hay, the women and children following behind, their brightly coloured headscarves rising and dipping as they gather up the fallen stems and tie them into bundles. Corinna notices the overseer in a baggy tunic, a brown dog at his side, who is watching these shabby workers from the shade of a tree, chewing listlessly on a blade of grass. She spies a house, a two-storey stone dwelling with crumbling steps leading up to a flat roof, its broken windows covered in sackcloth. The house could be deserted if not for the five or six chickens scratching around in the dust and the rag-doll children sitting on the front step, their dark impassive eyes staring at the train.

Corinna shifts her gaze once again, this time to the gentleman sitting opposite her, a distinguished-looking man in his early forties, with a shock of dark wavy hair, a well-trimmed moustache, a broad face and a cleft chiselled into the mid-point of his chin. One hand turns the pages of a slim blue volume as if he were counting banknotes, his attention so rapt that he seems oblivious to both the suffocating heat and the noises coming from Aunt Adelaide's throat. *What is he reading that is so utterly absorbing?* Edging forward, while ensuring her knees do not touch his, Corinna tilts her head, trying to make out the gold lettering on the spine. '*David Belasco.' Is this the author or the title?* She moves a little closer and discovers another word. 'Butterfly.' Perhaps he's a scientist, or a collector, a lepi- … lepido- …

Suddenly the book disappears and Corinna finds herself staring into a pair of eyes as brown and shining as September chestnuts. One eyelid sits a little lower than the other, as if giving her a conspiratorial wink. Then his moustache curls into the beginning of a smile. 'And may I ask what you are reading?' he says, his eyes still fixed on hers.

'What, this?' Corinna's book drops awkwardly into her lap. 'It's a text on administrative law.'

'Really?' He sounds intrigued. 'I didn't know young ladies read such things.'

'They don't,' she says, retrieving her book and placing it by her side. 'Not unless they have examinations to sit.'

'Ah,' he says, 'so you're at the university.' Then, glancing at Aunt Adelaide, 'And you are travelling with …?'

Corinna's gaze follows his to where her great aunt is still dozing, her lips quivering, her hand clutching the silver cross on the chain round her neck like a nun in a religious trance. 'That's my grandmother's sister,' she whispers, wondering if he can hear the shame in her voice. 'I'm staying with her and Grandma until the new term begins.'

'Really?' he says. 'What fun!'

Fun? Is he mocking me? 'I suppose it is,' she counters drily, 'if you care for embroidery and watching old ladies nod off in their armchairs.'

He glances once again at the slumbering form. 'I can't think of anything more entertaining!'

This time there is no doubt. A giggle slips out, which Corinna stifles with her hand, but not before the newspaper in the corner lowers a few inches and rustles in protest. 'Ooh,' she mouths, 'naughty me!'

Smiling to himself, the man reaches up to his breast pocket and touches his handkerchief. Several long seconds later, he leans forward. He smells spicy and male, his breath edged with tobacco. 'Look,' he says quietly, 'if the tedium becomes unbearable, drop me a line.'

As if by magic a calling card has appeared, which he slips expertly into her hand. 'We could go for a stroll or an *aperitivo* …'

Corinna slides the card between the pages of her book without looking at it. She knows it is dangerous. A whistle from the engine pierces the air, announcing that they are approaching their destination of Pisa.

'Wake up, Aunt!' Corinna says, shaking the old lady's arm. 'We're nearly there!'

Aunt Adelaide gives a start then sits bolt upright and looks around, blinking like an owl. 'Goodness me,' she says, 'I must have dozed off.' Adjusting her bonnet, she reaches into her large black handbag and starts rummaging around, pushing aside a comb, a pillbox and a magazine, the sort read by women with too much time on their hands. 'Here you are, dear,' she says, pulling out a small tin. 'Have one of these …'

Corinna takes a violet pastille and pops it into her mouth, then nods in the direction of the man.

'Perhaps, Aunt …?' she says.

Aunt Adelaide turns her head towards him and blinks again. 'But of course! I'm so sorry! Would you care for one?' she says, holding out the tin.

Half-rising, he picks out a pastille with his thumb and forefinger and holds it up like a jewel. 'Thank you so much,' he says. At that moment there is a screech, then a jolt, as the train lurches to a halt, and the man, caught off-guard, topples towards Corinna, saving himself by landing his hands on the panel above her head.

'Oh!' she cries, as his pastille drops onto the floor and she is left staring at his diamond tiepin.

Stepping back, he straightens his jacket and gives an exaggerated bow. 'My apologies, Signorina,' he says.

Corinna nods politely, the sparkle of his tiepin still playing in her eyes. Aunt Adelaide, meanwhile, is regarding him with more attention. 'Is it possible,' she ventures, 'that we have met before?'

The corners of his mouth ease into the faintest of grins. 'I don't believe I have had the pleasure.' Corinna looks away.

'Then I must be mistaken,' Aunt Adelaide says. 'At my age, one doesn't always remember.' The compartment door is opened, the ladies step down and there, pushing her way to the front, is

Corinna's grandmother, and with her a sheepish-looking porter in a bottle-green peak cap. Although well into her seventies, Grandma's bearing is straight and purposeful, suggesting the unassailable determination of a widow obliged to raise a child without the protection of a husband, a situation she never allowed to get the better of her. She has a thin face with well-defined features, yet in the high forehead framed by wiry grey hair, and eyes the colour of pond water, one can see that she and Adelaide are cut from the same cloth. Today she is wearing a light summer coat, a faded green garment entirely lacking any notion of fashion or style, its collar adorned with the green garnet broach given to her by her late husband, an army captain who died fighting the Austrian invaders before Corinna was born. Glancing round to see if the man on the train has witnessed this further humiliation, Corinna is relieved to see him, or rather the back of him, striding towards the exit.

'My dear, isn't this heat dreadful?' Grandma says, seizing Corinna by the shoulders and casting a quick glance over her. 'Isn't it dreadful? I don't recall it ever being so bad.'

The porter, as if to emphasise the point, lifts his cap and sweeps the back of his hand across his brow, sending drops of sweat to the ground.

Grandma frowns and turns to her sister. 'Good journey, Adelaide?' And not bothering about the reply, she swings around and sets off towards the luggage van at the rear of the train. 'Hurry up!' she calls out to the porter. 'Our taxi-carriage is waiting outside!' The cases are piled onto the porter's trolley and as the small party makes its way back along the platform, Corinna notices a young woman, about her own age, who is laughing happily as she strolls along on the arm of a curly-haired man. It is not the tinkling mirth though that has caught her attention, but rather the object in the young woman's hand, a parasol, furled up like baby's fingers, with a shiny white handle and a ruffle in a delicate shade of pink; a parasol that speaks of elegance and sophistication, of fine restaurants and balls, cruise liners and exotic travel … In summary, of all the bountiful gifts that life has granted to others, but not herself.

'Did you not hear what I said, dear?' Grandma asks sharply, for she does not care to be ignored.

'I'm sorry …?'

'I asked if that was Maestro Puccini getting off the train with you.'

Corinna's throat tightens in an involuntary spasm. 'Maestro Puccini?' she gasps. 'Getting off the train?'

'I hope you're not going to repeat everything I say, dear!'

'Puccini?' Aunt Adelaide cuts in. 'Really? Was that him?'

'Don't you start, Adelaide! And I can't believe you didn't recognise him, as his photograph has been in all the newspapers!'

Aunt Adelaide draws a defensive breath. 'You know perfectly well, Lavinia, that I pay scant attention to such things.'

'That,' Grandma says with a sniff, 'is because you are too busy reading those dreadful magazines of yours.'

'They are *not* dreadful.'

'That, my dear, is a matter of opinion …' *Puccini!* Knowing that her grandmother and great aunt will scrap like two small dogs until the very last word, Corinna lets her mind drift back to a freezing February evening some three years before, when she and her father (but not Mamma, who was going through one of her bad spells) were sitting in the gallery of the Teatro Regio, waiting for the lights to dim. Beneath them, in the boxes, men in dinner jackets chatted and smoked cigars while ladies cooled themselves with fans made of spangled silk or ostrich feathers, and discreetly searched out friends and public figures through their opera glasses. *La Bohème*. She remembers every second of Mimi's dying aria and Rodolfo's helpless grief, yet she only has the vaguest recollection of the man who received a standing ovation from the royal box, the very man whose card, she realises with a start, is pressed between the pages of her book.

'Does he live near here?' she asks, the words coming out too quickly.

'Who, dear? Oh, you mean Puccini. Yes, over at Lake Massaciuccoli. He has a villa there. Well, of course it's for him and his wife …'

'Only she isn't his wife, is she?' Aunt adds knowingly.

'Shh! Adelaide! *Pas devant les enfants*!'

Corinna looks from one to the other, since she can speak French, but understands the subject is closed.

Grandma, seeing the porter disappear through an archway, quickens her pace. 'Come along!' she says. 'He won't know which taxi-carriage is ours.'

The cases have been tied down, the porter tipped, and the ladies have settled into their seats. The cab driver raises his whip and *whoosh*, they are off, clip-clopping away from the kerb towards the fountain in the middle of the concourse, and around to the junction with Via Vittorio Emanuele, where a gleaming black motorcar pulls up beside them. Glancing across, Corinna sees a chauffeur, and next to him a familiar figure in a bowler hat who smiles as he tilts the brim in her direction. She smiles back, and he responds with a modest ironic bow, a gesture that sets off a flash near his throat, a moment of gold, then coruscating beams of diamond light that dazzle her eyes as they catch the shimmering rays of the afternoon sun.

Chapter 3
ELVIRA WAITS FOR IDA
IN THE DRAWING ROOM

The weeks leading up to Ferragosto are some of the busiest in the year, none more so than in Villa Puccini. The rooms must be aired and dusted, the floors swept and mopped, the rugs taken out into the garden and beaten with a wooden paddle, and the brass polished to a flawless shine. When that has been done, the crystal will be washed and buffed, the embroidered tablecloth and napkins lightly starched, sprinkled with rosewater, and pressed. After that, the *alzata*, a silver cake stand, will be decorated with unblemished peaches and plums, succulent white grapes, crystallised figs, dates, almonds and hazelnuts. Then, and only then, will the preparations for the five-course lunch be set in motion.

Usually for Elvira this is a joyful time, for she loves nothing better than bustling about the house ensuring that everything is in good order and seeing to the meal she has so carefully planned. This year, though, is an exception. Since her encounter with Renato a week ago, she has been suffering from a headache that grips her skull like the jaws of a vice. Now that breakfast is over, she would prefer to be lying down in a darkened room, a pack of orange leaves pressed to her brow, rather than waiting in the drawing room for her sister, Ida, to join her. But wait she must, for there is no one else that she dare confide in, and if she doesn't tell someone about that hateful meeting with her son, her head will surely split open. A ray of sunlight beams through the crystal-clear window into Elvira's eyes, slicing through her brain like a taut wire. Gripping the arm of her chair, she closes her eyes and waits for the moment to pass, then pulls a handkerchief from her pocket and breathes in eau de cologne.

Outside in the garden, beyond the vase of orange lilies on the windowsill, Elvira's daughter, Fosca, is crouched down, whispering to her younger cousins, Clara and Gastone. Watching this scene, Elvira manages a smile, thinking how lovely it is for Fosca, now nearly twenty-two, still with the dishevelled carefree look she had as a girl, delighting in the spontaneity of the children's company. But for how long? On a trip to Milan last winter, Fosca's head was turned by a young tenor, Salvatore Leonardi, and the pair of them have been writing to each other ever since, long letters, full of confidences that even a daughter as close as Fosca will not share. *It won't be long before she's married and leaving home for good.* Elvira's thoughts elicit a pain, an ache of sadness. And in her sadness her thoughts turn to her son – not Antonio, but Renato, the brother Antonio has never met.

When she arrived home from that recent terrible confrontation, Elvira went straight up to her room, tore the wrapping paper from the photograph and stared at it, trying to reconcile the docile toddler in the sailor suit with the scornful young man she had just met. And all the while she asked herself, *Who has done this? Who turned my affectionate child into a hateful youth?* But she already knew the answer. His grandmother, that's who! Old Ma Gemignani, who could stop a clock just by looking at it. The woman was a crab, a hard-shelled, vicious old crustacean, with claws that nipped and pinched when you least expected it.

It has been Elvira's custom since childhood to liken people to animals, a habit that began when darling old *Tata* Giulia was replaced by a younger nanny, one who didn't laugh out loud, go red in the face or sip smelly drink from a flask in her handbag. The new nanny was a large woman with slow-moving haunches that waddled from side to side as she walked, reminding Elvira of the hippopotamus in her story book. Then her younger sister Ida, with her quick little steps and love of ribbons and frippery, became a poodle. Her father seemed like an elephant, solid and dependable (until his business failed and he fled to Argentina, leaving them destitute), and her mother a canary, singing all the time but too terrified to leave her cage. Thoughts of her mother make Elvira glance up at the mantelpiece, where a woman with a heart-shaped face and a widow's peak looks timidly back at her from an ornate oval frame. The poor woman died shortly before Antonio was born, from a tumour that swelled up inside her like a marrow. Wicked tongues that revelled in causing misery to others claimed that the scandal of Elvira's elopement had contributed to her mother's death. It was nonsense, of course. Mamma had been ill for months before she even met Giacomo – although it was true, Elvira remembers with a guilty shiver, that her mother had fretted most terribly about Renato.

'Elvira, there is not a court in the land that will take a boy away from his father. If you leave without him, you may never see him again, not with Narciso and his mother lined up against you.' Elvira hadn't believed her but, in any case, by then it was too late. Already pregnant, she knew she would have enough on her hands caring for Fosca and the new baby, let alone a toddler. So she had bargained with Narciso that she would say nothing about his affairs or his lack of interest in her if he let her go quietly. Surprisingly he agreed, and even acceded to her request that Renato should spend the summer holidays with her once the divorce was settled. She should have known better than to trust him, should have suspected the hand of old Ma Gemignani at work behind the scenes, but so blinded was she by her love for Giacomo, she was prepared to think the best of everyone, even Narciso and his spiteful old mother.   Back then, the true nature of Elvira's situation came to light a few weeks later, when she consulted a lawyer, Avvocato Bertoli, in his cluttered office overlooking the Arno River in Pisa.

'Free yourself from your husband? But my dear Signora, the law allows for no divorce whatsoever, and only grants annulments in certain cases of adultery committed by a woman. The law, I should make clear, does not recognise adultery committed by a man ...'

Bertoli, a man with small eyes and sunburnt leathery skin, had stroked his chin as he uttered this pronouncement, which swirled around the vaulted ceiling and came back to assault her a second time.

'You mean to say that my husband can refuse me as his wife while courting women all over town, and yet I have no recourse against him?'

'Regrettable though it is, Signora, yes, that is indeed the case.' The words, delivered with an infuriating half-smile, were intoned in a voice so bland and insincere she understood instantly that Bertoli was not in the least opposed to a system which allowed men, as the old saying goes, to have their wives tipsy and their wine casks full. A *weathered fox, Avvocato Bertoli, duplicitous, mean-eyed.*

She is brought back to the present by a scuffling sound from outside, where Gastone, an impish smile on his face, is diving down behind a red hibiscus bush in a bid to hide from his sister. Deciding to join in, Elvira goes over and raps on the glass. 'Hey, Gastone!' she calls. 'I can see you, you know!'

An answer comes in the form of a shriek, not from the garden but from the kitchen, a high-pitched shriek followed by shouting and the smashing of plates. *Oh no! Cook and Maria are at it again!* Hurrying into the hall, Elvira sees Maria, the maid, disappear through the back door at the end of the corridor, her well-rounded silhouette outlined by a shaft of light before vanishing into the garden.

'Good riddance!' Cook yells after her in that rough country voice of hers. 'And if you set foot in my kitchen again, I'll slice off your ears with this carving knife. Believe it, I will!'

'*Her* kitchen?' Elvira's stomach gives an outraged flip-flip: 'The cheek of it!' Pulling herself up to her full height, she is about to march into the kitchen and remonstrate with her adversary when the front doorbell chimes. It is Mingo, the stick insect of a postman, and he is holding out a bundle of mail. 'Hot day,' he says, not moving his lips.

'Indeed it is!' Elvira replies, distracted.

Closing the door, she heads back to the kitchen, barely pausing to drop the letters on the hall table as she passes. It was Elvira's suspicious custom to sort through Puccini's letters. In this instance she would have found a green envelope giving off a faint trace of perfume, its woven surface inscribed with the large, curved letters of youth and desire. This she would have steamed open and read, her eyes narrowing into furious slits, before screwing it up and flinging it into the boiler, to curl and char at the edges before bursting into flames.

Chapter 4
THE MAESTRO STRUGGLES WITH HIS NEW OPERA

While Elvira is in the kitchen sorting out the latest outburst between Cook and Maria, Puccini is buried away in his studio, a slim blue volume open in front of him on his score table, his brow creased into furrows of frustration. It is over a week since he read *Madama Butterfly* on the train, and since then he hasn't stopped thinking about her, his butterfly. Her smile follows him through the day, and at night she comes to him in a perfumed gown, whispering that she is waiting for him. *Madonna!* He picks up a pencil and jabs it into his thumb. The point is blunt. He starts rummaging among the notebooks, articles, sheets of music and jottings that litter the surface of his table. *Where is it?* He moves the lamp, and then the clock. *Ha! Here it is*. He cups his hand over the missing sharpener as if it were a spider. 'Got you!' he says out loud, inserting the pencil and giving it a few sharp twists.

Behind him, the sun is streaming in through the open French windows, pouring liquid gold onto the marble-chip floor. And with it comes the sound of shrieking children, reminding him that at breakfast Fosca, his stepdaughter, promised to play hide-and-seek with her young cousins. Rising, he goes over to the windows, steps outside under the awning and peers around, expecting to see Clara or Gastone tucked behind a bush or tree, with Fosca creeping along the path in pursuit of them. But there is no sign of the children or Fosca, just the creaking of the iron gate as it slowly swings shut. Imagining that they have gone down to the jetty or are scrambling over the rocks to the boats tied up in the shallows, he wanders down to the railings and looks about, but the only sounds that reach him are the *churr* of the cicadas and the croaking of numerous invisible frogs.

That's a relief! Shading his eyes, Puccini looks towards the purple-green mountains, the sunlit peaks and the slopes dropping down to the lake in folds, like a woman's skirt. The water sparkles as it laps gently at the shoreline, and further around, a lone heron stands on a pole jutting out from the reeds. Wild ducks, coots, grebes, reedwarblers, godwits, teal and moorhens are there too, concealed in the dense undergrowth.

'Hey!' he calls to a bird with a long proud neck. 'Tell your friends I'll be after them as soon as the hunting season begins!' Turning, he crunches back along the path, allowing himself a moment's pride as he surveys the garden that is all his own design. No green lawns or luscious flower beds like the parks of London for him, but spiky native plants and palm trees from the south. His one concession, a rose bush bearing the scented buds he likes to tuck into his buttonhole on special occasions. And behind the house, out of view, a kitchen garden where Poldo, the gardener, grows vegetables and herbs. It had been slow work reclaiming the swampy land where the old medieval tower stood, but worth every lira. Stepping back inside, Puccini pauses to let his eyes adjust to the softer light, and in those few defenceless seconds he sees her again, kneeling in front of the fireplace gazing up at the triptych, her hair falling onto her shoulders, her hands clasped modestly in her lap. Words flood into his brain but nothing comes out, and it is she who opens her mouth as if to speak. And then she is gone.

'Madonna!' he cries out. Stumbling to the table that holds his score, he grasps a silver box, banging it into the ashtray as he pulls out a cigarette, lights it, draws the smoke deep into his lungs and counts to five before blowing it out towards the ceiling.

Enough! He can wait no longer. Jamming the cigarette between his teeth, he sits down at the piano and lets his hands hover above the keyboard as if they, not he, are deciding what to play. When they do drop down, a light, playful refrain fills the room – then stops. Swivelling back to the table, Puccini begins sifting through sheets of music, now yellowed by time. He soon discovers they're not in the order he left them. *Damn Elvira! She's been going through my things again!* He leans back and lets out a sigh, thinking about Elvira acting oddly over the past few days, ever since she went off to buy gifts for the children. She'd come back empty-handed and spent the rest of the day shut away in her room with a headache. *And now she's been sneaking through my papers, looking for what? Billets-doux, receipts for jewellery or flowers ... evidence that I'm a real man? As if I'd be so careless!* Grinding his cigarette into the ashtray, Puccini rifles through the music sheets until he finds what he is looking for. It is a flimsy document dated 1885, entitled *The Mikado*. He lifts it delicately by the corners and places it carefully on the music rack. The notes that emanate from the gleaming black piano this time are not tuneless exactly, but peculiar, like the call of a large exotic bird. He plays them several times, his face set in an expression of anxious concentration, as if trying to draw something from the strange sounds.

'Giacomo!' a voice sings out. 'It's ten o'clock. Time for your coffee!'

His fingers slam into the keys. 'Christ, Elvira,' he snaps, swinging round to face her, 'how often must I ask you not to sneak up on me like that?'

Elvira is not listening. She is bent over the side table, making room for the tray. 'Mingo has been,' she says, pointing to the letters propped up against the coffeepot, 'and I've cut you a slice of seed cake. It's light so it won't ruin your appetite. We're having chicken for lunch, and Cook is making a zuccotto for dessert.'

'Zuccotto?' Puccini imagines the dome-shaped sponge filled with chocolate, candied fruit, liqueur and cream – *a dish Elvira's waistline could well do without*. It is a sentiment he knows better than to express.

'The children are noisy today,' he says, for want of something to say. 'They were outside a minute ago, screaming their heads off.'

Elvira looks at him with her black eyes. 'Yes, well it is the holidays.'

Something in her tone makes his neck bristle, like the fur of a cat. 'That may be so,' he says, 'but we came here so I could work in peace, not so that you could fill up the house with your relatives.' He knows he is being unfair, for it was he who insisted on living in this isolated spot, and why shouldn't Elvira invite her family to stay in what was, after all, her home as well as his? 'Your problem is that you don't like Ida,' she retorts.

His mind flips up a picture of Elvira's younger sister, with her bow lips, prissy little walk and endless conversations about dressmakers and dinner service. 'That is simply not true,' he lies. 'It's just that I'm having a devil of a job getting started on this new opera, and I'd appreciate a bit of peace and quiet.'

Pinpricks of moisture have appeared on Elvira's brow. She pulls a square of lace-trimmed handkerchief from her skirt pocket and dabs them away. 'You wouldn't be saying that if Antonio were here. You'd be off for jaunts in the motorcar and playing about with boats, and not doing a skerrick of work.'

Puccini looks down, not wanting to admit the truth of what she says. He misses their son, who is away in Paris with a party from his boarding school, visiting the International Exhibition and Olympic Games. Without Antonio, the house reminds him uncomfortably of his own childhood home, where he, the first boy after five girls, couldn't take a step without one or other of his sisters wanting to pet him, dress him up, or fiddle about with his hair.

'Anyway,' Elvira resumes, 'Fosca adores little Gastone. This morning they made a boat and floated it on the lake. You should have seen his face!'

Puccini, supposing he has given Elvira enough of his attention, lets his mind drift off to another face, one with smooth skin, small features and oriental eyes. How was he going to capture his new heroine, transpose her charms, her sensibilities, from the page to his score? *I'm not Mahler, a fellow who can conjure music out of thin air. I'm a dramatist. I need words, verse, flesh and blood ...*

'... and Maria refuses to come back,' Elvira is saying, animatedly, 'because she's frightened of Cook. Honestly, Giacomo, all this just before Ferragosto! Anyway, I'm going to speak to Signora Manfredi, you know, Doria's mother ...'

Puccini, who doesn't know, decides (unwisely as it turns out) to pick up where he left off. 'It can't be much fun for Fosca being stuck with the children all day,' he says. 'Why doesn't she invite a friend to stay?'

Elvira goes very still, her expression darkening. 'You haven't been listening, have you?' she accuses. 'And if you mean some pretty young thing for you to make eyes at, no thank you very much! Not under my own roof.'

Puccini lifts his hands and shakes them like rattles. 'For goodness sake, Elvira, you're being ridiculous! I was thinking of Fosca. She's not a child anymore. She must be bored out of her mind.'

'Oh?' Elvira is fiddling with the edge of her handkerchief, rolling it tightly between her fingers. 'Why this sudden concern? It never bothers you when I am stuck here on my own.'

He hesitates, but only for a second. 'No,' he says, 'because it means I'm running round the country, not to mention half of Europe, earning money for you to spend on finery.'

'Earning yourself a reputation as the biggest dandy in town, more like!'

'So help me, Elvira, if you acted like a wife and came with me sometimes, you'd have nothing to complain about, but as you choose –'

She cuts him off with a scornful laugh. 'If I behaved like a wife? That's grand! Your high-and-mighty friends make sure I am never treated as your wife. Last time in Rome, if you remember, I was squeezed into a corner of the box where I couldn't even see the stage, and no one addressed a single word to me all evening! And now I suppose you're going to say it's my fault that they sneer at me and make me feel unwelcome!'

'Yes, I am,' he fires back, rattling his hands again. 'You've never made the slightest attempt to be civil to any of them.'

'And why should I cosy up to such superficial people?'

'Because I work with them, *for God's sake!*'

'Yes, that's right, you work with them, and I don't!'

Half-rising, he leans towards her and fixes her with a glare. 'You'd better go, Elvira,' he says angrily, 'before I say something I regret!'

'Fine!' Crushing her handkerchief in her fist, she flings it aside, turns and flounces through the door, slamming it so violently behind her that the barometer slips from the wall and crashes to the floor.

His reflection shimmering in the glass door panel, Puccini sinks back into his chair and reaches for the silver box, wondering, and not for the first time, just how a few misplaced words could lead to such an almighty row. But he already knows the answer, even if he doesn't care to admit it to himself: Elvira gets on his nerves. It hadn't always been so. Easing a cigarette from under the turquoise-studded lid, he thinks back to an earlier time, when he was just starting out as a young musician and still had to give pianoforte lessons to keep the wolf from the door. He hated it, wasting his time when he should have been getting on with his own work. He would have refused Narciso Gemignani's request to teach his wife had they not been old school friends. Every week he found himself a captive of the chilly sitting room that Narciso's horrible old mother refused to heat properly, and of Elvira. She was different from other women he had known, with a kind of audacity in her, a self-confidence, together with a passionate nature that had at first surprised and then overwhelmed him, the more so because she seemed uncomfortable with her husband and shied away from his touch. Even now, the thought of those first furtive encounters, raw with desire, makes him long to go after her and take her in his arms ... or would do if not for Ida, who would come nosing after them like one of his spaniels, sniffing them out like a pair of still-guilty lovers. Striking a match, Puccini sucks in, counts to five and shoots a plume of blue smoke into the air. He has finished his consideration of the past, a place he visits infrequently (and then in small measure) and has turned his thoughts to the future. There is a telephone call to make, and the sooner the better.

The air in the hall is misted with the delicious smell of roasting chicken, a smell that makes Puccini swallow hungrily as he twirls the handle and lifts the receiver. Hoping that the lunchtime bird will be served with crispy roast potatoes garnished with rosemary, a dish his mother used to make, he drums his fingers on the table and waits for the operator.

'Pronto?' The voice is young and perky.

'Milan 364, if you please ... Signorina,' he adds, rounding off the word with a flourish that he directs into the mouthpiece. There is a gasp, or possibly a stifled giggle, and then silence. Puccini shrugs and looks down at the table, where his daily newspaper, *Il Corriere della Sera*, is waiting for him next to the telephone stand. He picks it up and reads the headline, which is framed in thick black ink: *Funeral of King in Rome tomorrow*. 'Of course!' he blurts out, having quite forgotten the news. He runs his eye along a line or two of print, seeing fast-moving centipedes scurrying across the page instead of words. *Good grief!* he thinks, worried he might be losing his sight. Only this morning he'd discovered a strand of silver in his moustache! Searching around for a pencil to make a note to ask Ida's optometrist husband, Giuseppe, to check his eyesight, he is distracted by a noise from the doorway across the hall. The children are in his gunroom!

Just then there is a click on the line, which is followed by the unmistakable intonation of a voice from the north. 'Good morning. House of Ricordi.'

The composer drops the newspaper. 'Good morning,' he says. 'This is Puccini and I should like to speak to Signor Giulio.'

'Of course, Maestro. Please hold.' There is a pause, a crackle, then the clipped vowels of his mentor and publisher, the impresario Giulio Ricordi, the man universally considered to be the high priest of Italian music.

'Giacomo, dear boy! How is life treating you in the green marshes?'

Puccini's face relaxes into a smile. 'Very well, Signor Giulio, thank you, although in this heat they're a little more brown than green. Even the frogs have changed colour. You must come and visit us when you have time.'

'Time?' the older man retorts. 'What, pray, is that? You musicians are such a demanding lot, I rarely have a minute to call my own. Now, to what do I owe the pleasure of your call?'

'Signor Giulio, it's about *Madama Butterfly*.'

'Ah! The exquisite Cio-Cio-San. Yes, I rather thought it might be ...'

Puccini doesn't let him finish. 'I've read the play and ideas are flitting round my head like moths near a candle ...'

'But ...?'

'But I need a libretto! With all this delay over the contract, I'm going out of my mind, I swear I am. I need to get started, Signor Giulio. *Butterfly* is going to be my greatest work ever, the one to put all my other heroines to shame – Manon, Mimi,

Tosca – you'll see!'

'Gracious, dear boy, I do hope not! But I take your point.'

A thin, intermittent sound, like the clipping of toenails, derails Puccini's thoughts. He looks around and sees that it is coming from the floor outside his gunroom, where a brown object propelled by a broom handle is juddering slowly towards him: a decoy duck, one of the set of twenty he uses to entice waterfowl out of the shallows and into the range of his gun. 'Psst!' he hisses, in the direction of the duck.

'Sorry, Giacomo, did you say something?'

The composer clears his throat. 'No, Signor Giulio, nothing. Now, where was I? Ah yes. You see, the problem is that Illica and Giacosa won't write a word without your consent.'

A second duck has joined the first.

'Of course not,' Ricordi says, his tone matter of fact. 'I can't have my best librettists wasting their time on something that may not eventuate.'

'But Belasco agreed ...'

'You should know by now, Giacomo,' the impresario says slowly, as if explaining the situation to a child, 'that there is a world of difference between a playwright's word and his signature on a contract. However, your call is opportune because last night Belasco's lawyer rang from America to say that everything is in order, and we should have the contract in a few days.'

Puccini expels a sigh of relief. 'Thank goodness for that! When I met him backstage in London, he seemed genuine enough, but it's hard to tell when one doesn't speak the language.'

'Quite,' Ricordi affirms. 'Anyway, Belasco obviously grasped your intentions, Giacomo, because he told his lawyer that while holding his arms around the venerable composer, he could hardly refuse an Italian who couldn't understand a word of English, with tears in his eyes moreover. In retrospect the lawyer found the interaction not without a degree of charm.'

'Did he? Why is that?'

'I have no idea ... possibly the Anglo-Saxon sense of humour.'

Puccini considers this for a moment. 'Yes,' he says, 'perhaps so.'

Another duck is sliding round the door jamb.

'Anyway, Signor Giulio, I have to go, but thank you for setting my mind at ease.'

'Not at all. Love to Elvira.'

'Of course.'

Hooking up the receiver, Puccini bounds forward and aims a kick at the broomstick, sending the brown female mallard decoy skidding across the floor into the skirting board and ricocheting into the grandfather clock, then the umbrella holder and finally the leg of the hall table before coming to rest by the coat stand.

'Right, you little rascals, skedaddle!' In three strides he has reached the gunroom. 'Where are you, then? Come on, the game's up!' But there is no sign of the children, just the open door leading out into the garage. 'The little blighters! They've taken them down to the lake.'

Puccini pushes his dark chocolate felt hat firmly onto the crown of his head and writes *Madama Butterfly* on the frontispiece of a new notebook with his recently sharpened pencil. Then he leans back, clasps his hands behind his neck and stares up at the ceiling, panelled in black and white squares like a chessboard. A crawling sensation is working its way up his spine, as if something is living there, a scaly, reptilian creature, breathing fear through its sharp-tongued mouth. What if he should fail? What if the sounds that have been coursing through his brain have no merit, or worse still, elicit scorn and ridicule from his audience? This is how it begins: an idea, a rush of joy, the euphoria of certainty, followed by doubt and apprehension which can only be relieved by months of gruelling work where every note, every phrase, is tried and tested, perfected, and committed to paper. But they are never perfect, nowhere near, and so he goes over them time and again, back and forth, back and forth, a cigarette glowing in his ashtray, altering, adding, subtracting, reworking, until that extraordinary moment when time stills, his breath calms, and his body is flooded with a deep and visceral warmth, like a heavenly light beaming onto his skin, confirming that he has got it right. But even that is not enough; there is the orchestration to be added, the voices and textures of the various instruments to be harmonised and contrasted. And the final hurdle, the endless rows with his librettists, Luigi Illica, the creator of the storyline, and Giuseppe Giacosa, the old pedant who sets Illica's words into the verse that drives his music. They argue about everything, this unlikely triumvirate – the characters, the setting, the pace, the drama – furious arguments leading to icy silences that only Giulio Ricordi, using all his legendary tact and skill, can resolve. Alongside all this is Belasco's temper at the continual revision of dates.

For now, though, Puccini cares nothing of this. His first task, Promethean, is to coax Butterfly into existence. In order to do that, every feature of her must be known and understood, her longings, her fears, her strengths and frailties. Like seducing a new love, he must disarm her defences, then slowly, tenderly, uncover her, garment by garment, for only when she resonates in every fibre of his being can he bring her to life in the hearts of others. To this end, he closes his eyes and pictures a small woman in a silk tea gown reclining on a couch, a woman with a shy smile, pearly teeth and raven hair pinned into place by combs like conductors' batons. Reaching out to touch her, his hand instead finds the silver box.

Puccini has taken three puffs when he sees the envelopes propped up against the coffeepot, forgotten about in the upset with Elvira. He picks them up and shuffles them in his hands, examining the Eiffel Tower postcard from Antonio, the account from his shoemaker to be settled by the end of the month, a handful of invitations to events he will surely not attend, a program from La Scala, and a pale green envelope, the colour of a nightingale's egg, with the word 'private' printed in the top left-hand corner and underlined twice. He pauses to study the handwriting, which is large and curved, each letter heavy with ink, and although he is certain he has never seen it before, his fingers falter as they reach for the paperknife to slice open the flap.

Dear Maestro, it was a great pleasure to meet you ...

Who is this? He reads on.

Life with two elderly ladies is, as you predicted, not very amusing. So if your offer of a stroll still stands, I am free from 2 to 5 in the afternoon, when they shut themselves away for a siesta. We are staying in Viareggio, on the promenade, at the quieter end.

It was followed by a signature and an address.

'Well, well.' Puccini's face eases into a slow grin while at the same time his mind pulls together traces of the young woman sitting opposite him on the train, a pretty girl with not a dab of make-up on her face (unlike those painted gargoyles of chorus girls who would throw themselves at him these days), a soft voice tinged with the not unpleasant accent of Turin, curious eyes (which could bode well in the bed department) and wonderful dark, shiny hair, like the skin of a newly plucked aubergine … Oh yes, and now he remembers she was travelling with an old biddy who snuffled like a piglet the whole time. *Hmm … she might be a bit young … but there again, a modern girl, a university student no less … What was her name again? He looks down and checks the signature. Corinna. Ah yes… Well, well, well!*

Chapter 5
ELVIRA AND IDA VISIT
THE MANFREDI FAMILY

Ida Razzi has completed her *toilette*, an event to which she devotes a good hour each morning. She is now reclining in a comfortable armchair in Elvira's drawing room, the coffee tray on a low table by her side, waiting for her sister to sort out some dreary little contretemps that has just taken place in the kitchen. Setting down her fan, she straightens her fashionable bell-shaped skirt, embroidered with tiny blue forget-me-nots around the hem. She leans forward to lift the cup from its saucer, puckers her lips and takes a sip of thick bitter coffee. Stretching out a hand to the biscuits, her fingers hesitate above the plate before selecting a yellow triangle studded with almonds and dusted in fine sugar. At breakfast Elvira whispered that she had something to tell her. Ida, sensing gossip of the most delicious kind, had suggested they take coffee together after her bath. However, and rather annoyingly, her sister has now been drawn into an argument between Cook and the maid. *Heaven only knows when Elvira will be calm enough to return to that other, surely more interesting matter*, is Ida's only thought.

Nibbling the edge of her biscuit, she gazes at the windowsill where the morning light catches the vase of orange flowers, casting shadows from the small, trumpet-like blooms onto the floor. Her mind moves on. *Lilies delivered to the villa each week, the scented variety at that, surely contribute to the headaches Elvira so frequently complains of, she thinks. If only Elvira weren't so highly strung! Now that Giacomo has all the money in the world, what outings we could have to Forte dei Marmi and other fashionable resorts, not to mention shopping trips to Florence, and even to Milan.* But Ida realises that Elvira seems incapable of relaxing and enjoying her good fortune, choosing instead to remain yoked to the past like one of those oxen with their massive heads and rolling eyes that she had first seen working the fields when she arrived.

The clock on the mantelpiece sets off on its slow chime towards eleven. Ida turns her head towards the sound and sees the photograph of her own Mamma in better days, before Papa lost all his money and ran off to Argentina. Keeping her mother company above the fireplace are three bronze statuettes of Wagner, Verdi and Donizetti, the trio worshipped by her brother-in-law. Not her taste, the golden metal dwarves, but then neither, come to that, are the frescoed walls or the chandelier that looks like the crown of a crazed emperor. *But the Bugatti armchairs are tasteful ... and the Persian rug, of course.* Ida sets down her cup with a chink of envy. Elvira has done very well for herself, even if it has been slow in coming. Searching around for something to distract her, Ida's hand flops down on the arm of her chair. She scrutinises the weathered fabric, imagining a puff of fine dust being propelled into the air then floating back down to settle on the book by her side, Pellegrino Artusi's manual on the art of cooking and home management, a tome to be found in all well-run households. Blowing away the dust particles, she lifts the book and balances it in her hands, scanning the pages close to where it has fallen open: recipes for wild duck, braised pigeon, snipe and olives, all dishes Giacomo loves to eat. Shuddering, Ida recalls the lunch for All Souls' Day last November, when her brother-in-law had devoured a dozen little thrushes, picking them up by the beak and popping them whole into his mouth.

'Oh, there you are, Ida!' Elvira's head appears around the door. 'Let's go. If we hurry, we can be back in time for lunch.'

Ida, unable to follow this turn of events, sets the book down. 'But Elvira, I thought you had something to tell me ... the matter you mentioned earlier.'

There is a flinch in the black eyes – and then it is gone. 'I don't have time for that now,' Elvira says, flustered. 'With Ferragosto only a week away, I need to find another maid. Come on ...'

'But where are we going?'

'To the Manfredis'. It's only a short walk.'

The *scirocco* is a hot, dry disagreeable wind that blows from the south, bringing with it fine red sand from the deserts of Africa. It stings the villagers' eyes as they go about their tasks and covers the terrain like a sprinkling of dirty icing sugar. It is a wind that is known to excite the mind and stimulate the nerves, making wives shout at their husbands, husbands beat their dogs, and dogs cower in the shade of outhouses. And it is this wind that greets the sisters as they pass through the Puccinis' front door and make their way down to the gate.

Stepping onto the road, Ida coughs and brings her glove to her mouth, for the air is rent through with the terrible stench of rotting fish coming from the fishermen's huts, a cluster of stilted ramshackle sheds in the middle of the lake that could have been tossed there by a careless giant living in the skies above. Thank goodness she is too far away to see the slit throats and glazed eyes of the carp drying on the racks outside, she thinks. Coughing again, she pulls out a handkerchief to cover her nose, and sees that Elvira is doing the same.

They turn away and hurry on up the road, Ida lagging a few steps behind Elvira, unable to keep up with her sister's longer strides, both of them silenced by the cloying air and a sun that is sticking their clothes to their damp perspiring backs. How on earth, she wonders, can her sister survive in this backwater, where the nearest shop, or indeed any sign of civilisation, is half an hour up a dirt track? She pictures Florence, with its wide streets, noble buildings and expansive squares that proclaim the city's proud heritage. What could this village offer that compared with the galleries and shops displaying the latest fashions, artworks, furnishings, and toys for the children? Not to mention the cafes, with their enticing window displays of glazed tarts and crisply baked biscuits, where one could sip hot chocolate, listening to educated voices echoing off the marble floors and glass-fronted cabinets. The question, though, as Ida well knows as she steps around a patch of something green and disgusting, is hardly relevant, for Elvira has not been won over by the smelly marshes. Far from it. But following Giacomo's success with Manon *Lescaut* and *La Bohème*, she had willingly agreed to the building of a villa here, would indeed have agreed to one anywhere, so she could at last have a home of her own. Ida still remembers the excitement of those early shopping expeditions for curtain materials, bed linen and blankets as soft as spun sugar, the very best money could buy.

Onward the two women go, around the well and past the *capanne*, the thatched shacks where the reed-cutters live, onto a footpath that runs through the fields, their shoes kicking up flurries of dust that trail behind them long after they have passed. Together, they made a strange sight indeed, the well-dressed sisters, in this landscape of stunted trees and parched grass; Elvira in a ribboned bonnet and matching beige summer coat, Ida with her pink-lined cape thrown loosely around her shoulders, her elaborate chignon topped off by a far from demure pale pink hat with a chiffon bow, cherries pinned to the brim. On and on, until finally, just as Ida is beginning to wonder how much further she can walk in such heat, they reach a settlement of stone cottages built around a communal courtyard.

In winter, the barnyard, the *aia*, is a bleak place, grey, damp and deserted, the ground split into sticky clods of earth by the frost. But in summer, outside the mossy stone walls of the courtyard, the land bursts into life. During the day, the tenants dry corn and thresh wheat on its hard dusty surface, while in the evenings they sit around chanting the rosary or chatting; the women doing lace work and stitching clothes, the men drinking and playing cards, the children chasing around with the dogs, shrieking as if seized by a sudden madness. Seeing it now, as lively and colourful as a Brueghel painting, it is impossible to imagine the desolate, frostbitten place it will become again in a few months. Today being Monday, Filippo, the barber's assistant, is here to trim the hair of those too poor to afford a visit to his master's salon, an event that brings with it all the excitement of a summer fair. Boys rush around with stools tucked under their arms, not knowing where to put them down, while mothers shout their feverish instructions, arms waving, though little can be heard above the noise and confusion.

Filippo is a tall lad with a hawk's nose and a big round head, his countenance suggesting a good-natured overgrown schoolboy. But now he's caught up in a problem he recognises well, alongside two spotted dogs with floppy ears, one clamped against his leg in the unmistakable act of coitus, the other yapping its head off fit to wake the dead. 'Now then, everyone,' he calls, brushing the dog away and risking his hand in the process, 'a little order if you please! Let's start with the gentlemen. Line up here! That's it. Come on, Angelo, you're first!'

Filippo's scissors flash back and forth, *click, click, click,* as he moves from one man to the next with the speed of a magician pulling rabbits from a hat. 'There you are, Flavio. You've never looked so handsome in your life! Your wife will think she's got a new man!'

'She needs one!' someone shouts back. It is Giorgio, the ironmonger, a jovial fellow with an almost bald head and patches of russet hair.

'Thank you, sir!' Filippo calls, nodding to the ironmonger. 'And will you be needing a haircut?' A laugh goes up as Giorgio runs a hand over his smooth oily pate. 'No?' Filippo goes on, 'Then it's time for the boys. Come on lads, over here …'

The barber's assistant works efficiently, snipping away until he can see skin under his scissors; poor folk expect value for money, and hair razed to the scalp helps eliminate headlice.

'Hop up, Egidio! I won't bite you … Here, try this!' And he presses a hard round sweet into the boy's hand.

Waiting for Ida to catch her breath, Elvira sees the door of a nearby cottage open and an arthritic old man shuffle into view. It is Bernardo, the beekeeper, a bachelor with rasping breath and few words, reputed to be the meanest man in the village, whose bees produce a pale glassy honey from the hives among the acacia trees by the brook.

'Good day to you, Signora Elvira,' he calls weakly. 'Were you wanting some honey?'

'No thank you, Bernardo,' she calls back. 'Not today. We're here to speak to Signora Manfredi.'

'Is it to do with Doria?' The question comes not from Bernardo, who has lost interest and is stumbling back inside, but the barber's assistant.

'I don't believe that's any of your business,' Elvira says briskly, noting that Filippo's face has taken on the woeful look of a puppy about to lose its bone.

A whistle escapes from the crowd, a shrill sound, full of insult. The spotted dogs tense, their tails shooting in the air, before they bound towards Dario, the chimneysweep, a man with one leg shorter than the other, accompanied by three or four small children and cradling a baby still in swaddling clothes.

Elvira fixes him with a stare. He looks away, but not before sticking out an insolent tongue.

'Come on, Ida,' she says, taking her sister's arm. They cross the *aia* and stop outside a house with bundles of cane, chair frames and fishing rods stacked up outside. Swatting away the frenzied flies that are buzzing around her head, Elvira steps up to the door and bangs on it with her fist. There is a scraping sound from within, the door creaks open, and a pall of smoke billows past them in a desperate bid to escape. 'Ahem ...' Elvira coughs. 'Good morning, Signora Manfredi.'

'Ah, Signora Elvira, Signora Ida ...' The door opens a little further to reveal a stout woman in a black dress and grubby apron, her steel-grey hair tucked into a matching headscarf, except for the few greasy strands stuck to her cheek above a sooty smudge. Set against a room as dark and airless as a cupboard, with a low ceiling and one small window hidden behind a square of sackcloth, she has the air of someone reconciled to unflinching hardship. 'What can I do for you?' she asks cautiously, looking from one to the other.

'I wonder if we might come in and have a word?'

Signora Manfredi lets out a sigh, a heavy sound, weighed down by the burdens of the poor. She knows what this is about. The uncomfortable silence is broken by the clunking of a weaving loom, then Signora Manfredi moves aside to let them in. The room has a dry-earth floor, a trough in the corner for making bread, a few pieces of wooden furniture, a shelf above the hearth with an old photograph on it, and an oil lamp dangling down over a table where a rabbit, an onion, a pile of old potatoes and sprig of rosemary are waiting to go into a pot. Knowing that she and Ida will not be invited to sit down, Elvira opens with a little polite conversation.

'Where are the children?' she says with a smile, looking around. Signora Manfredi eyes her suspiciously, suspecting a double edge to the question. 'The younger ones are out in the *aia*, and Alice, as you know, works over at La Piaggetta.'

Elvira nods, picturing a short girl, stout like her mother, who is a housemaid at the villa of the Marchese Ginori-Lisci, on the other side of the lake. 'And Rodolfo?' she asks, referring to a swarthy lad of seventeen, recently arrested for nighttime poaching on the estate.

'He's on the railways. They wanted him to go over to Corsica, but I wouldn't let him.'

'Oh?' Ida cuts in, supposing the pay to be better. 'And why not?' Signora Manfredi gives her an old-fashioned look then says to Elvira, her voice catching. 'I need him here ... after what happened to his father ...'

'Of course you do,' Elvira says quickly. 'Such a horrible accident!'

Signora Manfredi turns to the smoky black crucifix nailed to the wall above the hearth, her eyes glazing over with an impenetrable sadness. Elvira shoots a look at Ida, who gestures for her to hurry up.

'*Ahem* ... Signora Manfredi,' she begins, 'I've come to offer Doria a job at the villa. The pay is twenty lire a month, live-in, with Sundays free.'

'I see ...' replies the widow, not shifting her gaze.

Now it is Elvira's turn to fall silent. She knows Emilia Manfredi to be a good woman, devout and God-fearing, who under normal circumstances would never let a daughter of hers work in a house where the master and mistress lived together without being married. But with her husband's recent death, his blood poisoned by a stray shotgun pellet, and mouths to feed, Emilia has little choice in the matter.

'Ahem!' Elvira repeats, much louder this time.

Now Signora Manfredi turns to face her. 'I suppose you'd like to speak to her?' she says wearily.

'Yes,' Elvira affirms, 'but before I do, there's something I need to mention. I can't have Doria's young man, that barber fellow, hanging around the kitchen door. Cook won't stand for it. The other day she even boxed the ears of Maria's intended, and there's been nothing but trouble ever since. I hope you don't mind my speaking ...' Elvira's words grind to a halt when she realises that Signora Manfredi is staring at her in shock, or perhaps disbelief.

'Doria is far too young to be courting,' she says sharply.

'Of course she is,' Elvira agrees quickly, not wanting to give offence.

The widow pauses to take in the expediency of this reply, then says, 'I'll call her for you. Doria! Come here a minute!'

The weaving loom falls silent, and a few seconds later a girl of about fifteen appears in the doorway. She is short like her mother, but thinner and finer boned, with a small hooked nose, flat expressionless eyes, like buttons, and a complexion that is unusual for a peasant; not ruddy from being out in all weathers, Doria's skin is smooth and pale, not anaemically so, but enough to give the impression that she spends most of her time indoors. Her long chestnut hair, her best feature by far, is tied up in a ponytail but if it were not, it would surely reach her waist. She wears a faded red blouse, straining at the buttons to stay done up, with dirty frayed cuffs that stop well short of her hands, whereas her skirt, a shapeless garment made from the same heavy hemp cloth as the curtain, is loose and dragging on the ground.

Doria regards the visitors without blinking.

'My dear,' her mother begins, 'Signora Elvira wants you to go and work at the villa.'

The girl, whose gaze has settled on Ida, appears not to hear her.

'Well, Doria, what do you say?' Elvira prompts.

The pot over the fire slurps something into the grate that gives off a loud hiss.

'Thank you, ma'am,' Doria mumbles, her eyes still fixed on Ida.

'Good, that's settled then. I shall expect you on Monday morning, at ten o'clock.'

Now the girl looks puzzled.

'What is it, Doria? Is there something you want to ask?'

Doria points at Ida's bonnet. 'Will I get a hat like that?'

'Doria!' her mother chides. 'That's enough!'

The girl looks down. 'Monday morning,' she mutters, 'Monday morning ...'

Elvira glances at Ida and sees that her sister has been struck by the same thought. Doria is simple.

Chapter 6
THE FEAST OF SAN LORENZO

Clang! Clang! Clang!
The blast of church bells bursts into the early morning dimness of Corinna's room. She lets out a groan, rolls over and draws the sheet over her head.
Clang! Clang!
'It's not even Sunday!' she wails, pressing her fingers to her ears. 'How am I supposed to sleep through this din?'
She isn't, and after a few minutes of tossing this way and that, Corinna gives up and grudgingly opens her eyes. Through the haze of netting, she can make out the shapes in the room, the washstand and jug, a hard-back chair, a chest of drawers, and a wardrobe with iron fittings that leans against the wall like an up-ended coffin. *Ugly, ugly, ugly! All of it.* How she longs to be back home in her own room overlooking the park, with its pretty brocade curtains defending her from the world outside, as they swish along the floor.
Clang! The air trembles again and then settles. Somewhere near her head a mosquito is droning, intent on exchanging its itchy poison for her blood. She flaps at the netting and for a moment there is silence. Then the bell strikes again, as malicious as thunder.
'All right! All right!' Easing herself out from under the sheet, Corinna slides her feet onto the rough tiles, crosses to the washstand and splashes water from the jug into the bowl. Further along the corridor, a door opens and shuts. Footsteps (too heavy for Grandma, too quick for Aunt Adelaide) clump past her room and fade around the corner on their way to the kitchen. They be-

long to Lucia, the butterball of a cook, who produces meals that are as bracing as the sea air on the deck of a ferry – pasta laced with oil and garlic, thick soups of cabbage and beans, tripe or rabbit, accompanied by wedges of heavy, tasteless bread. How Corinna craves the dainty sandwiches and moist chocolate cake of her home city, but the food in this apartment is as stolid as her day: study or a little shopping in the morning, a rest after lunch, a late afternoon *passeggiata*, supper at eight, and early to bed.

The soap smells of lemon. Corinna rubs a little onto the wash-cloth and cleans her face, pressing the towel to her eyes while she waits for her skin to dry. Loosening the ties of her night-gown, she lets it slip to the floor, steps into a fresh pair of drawers and turns to the mirror, which shows a girl with shoulder-length black hair, small breasts and ribs narrowing to a dainty waist. Corinna regards her form unselfconsciously, then an unbidden thought arises; she is thrilled in imagining Maestro Puccini eye-ing her all over.

A week has elapsed since she wrote to him, a week in which the lure of an adventure softened her hours, punctuating them with guarded smiles that at times made her look almost happy. Slow-ly, inexorably, though, her hopes have faded, for if the composer intended to respond, surely he would have done so by now? It is a conclusion that brings with it a sinking feeling, like the onset of seasickness. What had she been hoping for? She couldn't say exactly, but something, *anything*, to relieve the boredom that is worming its way through her like maggots in a slowly rotting apple. Each day that passes, though, confirms that for Maestro Puccini their encounter had just been a little entertainment, a way to make a train journey pass more pleasantly, and now she feels stupid and wishes she could undo her impulsive act.

Catching a second look at herself in the mirror, Corinna runs a slow hand down her body, feeling the smooth curves of her flesh. 'What will become of me?'

No answer.

'Will I marry?'

Silence. Reaching across to the chest of drawers, she picks up a bottle of violet water and sprays a little around her neck. *If only Aurelia were here!*

They had met, she and Aurelia, on their first day at university last October, in a lecture hall on the top floor of a white stucco building with arches overlooking a quadrangle where two pigeons circled a fountain, nodding their heads like a pair of peripatetic philosophers. Being the only girl from her school to continue with her studies, she was nervous about what she might find there. Would the other students be very clever, which she wasn't, although her schoolteachers had judged her 'promising'? And was it true, as Grandma insisted, that she would be better served learning to embroider and cook, as only those with family connections or important friends became lawyers, of whom very few were women? She supposed it might be, but still she pressed ahead. Embroidery and cooking could come later, if they had to come at all. Besides, the law fascinated her, with its elegance, its logic and certainties, elements that countered her own unsure destiny, a destiny that could change on meeting the right sort of young man. And where better than a law school? Although scanning the ranks of studious youths in jackets, stiff collars and ties, their hair neatly combed as if already practising the profession that awaited them, she feared she was in for a disappointment.

The lecture was already underway when Aurelia appeared in the doorway and leaned against the door jamb, gazing around, the corners of her mouth pulled down in an expression of obvious distaste. A young man in the front row was the first to spot her, and he nudged his neighbour who then nudged his, until an unsettled ripple ran round the hall. And who could blame them? At nearly six feet tall, her red hair crimped and worn loose, Aurelia looked like a pre-Raphaelite portrait, an impression enhanced by the frilled blouse, strings of beads and flouncy skirt that barely reached her calves.

'Ah, Signorina Pilotti,' the professor murmured, nodding in her direction, 'good of you to join us … at last.'

Ignoring the barb, Aurelia flashed him a winning smile, the sort that could only come from being in his confidence. 'I'm sorry I'm late,' she said, sweeping past him, '… and Papa says to say hello.' Plonking herself down next to Corinna, she pulled a notebook and pencil from her bag and leaned back, looking exquisitely bored. Then, without turning her head, she hissed, 'Dear God, just look at them all! Dull as ditchwater, the whole bloody lot!'

Later, over lunch in the *mensa*, Corinna learned that Aurelia's father was one of the city's top lawyers who counted leading businessmen and politicians among his friends, and even a cabinet minister in Luigi Pelloux's militarist government. Waving her long arms as she spoke, Aurelia described a world so very different from hers that Corinna found herself shrinking back from revealing the achingly dull circumstances of her own existence, lived alongside her parents. Poor dear Mamma, whose illness had reduced her to the dependency of childhood, to drinking straws, a walking frame, and outbursts of tears and frustration; and her architect father, whose response to all this had been to bury himself in his work, darting in and out of the house. Yet there was something in Aurelia's fiery character, in her unflinching eyes and no-nonsense approach that invited confidences, and so, unbelievably, Corinna found herself revealing secrets which previously she had kept bound up inside her, hostages to their own fortune.

When Corinna finished her story, Aurelia said, 'Dear thing, what a dreadful time you've had. But don't despair! You, too, have a part to play in the grand theatre of life. The future of this country depends on people like you.'

And Corinna, incredulous, laughed out loud.

'No, no,' Aurelia insisted, 'believe me, the ruling classes have had their day. The arrogance of them! Really! They believe they have a God-given right to arrange everything to suit themselves, and don't give a fig for the common man. Anarchy, that's what we need, with everyone thinking and acting for themselves. To hell with the church and state! To hell with middle-class morality! Free love for all! ... Dear thing, don't look so shocked.'

But Corinna was shocked, for she had never heard anyone speak like that before. It was dangerous, seditious, yet despite this, Aurelia's ideas intrigued her, and so in the evenings, after supper, she sat at her desk in her bedroom and devised questions, lists of them, which she fired off as they strolled along the corridors, arm in arm, the discrepancy in their stature drawing looks from the other students. Aurelia's daring and enthusiasm crackled with an infectious energy, so that when she was with her, Corinna too could believe in a future beyond the tedium of her daily existence, a tedium reeking of camphor and decay that coated her tongue and lingered in her nose, making her want to vomit.

The church bells have finally stopped their frightful din. Corinna crosses to the window, slides a bolt and opens the shutters onto the dusty lane at the side of the house that is overlooked by the roofs and chimneys of once-grand *palazzi*. A jumble of noise is coming from the promenade where merchants drive their carts to the marketplace in the centre of town. Later, if she finishes her studies in time, she and the old ladies will stroll around the colourful stalls of fruit and vegetables, house linen, ribbons and buttons, and pens confining chicks, ducklings, rabbits and kid goats. The vendors will shout at the tops of their voices, as Grandma feigns anger at the prices, a tactic essential to any successful bargaining. But for now, Corinna must finish dressing. Pulling a cotton frock over her head, she reaches for her hairbrush and tugs it through her hair, easing one pin at a time from her hairpin box as she fixes the twisted skein to the top of her head. Then she pauses, picks up the box and peers at the small, gold-embossed card that is tucked inside the lid. *Maestro Giacomo Puccini, Torre del Lago.*

She has read the words dozens of times over the past week, words that previously signified hope and excitement, but now only disappointment. If only Grandma hadn't insisted she spend the summer here, she wouldn't have been on that wretched train in the first place! She would have been in the hills of Monferrato, many kilometres to the north, picnicking in soft, grassy fields full of wildflowers with butterflies flitting about in the cool air, or watching Aurelia and the other house guests play tennis, and even having a game herself. Perhaps with Maurizio.

Older than herself by three years, Aurelia's brother is also studying law at the university, on his way to a place in the family practice. Tall and good looking in a bland sort of way, he likes her. She knows this by the fumbling way he helps her on with her coat, by the flush that reddens his ears and cheeks when she accidentally brushes up against him as they stroll together in the beautifully landscaped gardens of his home on the fashionable side of the park. Corinna should be delighted and flattered, for it would be hard to imagine a better match, one offering security as well as cementing her friendship with Aurelia. But there is something about Maurizio, a soppiness, a sort of pleading melancholy, like a consumptive poet, that sets her teeth on edge. She wants to shake him, tell him to be bolder, more of a man, not mope around after her like a lovesick youth. Yet all she can do is regret not having the right sort of feelings, and hope that sooner or later he comes to his senses.

Grandma sets down her coffee cup and looks around the breakfast table, a sure sign that she is about to make a pronouncement. 'As today is the feast of San Lorenzo,' she says, 'I propose that after supper we take a stroll along the promenade to see the shooting stars.'

So that's what all the bell-clanging was about!

Aunt Adelaide nods her head vigorously. 'Oh yes!' she says. 'They say if you see one fall, it brings good luck for a whole year!'

'They also say they're the saint's tears,' Corinna mutters under her breath, regretting it when she sees her aunt stick a piece of bread into her mouth and begin chewing it with offended little hamster bites. 'Sorry, Aunt, I didn't mean to be rude.'

'Good!' Grandma continues, oblivious to the diversion, 'that's decided then. Now, I need a length of new ribbon to trim my bonnet. Adelaide, you can come with me to the market while Corinna gets on with her study.'

'But Lavinia,' Aunt Adelaide says, offering her sister an apologetic little smile, 'I have my tapestry to do. You said yourself that the screen for the fireplace must be finished by September.'

Grandma is caught in her own net. 'Bah!' she says. 'Very well, I'll go by myself.'

And so shortly afterwards, with Grandma safely out of the way, Aunt Adelaide positions herself by the window in the parlour, pulls a magazine from her handbag, pops an aniseed drop in her mouth and settles down to a little guilty pleasure, leaving Corinna to do the same.

In the drawer of her bedside cabinet is the copy of *Madame Bovary* that Aurelia had pressed into her hands when they parted for the summer: 'Dear thing, if you really must go into hibernation, you'll need something scandalous to keep you from going mad. But for goodness sake don't let anyone see it!' And Corinna, true to her word, had folded the novel into the dust jacket of a textbook, and hidden it under a pile of handkerchiefs. Now, leaving the door ajar, she perches on the end of the bed and turns to chapter four. Emma, a young farm girl, is about to marry Charles Bovary, a widowed doctor older than herself, who can offer her a place in society as well as an escape from the dreariness of life on the land ...

Rat-a-tat-tat! Rat-a-tat-tat!

'Heavens! Grandma must have forgotten her key!' Pushing the book under the pillow, Corinna hurries down the corridor and opens the front door.

'Good morning, Miss!' It is the postman, a young fellow with pockmarked skin and a cheeky smile. 'You're in luck today,' he grins, holding out a letter.

Corinna takes the envelope, and shadows from the tiny mauve flowers above the doorway flutter as she discerns her name, then the postmark. 'Thank you,' she whispers, her words swept away by a gust of salty air.

Her heart thumping as she hurries back along the corridor to her room, Corinna sinks onto the bed and fumbles open the flap of the envelope. *How lovely to hear from you!* he begins, his words small and angled to the right. *I shall come to meet you on Saturday, by the footpath at the end of the promenade, on the far side of the canal.*

'Saturday ... tomorrow!' The thumping quickens, sending a surge of blood to her head. Stumbling to the window, Corinna throws it open and leans out, gulping down mouthfuls of dusty air.

You can't meet a man without a chaperone! What if Grandma finds out? Your reputation will be ruined, your family disgraced! The accusations come to her with the intensity of a Greek chorus, the voices swelling into a deafening crescendo as the players grind out their shrill, insistent chant. *Slut ... Slut ... Slut ...*

Corinna clamps her hands to her ears. 'Stop it! Stop it! I'll cancel ... I'll send him a telegram – right now!'

Her tormentors, satisfied, stop their performance and start to pack up. But she won't cancel. Of course she won't, because at the same time there is another voice at work, that of her friend Aurelia, telling her that this is nothing but a construct coming from her own imagination, one designed to keep her firmly in her place. *Carpe diem!* Besides, when else will she have the opportunity to glimpse life beyond the parapets of obligation and duty, where everything she longs for so surely resides?

Turning to the coffin wardrobe, Corinna opens the door and runs her hand along the rail, passing over everyday blouses and frocks until she comes to a soft blue dress with a square neckline, pintucked bodice, and full skirt. Lifting it out, she holds it up against herself and consults the mirror. *The style is good, the colour perfect, not too bright, and the shade tones in with the tie of her bonnet. But something is missing ... a brooch? ... a necklace?'* She cannot decide what, and so she turns this way and that, examining herself in the minutest detail. And then she has it! With a quick glance at the clock, she drops the dress onto the chair and hurries along the corridor to the parlour.

'Aunt Adelaide!' she cries, throwing open the door. 'Let's go and look at the boutique on the corner, the new one that's just opened. Hurry now, before Grandma gets back!'

Chapter 7
ELVIRA AND IDA HAVE
A HEART-TO-HEART

It is Saturday morning, and although there are still four days to go until Ferragosto, Elvira is already run off her feet. Not only is she having to fill in for the missing maid, but yesterday a Japanese actress (a tiny woman called Sada Jacco) came to lunch and ended up staying for dinner. Giacomo had invited her weeks before because he wanted to record her peculiar way of speaking on his phonograph machine, but with one thing and another, she had quite forgotten to mention it to Cook, and when the visitor arrived, Cook, as rude as ever, had planted her hands on her hips, glared with those bug eyes of hers, and declared in a voice loud enough to carry into the hall, 'Rice? Dry with a little beef and ginger? I'm not cooking such a thing! You won't crap for days. Have risotto, with asparagus and parmesan, much nicer. Dry rice! Never heard of such nonsense in my kitchen. Such a funny colour ... *mal*!' Cook is still in a bad mood and Elvira is in the kitchen helping to prepare lunch. She has just spent half an hour cleaning up after Dario, the chimneysweep, who caught his gammy leg in the fender in the drawing room and tipped coaldust all over the rug, a circumstance she suspects might not have been entirely accidental.
'What is there to do?' she asks, seeing the knives laid out by the chopping board, the mortar and pestle, the waiting onions, garlic and chili.
Cook slaps a roll of tripe in front of her and says, 'You'll need to slice this!'
A pungent, slightly sweet smell, edged with dead animal, reaches Elvira's nostrils, making her stomach turn. She closes

her eyes, trying not to look at the rubbery grey stomach tissue that Enzo, the butcher, had recently excised from an ox. 'You can do this, Cook,' she manages, her throat suddenly dry, 'while I see to the pudding.'

Pretending not to hear, Cook grasps the handle of a meat cleaver, raises it high above her head and slams the blade into a shinbone with the force of an executioner severing a head. Elvira closes her eyes again. The noise of the splintering bone is like a volley of darts finding its target in her scalp. It is outrageous that she must tolerate this *scrofa,* this sow, in her house, but with no one else in the village capable of doing the job, what choice does she have? The woman despises her. She has even said so. Not to Elvira's face, of course, as that would require courage, but in whispered conversations with Silvia, the laundry girl.

'They haven't been blessed by the priest, now have they? Who does she think she is, Miss High and Mighty? He'll leave her one day, you mark my words ...' And Silvia, who hasn't a grain of sense in her head, reports every detail back to her father Mingo, the postman, and it's all round the village in no time. They look down on her, every single one of them, even that witless fool, Renzo, with his slack mouth and twisted body, who goes limping from door to door begging for coins in return for tuneless renditions of Giacomo's arias. They all know the truth, whispered from one to the other behind their hands as she passes. *Signora Elvira is a fallen woman, a harlot, a pretender to the throne ... call it what you like, she is not married to the Maestro.* Cook, the fleshy padding of her chin still wobbling from her exertions, pulls the tripe onto her chopping board, angles her knife and starts cutting off long thin strips, which she drops onto a plate. Despite herself, Elvira finds her gaze drawn to the lengths of tripe curling around each other like newborn vipers in a nest ... like the people in this godforsaken village, whose lives slide round in a listless mess of dirt and tittle-tattle.

'Urgh!' Turning her back, she goes to the pantry to fetch the eggs.

Elvira is going to make *latte alla portoghese*, a rich, baked custard that had been introduced to Giacomo's grandmother by the cook in the family home in Celle, a village in the hills to the north. Selecting a bowl from the dresser, she taps each of eight eggshells firmly against the rim, separates off the white with a cup and spoon, and pours the yolks into a jug of sweetened cream. Whisking them together, she wonders why the dessert is called Portuguese milk when there isn't a drop of milk in it, a thought she realises she must have articulated out loud when Cook drops the lemon wedge she is squeezing over the tripe, and says sourly, 'Questions, always questions. What would I know what them foreigners get up to?'

Elvira shrugs. 'Indeed. Who is to know what anyone gets up to?' A question that goes no further because it is interrupted by the doorbell. Running her hands down her apron, she disappears into the hall, returning a minute later with the mail, which she will inspect when Cook goes outside for the vegetables.

Today there is a registered packet from the House of Ricordi (the contract Giacomo has been expecting, no doubt), and a second postcard from Antonio describing a tennis match at the Olympic Games. Turning it over, Elvira inspects the photograph of a young woman holding her tennis racquet triumphantly aloft; an English girl, most likely, judging by the fair hair and flawless complexion, who is wearing a high-necked blouse and – *good grief!* – a man's tie. Mesmerised by what she sees, Elvira lowers herself onto a stool, all the while scrutinising the athletic physique, the ecstatic smile, the striped tie. *What sort of woman would parade in public in men's clothing?* But she already knows the answer: one with no sense of propriety, no shame, that's who! The same breed that throws themselves at Giacomo, intent on the pleasure of the moment, with not a moment's consideration for herself or the life that entwines them like a pair of underground streams. Where were those hussies when Giacomo was a penniless musician, moving from one set of lodgings to the next, while she and the children stayed with Ida in Florence? *In their cradles, that's where! Shame on them! Shame! Puttanas, the lot of them, with nothing better to do than steal other women's husbands!* Elvira's hands are trembling; her skin has begun to itch. The postcard is contaminating her! She must get rid of it, but first she must show it to Giacomo.

He is sitting at his music score table, his back to her, his pencil moving steadily across the surface of his notebook. Elvira coughs, and he, in turn, pretends not to hear, a ridiculous tactic because she knows he has the finely tuned ears of an owl. When he does swivel round, she is surprised to see that instead of his usual house attire of baggy trousers and open-neck shirt, he is wearing pale maroon linen and silk.

'You look very smart,' she says, handing him the postcard.

He looks down at himself, bemused by her comment. 'I suppose I do,' he says. 'I'm popping over to La Piaggetta after lunch to see Carlo. He's thinking of buying a motorcar and wants my advice. I can't barge into the home of a marquis looking like a tramp, can I?'

'No, of course not,' Elvira says, forcing a smile. She isn't fond of the Marchese Ginori-Lisci or his wife, who treat her with a sort of cool politeness that borders on contempt.

Handing the postcard back to her, Giacomo reaches behind him for a glass that contains red wine. 'What are we having for lunch?' he asks.

'Tripe ... and isn't it a little early to be drinking?'

'I hope there isn't too much garlic in it,' he says, disregarding her question.

'No, just a little, and some onion. But you like garlic ...'

He pats his stomach. 'I've still got a touch of indigestion from the *agnellotti* we had for supper last night.'

Elvira frowns. 'I don't see how drinking wine is going to help. And it'd better be cleared up by Wednesday.'

'Wednesday?'

'Ferragosto, Giacomo. Don't tell me you'd forgotten!'

'Of course not,' he says, his tone brightening. 'Is Giuseppe coming? I need him to check my eyesight. I'm getting as blind as a bat.'

'Yes, he'll be here for three days. The children are so looking forward to seeing him. The only one who'll be missing is Antonio ...' And here Elvira pauses, her eyes drawn like magnets to the panels above the fireplace, where a chubby little *amorino*, a naked boy-child, is entwined in ribbons and clusters of pale, peony-like blooms. She closes her eyes, knowing that in a second or two another small boy will emerge from the shadows of her mind. *Oh, Renato ...*

There is a cough followed by the sound of spitting. Giacomo is dabbing a red streak from his chin with the edge of his handkerchief.

'Did you get any on your shirt?' she asks, unable to look him in the eye.

'No,' he says. Then, 'Elvira, are you all right?'

It is a question she cannot answer, and so she turns to the French windows, where the sun is shining through the glass, filling the room with a bright, creamy light that for some reason seems to attenuate the grief she is nursing for her lost son. *Are you all right, Elvira?* How she longs to tell him the truth, to shout it in his face, to see his eyes widen with shock, the guilty realisation of what he has done to her. No, *I'm not all right! How could I be when I've given up my child for you!* But what would be the point? And so instead she forces a note of jollity into her voice and says, 'Of course, I am. Why shouldn't I be?'

And he, visibly relieved, answers, 'Oh, no reason.'

The clock on the score table ticks round to the hour. 'Goodness me, is that the time?' she says. 'Ida will be wondering where I've got to.'

Ida watches her sister pour thimblefuls of black coffee into the small cups, reach for the delicate tongs and carefully drop a sugar cube into each one. Through the window behind Elvira's head, she can see Poldo stumbling past the front gate with a milk churn on his back, on his way round to the kitchen. Earlier it had been the butcher's boy, his arms loaded with blood-stained parcels, and before him, the chimneysweep, an oaf of a man who managed to dirty the rug. With all this to see to, no wonder Elvira is looking worn out, a situation not helped by the blouse she is wearing, which is a pale primrose, ruffled at the neck and puffed out in front like a pigeon's breast. Ida knows only too well that in men's eyes forty is not a good age for a woman, and for a moment Ida feels sorry for her sister, a sentiment that calls up memories of a younger Elvira. A spirited girl with a laugh too quick to hide behind her fan, who loved to dance and stay out as late as she could. What fun they'd had! The parties, the summer days at *Salsomaggiore*, sipping the bitter health-promoting water while planning the evening's entertainment, the trips to the ballet and the opera – outings designed to introduce them to the right sort of young men. When father fled to Argentina to escape his creditors, their mother gave up, taking to her bed with a pile of handkerchiefs and a bottle of smelling salts. Elvira, too, seemed to lose interest in everything except some harebrained scheme to join him as soon as she could. Of course, there was no money for such a venture, and within a year, a few months short of her eighteenth birthday, Elvira had been married off to Narciso Gemignani, him with his shopkeeper mother …

Ida turns to her sister, thinking to reminisce a little and sees to her dismay that Elvira is weeping. 'My dear,' she says, putting down her cup and taking Elvira's hand, 'what on earth's the matter?'

Elvira, unable to speak, gulps instead. Ida, who has witnessed a number of these scenes over the years, nudges her a little. 'It's *Ferragosto*, isn't it, making you think of Renato?'

A sob rasps from the back of Elvira's throat. 'Oh Ida, I'm *always* thinking of him. I can't seem to stop … now that Antonio's away at school and Fosca's taken up with that fellow in Milan … I saw him, you know.'

'Who, dear?'

'Renato.'

'Elvira, you didn't! But when? Where?'

Through her tears, Elvira blurts out the story, word by horrible word.

'Oh, my goodness!' Ida says, when the story has ended. 'You poor thing! But Elvira –'

'I know, I know!' Elvira says, straightening up and wiping her nose. 'You make your bed, and you lie in it. That's it, Ida, isn't it?'

Ida shakes her head. 'I wasn't going to say that at all.'

'So, what were you going to say?'

Ida pauses, filtering out thoughts that would only add to her sister's anguish; that children rarely forgive mothers who abandon them, no matter what the reason, that Elvira should never have run off with a man driven by an artistic temperament …

'And that's not all,' Elvira adds in a whisper.

Ida leans closer, so as not to miss a word. 'There's more?'

'Isn't there always?' she says with a bitter laugh.

'Well?'

Elvira's gaze turns towards the window, and the lilies in the crystal vase. 'Since Giacomo started work on his new opera, he hasn't shown any interest in me … you know … as his wife …'

Ida pauses to take in the significance of this revelation. 'And you imagine …'

'… that he's up to his old tricks?' Elvira finishes for her.

'But, Elvira, who with?'

Now Elvira turns to look at her. 'Some local woman, I suppose.'

'Don't be silly, dear, there are no local women, just peasants.'

'Well then, it's some little strumpet he's picked up somewhere else.'

There is a silence in which Ida pulls a loose thread from the seam of her cuff and winds it around her little finger. She is thinking how best to respond; give the matter too much weight and it will inflame Elvira against Giacomo, too little and the ire will come her way. Unwinding the thread, she remembers how trusting of Giacomo Elvira had been at the beginning, how reluctant to consider his true nature, his fascination with the gentler sex, his delight in cultivating his 'little gardens'. Knowledge that a clever woman would have used to her advantage, exacting diamonds, fur coats and trips to Paris and Monte Carlo in exchange for her acquiescence. Not Elvira. She wanted him all for herself, and deep down, sensing that she could never have him, a part of her had turned sour and angry, provoking outbursts of fury that at times drove all reason from her mind, replacing it with thoughts bordering on madness.

'But Elvira, dear,' she says gently. 'Giacomo has been working day and night and hardly ever goes out.'

Elvira stiffens. 'I knew you wouldn't understand.'

Ida gives her sister's hand a reassuring squeeze. 'No, I promise you, dear, I do. It's just that thinking about Renato always upsets you, and although we both know Giacomo isn't a saint, I really don't see that you have cause for alarm.'

'Alarm!' The word splinters like glass. 'He's going to leave me, Ida, I know he will! The shame of it! Just imagine! After all these years …'

Ida has been patient long enough. 'Come on, Elvira, this will never do! You're tired and overwrought. You've been doing too much, and quite frankly, you need to get out of the house a bit more. How about a shopping trip? There's a new boutique on the promenade in *Viareggio* – you remember the one I was telling you about? It has some lovely dresses … divine colours, pinks and blues, and those yellows you favour …'

Elvira is not to be so easily deflected. 'I'm sick of it, Ida,' she says, her tone changing, becoming angrier, 'sick of steaming open letters and listening in to telephone calls, sick of questioning maids and sniffing Giacomo's shirts …'

'Shhh, Elvira! He'll hear you!'

'Let him!' she says, triumphantly. 'It's time he knew the truth! I'm going to confront him, get everything out in the open.'

Ida grabs her wrist. 'Stop it, Elvira! You're talking like a scema, an idiot. You know how much he hates a fuss, and what's the point of starting a row you can never win? Listen to me … If you want Giacomo back in your bed, you'll have to use your head a little, and your powers as a woman.'

Elvira regards her through blotchy uncertain eyes. 'Whatever do you mean?'

Ida gives Elvira's hand an encouraging little pat. 'Be gentle, dear, alluring even. Don't raise your voice and indulge him for all he's worth. Plan his favourite meals, you know, all those ghastly birds and things, order good wine, cigars, and the very best chocolates. And dearest …' – here she pauses, choosing her words carefully – 'as a woman gets older, she must take more care of her appearance. Face cream, Elvira, a dab of rouge, a little more colour on your lips. You've got wonderful breasts, have your blouses cut a little lower so he can see what he's missing …'

Elvira is staring at her in disbelief. 'You mean dress like a puttana?'

'No, no, of course not!' Ida says quickly. 'But instead of crossing Giacomo, try pandering to his male instincts a little more … Now dear, what about that outing I suggested? Once Ferragosto is out of the way, we can get Poldo to take us to Viareggio in the carriage.'

Chapter 8
A SPIN IN PUCCINI'S MOTORCAR

Corinna crosses the bridge over the canal at the far end of the promenade and continues until she reaches Pineta di Levante, a pinewood that sweeps south along the coast towards the mouth of the river Serchio, and from there through the grounds of San Rossore, the royal park that houses the hunting lodge favoured by the old King. In years gone by, before the town became fashionable, the pines were cultivated for industrial purposes, the bark to produce dye, and the resin (a pungent, gluey sap, thick and transparent) collected in flasks and poured into drums, themselves loaded onto barges and floated downstream on their way for processing. But Corinna's thoughts are far away from such things as she stops and looks around, her gaze shifting from the bleached sand, where two bathing pavilions strut out like wading birds into the foam, to the vegetation in front of her. *Where is the path?* And then she sees it, a little further up. Lowering her parasol, she hurries towards it, and into the blissful shade of the trees.

A seagull enjoying the cool air under the dense green panoply looks up and sees a slight figure, the colour of a summer sky, holding one of those infernal sticks the ladies use to chase him away. He lets out a squawk. This could be his revenge, to splatter her bonnet and mark her dress. Thinking better of such a show, he squawks again and takes off, aiming towards the shoreline in the hope of finding some salty little morsel washed up by the tide. Corinna watches the gull fly off into the distance and closes her eyes. The air is cool and damp, tinged with the heaviness of pine, a smell which transports her back to childhood afternoons spent near the water, piling sand into mounds and decorating them with shells shaped like finger-nails and strands of seaweed from far-off shores, with Grand-ma's voice calling over the waves. 'Be careful, dear. Don't get wet. You'll catch a chill!' Opening her eyes, she digs the toe of her shoe into the mat of fallen pine needles, watching the ants scurry about in confusion. 'Come on!' she mutters. 'Hurry up! Hurry up!'

While she is waiting, Corinna considers how she should pres-ent herself to the composer – not to be too coy, for then she will be dismissed as a boring little provincial. On the other hand, if she is too forward, she risks being taken for the sort of girl who ends up giving birth to a nameless child in a faraway convent. How very confusing! And in her confusion, Corinna's thoughts return to another occasion, just before Christmas, when she had sneaked out of the house in Turin on her first secret assig-nation, one that would have equally scandalised her family had it become known.

'So, what do anarchists actually believe in,' she had asked Aurelia over lunch in the cafeteria one chill December day towards the end of their first term, '... if there's no God, no government and no society?'

Aurelia, had ripped a piece of bread with her fingers, and fixed her with a challenging look. 'Listen, dear thing. Instead of grilling me like a piece of fish, why don't you come along to one of our meetings? There's one on tonight, with a talk by Luigi Galleani, a leading light in our movement.' The meeting was held in a bar near Porta Susa railway station, a smelly place with sawdust on the floorboards and a spittoon like a yawning mouth in the corner by the counter. Behind the bar hung a framed mirror, so covered in dust it hadn't reflected anything for years, and the candlelit tables were packed with men who turned to stare at them as they entered.

'Aurelia! Where are the women?'

Her friend screeched with laughter. 'Women! In a place like this? Come on! Let's go and sit over there, by the fire.' There were two groups, factions Aurelia called them: working men with badly shaven faces and calloused hands, and the pale in-tellectual type with spectacles and floppy forelocks, some of whom Corinna recognised from the university. They huddled around the tables, each keeping to their own kind, but united by a hatred of the country's militarist government and an interest in the two women who had just entered. The working men stared openly, eyeing them shamelessly up and down, as if by coming to this place she and Aurelia had relinquished any right to the considerations normally granted to their sex. The students peered out timidly from behind their beer mugs, which Corinna found equally disconcerting. All listened patiently to Luigi Galleani, a long-faced bearded man in his forties with low-slung ears that looked as if they had slipped from their rightful place, while he recounted stories of his exile in France and Switzerland, and his banishment to a remote island off the coast of Sicily. But when he moved on to his main topic, the assassination of tyrants and other enemies of the people, the mood swiftly changed, the men acting like hungry lions devouring the clumps of meat thrown through the bars of their cages. And how they roared, clambering onto the benches, waving their fists and shouting at the tops of their voices. It all made Corinna's head spin, as it does when she stands up too quickly.

'What did you think?' Aurelia asked her afterwards, as they crossed the road back towards the station.

Corinna hesitated, unsure how to respond, for in truth she had been sickened by Galleani and his feverish exhortations to violence, his assertion that the slaughter he proposed could be justified by the nobility of its aims. *He was mad, unhinged.* Yet within his madness, there was a glimmer of something that had struck her as both true and useful: that one should not blindly accept one's fate, but instead react, respond, and ultimately rise up and break the chains that bound one to it.

Here and now, Corinna digs her shoe into the pine needles and makes a little pile with her toe, listening to the crackle and snap underfoot. She looks around at the silver threads spinning across the path, the undergrowth shifting with unseen life, the small green lizard that darts out then freezes like an ornament on a mantelpiece. To her right, in a thickly wooded area, a pool of sunshine is striking through the trees, illuminating the clusters of berries that hang like rubies from a bush.

Where is he? Come on! Come on!

A sudden noise, a *whiz* then a *bang*, like the firing of a rifle, startles Corinna from her thoughts. She jumps back, grasps hold of a tree and peers out from behind it, thinking to see a hunter in pursuit of a rabbit or pheasant. There is nothing, only the pine cone that has landed near her feet, sprouting pods shaped like garlic cloves covered in fine soot. Crouching down to inspect them, Corinna hears another bang, the backfiring of a motorcar, then quite unexpectedly Puccini has breached the distance between them and is standing in front of her.

'My dear, how lovely to see you again,' he says, in a tone suggesting she is the only woman in the world. He is wearing a pale maroon linen suit with a spotted beige bow tie, and a straw boater placed at a rakish angle on his head, where a strand of hair has escaped from the mass and is curling on his brow like a question mark. Taking her hand, he lifts it to his lips, and as he does so, a ray of sunlight penetrates the awning above, illuminating them.

'You're lucky to find me alive,' Corinna says, blithely. 'I was very nearly struck by a pine cone.'

'Good Lord!' he says, leaning back and looking up at the tree.

'Really, it was nothing …'

'Nothing? They come down at the speed of light! I have a chalet near here, and some years ago a friend of mine was knocked clean out of his senses.'

Wanting to know more, Corinna is momentarily distracted by the touch of his hand on her arm.

'I thought we could motor along to a little place I know near Lido di Camaiore,' he says, guiding her towards the automobile. Stopping by the passenger door, he takes her parasol and twirls it expertly in his hands, spinning the ruffle into a hazy pink pom-pom. 'What a fine object!' he says, placing it in the back of the car. 'Is it new?'

'Oh no! I've had it for ages.' Then she swallows, wondering why she'd told such a stupid little lie.

He steps forward and swipes the air, striking at an imaginary ball. 'The thing about parasols,' he says, 'is that they make excellent bats. I've ruined dozens in my time … My sisters used to get furious with me.'

'And what about your brothers, did they join in?'

He looks down, but not swiftly enough to hide the flinch in his eyes. 'I have no brothers,' he says quietly.

Now it is her turn to look away, struck by the profound sorrow in his expression.

'Here,' he says, 'pop this dustcoat on. It will stop your pretty dress from getting dirty.' He is holding open a garment like a summer bathrobe, smiling happily, so happily that Corinna wonders if her mind is playing tricks on her.

The car seat is an elegant pale tan, the warm leather giving off the musty-sour smell of newness and expense. Corinna arranges herself on its smooth surface, feeling the heat working its way through her dress, her underskirt, her drawers, until it is scratching uncomfortably at her bottom and thighs. She shifts about, edging this way and that, while Puccini cranks the handle at the front and brings the engine to life. Climbing up, he sits beside her and fiddles about with the controls. He seems larger than before, more solid somehow, and now that he is so close, she can smell the spice on his skin, a smell that makes her shuffle closer and breathe in again.

'Are you ready?' he asks, as they jointly adjust their goggles. She nods. The motorcar shudders, jolts, then slides forward, and suddenly they are bouncing along the esplanade in the shade of the palm trees.

'It's a De Dion-Bouton,' he calls proudly, heedless of the breeze and accelerating past cafes and boutiques with awnings flapping.

'Really?' she cries, her voice barely audible above the noise of the engine.

'Yes, it's only two months old. Five horsepower – one of the first in the country.'

'Really!' she calls out again, wondering if he realises she has never been in a motorcar before. On he drives, past villas, pensioni and hotels with walled gardens of parterres, statues, clipped hedges, and fountains, all shuttered and eerily deserted, as if the inhabitants have been swept inside and the doors barred against an invisible enemy. They pass a lone workman attending to a gas lamp who turns to look in the direction of the unfamiliar roar, and then a group of young men, tall, pale and badly dressed, gathered around a stone monument.

'Look at the English!' Puccini shouts. 'These are the students who cluster, ant-like, at the place where the poet Shelley's body was washed up on the shore.'

Corinna clutches the brim of her bonnet and nods. 'He drowned.' She, too, is shouting. 'There was a storm ...'

'Yes. Poor fellow! His boat sank.' Corinna gives up trying to converse and looks about her, at the jagged line of mountains to the north, at the white crested waves rolling in slowly, one after another, at a sky that dazzles her eyes. Her body is swaying with the motion of the vehicle, and now that she is becoming used to it, she finds it quite soothing, so that by the time the motor swerves off the road onto a sandy track and comes to a juddering stop, she is breathing quite normally again.

They have pulled up outside a shack with a flat roof and a gangplank leading up to a verandah, itself stacked up with broken chairs, empty flagons and a perambulator full of dusty beer bottles. Corinna looks around for the cafe of her imagination, which has arched windows, a vine-covered pergola and a terrace decorated with pots of cheerful red geraniums. Instead, there is nothing but this sun-bleached cabin set among the sand dunes. Puccini precedes her up the gangplank and pulls open a flimsy door, where a blast of air, like a gust from an oven, greets her as she steps inside and looks from the scuffed wooden floor to the faded hessian walls.

'I'm sorry it isn't very glamorous,' he says, sensing her disappointment, 'but we won't be disturbed here. It's quiet at this time of day.'

'Quiet?' Corinna looks at the empty tables in the small, cramped salon. 'Deserted would be a better word.' There is a bar, and behind it glass shelves holding bottles of brightly coloured liquid that wink at her from the mirrored wall. At the far end, a coffee machine sighs and blasts a jet of vapour towards the ceiling. A warm, sweet smell fills the air, and suddenly Corinna feels ravenously hungry.

'Let's sit there,' Puccini says, indicating a table in the corner by a window. 'It's cool, and the view is pleasant.' Corinna lowers herself onto a seat next to curtains that would make her grandmother gasp at their threadbare state and looks out over mounds of sand anchored down by rope-like grass.

'Maestro,' a thin voice pipes, 'what a pleasure! We haven't seen you here in ever such a long while.' Corinna turns and sees what is either a very old man or a living corpse, a small creature, frighteningly thin, with skin like parchment, tufts of hair sprouting unevenly from his skull, and a pitted nose the colour of vintage wine.

'Arturo! Good afternoon to you!' Puccini says, grasping him by the hand. 'No, I'm afraid not ... my work, you know, keeps me very busy. And how is the family, your wife? All well, I hope.'

The man raises his first and little fingers and jabs them in the air. *'Tocca ferro!'* he croaks, 'although none of us is getting any younger.'

Puccini agrees, leaning back in his rickety chair. 'Now, what can you offer us by way of refreshments?'

The old man wheezes in a breath. 'We have some savouries ... my wife made the paté only this morning ... a little salami, a few olives, peppers *sottolio*, perhaps ...'

'My dear, how does that sound?'

'Wonderful, but ...'

'But?' He looks at her, reading her eyes. 'Ah! ... and what,' he says, turning back to the proprietor, 'can you offer us by way of *dolci*?'

Arturo shifts his weight and gives a rasping, metallic cough, as if there is loose change stuck in his gullet. 'Quince crostata and sorbetto di limone ... The lemons are from our own trees.' Corinna smiles her assent.

'Done!' says Puccini. 'Savouries for me, crostata and sorbetto for the young lady, and a bottle of your best champagne, right away!'

The old man turns and shuffles back to the kitchen while Puccini reaches into his jacket and pulls out a cigarette case, which he flicks open and holds out to her. Corinna hesitates, then shakes her head. She is searching around for some tidbit of conversation, something bright and witty, but her mind has gone blank.

'Do you stay in Viareggio every summer?' he asks, anticipating her.

'Oh yes!' The words come out as a sigh.

'You don't sound too happy about it.'

Corinna shrugs. 'A little variety would be nice.'

He puts his cigarette to his mouth, watching her. 'Variety being the spice of life, you mean?'

She hesitates, unsure of his tone. 'Something like that.'

'What about university?' he presses on. 'Surely it's full of bright young people having fun?'

She shrugs again. 'That's what I'd imagined, but I can assure you it's not. The boys are pasty-faced bores, and the girls, all five of them, are swots. Except for my friend, Aurelia,' she adds, 'who's mad.'

'Mad?' he says, intrigued. 'In what way?'

'In a certifiable way,' Corinna says.

'That's not a very well-argued case,' he says, teasing her with his eyes.

'No, I suppose not. But what if I told you she can't abide authority in any form, or "middle-class morality", which seems to encompass just about everything else.'

He thinks for a moment. 'Perhaps your friend is more modern than mad?'

'Oh no. She says one day women will be doing the same work as men.'

His eyes widen. 'Does she really?'

'Yes, but as her father is a top lawyer …'

'She can say anything she likes,' he finishes for her, a lick of smoke slithering from his mouth. A hand with pebbles for knuckles smooths two squares of straw paper on the table in front of Corinna and Puccini, then adds a bottle of champagne in an ice bucket. Reaching out for the bottle, the composer pops the cork and swoops the liquid into their glasses.

'Salute!' he says, raising his flute to hers.

'Salute!' Corinna tips the glass to her mouth and takes a tentative sip, swirling the champagne round with her tongue to appreciate the unfamiliar taste. Delicious! Tipping the glass again, she takes another sip.

'And what do you intend to do when you finish your studies?' Puccini asks.

She pulls a face. 'I'll probably end up a schoolteacher.'

'Is that so bad? Two of my sisters taught at elementary school before they married, another is a *maestra* of French, and Otilia, the eldest, gives piano lessons. They all seem to like it.'

'Oh, please don't misunderstand me,' she says quickly, 'I think teaching is an admirable profession. It's just that I was hoping for ...' her voice trails off.

'Something a little more exciting?' he suggests.

She nods, adding in a cheerful tone, 'At least one only works mornings, and there are the holidays for doing other things ...'

Now the old man is placing food on the table: a basket of bread, a platter of salami and olives, and a dish of red and green peppers floating in oil like tropical fish in a viscous yellow sea. And for her, a pastry along with two rounds of sorbet which are rapidly dissolving.

Stubbing out his cigarette, Puccini reaches for the champagne and tops up her glass. 'Other things? What sort of other things would you like to be doing?'

'Oh, I don't know ... I should love to travel, for example.'

'Really?' He sounds surprised. 'I seem to be travelling all the time. In fact, I only got back from London a few weeks ago.'

'London!' she breathes enviously. 'Is it as wonderful as they say?'

He sucks in his lips. 'I suppose so, but as I was working most of the time, I hardly noticed. Of course, Covent Garden is one of the lovelier opera houses, and the city does have its own particular style with its fine architecture and vast green parks. It's ...' his thumb and finger click together searching for the missing word ... '*imperial*'. Yes, that's what it is. But after a few days, I was dying to come home.'

Corinna is astonished. 'But why?'

He smiles. 'Because they speak English – an unfathomable language – and drink tea all the time. Tea! I ask you! I never touch the stuff, although they do say it is good for fevers.'

'And feet.'

He blinks. 'I'm sorry?'

'Feet,' she confirms. 'Surely you've heard of the beneficial effects of tea on the feet?'

'I don't believe I have,' he says. 'I must try it.' Then he leans forward, as if sharing a confidence. 'Do tell me, do you dip your toes directly into the teapot?'

'Of course. How else?'

His grin is like a light being switched on. 'Marvellous!' There is a complicit pause, then Corinna picks up her spoon and plunges it into the tart. 'You make your visit to London sound very dull,' she says, 'but what about the wonderful shops?'

He covers a corner of bread with paté. 'Shops? Well, I certainly had a fine old time in Liberty's browsing through their selection of Chinese bronzes.'

'And Harrods? Did you go there?'

'I wouldn't go near the place!' he shudders. 'They have a moving staircase that is so bumpy the staff hand out nips of brandy to customers at the top!'

'You're scared of an escalator?'

'Not scared, terrified. But I did go to the theatre –'

'When you don't speak the language. Isn't that even more frightening?'

'It certainly is,' he smiles, 'which is why initially I refused. But my friends insisted, and thank God they did because the play turned out to be *Madame Butterfly* …'

'*Madame Butterfly* – the book you were reading on the train?'

He regards her with a mix of surprise and delight, as if she were a dog that had just performed a particularly clever trick. 'My dear, what an excellent memory you have!'

'It comes in useful for the exams.'

'I imagine it does,' he says. Then he gives her a look that lingers like a caress. Corinna, unnerved by what she sees, lifts her glass and pours the contents into her mouth.

'It's going to be my next opera,' he says, breaking off a piece of bread.

'What is? … Oh, you mean *Madame Butterfly*. The playwright must be pleased.'

'Belasco? It's hard to tell, he's such a strange fellow. An American with lots of hair who dresses like a priest.'

'A priest? Really? And what is Mr Belasco's play about?'

Puccini is sliding more champagne into her glass. 'It's about a young Japanese girl who becomes a geisha after the death of her father, falls in love with and marries a US naval officer in defiance of her family, only to be abandoned by him shortly after the wedding.'

Corinna's spoon stops halfway to her mouth. 'But that's terrible!'

'It gets worse,' he says.

'Worse?'

'She waits for him, convinced that he will return.'

'And does he?'

'Yes and no.'

'Yes and no? It can't be both.'

'Why not?' he says, his mouth curling into a smile.

'It just can't be! Do explain what you mean.'

'But that would spoil the surprise.'

'Aah,' she yelps, 'a secret! I hate secrets!'

'Do you? His hand slides across the table and settles on hers. 'But can you keep them?' He is looking at her, his eyes suggesting that it is the answer to another question that he really wants. But before she has to reply, he pulls away his hand, picks up his fork and spears a green olive. *'Buon appetito!'* he says, popping it into his mouth.

Corinna reaches for her glass and takes a nervous gulp. Can she keep a secret? *What does he mean exactly? And that look!* Oh, if only she had more experience! But she has so little. None, really, Corinna recalls, except for that one time at Aurelia's house when Maurizio held open the door to the conservatory, bent down and clumsily pressed his mouth to hers in a frantic sort of kiss …

There is a clink as Puccini drops his olive stone, sucked clean, onto his plate. 'Do you like cooking?' he asks, wiping his mouth on his napkin.

'Cooking?' The question is so unexpected that it propels her straight back to the yellow, high-ceilinged kitchen where she spent so much of her childhood. There, under the marble-topped table, is the stool she clambered onto to draw patterns on the steamy window glass, or watch starlings devouring bloated orange persimmons from the tree in the garden next door. She had knelt on it, too, while her floury hands shaped soft little gnocchi, and the cook (she can't remember which one) prepared a sauce of melted butter and sage. Later, when she was a student at the *liceo*, she had perched in the warm angle near

the stove, reading the novels of D'Annunzio and Pascoli and dreaming of the life she one day hoped to lead. Does she like cooking? She doesn't really know, but the kitchen had certainly been a haven for a child whose father was always working, and whose mother lay in a darkened room that smelled of medicine and disinfectant.

'At home in Turin, I sometimes prepare simple dishes, but my grandmother won't let me near the kitchen here for fear of upsetting Lucia, our cook.'

'Very wise of her,' he says, grasping the bottle round the neck and aiming it at her glass. 'So, what do you do with your time?' Corinna searches for things to describe other than the helpless hours spent on shady benches, watching the passersby.

'We go for walks, shopping ... I like to read ...'

'Oh yes, I remember, law books.'

'Not only. There are the newspapers, which my grandmother edits.'

'Oh?'

An unexpected giggle rises up in Corinna's throat, which she manages to swallow. 'She cuts out pieces she considers detrimental to my young mind.'

He smiles. 'I see.'

'And novels, of course,' she goes on. 'I'm reading Flaubert at the moment – *Madame Bovary.*' Then she pauses, shocked at her own boldness.

'Your grandmother's scissors would find plenty to do there!'

'That's why I keep it well hidden from her.' *What is she saying?* She looks down into her lap and sees her napkin shifting about like the sail of a restless boat.

'I envy you the pleasure of reading,' he says. 'My mind tries to turn everything into an opera, even *The Hunchback of Notre Dame.*'

'What? Quasimodo as a tenor role?'

'I know! I know! The trouble is, I can't turn a page without seeing the characters on stage and hearing the music. It's a curse, really it is ...' He has found a subject dear to his heart, and as he explores it, his hands waving in small circles, Corinna watches the way his mouth tightens at the corners and his moustache twitches up and down, keeping time. His words drift past her like wispy clouds in a windswept sky, making no sense at all. Do they have substance, she wonders, and if she reaches out, will she feel something solid, or just the cool mix of vapour and air? Leaning forward, she stretches out her hand like a child trying to catch a beautiful ephemeral insect. And that is when the most extraordinary thought occurs to her – what would his lips feel like pressed to her own? This time there is no stopping the giggle that bursts from her, despite the napkin hurriedly stuffed to her mouth.

Puccini, though, appears not to notice. Tugging at his watch-chain, he glances into his hand. 'My dear,' he says, 'we must be going or you'll be late.' Corinna is standing by the motorcar pulling on her glove, one finger at a time, when she makes a re-markable discovery: there is no hole for her thumb, but instead an extra floppy rabbit's ear beside her little finger. Twisting her hand, she examines the front then the back, trying to resolve the problem.

'Here!' Puccini says, holding open the dustcoat. Forgetting all about the glove, Corinna turns to slip her arms into the sleeves. Which is when her foot catches, or perhaps she slips – exactly what happened isn't clear – but from one second to the next she is lurching towards the ground and he, with the reflexes of a fencer, jumps forward and catches her.

'Oh!' she cries, kicking her feet back onto the path. 'How clumsy of me!' The dustcoat has twisted itself round her shoulders and one of the sleeves is tangled up with the tie of her bonnet. She shakes her head, but perhaps a little too vigorous-ly, for now her hair is snagged on his tiepin. She gives a tug, and then another. Ouch! Now she is free, but before she has time to compose herself, his hand is running along her cheek, sweeping a strand of loose hair behind her ear.

'I hope we can do this again,' he murmurs, his handsome eyes close to hers. And Corinna, unable to speak, nods instead.

Chapter 9
PUCCINI PAYS A VISIT TO THE CLUB DELLA BOHÈME

Puccini enters through the back door and treads quietly along the corridor to the hall, where he stops and listens to the murmur of voices coming from the verandah beyond the dining room. It is five o'clock, and sure enough, Elvira and Ida are taking afternoon tea. Slotting his boater onto the hatstand, he pauses for a moment to study Ida's bonnet, a ridiculous confection of frothy netting and cherries, reminding him of the cakes he used to gaze at longingly through the window of the *pasticceria* in Milan when he was a student. Reaching out, he runs a finger over a glossy red fruit, which is waxy and leaves a residue on his skin and, resisting the urge to pluck it off and stick it in his pocket, he drops his wallet on the telephone table and continues up the staircase to the bathroom, pushing the door to behind him.

A row of bottles containing cologne, astringents and Acqua di Parma sits on the shelf under the mirror. Stretching out his hand, he selects a dark green sphere and squeezes the bulb, sending a mist of spice shooting through the air and onto his skin. Then he picks up his comb, runs it through his hair and regards himself with a contended nod. The encounter went better than expected. The young lady from Turin was a breath of fresh air compared with all the theatre types he was meeting these days. She was more like Fosca, bright and amusing, with hidden depths to be sounded …

The composer lifts a tumbler of salt water, takes a swig and swishes it round his mouth, then tips back his head, gargles up and down a scale and spits into the hand basin. … And the odd thing is that when he took her parasol and twirled it in his hands, he was struck by a sense that he already knew her – *her*, properly her, not some girl he'd met on a train. And even odder, the sensation kept coming back, although he had no idea why. Perhaps she reminded him of someone? Like that little ballerina he'd entertained all those years ago in Milan when he was sharing rooms with Mascagni, paying his friend to wait outside until dawn. *Oh boy, hadn't it been worth it!*

There is a smile on Puccini's face as he leans forward and peers into the mirror, checking for stray hairs on his jacket and collar. No matter what, he must tread carefully; no compromising notes or letters, no gifts or flowers that can be traced back to him ... and with a bottle of champagne always at the ready! He straightens up with an image in his mind of a tipsy Corinna tripping over her own feet and crumpling into his arms with the look of a startled kitten. Sauntering downstairs, the composer makes his way through the dining room to the verandah, pausing in the doorway to listen to the clinking of teacups from within. The blinds have been lowered to defend the ladies from the afternoon sun, and in the soft, filtered light a few stray beams pick out a three-tiered, gold-rimmed cake stand offering a selection of small pastries. Perfumed steam rises from the curved spout of a teapot, and as he watches it drift towards one of the ornamental palms, Puccini wonders how anyone in their right mind could drink tea on such a hot day.

'Giacomo!' Ida calls gaily from a cane chair that looks as if it has swallowed her whole. 'Come and join us! We're christening the new tea service.'

'No thank you,' he says, stepping into the room. 'I never touch the stuff, although they do say it's good for the feet.'

'Feet?' Now Elvira turns to look at him. 'What are you talking about? Well at least have some cake,' she insists. 'It's the one you like with semolina and honey. Cook baked it for you this morning.'

'No, really, Elvira, thank you. I'm not hungry.'

Her eyes narrow suspiciously. 'But a spin in the car usually stimulates your appetite. All that fresh air ...'

'I know,' he says, patting his midriff, 'but I still have a touch of indigestion.'

Thankfully the conversation goes no further because at that moment the door to the garden flies open, banging into the doorstop, and there on the step, backlit in gold like an angel from heaven, is Fosca. This angel, though, has flushed cheeks and the windswept look of a scarecrow. One shoe is missing, and her blouse and skirt have parted company, exposing an expanse of firm young flesh. With her, yelping and pulling excitedly on his lead, is Nello, Puccini's brown and white spaniel.

'Goodness me, Fosca!' Ida exclaims, 'you look as if you've been dragged through a mulberry bush backwards!'

Ignoring her, Fosca turns to Puccini and gives him a smile of such warmth that something catches near his heart. 'Papa, thank goodness you're back! Gastone let go of Schaunard and he's run off into the woods. Poldo is helping us search for him …'

'What? He'll cause havoc! Where are the other dogs?'

'With Clara, but Schaunard won't come to anyone but you.'

The spaniel, who had been quietly sniffing the delights of Fosca's bare foot, suddenly catches sight of the finches in Elvira's aviary at the end of the verandah. He shoots forward, yapping with excitement, and careens into Elvira's chair, where a wave of pale tea, about to be poured into her mouth, slops from her cup to her saucer and into her lap. 'For goodness sake!' she cries, flapping her hand at the dog. 'Get that animal out of here!'

Grabbing the lead, Puccini squats down and ruffles the spaniel's silky ears. 'Come on, Nello,' he says quietly. 'This is no place for you.' The dog rubs against his leg with a happy whine and wags his tail.

'By the way, Giacomo,' Elvira says, busily dabbing the tea from her skirt with a napkin, 'another one of those packets arrived from the Japanese embassy while you were out. It's on your score table.'

The composer pushes himself to his feet. 'It'll have to wait until I get back.' Like all good hunting dogs, Schaunard respects and fears his master, so after only a couple of whistles and a short wait, Puccini hands him back to Gastone, with a stern warning to be more careful in future, then makes his way through the soft-scented trees towards the lake. He ambles slowly, breathing in the woody dankness while listening to the whispers of the landscape, the rustling leaves, the twigs that snap under his feet, the woodpecker *click-click-clicking* its way into the bark of an oak in search of insects. He knows them all, the wrens that nest in the bushes, the partridges that cry out as they rise into the air on rounded wings, the tits, blackbirds and grouse, the hoopoes with their orange crests and striped throats, the jays that feed on acorns, the song thrushes whose notes soar above the trees, the turtle doves cooing their fidelity to the world, and the owls that hoot into the night. This is what he yearns for when he is far away in grey bustling cities: the joyous, disorderly cascade of birdsong, the air perfumed by nature, and a sense that he is in a place as timeless as the sky above his head.

Drawing a breath, he remembers coming here as a boy with his brother, Michele, to spend the long summer days fishing and trapping birds. Michele! He was cursed from the start. Born three months after their father's death, he too had studied music, but lacked the determination to become a musician. And so in his early twenties he had set off to teach in South America where, he discovered, life was difficult and the cost of living high. After nine long years, Puccini still has the words of his brother's last letter imprinted on his mind.

I crossed the Andes, and after innumerable sufferings came at last to Jujuy. But America does not suit me. If the gold market improves, I shall return to Italy. Meanwhile I am a little worried by the epidemic. My classroom is empty …

The composer pulls out a handkerchief and presses it to his eyes. Stepping up his pace, he strides through the trees until he reaches the path, where he turns left, alongside the lake, away from the villa.

There are voices coming from the rocky inlet where the peasant women wash their laundry, and as the composer approaches, he imagines them there, squatting down in the shallows, pounding and rinsing, their skirts hitched up to reveal sturdy thighs that have borne child after child. On rounding the corner, it is not women he sees but four or five children who are dragging lakeweed from the water. With them is Rodolfo, son of his poor dead hunting pal, Emilio Manfredi, and brother of that girl with the beautiful hair, the strange one who's coming to work at the villa. What was her name again? Puccini clicks his fingers searching for the answer and is still clicking when he arrives at a large, thatched wooden shack, known to all as Club della Bohème. Club della Bohème, a bar of sorts, is run by Andrea Gragnani, a man in his fifties, whose spindly calves and strangely jointed knees have earned him the nickname 'Blackbird Legs'.

He is a cobbler by trade, skilled at his work and renowned for charging a fair price, but labouring over a bench is a solitary affair, and Blackbird Legs likes nothing better than a good yarn about how to put the world to rights. And so, over the years, he started offering a glass of wine to the fellows who stopped by while he was restitching their boots or hammering nails into their clogs, and to hunters at the end of a thirsty shoot. One day, a table and chairs appeared in his workshop. Word spread through the village like lightning, and in no time at all the seats were taken up by men playing a hand or two of cards, or a game of dice or draughts. It would have been uncivil not to offer them a drink and a little something to eat, and so in that insidious way in which the devil goes about his work, it wasn't long before Andrea was replacing his tools with bottles of wine, *digestivi* and grappa, and converting his workbench into a bar. Salamis and dried fish hung from the smoke-blackened rafters, and olives, cheeses, and wheels of heavy bread found their way into the cool chest under the north-facing window. In winter, the men (for no woman would be seen dead here) stay indoors near the wood burner, while in summer they sit outside to catch the breeze off the water. The modest hut has no bathroom and so in all seasons patrons can be seen lining up along the foreshore, pissing arcs of fluorescent yellow into the lake. Puccini thinks he'll have a quick word with Andrea before returning to his package from the Japanese embassy, but changes his mind when he sees his friend, Ferruccio Pagni, an artist lured to the village by its soft light and ever-changing colours, hunched over a table in the shadow of the doorway.

'Ferruccio!' he calls, cheered at the prospect of a little earthy banter that men can only enjoy well away from the disapproving ears of their womenfolk.

The battered straw hat turns, revealing young eyes with tobacco strand eyebrows fixed to a deeply lined brow, itself fringed with dark hair that gathers in clumps, like untreated wool, and a face that has a racked, exhausted look to it. 'Hey, Giacomo!' the artist slurs, gesturing vaguely towards the chair on the other side of the table. 'Come 'n have a drink!' Ferruccio's eyes are red-streaked, his eyelids blinking out of phase as if not connected to each other.

Puccini lowers himself onto the dusty seat. 'Everything all right, Ferro?' he says, knowing it is not.

'Awright?' Ferruccio echoes. 'Women! First she was screaming that I should drink less and paint more ... then she started throwing things at me!' To confirm the point, he slaps the arm of his jacket, which is caked in thick red paint, as if he has received a lacerating wound to the elbow. 'What would she know? Bloody peasant ...'

Puccini nods. It is well known that the artist's lover, Giulia Grassi, a woman with haughty eyes and large breasts, has a violent temper. 'The curse of the female,' Puccini says, not really thinking, 'is they don't understand that men need to be left alone to be men sometimes.'

Ferruccio bangs his fist on the table, making his glass jump. 'How true is that! I told her that her nagging was driving me to drink, but d'you think she'd listen?'

The composer sighs. 'Believe me, Ferro, there's no point fighting it. Let's get another flask ... and you need to eat something. It doesn't do to drink on an empty stomach.' Twisting around, he sees Andrea at the bar, glued to his newspaper, apparently impervious to the deafening whoops and groans coming from the cardplayers inside his shack. 'Garçon!' he calls.

Andrea's balding head rolls unwillingly on its axis. 'Oh no!' it mutters in a fruity baritone voice. 'Not two crazy geniuses!'

'That's enough from you! My friend here is in need of a little more ruby liquid, so if you'd be so good as to bring us another flask, and some bread with a few of those anchovies you've got hidden away ...'

'Going to feed the multitude, are you?' Andrea quips, booming out a laugh at his own joke.

Not bothering to reply, Puccini turns back just in time to hear Ferruccio belch out a mouthful of swampy air.

'That's better!' the artist says, patting his chest with the flat of his hand. 'So, tell me, Giacomo, how's life in your turris eburnea?'

Surprised at his friend's use of Latin, Puccini takes a moment or two to unravel these last words. 'My ivory tower,' he replies, 'has been invaded by women and children. I cannot take a step without falling over a toy or some article of female apparel, and the whole place stinks of perfume and tea!'

Ferruccio whoops with delight and throws open his arms, sending his glass spinning to the ground. Bending down, he starts clawing about in the dirt in an attempt to retrieve it. 'Lucky old you!' he mumbles from somewhere between his legs. 'I think I heard Antonio had deserted you …'

'And Giuseppe.'

Giving up on the glass, Ferruccio straightens up and starts fumbling about in his pocket, bringing out a half-smoked cigar, one that Puccini had given him weeks ago.

'For goodness sake, Ferro, you can't smoke that old charcoal stick! Here, have one of these.' He pulls out a packet of cigarettes and taps one into his hand. Ferruccio grabs it and sticks it in his mouth, and after several clumsy attempts, manages to light it from the flame Puccini has produced from a match.

'His wife's a bit of all right,' he mutters, sucking in and making the tobacco glow red.

'Whose wife is?'

'Giuseppe's …'

Puccini leans back and groans. 'Signora Ida? You must be joking! She's just an empty little shell – a trinket to go on a mantelshelf to be looked at, not enjoyed. I like a woman with some fire in her, something to stir the blood …'

'Ooooh!' Ferruccio sighs, in a mock swoon. 'How utterly divine …'

'What is?' a third voice joins in. Andrea has arrived with a tray, which he sets down on the table.

'This is!' Ferruccio replies, grabbing the flask and tipping it towards a glass, which he drains in one long slurp. 'Your health, old man!'

Andrea looks disapprovingly at the artist and then at the pool of slopped wine on the tray. 'Watch your manners!' he barks.

Then to Puccini, 'I'm reading about the trial of Gaetano Bresci, you know, that silk weaver fellow who shot the King. They say his sister was trampled to death in those food riots a couple of years back, poor girl. Terrible business, that was, sending in the army against all those starving folk.'

Puccini reaches for a glass and half fills it. 'Yes,' he says vaguely, 'very distressing.'

'Don't waste your breath talking politics to him,' Ferruccio says, his eyes fixed on the anchovies as if trying to figure out what they are. 'He's a composer, for God's sake, he doesn't even know the name of the prime minister ...'

'Shut up, Ferruccio!'

Andrea ignores them both. 'It's a disgrace, so it is, a wretched disgrace. And it's all the fault of that finance minister, Sonnino. It was his idea to put up taxes to pay for factories and suchlike. "Get the country on its feet," that's what he said. And who pays? The poor devils on the land, that's who, who can't even afford a crust of bread. While he, Signor Sonnino, lives in a castle! Half the fellows called up for national service are undernourished! Did you know that? Half of them! There's not enough food, the water's undrinkable. This country isn't on its feet, it's on its knees!'

Ferruccio lurches to one side and grabs Andrea's sleeve. 'What're you talking about, you old fool? Sonnino's a genius! Follow the Germans – industry and education, that's where our future lies.'

Andrea shakes his arm free, his cheeks reddening. 'There won't be anyone left to work in Sonnino's bloomin' factories at this rate! Maestro, you tell him ...'

'Boys, boys, calm down!' Puccini urges. 'You're never going to agree, and I can't help you because I've been too busy working to follow the arguments.'

Ferruccio burps again and wipes a dirty hand across his mouth. 'Not this afternoon, you weren't. I heard your motor go past.'

Puccini shoots him a look.

'Oh, I see!' Ferruccio says, smirking. 'My mistake, it wasn't a motorcar, it was ... let me see ... a chariot, yes, that's what it was. Elijah in his chariot of fire, off to heaven ... ha ha ha!' And with that, he sprawls headfirst onto the tray, tipping over the plate of anchovies.

Puccini has had enough. 'It's time to go,' he says, standing up. 'But Maestro …' Hands pressed together in a gesture of supplication, Andrea nods at Ferruccio. 'Please! He's been drinking like a pike all afternoon …'

'Don't worry, Andrea,' Puccini says, catching the meaning, 'I'll settle the bill.' Inside the shack is as dark and gloomy as a cave, the dense air illuminated by a small window overlooking the water and the glow-worm lights from the cardplayers' cigarettes. Among the shadowy figures around a table, concentrating on the game in hand, are: Beppino, the ox-like blacksmith, his head driven into his immense shoulders like a nail into a block of wood; Dario, the chimneysweep; Giorgio, the bald ironmonger; Bruno, one of the reed-cutters (a bully of a man who beats his wife, having first drunk the day's earnings); and with them an assortment of silhouettes too indistinct to be identified. Giorgio is the first to speak.

'Ragazzi! Look who's here! Just the man! Hey Maestro, give us a tune!' Necks twist and crane in Puccini's direction as the players throw down their cards and take up the chant. 'Give us a tune! Give us a tune!'

Puccini inwardly groans. 'Not today, boys. I'm in a bit of a rush …'

The response is stamping feet and the banging of glasses on tabletops. 'All right, all right,' he says, raising his hands in surrender, 'but just the one.' Blowing the dust from the keyboard, Puccini runs his fingers up and down the keys then breaks into a popular tune, one of the many he learned earning pocket money as a teenager playing piano in the bawdy house in Via della Dogana. It is a simple song, full of pathos, about a young man who longs to touch the rosebud skin of his beloved. But for him, it signifies the sound of giggling laughter, high heels clicking on a brick floor, the reek of cheap perfume, and the wonderful feel of soft flesh being pressed against his own as the girls leaned over to pop lighted cigarettes between his lips. Closing his eyes, he plays three more verses, lost to the memory of a chilly December evening when Silvia, a small girl with shapely legs and the face of a Botticelli angel, guided him into one of the cubicles, and whispering, 'This is your Christmas present,' revealed with her hands and lips what until then had only been a glorious possibility. Rounding off the last verse, Puccini bangs down the piano lid and stands up.

'Now, I really must be off. You don't want me to get on the wrong side of Signora Elvira, do you?' Jeers and laughter follow him to the bar, where Andrea has resumed reading his newspaper. 'How much do I owe you?' Puccini asks.

Andrea glances up, picks up his pencil and scribbles on a docket. 'Five lire,' he says, skewering the paper onto a spike.

Puccini reaches into his jacket, and not finding his wallet, pats his trouser pockets. 'I'm sorry, my friend,' he shrugs. 'I must have left my money at home. I'll fix you up next time.' Andrea opens his mouth to protest, but Puccini is already making his way to the door. Then he turns back. 'By the way,' he calls softly, 'if any letters arrive for me here, just pop them under the counter, would you?'

And Blackbird Legs, who's had it in for Signora Elvira ever since she acted all high and mighty over the re-heeling of a pair of shoes some years back, gives him a wide, complicit grin.

Back home, Puccini opens the door of his drinks cabinet, takes out a bottle and splashes red liquid into a tumbler, swirling it around so he can hear the clinking of the ice cubes. He holds his glass up to the light, appreciating with a wry smile the bright crimson that is usually associated with poison. The *aperitivo*, produced in Novara, a town not far from Milan, is a gift from Giulio Ricordi, sent to celebrate the arrival of Belasco's contract from America. Taking a swig, he holds it in his mouth before swallowing it down; not bad, a little bitter perhaps. Taking another mouthful, he goes over to the piano, rests his glass on the score table and picks up the package, pausing for a moment to examine the delicate chrysanthemum seal.

Following his trip to London and fortuitous visit to the Duke of York theatre, Puccini had travelled to Milan to discuss his plans for *Madama Butterfly* with Giulio Ricordi, only to find his mentor firmly against the idea.

'Giacomo, dear boy, I see nothing but obstacles in the way of a work set in Japan. For a start, the values of a country that has been locked away for centuries will be hard for westerners to grasp. You yourself are the first to say that an audience must believe in its characters. How on earth are they going to cope with a fifteen-year-old girl falling for a man old enough to be her father, let alone the concept of geisha and ritual suicide? And what about the music? Are you going to use eastern elements? Because let me tell you plainly, the public won't stand for it.' Puccini had stared across the desk into Ricordi's cool grey eyes, reluctant as ever to cross the man who had been like a father to him, guiding, cajoling, encouraging and praising, always with the best of intentions. He owed Ricordi a great deal, some would say everything, but that didn't mean he was always right. In fact, there was one thing Signor Giulio seemed utterly unable to grasp – Puccini didn't choose his heroines, they chose him. They tapped him on the shoulder as surely as the Angel of Death, and like that ethereal figure, they took him over, possessed him and never let him go, no matter how hard he struggled.

'The public aren't having any difficulty with The *Mikado*,' Puccini had countered weakly.

'Please Giacomo,' Ricordi said, straining to keep the exasperation from his voice, 'never compare your work with all that *tonkety-tonk-tonk* from Gilbert and Sullivan.'

The impasse had lasted two weeks, until Ricordi, astute as ever, arranged a luncheon with the Japanese ambassador in Rome, certain that when the difficulties of staging a work set in the orient became clear, Puccini would lose heart. It was a plan that seriously misfired.

Luncheon was a quiet affair, just Ricordi, himself (but not Elvira, who had one of her headaches) and the ambassador and his wife. A tiny woman with porcelain skin and a curious *pizzicato* way of speaking, she was so enthused by the idea of an opera set in her own country that she presented him with music penned on tree bark paper so old he feared it would crumble to dust in his hands. These, she explained, were folk songs that had once been sung by her grandmother, who would smile from heaven to know that they were in such illustrious hands. (Puccini later became fascinated by the odd-sounding pentatonic scale in which they were written, and despite Ricordi's objections, decided to use it to create a *leitmotif* for his new heroine.)

Since then, hardly a week has gone by without a package arriving from the ambassador's wife containing articles, journals and magazines, as well as books he might wish to consult. Puccini has studied this stream of information with great care, becoming something of an expert on Japanese culture, the art of geisha, the kimono, white paste for the face, elaborate wigs, and the precise unfathomable tea ceremony.

Breaking open the chrysanthemum seal, he tips the contents onto the table, sits down and riffles through them, selecting a magazine with a symmetrical arrangement of ornate fans on its cover. The caption tells him that a passion for all things Japanese is sweeping through Europe, and that to be considered stylish, one must own teak furniture, lacquered screens and finely painted vases. Imagining the sturdy walls of his studio replaced by rice paper, a red lantern glowing where the candelabra used to be, Puccini gives a derisive snort, picks up a second magazine and leafs through it, flicking quickly from page to page. He is searching for something, a task made all the more difficult because he cannot say precisely what. If he were to say anything, it would be to concede that Giulio Ricordi is right, at least in one respect: for *Madama Butterfly* to succeed, it must blend western taste with an oriental sensibility. But how? Puccini has pondered this question long and hard, deciding that the answer lies in a symbol, an element to bind the cultures together that is recognisably eastern yet still pleasing to Europeans. This is what he is hoping to find among the articles on rice-growing, carved ivory figurines, obscure poetry, and the enchanting but improbable notion of mixed bathing.

Puccini lifts his red-filled glass, takes a sip and continues turning the pages of the magazine. He pauses at an illustration of trees covered in luxuriant blooms, which, he learns, are the Shimidsu Sakura, the flowering cherries that have been cultivated in Japan since the seventh century for the beauty of their blossom, not their fruit. But it is not this curious fact that draws him from his chair, it is the following: *The transience of the blossoms, their extreme loveliness and quick death, has frequently been associated with mortality. For this reason, they are often used in artistic and musical representations ...*

Puccini waves the magazine in the air. 'Cherry trees! Of course!'

Why hadn't he thought of it before? Pink and white blossoms all over the stage … bucketfuls of the stuff everywhere!

Draining his glass, he jigs happily over to the drinks cabinet, and is about to pour himself a top-up when he slams the bottle down with the force of a judge's gavel. 'Oh Christ! The parasol …'

The blood drains from Puccini's head and his face takes on the pallor of death. He leans against the drinks cabinet, icy waves shivering up and down his spine, and stares into the room, seeing the furniture swimming around him, watery and loose. He closes his eyes, this man at the zenith of his creative power, loved by his countrymen and admired the world over for the passion and beauty of his music, frozen to the spot at the thought of what Elvira would do if she found another woman's parasol in the back of his motorcar.

And then he has an idea.

Chapter 10
SUNDAY AT THE SEASIDE

'There, that's better!' Grandma sticks the last pin back into the pincushion and holds up her bonnet, now neatly trimmed with a length of jade ribbon. 'What do you think, dear?'

Corinna glances up from her book. 'Lovely, Grandma ... very smart,' she says, giving the hat barely a second of her attention. 'Yes, I do believe it is,' Grandma agrees. 'And it will go very well with my garnet brooch, the one your grandfather gave me.' It is Sunday morning and the ladies are in the parlour, whiling away the hour or so before they set off for church. Sunlight, which even at this early hour has a white intensity to it, is filtering through the net curtains, showing up dust on the fringed lampshade, the china ornaments and the dark oversized furniture.

'You shouldn't be studying today, dear,' Grandma says, sucking in the corners of her mouth. 'Why not write to your mother instead? There's still time before Mass.'

Corinna lifts her head again, her fingers silently drumming the page of her book. Having dared bring *Madame Bovary* into this stuffy room, she wants to be left in peace to read of Emma's unfolding desires, not scour her mind for things to say to her mother. 'I'll do it later, Grandma,' she says, playing for time.

An eyebrow arches upwards. 'I don't think so, dear!'

There is no point arguing, and so Corinna gets up and crosses to the bureau, scraping the chair along the floor as she sits down. 'There's no need for that!' Grandma chides.

Pretending not to hear her, Corinna pulls a sheet of paper from a pigeonhole and starts doodling. The sharp little strokes soon form a motorcar with a starting handle perpendicular to the radiator grille and two lanterns hooked on the body, beneath the windscreen. She gazes at it for a second, then angles her pencil and shades in the mudguards. *Why do I feel so different this morning when nothing has changed?* Breakfast was the usual taciturn affair of coffee, bread covered with dark, glossy chestnut honey, and the sound of Grandma's scissors clipping the best bits from the newspaper. Even Aunt Adelaide's daily observation, 'There's not a cloud in the sky!', was repeated on the dot of eight with no change in tone or inflection.

'As it is Sunday,' Grandma continues, a little stiffly, 'I thought we might have a treat later at Gran Caffe Margherita.' Her words are met with a chirp of delight from the corner, where Aunt Adelaide is imagining sinking her teeth into a marzipan slice dusted with vanilla sugar.

Corinna rolls her eyes and draws a stick man, giving him two small ears, a prominent nose and a mouth shaped like a slice of watermelon. Perhaps she is sickening for a fever? What else could explain how Maestro Puccini has insinuated his way into her thoughts, as if every word and gesture of their short encounter held some special significance. *It was just a little outing, over and done with, and never to be repeated, not after the ridiculous way I tripped and stumbled on top of him. She adds a moustache and bow tie then leans back to contemplate her work.*

The smell of fish drifts through the doorway, a smell so revolting it quickens the pulse in Corinna's head, making it throb even louder than before. How is she going to face the lunch of *cacciucco*: squid, cuttlefish and other bibs and bobs trawled from the sea, cooked in tomato and red wine, then ladled onto garlic-smeared bread. Easing her neck backwards, she massages her temples in slow circles while gazing at the needlepoint picture on the wall of a little girl sitting on a garden swing, an inane smile on her apricot face.

'Have you run out of things to say, dear?' Grandma sings out.

Corinna reaches for a fresh sheet of paper and slides it on top of her drawing. 'No, Grandma,' she says. 'I'm just thinking.' If only she didn't have to go to Mass, but could instead lie on her bed and let her mind wander back to the cabin in the sand dunes, reliving each moment of yesterday's adventure. Grandma, though, would accept no excuses. Soon they will put on their hats and gloves and walk to the end of the street, through the *piazza* in the shade of the oleanders, then across to the basilica of Sant'Andrea. There, an elderly priest will mumble in a language that no one has spoken for centuries, and Signora Sandrelli, the young widow who lives upstairs, will lustily chant out the responses in a way her grandmother considers vulgar. Corinna, meanwhile, will stare at the columns supporting the roof, or count the statues of long-dead saints gazing solemnly down from their pedestals, while the fumes of the incense turn her stomach even more than the prospect of today's fishy lunch. As a child, she had been fascinated by the idea of God, a benevolent, all-present yet invisible being – a sort of universal magician – who, with the right kind of entreaties, would restore her mother's health and release Corinna, Cinderella-like, from the kitchen. She had accepted the fact of his existence without question. Why not? Adults didn't lie, her mother, her grandmother, the priest, the teachers at school, while all around her, at home and in churches and public buildings, was proof in the form of crucifixes, religious paintings and statues. It wasn't until she was at the *liceo* that it dawned on her that it might not be true. Why, she began to wonder, did her prayers go unanswered year in, year out? Did God not hear her? If not, he must be deaf, and thus imperfect; or somewhere else, and not omnipresent. Worse still, if he could hear her, what sort of indifference made him ignore her? Either way, her patience had run out. God could exist if he wanted to, but he would make no difference to her life. She was going to have to do that for herself.

After what seems to Corinna an almost interminable church service, Grandma finds her cafe of choice. The Gran Caffe Margherita is the most imposing of the Liberty-style buildings along the promenade, with its twin cupolas, arched entrances and impossibly high ceilings. Opaque blue-white nymphs recline in curved recesses, their hooded eyes observing the waiters who glide across the floor like ice-skaters, balancing silver trays that flash sparks of light from the orb-shaped wall lamps. Strains of music – a string quartet playing honeyed songs from the south – drift above the ferns to mingle with the voices of the patrons who have gathered to take tea or an *aperitivo*, to smoke a *Mezzo Toscano*, or simply to see and be seen.

The ladies are offered a table on the terrace and Grandma, having looked carefully around, nods her assent. The position – on the corner facing the *passeggiata*, nicely protected by an awning, and not too close to the miniature lemon trees which could harbour annoying insects – is acceptable to her.

'Now, ladies,' the waiter says briskly. 'What can I bring you on this lovely afternoon?'

Aunt Adelaide is the first to speak. 'A marzipan slice, if you please. And do you have any of those puffy cakes filled with custard cream?'

'Sfogliatelle,' he confirms, bowing his slicked-back head. 'Certainly!'

'And perhaps an almond biscotto or two,' Aunt Adelaide adds, giving her sister a quick glance, 'and a glass of sweetened water, fizzy not still …'

The waiter's postage-stamp moustache has begun to twitch. Time is money, depending as he does on tips to earn a living wage. He turns to Grandma. 'And for you, Signora?'

'The sfogliatelle, are they fresh?'

The waiter, who under different circumstances might take offence at the question, gives her a winning smile. 'But of course! Every morning, fresh as the dew.'

'Very well. One for me … a pot of tea for three … And for you, dear?'

Corinna is not listening. She is staring towards the promenade, where a man so like Puccini that her heart has begun to race is sauntering along, looking around him, scrutinising faces in the crowd. The waiter gives an insistent little cough, and Corinna, hearing a sound like the bark of a small dog, turns her head and sees a short man with a film of oily perspiration on his brow.

'And for you, Signorina?'

'Oh … the same … thank you.' She glances back at the promenade but the man has disappeared, leaving couples arm in arm, little girls in frilled smocks with ribbon-tied hair, and boys in sailor suits or jackets and pantaloons. Drawing a breath, she reaches for her napkin and smooths it onto her lap, wondering if she isn't becoming a little unhinged. There is a single, deep-cupped rose at the centre of the table, with burnished leaves curling away from its stem. The petals – a soft, peachy pink, tinged with yellow – are like the afterglow of a sunset, and as she looks at it, Corinna is filled with sadness for this beautiful flower that has ended up on a cafe table, to be ignored by customers and waiters alike. She will rescue it, she decides, hide it and take it back to her room, to savour its graceful perfection and heady scent. Now would be a good moment. Stealing a quick glance at Grandma, who is chiding Aunt Adelaide for being greedy, she reaches into her pocket for her handkerchief to wrap it in. She stretches out her hand, as casually as possible, and glances up to see if Grandma has noticed, but instead sees him, Puccini, standing at the entrance of the terrace, watching her. *Oh Lord …*

With a barely perceptible wave, he starts walking towards them.

He's coming over here! Surely not …

Heads turn, but still he keeps coming. Corinna closes her eyes and when she opens them, he is standing beside her.

'Maestro!' a voice oozes. 'What an honour!' It is the waiter, appearing from nowhere.

Puccini ignores him. He has eyes for one person, and one person only. 'Signora,' he says, sweeping off his hat and bowing to Aunt Adelaide. 'How delightful that we should meet again!'

Aunt Adelaide looks nervously around her. This time she has recognised the elegant figure, but surely his words aren't directed at her?

The composer, meanwhile, turns to Grandma. 'Signora, may I present myself? Giacomo Puccini … your sister and grand-daughter kept me company on a recent train journey.'

'Oh yes,' Grandma says, collecting herself. 'I believe I did hear something of the sort.'

'And Signorina,' he murmurs, offering his hand to Corinna. 'What an unexpected pleasure!' His fingers are touching hers, pressing them in a gentle squeeze. Corinna looks down to hide the confusion that has flared in her cheeks.

'Would you care to join us?' Grandma offers. 'We're about to have tea.'

'Tea?' No, no, no … thank you so much. I'm just taking a little sea air. I must be off. So nice to see you again. Good evening …' Later, in the safety of her room, Corinna unfurls the note that he had pressed into her hand, and which she had so carefully transferred to the pocket of her skirt. *I have your parasol. Meet me under the tree tomorrow afternoon. Giacomo.*

Chapter 11
DORIA COMES TO WORK AT
VILLA PUCCINI

It is a Monday morning in early spring, and the church bell has just tolled the sonorous peal that denotes the half hour, an event of little interest to the peasants who are governed by sunlight and shadows, not pendulums, weights, ropes and wheels. Today though, Doria is listening out for the chime, and when she hears it, she leans her twig broom behind the door, pulls off her apron and clicks open the latch. Then she recoils, a sudden look of apprehension in those button eyes. Today she, Doria Manfredi, is going to work at the big house of Maestro Puccini. On the table that Doria recently scrubbed clean is a bundle containing a missal with loose yellow pages (which she likes to thumb through, pretending to read), a comb, a spare pair of bloomers, one of Alice's old nightgowns, a marble given to her by her younger brother, Paolo, a clothes-peg doll from Lucia, and a pebble from Eva. From Rodolfo there is nothing, but Doria doesn't mind because it means she won't have to thank him. Talking to her older brother sets off the grasshoppers, the ones that jump about inside her when she's nervous, and she gives him a wide berth. Another one to avoid is Bruno, the reed-cutter, with his thick neck and scarred face, who lives in a shack near the well and beats his wife. Doria knows this is so because after Mass one Sunday she heard the women whispering about it outside the church. People often say things in front of her they shouldn't. That's because they think she's an idiot, a *cretina*, but that doesn't make her deaf. She knows that Signora Pezzi goes to Poldo for herbs to help her make a baby, that Bernardo, the beekeeper, is so mean he wouldn't give his own mother a pot of his honey, not even if she were starving, and that Settimelli, the barber, is a lecher who puts on 'airs and graces', although she has no idea what this means.

Doria takes a breath and once again raises the latch, opens the creaky door and steps out to look across the *aia*. She is hoping to see Filippo, the barber's assistant, who should be bumping along the path on his bicycle, his bag slung loosely across his back. She likes Filippo because he always smiles at her and sends Paolo across with one of his boiled sweets. She's not allowed to talk to him, though, because she's too young, and Signora Magrina, who jabbers like a magpie, told Mamma he probably had funny ideas in his head, put there by his jumped-up skirt-chaser of a boss.

The barnyard is bathed in bright summer sunlight, the corn laid out in rows, but there is still no sign of Filippo, just a group of small children in the shady corner playing with a rope, laughing and pulling, legs and arms tangled up as they drag one another about in the dust. *Ouch! Aiyeee! Get off me!* Signora Cioni's cat is curled up asleep on the front step next door, its black fur gleaming in the sun. Bernardo found it in his wheelbarrow one spring morning when it was still a fluffy ball of kitten, and he was all for taking it down to the lake to drown. But when Signora Cioni saw how sweet it was, with its wheat-coloured eyes and helpless little *miaows*, she said she'd keep it for company. She's a widow, Signora Cioni, and very, very old, with whiskers on her chin and her back bent double like a weaving shuttle so she's always looking at the ground. She lives alone, except for her cat, and she hardly ever speaks because she's deaf as well as old. So old there's nothing left to say, or hear, come to that.

A flash of white against blue draws Doria's gaze to the sky, and the little egret that is soaring towards the fields where her brothers and sisters are helping bring in the hay. Then she looks across the *aia* and sees Bernardo stumbling about in the shadow of his house, pouring dirty water from a watering can onto the herbs he grows in pots and jars, all higgledy-piggledy. If they were hers, she'd line them up neatly in rows, the sage and rosemary at the back, then the basil and oregano, and the calamint and parsley at the front. But Bernardo doesn't do anything properly. Like not going to Doctor Falli to have his teeth pulled, even though they're all brown and chipped, and his mouth smells like rotting potatoes. Setting down his watering can, the old man disappears round the side of his house, off to the beehives by the yellow trees that make Doria's nose itch, and the brook where yesterday she'd had a bath, the second in a month.

'You want to be nice and clean for tomorrow,' Mamma had said.

Rodolfo, who was sitting on the step whittling a yew branch into a bow, stopped what he was doing and said in his nasty voice, 'Clean for a dirty set-up!'

'That's enough!' Mamma scolded him. 'Doria doesn't know about such things.'

'No, that's because she doesn't know anything except that nonsense put into her head by the priest!'

Mamma crossed herself. '*Zitto!* I won't have you speaking against Don Zeno in this house.'

'I'll speak any way I please now I'm head of the family!'

Which is true because Papi's gone to heaven. He's been there since Christmas. For as long as Doria can remember Rodolfo has given her the grasshoppers, and that's because of the way he curls his lip when he looks at her, like she's a crawling insect to be stamped on. Alice says he's jealous, what with her being Papi's favourite and all, and not having to go to school. Alice lives at La Piaggetta, the big house on the other side of the lake. Yesterday she was home, and when they got back from church, she showed Doria how to braid her hair, curling it round her fingers then pinning it up. It's how Doria has it now, but she doesn't like it because it's pulling at her scalp and doesn't move when she shakes her head.

When she'd finished with Doria's hair, Alice had said, 'When you open the front door to visitors, you give a little curtsy, like this ... see? Then you take their hats and coats and hang them up.'

'Why don't they do it themselves?' Doria had asked.

Alice thought for a moment then said, 'Because they're rich, Doria, that's why.'

Doria has never met a rich person, except for the Maestro, and she hasn't met him, not properly. But he did come to the house the day after Papi died with a letter in his hand for Mamma, a thick letter, which seemed odd seeing as she can't read. Mamma asked him if he'd like to step inside to see Papi, who was in his coffin with a candle that burned night and day, but he said he was in a hurry to get back to villa. Later, when Mamma opened the letter, she gave a little cry, went into the bedroom and hid it away in her special box, the one no one's allowed to touch. 'Don't tell anyone about this, Doria!'

'Not even Rodolfo?'

'Especially not him.'

Mamma has come up behind her this morning. 'It's time to go, Doria! Here, put the bundle on your back and carry the eggs in your hand. There's one for the Maestro and one for Signora Elvira.'

Doria slips the bundle over her shoulder and takes the eggs, which are still warm and covered in dirt. 'One for the Maestro, one for Signora Elvira,' she says.

Mamma nods, then leans forward and kisses her on both cheeks. 'Now, Doria, remember to listen carefully to what Signora Elvira tells you, and say your prayers morning and night.'

'Yes, Mamma.'

'Off you go then, you don't want to be late.'

'But Mamma ...'

'Go, Doria, please.' There is a tear rolling down Mamma's cheek, as round and silent as a mistletoe berry. As soon as she reaches the path through the fields, Doria crouches down and rests the eggs on a tuft of grass because the bloomers under her skirt, the ones her mother stitched from a piece of old sheeting, are scratching the top of her leg like a sharp twig. She gives them a tug, when what she really wants to do is pull them off and throw them into the stinging nettles. But she mustn't because in the big house everyone wears bloomers, that's what Mamma said, and so must she. Doria doesn't see the sense in it, it's much nicer having fresh air against your skin, and easier to squat down and pee. Giving the bloomers another tug, she gathers up the eggs and sets off again.

'Hello, Doria!'

'O Santa Zita!' Doria freezes, then slowly turns around to seeing a tall figure with a large head and a nose like a handle.

'Filippo!' A shy heat rushes to her cheeks, turning them pink.

'I'm sorry, I didn't mean to scare you,' he says. 'I just wanted to wish you good luck.'

'Good luck?' she echoes, forgetting she's not supposed to speak to him.

Filippo is staring at her, his mouth open wide enough to take in one of the eggs. 'What have you done to your hair?' he whispers.

'My hair? I had to tie it up.'

He rocks back on his heels and laughs. 'Thank heavens for that! For one terrible moment I thought you'd cut it all off.'

'Oh no, I'd *never* do that!'

'I should hope not because it's the most glorious hair I've ever seen ...' he laughs again, 'and believe me, I've seen plenty.'

Doria, not quite following, asks, 'What does "glorious" mean?'

Filippo thinks for a moment, then says, 'It's a kind of miracle.'

'Oh ... like turning water into wine?'

'Sort of,' he says, looking unsure. There are footsteps coming along the path. He flashes her a smile. 'Good luck then ... and don't drop those eggs!'

'Glorious ... glorious ...' Doria rolls the word up and down her tongue as she strolls along, past stubble fields, domed haystacks and dry ditches whirring with noisy insects. Imagine! Her hair a kind of miracle! Then she has another thought: but even when Mamma douses it in paraffin to kill the nits? It smells horrible, the paraffin, and makes her throat go dry. 'Glorious ... glorious ...' Nearing the well, Doria's footsteps once again slow to a halt, for there are pools of green goose-droppings splattered across the path. Samuele has been taking his birds to market. She doesn't want to get that on her skirt, so she lifts one foot, placing it carefully on a clear patch, then the other foot, until she looks up and sees that she is outside the hut of Bruno, the wife-beater.

Tucked inside the pages of Doria's missal is an *immaginetta*, a small picture card of her favourite saint, Santa Zita, a young girl like herself. It was given to her by Don Zeno, the priest, who explained that Santa Zita protected young servant girls. He taught her the words of the saint's special prayer: *Dear follower of Jesus, you became a faithful maidservant and helper of the poor. Help other servants to be just and charitable, and see their masters as children of God, as you are yourself.* Reciting these words, Doria lowers her head and hurries past Bruno's *capanna*, around the well, and onto the road that leads down to the villa. She looks up and sees her new home berthed on the edge of the lake like a great white ship. The gate is closed and Doria, in no hurry to open it, stares up at the vast, flat-roofed building. She narrows her eyes, trying to see the old tower, the one they pulled down to make way for the new house. Everything about it had been the talk of the village, the radiators that warmed the rooms in winter, the taps that spat out bubbling hot water, the telephone (a devilish thing for talking to people you can't see), and walls covered with story paintings, like in church. But still Doria doesn't open the gate. Instead, she runs her eye along the windows on the upper floor – 'one, two, three, four, five, six' – one with a balcony of black metal lacework.

A sudden, clamorous screeching behind her has Doria spinning on her heels, as a cloud of ducks lifts from the shallows of the lake and swoops over the water towards the mountains. *Bang! Bang! Bang!*

'*Coraggio*!' Taking a deep breath, she fumbles open the gate and heads down the path to the front door.

'Ah good, Doria, there you are!' Signora Elvira says, rubbing her hands together. Her new mistress has eyes like two lumps of coal, and a voice that is deep and rasping, although not unkind. She is tall, at least a foot taller than Doria, her broad shoulders and ample bosom covered in a light cotton blouse the colour of cowslips, with sleeves like legs of mutton. Doria looks at her, taking it all in, then curtsies and hands over the eggs. Signora Elvira looks at them and smiles weakly. 'Why, thank you … Now then, come in! Come in! Leave your clogs by the step.'

The hall is yellow and blue, like an April sunrise over the lake. 'Oooh!' Doria sighs.

Signora Elvira gives her a no-nonsense look with those black eyes and says, 'Come along now! You can get changed and then we'll have a tour of the house.' She leads Doria past door-ways, a staircase, around a corner and along a corridor to an-other small door, which she pulls open. 'Here you are, this is your room.'

Doria steps inside and looks around at the bed with a crucifix above it on the wall, the washstand, chair and small wardrobe, all spotlessly clean. 'Am I to sleep here alone?' she asks, her voice catching.

'Yes,' Signora Elvira says. 'But don't worry, you'll get used to it.' Doria looks down and shuffles her feet. She is thinking of her home, where everyone sleeps in one room, and even the chickens come inside at night to avoid foxes and thieves.

'Tut-tut,' Signora Elvira says, making the noise of a cricket. 'Hurry up now! Your uniform is in the wardrobe. I'll be back shortly.' And with that, she is gone. The black skirt sits com-fortably on Doria's hips. The white blouse, too, is the right size, and there is a small square of clean cotton in the pocket of the pretty frilled apron, its purpose unclear. Peeling off her socks, she slips her feet into the house slippers and pins the little white cap to her head the way Alice showed her. Then she turns to the mirror and tries out a bobbed curtsy, then a lower one. If only Papi could see her now! She twirls round, looking at her reflection, and there is Signora Elvira in the doorway, watching her. 'Good, you're ready! Let's start downstairs.'

'This is the gun room,' Signora Elvira says, opening a door onto a room that smells of cartridges and gunpowder. There is a deer's head high up on the wall, its antlers casting strange, branch-like shadows on the floor, its dead eyes staring into the distance. Underneath it, on a row of horn hooks on a shiny board, hang hunting jackets, capes, hats, brushes, knapsacks, and a small pair of bellows. There are racks of guns and boots and a central table, covered in an oilcloth, with photographs of hunters holding up small, limp corpses. Although there is so much to look at, Doria's gaze keeps returning to the deer that looks like it has butted its head through the wall. Her insides feel a bit funny. *It's ever so hot in Villa Puccini!*

'Come along now,' Signora Elvira says, tugging at her sleeve. The drawing room is beyond anything Doria is capable of imagining with its well-padded armchairs, fat cushions, side tables, candlesticks and ashtrays, and strange orange flowers in a vase. There are cabinets and rugs, shelves stacked with books, and striped curtains, edged with gold, trembling at the window. 'Oooh!' she breathes, looking down at the floor, which shimmers like river pebbles.

'And there's the kitchen,' Signora Elvira says, pointing across the hall. Cook is standing with her back to them, stirring a pot on the stove, her thick, solid arm straining against her sleeve. Doria swallows down a grasshopper. This is the woman who, many years ago, had picked up her sweetheart like a baby and thrown him into the lake, just for smiling at another girl. After that, no fellow would step out with her, and even today the boys follow her down the road, daring each another to tug at her skirt.

'That's the pantry,' Signora Elvira says, pointing to a door at the back of the room, 'and the washhouse is outside.'

'The washhouse?' Now Doria remembers that Alice's friend Silvia is the laundry maid here. 'Where's Silvia?' she asks.

Now Cook's head turns. 'Minding her own business,' she scowls, 'that's where.'

Signora Elvira opens her mouth to say something, then changes her mind. 'Come along, Doria. The dining room is next ...'

The dining room contains a long, shiny table, red and gold striped chairs, a sideboard with plates displayed on it and a chandelier of clear glass formed into leaves and flowers. 'This is where we have lunch and supper,' Signora Elvira says, 'and that,' pointing to smaller room through a doorway, 'is the verandah where we take afternoon tea. '

Doria nods, only half listening because through the doorway she can see flashes of bright blue, red, purple, green and yellow. 'That's my aviary,' Signora Elvira says, following her gaze. 'Birdcage, Doria. My husband doesn't care for it. He says finches are too fast to shoot and too small to make a good meal.'

'Oh ...'

'Let's go upstairs.' There are arched doors at the foot of the staircase containing panels made of circles of rimmed glass, like the bases of wine bottles. Doria pauses to run a finger around one of them, which feels cool and smooth. Inside the room a man is singing … and she knows this song! It's one that Renzo hollers out as he goes round the village begging for bread and small coins. But this voice isn't like Renzo's. It's like … Bernardo's honey.

'Caruso again!' Signora Elvira says, rolling her eyes to the ceiling. 'My husband is listening to his new gramophone, so I'll introduce you later. Hurry up, now!'

The banister rail is trimmed with purple, like Don Zeno at the Easter Mass. Doria clutches on to it and pulls herself up carefully, one step at a time, as she has never climbed stairs before. Nearing the top, she sees Signora Elvira disappear around a corner, and not wanting to lose her, she takes the last stairs two at a time and scampers after her, down a passageway and through a door. There is a bed, the largest Doria has ever seen, with yellow sails and at its foot, a wooden chest with gold corners and a giant lock and key.

'This is our bedroom, my husband's and mine.'

Doria blinks. 'Is that bed just for two people?'

The walls are painted with babies and flowers, and near the window is a low piece of furniture with mirrors that, when Doria moves her head, makes it look as if Signora Elvira has been sliced into three. *Oh look! There are three of everything – hairbrushes, little pots, even the photograph of the woman in the fluffy dress.* Stepping forward for a closer look, Doria gasps as the images merge back into one. The dress in the photograph is made of lace, the shawl spun from spiders' threads, and there is a jewel the size of a walnut on the woman's high bosom. A youthful face peers out from behind a fan made of peacock feathers. *It can't be … it's Signora Elvira!* Doria looks around and sees that her mistress has gone.

'This is our bathroom,' Signora Elvira says, holding open the door to the next room, which has a handbasin, a bathtub, and a smaller tub containing a little water. 'That's the toilet, Doria,' Signora Elvira says, 'where you do *pipi.*'

'Oh …' Doria takes a breath of perfumed air and stares at the handbasin, and the oval of soap that looks like a goose egg laid on a pretty china dish. She thinks of the soap scrap she'd used yesterday, made from pigskin, olive oil and embers from the fire, which left her hands fatty and smelling of old bacon.

'And here we have the dressing room,' Signora Elvira says, moving along the corridor, 'the guestroom and bathroom, Miss Fosca's bedroom, Master Antonio's, and the boxroom.'

'I don't think I'll remember ...' Doria begins, her words cut off by the blast of a bell.

'That's the front door,' Signora Elvira says, hurrying towards the sound. 'Pull the doors to, Doria, and meet me down in the hall.'

Doria stands in the doorway of the yellow sail bedroom watching the crisscross threads of the curtains catch the morning light. *Meet me down in the hall*, Signora Elvira said, but what if she should stumble and fall down all those stairs? The thought sends a shiver through her spine, a shiver that causes a dribble of warm pee to escape into her bloomers and run down her inner thigh. *Oh no!* Clutching herself, Doria turns and looks along the passageway, trying to remember which door leads to the shiny white toilet. *One, two, three ... that one!*

Doria is well inside before she realises that there are no pink birds on needle-thin legs chasing round the wall tiles, and then *whoosh, clunk,* the door shuts behind her and suddenly it is night-time. Slowly, though, through the dark, she sees in the corner something long and thin ... A rake? A pole? She moves closer. Not a pole, but a broomstick. A broomstick in the hand of a person wearing a cape and hat – a pointed hat! *O Santa Zita in heaven! It's a witch!* The scream that comes from Doria's mouth is a terrible sound, barely human, the sort to make your scalp tingle and your blood run cold. Her knees buckle, her legs give way and she slumps to the floor, where she lies whimpering like a lost puppy in the puddle that has seeped out from under her skirt.

Chapter 12
A WALK IN THE WOOD

It is shortly after two o'clock, and having just finished a delicious lunch of bean soup, fillet of beef and a slice of tart made with Elvira's own cherry jam, Puccini is standing behind his studio door, his ear pressed to the glass, listening for signs of life. Cook has left for the day. Elvira, Ida and the children are upstairs taking a nap. And Doria, the funny little maid, has been sent to her room. But one can never be too careful. Sliding the door open a little, he waits, and hearing nothing but the ticking of the grandfather clock, tiptoes into the hall, flicks his boater from the hat stand and makes his way quietly down the corridor to the back door.

The sun is high above him, a great shimmering disk set against blue, and as Puccini steps into the garden, he is blinded by its piercing white light. Pausing to rub his eyes, he picks his way around to the front of the house, taking care to avoid the noisy gravel path, until he reaches the rose bush. He plucks a fresh open bud with a soft pink hue, and slips it through his buttonhole. Retracing his steps, he slows down as he rounds the laundry and comes to the vegetable patch, laid out before him like a parade ground. A hoe leans against a clump of still-green tomatoes, and next to them French beans climb doggedly up the cord that Poldo has strung to a frame. The 'sparrow frightener', a figure in a shabby jacket and cloth cap, very much like the gardener himself, stands amongst the lettuces, its arms fixed to a wooden cross like a blasphemous crucifix. Cicadas shrill in the blaze of the sun, and a lone butterfly, yellow and black, hovers round the feathery leaves of the chickpea plants.

Struck by its beauty, Puccini pauses to watch.

The air has a sweetish smell which he recognises as the hay and manure that Poldo digs into the soil. The old man has been on his weekly mission, shuffling up the road with a pail in one hand and a spade in the other, his tortoise neck straining forward as he shovels up deposits left by the horses that pull cartloads of reeds from the lake to the village. Recently, when Puccini suggested they should order fertiliser and have it delivered directly to the house, Poldo eased his nut-brown face upwards to look him in the eye and said, in a voice tinged with offence, 'Fertiliser? And what should I do with the manure? Eat it?'

Puccini cranks the motor into life, climbs up into his seat and chugs out of the garage, whistling in relief as he looks over his shoulder and sees the shutters to the upstairs bedrooms all safely secured. On he goes, clattering up the road, his tyres swirling up clouds of dust that obscure his view of the low-lying fields where rice was once grown, the conditions perfect for the malaria-carrying mosquitoes that infected so many. Now that the land has been drained, the crops are wheat and corn. At this hour the peasants will be resting in the shade of the trees and haystacks, leaving no one to cross themselves or hop out of the way like rabbits as he passes.

Beyond the well, set back from the road in a large shed emitting an eerie orange glow, Beppino the blacksmith, is still hammering at his forge. Puccini drives on, past the ironmonger's, the *fiaschetteria* with its assortment of bottles and flasks, the shack that is home to his artist friend Ferruccio, the haberdashery which supplies gossip as well as needles, thread, buttons and ribbon, the post office, the coal merchant, and the cottage where Cook lives with her sister, another 'liverish old biddy', according to Puccini. Slowing to a halt at the junction with the main road, he sees Don Zeno, the friendly old priest, hobbling towards him across the *piazza* outside the church. But today Puccini has no time to spare, and so he gives the priest a cheery wave, pulls the steering wheel to the right and heads toward the coast.

Making his way alongside fields of densely packed corn, Puccini thinks back to yesterday's encounter at Gran Caffe Margherita: Corinna's hand reaching out to touch the rose so similar to the one he now has in his buttonhole; the touch of her fingers as he pressed the note into them; the coyness with which she avoided his eyes, and the sense of her gaze following him back along the promenade. These memories had inspired him to work like a man possessed. All evening and into the night he toiled, long after everyone else had gone to bed, the damper fitted to the piano (at Elvira's insistence) ensuring that he disturbed no one. And so it was that slowly, inexorably, the sounds came to him, the verses that Giacosa had crafted calling forth melodies that had been hovering on the edge of his consciousness for weeks. As the phrases unfolded and revealed themselves, suddenly he could see it all, the bamboo house with the sliding doors and rush-matting floor, the terrace and the shrine, the blossom-covered trees, and a small, black-haired figure, her downcast eyes concealing a love that licked at her heart like flames.

It was well into the small hours when the composer finally crawled into bed and lay there listening to the wavering hoots of a tawny owl coming from the wood by the lake. He could feel the heat of Elvira's body, smell the musky talcum powder she dusted on herself after a bath; an invitation to turn to her, ease up her nightgown and run his hands over her body. But he was too tired. Turning away, he closed his eyes and drifted off, thinking of Corinna.

She is standing under the tree in an apricot and cream dress with a tightly cinched waist, the chiffon scarf securing her bonnet fluttering away from her, caught on a light breeze. Her hair is smoothed back, and the front of her dress shows off her collarbones and the paleness of her chest. 'Madonna!' Puccini murmurs, feeling his innards slip and tumble. He reaches into the back for her parasol, and when he looks up, she is smiling at him, a luminous smile, full of shy intimacy. He climbs down and stumbles the few yards to reach her, grasps her hands and raises them to his lips.

'My dear,' he says, his voice catching, 'I do believe you've bewitched me.' He swallows. This is not what he meant to say. *It is too forward. It will frighten her.* But she just nods, as if these were the very words she was expecting. *Madonna! What should I do now? Give her back her parasol and go? That would be the best thing.* But he can't bear to leave her. Something has worked loose inside him. But what? He has to find out.

'Shall we …?' Taking her arm, he leads her to the path that curves into the woods. They stroll along in silence, the dapper man in the navy blazer and the slip of a girl in a cotton frock. There are so many things he wants to say to her, but he can find no words, and so he lets his mind drift off to an imaginary realm where he is unpinning her hair and covering her face with his kisses …

'Did you always want to be a musician?' she asks.

And he, jolted from his reverie, answers truthfully. 'No, not at all. I wanted to be a mechanic. I loved anything with gears and an engine – I still do.'

'So, what made you change your mind?'

He turns to her, seeing for the first time that the brown of her eyes is flecked with gold. 'When I was a boy, I saw a production of *Aida* and I knew then and there I wanted to write opera, although I had no idea how because there was no money to pay for the *conservatorio*.'

She looks surprised. 'I thought yours was a well-off family, like my friend Aurelia's.'

Now it is his turn to look surprised. 'No, not at all. I come from a long line of musicians who all lived in genteel poverty. My own situation wasn't helped by the fact that my father died when I was five, leaving my mother to bring us all up on her own. She was determined that I should follow in the family tradition, and so she arranged for her uncle to teach me piano.' He looks at her, hoping that this is enough, and sees that it isn't.

'There's still a step missing, though, isn't there?' she says. 'How did you get from wanting to write opera to actually doing it?'

There is something in her voice that makes him wonder if she is seeking the key to her own thwarted ambitions. Not wishing to disappoint her, but also not wanting to go into the details (how his mother wrote to Queen Margherita requesting a grant, and how, by sheer good luck, Giulio Ricordi heard and liked his graduation piece, rejected a few years earlier in a national competition), he makes light of it. 'Giulio Ricordi felt sorry for me when my first opera was ignominiously thrown out of the Sonzogno competition,' he says with a wry smile. 'So you see, I owe everything to him, Ricordi, my mother and my hat.'

'Your hat?'

'Yes, a shabby old brown felt thing. I can't write a note without it!'

She laughs, and it is a happy sound, like the tune of a fairground carousel. 'And is your brown hat helping to inspire you with *Madama Butterfly?*'

'You really do ask a lot of questions!'

She laughs again, making the corners of her mouth dimple. He can resist no longer. He reaches out to touch her …

'Oh look,' she cries, pulling back, 'Is that the chalet you spoke of?'

The spell is broken. Puccini turns, knowing that in the middle of a small clearing he will see a wooden house badly in need of repair. Sure enough, the paint is blistered and cracked, the shutters are broken (one hangs from its hinges like a flag at half-mast), the front steps have rotted away, and the verandah, too, with gaps in its railings like the teeth of an eight-year-old child. To one side, butted up against a wall, is a rusty water tank, choked with ivy.

'Yes, it is,' he says, wishing he hadn't brought her here.

'But it's charming!' she cries. 'A proper American cowboy ranch. What a shame we can't see inside!'

Puccini, used to the tastes of more sophisticated women, can hardly believe his luck. Digging into his pocket, he produces a key tied to a length of red ribbon, which he dangles in front of her. 'We might just be able to!' The door opens onto a room that threatens to suffocate them with its hot, fetid air. 'Wait here,' he says, striding across to the window where he slides a bolt and wrenches up the frame. When he turns back, he sees his own footsteps following him across the dusty floor like tracks in the desert. 'Let's wait for the air to clear …' The kitchen, screened off from the main room by a faded floral curtain, contains a stone sink, pots and pans on a shelf, and a table with a bottle anchored to its grubby surface by a rigging of cobwebs. There are cobwebs, too, hanging in strands from the ceiling and tightly woven into all the corners.

'Where's the stove?' Corinna asks, looking around.

'Behind the water tank outside,' he says. 'It's too hot to cook in here. Come on ...' He takes her hand and leads her into a corridor. The first room is a bedroom, dark and sparsely furnished, with a crucifix on the bare wall above the narrow bed, a paraffin lamp on a table, and a marble-topped washstand.

'It reminds me of the convent where my sister Iginia, lives,' he says, 'in a closed order not far from here. Sometimes I go over and play the organ for them, sacred music only, of course.'

'Of course,' she echoes, absentmindedly running her finger along the surface of the marble, leaving an arc in the powdery dust. 'I can't imagine being shut away like that.'

'Neither can I.' Reaching into his pocket, he pulls out a calling card. 'I want you to have this.'

She glances at it. 'But I already have one ...'

'Turn it over.' There is an address scribbled on the back in small, slanting letters. 'You can write to me there.'

She looks at him, holding his gaze, then slips the card into her pocket.

'And I was thinking,' he continues, 'that you might like to come here in the afternoons. You can have the key, and I'll book a taxi-cab to run you back along the promenade. It's safer ...'

She gives him that smile again, the shy one edged with knowing. *It is too much.* Reaching out, he touches her cheek, finding skin so soft it makes him want to weep. '*Sei bella* ... You are so beautiful ...'

So many corners, so many cobwebs.

Chapter 13
FERRAGOSTO

Celebrated since pagan times to honour the cycle of fertility and ripening, Ferragosto has come at last. And what a wonderfully bright, sunny day it is – a blessing temporarily lost on the villagers who are jammed inside the church, shuffling about trying to find more space for themselves on the hard pews, or standing by the columns, waiting for Mass to begin. The bell, its job done, has fallen silent, the great belfry rope left to trail sinuously on the ground. At the eastern end, light pours in through the stained-glass window transforming Saint Joseph's robe into a coat as glossy as a gentleman's horse and turning his halo to gold.

Don Zeno enters from the sacristy and genuflects towards the altar in a slow clumsy movement as if his vestments, the amice, chasuble and surplice, are too heavy for his back. Long rays of light beam above his head, throwing the recesses of his church into darkness, while in a niche in the chancel wall, a misty white vapour quivers above a night wick. The priest stares at it for a second, sensing in the dense trembling air something of the mystery of the Eucharist he is about to celebrate. Then he turns to bless his parishioners.

They are all here except for the few souls who hold themselves beyond the reach of divine providence (the doctor, for one, and Ferruccio, that loose-living artist, for another), wanting to earn themselves a place not in heaven, but at the communal lunch to be held in the piazza after the procession, a lunch that the women of the parish have been preparing since dawn. Later, after a good dose of liver salts and a reviving snooze, everyone will return to the piazza for a light supper and an evening of music and dancing, an event eagerly looked forward to by the widows and widowers, giving them as it does the rare and delightful opportunity to snuggle up in the arms of a person of the opposite sex. But before Don Zeno presides over the feast, four of the tallest men in the parish – Beppino, Sandro, Flavio and this year, for the first time, Filippo – will carry the Virgin in a candlelit procession around the precincts of the church (still dusty, despite the best efforts of the verger and his broom). The statue is a new plaster version with the brightly painted face of a doll, replacing the centuries-old wooden figure smashed to splinters in an unfortunate incident involving the verger and a bottle of communion wine left unguarded in the sacristy.

While the villagers are praying for the forgiveness of their sins, Elvira is in the dining room with Doria, unfolding the tablecloth and counting out napkins while trying to ignore the sinking feeling that has been in the pit of her stomach since dawn. She now knows that the dream she has been nurturing all these years of having Renato with her on this special day was nothing more than a fantasy, and with the realisation comes a stinging reminder that she cannot even seek solace for her loss in the comforting arms of the church. Don Zeno, an avuncular man, mild mannered and down-to-earth (malign tongues have suggested a little too down-to-earth, for surely his housekeeper does more for him than cook his meals and press his vestments), comes to visit her from time to time, but they both know she may never set foot in his church. And so, with Ida and the children at Mass, and Giacomo and Giuseppe out on the lake, Elvira busies herself showing the new maid how to lay a festive table.

'Now Doria,' she begins, 'the tablecloth must be pulled straight, like this – do you see? – and a tablemat goes in front of each chair. Then the swan is placed in the middle, facing the head. Is that clear?' Doria nods. Elvira looks at her, trying to gauge if anything has sunk in. 'Very well,' she says, uncertainly. 'You carry on here while I go and check in the kitchen.' Cook doesn't work on public holidays, so there is a bounce in Elvira's step as she goes into the pantry to inspect the chicken liver paste for the crostini, the little meat tortellini to go in the broth, and the tart of glazed peaches decorated with sweet little Cesena strawberries. Lifting the lid off the *fegatelli*, she dips in her finger and holds it to the tip of her tongue, tasting salty smooth liver with just a hint of marsala ... Good! Cook may be a devil to have in the house, but she certainly knows her job. And now to the goose. Crossing to the oven, she pulls open the door and crouches down to spoon spitting oil and meat juices over the puckered breast and the potatoes sizzling around it. Returning to the dining room, Elvira is surprised to see the tablemats in the correct position, the napkins neatly rolled in their rings, and the chairs lined up square to the table. 'Well done, Doria,' she says, giving her a smile. 'Now for the cutlery. We'll be using the set my husband brought back from London. They're on the sideboard in the case marked Mappin & Webb.' Doria looks down and shuffles her feet.

'What is it?'

Silence.

Elvira rolls her eyes to the ceiling, looking to someone or something for help. 'Answer my question, if you please!'

More silence.

Elvira is struck by a thought. 'You can read, Doria, can't you?' The maid mumbles a few words that Elvira doesn't catch. 'For goodness sake look at me when you're speaking!' Now the girl looks up, her lip trembling. 'Didn't you do your three years of schooling?'

Doria fiddles with the frill of her apron, twisting it, releasing it and twisting it again. 'No,' she whispers.

'And why not?'

'Mamma didn't see the sense in it.'

'Really? So how did you learn your catechism?' No response. 'Yes?' Elvira prods.

The button eyes look towards the doorway into the verandah. 'I got it off by heart from Don Zeno.'

'What, *all* of it?' Doria nods. Elvira thinks for a moment then says. 'You know it's wrong to tell a lie, Doria, don't you?'

'Oh yes, Signora!' Doria says, looking back.

'Very well, then,' she sighs. 'We'll just have to work around it. I suppose you can always draw little sketches to help you remember, like an artist.'

Now the maid beams. 'An artist?' she says. 'Me?'

And despite herself, Elvira smiles. Two days earlier, when she found Doria on the floor of the boxroom lying in a puddle of her own making, Elvira resolved to send her home straight away. She needed a girl made of sterner stuff, someone who could think for herself and be trusted not to break the valuable china and glass. But when she told Doria to pack her things, the girl started to wail, pointing at the dressmaker's dummy in the corner. 'That's what scared me! Please don't make me go, Signora. It'll break my mother's heart!'

Elvira peered into the corner, thinking to see a mouse or a big black spider. There was nothing, only the mannequin storing the costume of La Befana, the old crone who brings coal to naughty children on Twelfth Night. Then the penny dropped. 'But Doria, that's not a real witch, it's the Befana.'

Doria stole a nervous glance at the dummy. 'Oooh,' she said, 'it gave me such a fright!' It was easy for Elvira to understand how a simple girl like Doria, unused to switching on the electric light, and with a mind stuffed full of silly superstitions, could make such a mistake. The realisation reminded her of another girl, a little older than Doria, whose father's disappearance had forced her down a path she would not have chosen for herself. And with it came the memory of old Ma Gemignani, Narciso's mother, whose cold eyes had followed her from room to room, silently criticising her every move, her choice of clothes, her manners, the way she handled the children. There was no pleasing the woman, and there was no escape, not until she met Giacomo. But for Doria, there would be no man to sweep her off her feet. The best she could hope for was some poor ignorant hobbledehoy, like that barber's assistant, a young man all too happy to yoke her to the mill of childbearing, endless toil and indifferent health. And in that instant, something in Elvira shifted. She wouldn't treat Doria as she herself had been treated. Instead, she would be kind to the girl, show her some of the charity she had so longed for herself. And at the same time, she would try to bring her on a little, for God knows she could do with an ally, someone to act as a buffer between herself and the disagreeable Cook. Lifting a stemmed glass from the sideboard, Elvira inspects it. 'We'll be using these, Doria. They just need a quick rub. Be careful, though, because they're Bohemian crystal, and if you drop one it will shatter.'

The maid, copying her, takes a glass by the stem and runs a finger round the inside. 'Ooh,' she says, 'it feels like water …'

'You mean ice, don't you?'

Doria thinks for a second, then says, 'Yes, but ice that's warm.'

Elvira closes her eyes and sucks in a breath. 'All right,' she says. 'Now, pay attention while I lay a setting, like this … and then you do exactly as I do.'

They work in silence until the ringing of the telephone obliges Elvira to set down the soup spoon she is holding and hurry into the hall. It is Ramelde, Giacomo's younger sister. A cheerful, plain-speaking woman, she lives with her husband and two daughters near Pescia, on the way to Florence, in a house surrounded by vineyards that produce the light sparkling wine Giacomo likes to drink.

'*Buona festa* to you, too,' she says in response to Ramelde's greeting. 'But I'm afraid your brother isn't here, dear. He and Giuseppe have gone off in a boat and won't be back until lunchtime. It's a shame you can't join us, but with your mother-in-law to look after …' After a conversation about the state of the old lady's health and the goings-on of the children, Elvira hangs up, saddened that she and Ramelde don't live closer to each other. She is fond of Giacomo's younger sister, the only one (apart from Iginia in her convent) who hadn't banished her from their house all those years ago, but instead had offered words of comfort and support. Not that Ramelde had approved of the elopement, that would be going too far, but her heart was less inclined to judge, and she could see no reason to punish Elvira for falling in love with her brother. Pausing before entering the room, Elvira sees the maid standing in front of the sideboard, staring into space. 'Doria!' she says sharply.

The girl jumps in the air like a baby deer, then says, 'They're really sad, those eyes …'

'What eyes?'

Doria points to the photograph behind the cutlery case of a plump woman with large eyes, a narrow forehead and scraped-back hair, with pearl earrings clipped to her small earlobes.

'That's my husband's mother,' Elvira says testily, forgetting her pledge to be nice to the girl. 'She had a horde of children to bring up on her own, so I don't suppose she had much time for smiling.'

Doria's gaze remains fixed on the photograph. 'Is she dead?'

'That's not quite the way one puts it. Oh, never mind … Yes, she died the year before I met the Maestro. He worshipped the ground she trod on.' And here Elvira stops, for a doubt or a question is forming in her mind, in that dark region where it is safer not to travel. Besides, what was the point in speculating whether Giacomo would have eloped with her had his mother still been alive?

'Now then, Doria, enough of this chatter,' she says briskly, turning to face the table. 'How are you getting on?' And there it is, perfectly laid out, the knives and forks as straight as soldiers and beside them the shapely soup spoons, the napkins neatly rolled alongside, the plates centred on their mats, crests facing north, the glasses lined up in a row beside them. 'Doria,' she says, 'you're a wonder!' And she means it.

Doria has cleared away, washed up the lunch dishes and put everything back in its proper place, and is now lying on her bed gazing up at curtains that glow at the edges, trimmed by the sun. She has never been so tired in her life. Never. Everything aches, her arms, her back, her legs … Her head, too, which is fit to burst from all the new things she has learned: which wax to use on the floors and which on the tables, how to wash the chandeliers without getting soapy water near the light bulbs, which items to dust, which to rub with a soft cloth, and which not to touch at all. There is bicarbonate of soda and lemon juice to lift stains from the handbasins, and vinegar water to bring the mirrors and windows to a perfect shine. Doria has taken it all in, drawing sketches to help her remember, and looking at them, one by one, before she drops off to sleep. Bleach, sugar soap, disinfectant, lavender bags, she knows the proper use of them all. Rolling over, Doria looks down at the floor, where the light from the curtain is casting a long, thin shadow that reminds her of Filippo's dog, a bad-tempered animal with flap ears and stiff little legs that likes to hunt rabbits. Thinking of the dog pushes her to another thought, and then another, until memories of what happened one afternoon last summer come flooding into her head.

Mamma was going to make jam to sell at the market, so she sent Doria with her younger sister, Lucia, to pick blackberries from the hedge near Beppino's forge. 'Take the bucket, Doria, and don't come back until it's full, mind!'

They had worked all afternoon, pulling at the brambles, plucking the ripe blobs from their stalks and dropping them into the pail, their hands scratched and stained purple. Then, as the sun started to move behind the forge, the mosquitoes came swarming out.

'Come on, Doria,' Lucia said, 'I'm getting bitten! Let's go!'

'But we haven't finished …'

'Doesn't matter, come on.'

It was then that Filippo's dog appeared from behind the hedge and ran at them, snapping with its pointy mouth. Lucia gave a shriek, jumped behind Doria and grabbed her tightly round the waist. Doria, too terrified to move, closed her eyes and began to pray.

'Oh no!' Lucia howled. 'Look what it's done!'

Doria opened her eyes, and there was the bucket, lying on its side, the blackberries scattered around it in the dirt. It was then that she kicked Filippo's dog, or rather when her foot, of its own will, swung forward and landed a blow on the animal's flank. The dog yelped and cringed away from her. But only for a second. Then it was back, darting forward, an evil look in its beady black eyes as it sank its teeth into her ankle. Lucia shrieked again and the dog, as if jolted to its senses, turned and bolted towards the hedge.

'Oh my God! Are you all right?' It was Filippo, hurrying towards them, a leash in his hand. 'My mother forgot to shut the door and the damn thing got out again!' he said in breathless gasps. Crouching down, he examined the puncture marks on Doria's ankle, which had started to ooze thick red blood. 'Come on,' he said, straightening up, 'you can't walk like that!' And swinging her onto his back, he carried her all the way home.

'Mamma, why am I simple?' Doria was resting her foot on a low stool in front of the grate while her mother ground marshmallow root into a poultice for her ankle. Next to her, Lucia was also sitting with her foot up, determined to grab some attention for herself.

Mamma stopped what she was doing and said gently, 'You're not simple, Doria, you're special.'

'But Rodolfo says she's simple,' Lucia said, helpfully. 'He says she's *scema, deficiente, credulona …*'

'That's enough, Lucia!'

'… *tonta … fessa … stupida …*'

'I said that's enough!'

Lucia closed her eyes, shutting out her mother's angry face.

'Special?' Doria said, picking up where Mamma left off. 'But why?'

Her mother's tone changed, becoming kind. 'Because you were born upside down, Doria, and by the time the birthing woman pulled you out, you'd gone purple and couldn't breathe.'

'Purple!' Lucia piped. 'Like a damson?'

Mamma nodded. 'Just like a damson.'

Doria stared at her ankle, trying to make it dusty blue. Giving up, she said, 'Why was I upside down?'

'Nobody knows …'

Nobody, that is, except Lucia: 'Because she's the devil's child, that's what Rodolfo said.'

The pestle slipped through Mamma's fingers and glanced off the grate. 'Lucia! Never let me hear you say that again!' Lucia looked down and stuck her thumb in her mouth, sucking it furiously. 'Take no notice of her, Doria,' Mamma said. 'Do you hear me?'

Doria nodded. The devil didn't have any children, Don Zeno had already told her that. Besides, she was Papi's girl. That's what he said when he brought her the first ripe fig from the tree behind the aia, splitting it with his fingers to let her suck out the pulp, or when he picked a May poppy from the fields and twisted it into her hair like a butterfly …

'Butterfly!' Doria's thoughts jolt back to the present as she lies on her bed. 'That's what the Maestro was talking about at lunchtime while he was carving the goose. "I think I've found my butterfly",' he said. And Signora Elvira replied. "That's good, dear," like she wasn't really listening. She's funny, Signora Elvira, the way one minute you think she's cross with you, and the next she's all smiles and patting your arm. Like at lunchtime, when she rang the bell and said, "We've finished in here, Doria, so you can help yourself to anything you like".' And that's just what she had done, piling up her plate with slices of tender goose, roast potatoes and a vegetable that tasted like thistle, then a large piece of peach tart topped with strawberries, which she picked off with her fingers. When she'd finished her meal, Signora Elvira asked her to take the coffee into the studio, where the Maestro and Signor Giuseppe were sitting with their feet up, smoking cigars the size of cucumbers.

'Ah, there you are, Doria,' the Maestro said, smoke coming from his nostrils. 'Signor Giuseppe and I were just saying what a good job you did at lunchtime. Well done, my dear!' Doria looked down and shuffled her feet. 'After all your hard work, you deserve one of these. Here ...'

A sweet, tempting smell reached her nose. She looked up and saw a chocolate box decorated with a gold ribbon. 'Ooh!'

'Take two,' the Maestro said. So she did, scooping them into her hand and then into her mouth. A look passed between the Maestro and Signor Giuseppe, a look Doria didn't understand. She gulped, losing one of the chocolates.

'Do you have an admirer, Doria?' Signor Giuseppe asked, 'a fancy boy of some sort?'

Doria stared at his mouth, at the pink tongue pushing out a stray brown tobacco strand.

'Don't tease the girl!' the Maestro said.

Doria looked from one to the other.

'Daarling ...' Signora Ida was in the doorway, wearing a gown you could almost see through. 'I'm waiting for you!'

'I won't be a moment, my love,' Signor Giuseppe said, winking.

'Well, don't be too long ...' and with that she vanished.

Seizing the moment, Doria curtsied and hurried after her. Doria rolls over and looks up at the sun-edged curtains, running her tongue around the inside of her mouth in search of any leftover hint of chocolate. 'What a nice man the Maestro is ...' And with that thought in mind, she finally drifts off, brought back again (but only for a second) by the rumble of his motor-car leaving the garage.

Chapter 14
CORINNA RECEIVES
ANOTHER LETTER

The seagull swoops towards the paving stones where a small puddle glistens, and lumps of something, possibly edible, form a trail on the path around the white church with the square tall belltower. He has learned to be cautious of this place with its bursts of terrifying sound that shake his innards like the jaws of a voracious cat, but he can no longer ignore the hunger that is sucking out his insides, robbing him of what little strength remains to him. Yesterday the town was crowded with holiday-makers, but each time he found a crumpled paper containing leftover crumbs of bread or biscuit, he was chased away by unruly children.

Shriek! Shriek! The seagull lands just short of the arched door-way, looks around, then pecks quickly at the ground. *Ugh!* A thick lump of whatever-it-is has stuck to his beak. Striking the offending item on the paving stone until it drops off, he flaps his wings and takes to the air, gliding towards a promenade littered with streamers, drink bottles (their stoppers taken by small boys to use as marbles), cigarette ends, straw, pieces of string, crate fragments, and other objects that look as if they have been washed up by the tide. Thank goodness the squeeze-box players have gone, along with those devils costumed in black and white who twirl flaming sticks in the air without a thought for the danger they pose to airborne creatures. Not to mention that dancing bear, with its greedy eyes, who could crush him with one swipe of its massive paw. Spying a pair of nervous little sparrows bobbing near the table-legs of an outdoor cafe, the seagull wheels around and comes in to land just in front of the table. Puffing out his chest, he struts towards them, shrieking like a drunk shouting at no one, determined to get some crumbs for himself before the barista chases him away with a broom. It is nine o'clock, and many of the shutters along the promenade are still closed, a testament to the amount of alcohol drunk by the inhabitants and the late hour at which they staggered to their beds.

Excess, though, plays no part in Corinna's grandmother's life, so yesterday evening she and her two companions retired only slightly later than usual, and are now in the parlour anticipating their morning stroll.

'Are you not studying this morning, dear?' Grandma asks, picking up the scissors to attack the front page of the newspaper. Corinna is staring dreamily towards the window, where the breeze is lifting the net curtains, billowing them out like the skirt of a bridal gown. The scissors stop snipping. 'Your studies, dear!'

'Oh ... but I have a slight headache,' Corinna offers, by way of an excuse.

Grandma sniffs and resumes her task. 'You're probably still tired from last night. Eleven is a little on the late side.'

At this Aunt Adelaide looks up from the yellow rose she is embroidering. 'Yes, but weren't those harlequins fun? And I do so love a dancing bear ... and a *cantastoria*, of course. How clever to banter with the crowd in rhyming couplets like that!'

Before anyone can comment, there is a knock on the front door that has Grandma rising and bustling out into the corridor. When she returns, she is waving a letter in each hand, like two small flags. 'Here you are!' she says, passing one to Corinna.

The envelope, addressed in Aurelia's handwriting, rests in Corinna's lap as her mind continues to follow grainy images that are jerking from one frame to the next, like the moving pictures in the Lumière cinema back home in Turin ... A golden afternoon full of promise, a small house set among trees, a tall man with liquid eyes, his breath on her cheek, his thumb running enticingly along her lower lip, the faint prickle of his moustache ...

'I do wish your mother's nurse would take more trouble with

her script!' Grandma complains. The film in Corinna's head judders to a halt, to be replaced by the smell of dusty furnishings and slowly stewed mutton. 'The new priest has been to visit,' Grandma reads out, pushing her spectacles onto the bridge of her nose. 'He's young and a little shy, but *simpatico* … And the curtains have arrived, red velvet …'

'Red!' Aunt echoes. 'A perfect colour for lifting the spirits!'

Ignoring her, Grandma goes on. 'The doctor has recommended a stay at the thermal springs at Salsomaggiore …'

Aunt Adelaide's needle slips, inadvertently stabbing her little finger. '*Aiyee!*' She puts it to her lips and sucks it, then says anxiously, 'But that will cost a fortune. Who is going to pay?' The question provokes an uneasy silence in which Corinna examines Aurelia's handwriting as if it is new to her, and as she contemplates the loops and downstrokes rounded off with a flourish, she thinks back to her childhood, and better times, when Mamma was not yet confined to a darkened room where neither she, nor anyone else, wanted to be. On warm days, they would take the tram to the city centre and sit eating pastries under the porticos of Caffe San Carlo, where patriots had once met to plan the unification of their country. Mamma would make up stories, or recount episodes from *The Adventures of Pinocchio*, putting on silly voices for the cricket, the fire-eater, and the terrifying shark. There had been cold days, too, with violet-tinged skies, when they'd wrapped up in coats and scarves and crossed over to the park, their breath turning milky in air that smelled of chestnuts and damp leaves. She remembers the mud squishing under her boots as she jumped up and down or hopped alongside her mother's uneven footsteps. But they never lasted, those happy interludes, and soon it was back to playing quietly in the kitchen, and hoping Papa would come home before she went to bed.

Grandma is the first to break the silence. 'Aren't you going to read your letter, dear?'

'Oh yes …' Prising open the flap, Corinna scans the first few lines which, true to Aurelia's character, waste little time on pleasantries.

Dear thing … I miss you! How is life among the jellyfish?

Here the newspapers are full of the trial of Gaetano Bresci. You should hear the travesties they accuse him of, when the only question worth considering is how we tolerated a monarch who sanctioned the use of force against his own people! And yet it was left to this one poor fellow to carry out the final heroic act. He has a wife and child, and although Francesco Merlin (a brilliant man) is leading the defence, we all know he will never see them again ...

Corinna pauses, struck by the discordant tone of Aurelia's discourse; one that had sounded so convincing at university, but which seemed like feverish nonsense in this quieter world of seagulls and lingering sunsets. And so, folding the notepaper, she slides it back into the envelope and lets her mind drift back to the film in her head. Grandma insists on an early lunch, and so it is barely half-past one when Corinna takes her parasol from the wardrobe, treads quietly along the passageway, through the door into the courtyard, across to the side gate, and from there down the lane and around the corner onto the promenade. She walks quickly, paying scant attention to the two women who are standing outside the new boutique, gazing into the window.

'Look, Elvira!' one of them says as Corinna passes. 'Isn't that blue jacket with the stand-up collar charming?'

'You don't think it's a bit young?'

'One can never be too young, dear.' It takes Corinna less than fifteen minutes to reach the chalet, and once there she gazes around with the satisfaction of the most houseproud wife. The dustsheets have gone, the surfaces have been wiped, the floors swept, and the dresser decorated with a vase of the pink amaryllis that thrives in the sandy soil. Crossing to the window, she pushes it up and leans out, feeling a welcome breeze on her face. She is beginning to know the rhythms of this place, the squirrels that live in the pine trees, tirelessly leaping from one branch to the next, the tortoise that strolls across the clearing, the sparrows that flutter away at the slightest sound, and the bright blue bird with the brown crest that flashes through the trees, mewling like a kitten. In the kitchen, the cobweb bottle has been replaced by a new one containing lemon cordial, purchased from the grocer on the corner. Corinna fills a glass and takes it over to the chair by the window, where she settles down to read.

Emma Bovary is becoming disillusioned with her new life. Her husband, Charles, is a bore and the company they keep has none of the brilliance she'd imagined. When she finds herself expecting a child, she longs for a son, certain that this will put everything right. The birth of a daughter, however, convinces her that her life is all but over.

Corinna follows the words quickly, not concentrating as fully as she should. Emma, whose story had previously enthralled her, is beginning to annoy her. For surely a woman who has come from so little and achieved so much should be happy with her lot, or at least content? Flaubert's heroine, though, seems incapable of such a state. Or perhaps she is just petulant and stupid? Corinna fingers her bookmark, pondering these questions. Is it possible that the yearning for more than we have is embedded in our nature in some way? Does that explain why men voyage to uncharted continents, or into jungles seething with serpents and wild animals? And women? Instead of finding fault with Emma, maybe she should applaud her, for isn't Corinna, like Madame Bovary, opposing her fate by refusing to consider a man like Maurizio, who would give her security and social position in return for a child or two and a well-organised life?

Lifting her glass, Corinna takes a long sip of lemon. Then she picks up her bookmark and runs a fingertip over the letters, tracing each word with care. And Maestro Giacomo Puccini, what is his true nature? She may be young and inexperienced, but she isn't a fool. She knows there are men who prey on women, who charm and court them with silver-tongued promises of love and happiness. But what she sees in his eyes is something deeper, more elemental, edged with a melancholy he tries to hide. And that kiss! It was like being touched by an angel … Corinna takes another sip, hoping he will visit her this afternoon.

A sudden squawk startles her from her thoughts. There is a seagull perched on the verandah railing outside, staring through the back window with black-lined eyes. On it goes, squawking and shaking its head, until Corinna, convinced that something is wrong, goes to investigate. She edges around the verandah, taking care to avoid the planks that have rotted to nothing, but by the time she gets to the back of the house, the bird has vanished. She leans over the railing and scans the ground as far as the thicket, then looks up into the trees where the pine cones are lined up along the branches in pairs, like Noah's animals waiting to board the ark. A movement catches her eye, and there's the gull by the water tank, stomping his feet as if performing some native rain dance. She watches him drive his beak into the earth and pull out a puce wriggling worm, which he waves around before swallowing the life out of it. He dives again, but this time he strikes something solid that reflects the light, like a mirror or a prism.

It is small and spherical, and as Corinna prises it from the dirt, she sees that it is a crystal jar with a badly tarnished lid that gives way at the first twist. Inside is a blue casing, and inside that a small piece of cloth, folded on itself, which she slides onto her hand and peels open. And there, before her astonished eyes, is a pair of beautiful pearl earrings. *But who do they belong to?*

Corinna rolls the pearls back and forth on her palm, studying the creamy texture, the delicate setting. She holds one up high, the better to appreciate its flawless white glow. And all the while, she hears the words Aunt Adelaide let slip on the railway platform: *Only she isn't his wife, is she?*

Corinna shuts her eyes, willing them away. She refuses to think about the woman she now considers her rival, even though she knows nothing about her; refuses to question and delve, to discover details that would only give her more substance and make her real. No, Giacomo has chosen her, Corinna, and she is going to bask in the thrill of his kisses, lose herself to the memory of his embrace as he draws her to him, his eyes misted with desire. One little kiss, that is all it has taken to unbalance her mind, to call forth a torrent of hopes and dreams from her imagination that have swept away all common sense, leaving her as vulnerable as a newborn animal, victim to its own instincts. *Just one little kiss.*

Corinna clears the ivy away from the water tank and gives

the lever a sharp kick. There is a splutter like a consumptive cough, then a slow trickle that forms a dark rusty pool on the sunbaked earth. When the water runs clear, she crouches down and holds the pearls under the thin silvery stream to see their beauty emerge.

Chapter 15
PUCCINI RUSHES BACK TO THE CHALET

Three days have passed since Puccini took Corinna in his arms, three days since he pressed his lips to hers, sensing her hesitancy as well as her willingness. Oh, the waxing and waning of those first delicate moments that can lead to the most thrilling of conquests or the cool wind of a change! Yet this morning, as he gazes through the French windows, a pensive expression on his freshly shaved face, the composer is not thinking about the young woman from Turin, whose image has begun to haunt his every waking hour. He's thinking of Elvira. Something is wrong. Not in a bad way; in fact, quite the reverse.

Elvira is smiling too much, and yesterday, after supper, when I complained of a burning stomach, instead of accusing me of eating like a pig, she brought me a glass of warm bicarbonate and a cushion for my back. Not only has her mood improved, she has also taken to dusting pink powder on her face and leaning towards me in a way that, were it another woman, I might consider provocative. No, Elvira is up to something, all right, although I have no idea what!

The composer's ruminations are interrupted by the sight of Poldo on his way round to the vegetable patch, a wooden basket clutched in his crab hand, and suddenly, ridiculously, Puccini is overtaken by a wave of envy for the old man with the stooped back whose life is as solid as the ground beneath his sad old leather boots. For surely there could be no greater contentment than having one's days governed not by the whims of other people, but by the immutable rhythms of nature itself. And when it comes to the land, there is little the gardener doesn't know. Under his care flowers bloom, peaches and mandarins swell to perfect ripeness, and vegetables appear on the table every day of the year. His knowledge of local flora, passed down from generation to generation, is exhaustive and, in all weathers, he can be seen going about gathering berries and herbs to make those potions of his. Puccini isn't always convinced of their curative properties. He remembers with a smile Elvira's look of horror when the gardener suggested inserting sprigs of parsley into Antonio's bottom to cure a case of childhood worms; but the onion and honey syrup certainly eased his winter cough, the ointment of olive oil and cuckoopint leaves drew the pus from that boil on his neck, and the myrtle leaves in his hunting boots did seem to lessen the smell.

So carried away is Puccini by his contemplation of Poldo's life, by the time he flicks his watch from his breast pocket and glances at it, he has all but deluded himself into believing that the gardener's hard but simple existence is preferable to his own. Checking his watch again – eleven thirty, plenty of time to get to Club della Bohème and back before lunch – he steps through the French windows and into the garden.

Pausing to catch his breath by the oak tree where the path curves towards the lake, the composer glances up at branches that have been stripped of their acorns by the villagers, who will use them as fodder for their pigs. And as he stands there, a bird comes crashing out of the undergrowth, darting this way and that, its dirty yellow plumage blending in with the parched grass, its black-tipped wings whooshing the air like the bow of a violin. It is an oystercatcher, prized by hunters for its swift and complex flight as well as its abundant flesh. Cursing that a gun is not to hand, Puccini watches it loop and dive like a trapeze artist before it flies off into the distance.

There is birdsong in the air, the notes so pure they pass right through him like rays of ethereal light. 'Madonna!' This is the melody Pinkerton must sing to Butterfly on their wedding night, to charm and reassure her, sweep away her uncertainties and fear. But can he capture it? Closing his eyes, he concentrates with every fibre of his being, letting the notes seep into that deep still part of him, and then, when he can stand it no longer, he turns and jogs back along the path to his studio, grabs a pencil and starts scribbling as if his life depends on it. His plan for a pre-lunch visit to Club della Bohème abandoned. The sun has begun its slow descent towards the watery blue horizon when Puccini arrives at the chalet, his fulsome lunch still settling in his stomach – a pike with sharp teeth and irides- cent skin that had stretched the length of the kitchen table, its head, tail and bones boiled into stock for fish stew with toma- toes and peas, followed by a creamy tiramisu. The composer, though, cannot recall one mouthful of what he has swallowed. Nor does he remember Elvira's pinched lips, Ida's curious stares, or the giggles of the children, silenced by nudges from Fosca, as he gulps down glass after glass of Ramelde's vino frizzante, before rising and rushing back to his chalet.

'The room smells musty. It needs more air!' He crosses to the window and throws it open. The frame is hot and there is a crack through the glass like a bolt of lightning. A seagull on the verandah rail stares at him insolently. 'Shoo!' he hisses. 'Clear off!' The bird flutters to the ground and stalks haughtily away on splayed orange feet.

Puccini turns to face the room, and there she is in the doorway, outlined in a veil of light. Madonna! Her hair is falling loose in a dark satin curtain, and she is wearing blue, the colour of their first outing a lifetime ago. Small pearls, like droplets of cream, are fixed to her ears. Gazing at her, he finds he cannot breathe, overcome by a sense that he has known her forever. 'Come here,' he whispers, moving towards her.

She tilts her head, her eyes meeting his. There is a strange mes- sage in them, calm and full of joy.

'Oh God … come to me …'

Chapter 16
ELVIRA FIGHTS BACK

Several weeks have passed since Elvira's heart-to-heart with her sister, and in that time the sharp light of summer has softened to more mellow hues. Gone are the mosquitoes that swarm up from the lake at dusk, attacking every inch of her flesh not covered by clothing or oil of citronella. Gone, too, are Ida and the children, taking Fosca with them back to Florence. A village is not a suitable place to refine the manners of a young lady, and although Elvira has done her best, her daughter's behaviour at times can be a little wild. Now that Fosca is to marry Salvatore and settle in Milan, it's been agreed that she needs more polish. And so, with a heavy heart, Elvira has waved the little group off at the station, and now finds herself rattling round the big house feeling very much alone.

For some women, a period of tranquillity would be a blessing, leaving all the time in the world for appointments with the dressmaker, the hairdresser and the beautician, for visits to friends and neighbours, for browsing through copies of Women & Home, learning how to run their household in the inimitable style of the British. None of these activities appeals to Elvira, whose sensibilities, like a mother hen's, revolve around her family. Without children and relatives to fuss over, an emptiness opens up inside her where her heart should be, an emptiness she has tried to fill with the education of Doria in needlepoint, testing new recipes, even dabbling in watercolours. She is a sweet-natured girl, but with no conversation at all. Nothing seems to work. And so, in the afternoons Elvira goes for walks around the village, the brim of her hat pulled firmly down over her brow, ignoring the bite in the air and the smoke from the shacks that hangs over her like a deep winter fog.

Lost to thoughts exaggerated by solitude, Elvira doesn't notice the figtrees heavy with their pendulous load, nor the plums, apples and pears, juicy and ripe for picking, the chestnuts swelling in their spiny green casings, and the olives, which (if there is rain between now and November) will produce enough oil to see the villagers through until next year. She doesn't see that the grape picking has begun on the hillsides, the fruit clipped from the vines and carried to the *cantine* in baskets, tipped into tubs and crushed underfoot, then left until it starts gurgling and spitting like a monster rising from the depths of the lake, before being poured into barrels and kept cool until springtime. No, Elvira is unaware of nature bubbling away like the new wine, working its miracles around her, because her mind has become unhinged by enforced loneliness, day after day.

It is early morning, and the lady herself is seated at her dressing table examining the lotions and face creams from the apothecary of Santa Maria Novella in Florence, a gift from Ida. Lifting a small pot, she unscrews the lid and sniffs the sweetness of apricot. The creamy contents promise to rejuvenate her complexion, restoring the lustre and sheen of earlier years, yet despite using it daily Elvira can discern little difference. Peering into the mirror, she inspects the lines etched beneath her nose like the teeth of a small comb, and although she knows in her heart that no substance on earth will reclaim her youth and former beauty, she unscrews another pot and begins vigorously rubbing cucumber essence into her skin. Ivy shampoo, chamomile drops for her eyes, malva paste to whiten her teeth. Ida has thought of everything.

Reaching for the wedge of lemon on a small saucer, Elvira rubs it across the back of her hands, and while she waits for the juice to perform its magic, she listens to the sounds of the house, the throb of the boiler, the rattles and bangs from the kitchen signifying that Doria is preparing breakfast. Soon the smell of coffee and warm pastries will be wafting up the stairwell, offering her some small comfort … but what is that on her chin? Leaning forward, she stares at the mirror, then lets out a horrified gasp, grabs the tweezers and plucks a dark hair from the fold of her skin.

Hanging in the wardrobe of the dressing room next door, neatly pressed and protected by covers, are Elvira's latest acquisitions, purchased from the boutique in Viareggio, and it is to these that her thoughts now turn; the fine cotton blouse with a daring neckline, the blue French-style jacket with a stand-up collar and puffed sleeves, two skirts with sash waists and ruffles at the hem. The saleswoman had tried to interest her in a parasol, a white-handled flouncy thing in a common shade of pink, which she had rejected in favour of a fan made of Dutch goose feathers. And in the drawer of the dressing table, where she is now sitting, is her new lace-edged silk underwear, garments she would never have bought without Ida's encouragement, not in a million years! For Giacomo, it seems, must be handled like Poldo's donkey, enticed forward, not with an apple or a carrot, but with perfume and low-cut gowns, while being nudged from behind with compliments and sweet words. And she, instead of giving vent to her feelings, must smooth her hair with rosewater and oil. Are these really the tactics women employ against men, and if so, how has Ida gained this knowledge while she remained ignorant of it? Circling the rouge stick onto her cheeks, Elvira turns her head this way and that to check the result. Whatever the answers, Giacomo is very slow to respond.

Lunch is over (a quiet affair of tagliatelle with porcini mushrooms, braised beef, and chard tossed in a little chilli oil) and Elvira is in the pantry putting away the leftovers when she hears Giacomo shout out from the hall. 'I'm just popping over to see Carlo!'

Stepping into the kitchen, where Doria is busy washing up at the sink, Elvira catches a glimpse of his boater heading towards the back door. 'Wait a minute!' she calls, in keeping with her new resolution. 'Why don't I come with you? We can pick up the honey from Bernardo on the way.' There is no reply. It's too late … or is it? Hurrying into the hall, Elvira grabs her hat and makes her way quickly to the front gate, where Giacomo's motorcar is already chugging out of the garage. Certain that he will not hear her above the roar of the engine, she raises her hand to wave, but instead snags the cuff of her new blouse on a railing spike. 'Aiyee!' she cries, seeing the cuff is torn in the shape of an arrowhead, which will require the cuff to be turned. *But what is this?* There is a piece of paper wedged into the jasmine hedge. Tugging it out, Elvira sees that it is a letter, addressed to *Maestro Puccini, Club della Bohème, Torre del Lago.* A cheap, flowery scent reaches her nose. She stares at the pale green envelope, the large, insolent handwriting. Her pulse has begun to race, her head to hammer like Beppino at his forge. 'Aiyee!' she cries again.

Ripping open the envelope, she snatches out the notepaper and reads what is written there, then reels back, clinging to the gatepost for support. *Puttana! Filthy whore! Who could write such things?* Despite her shaking hands, she scans the page again, searching for a signature … and then she has it. *Corinna! Who is Corinna? Come on! Come on! Think!* But the name means absolutely nothing to her. *What should I do now?* she thinks. *Telephone Ida? No … no … Fosca might hear. Giacomo's sister, Ramelde? Giulio Ricordi? Oh God in heaven …* Closing her eyes, Elvira tries to concentrate, but there are firecrackers bursting into the blackness of her mind, shattering her thoughts into shards of deafening nothingness. She heaves in a breath, willing herself to stay on her feet, and slowly her mind begins to clear. Thrusting the letter into her pocket, she pulls open the gate and sets off toward the village. Elvira's jaw is grinding as she strides along under the red and yellow trees, her shoes stamping fallen leaves into the moist scented earth. When she reaches the well, she veers right, onto a path that will take her through orchards of apple and plum trees, and mulberries left over from the days of the old silk farms. On she goes, ignoring the stone that has worked its way into her shoe, until she comes to the cottage where Poldo lives with his wife, Concetta.

The gardener's donkey is tethered to a post, nuzzling the ground in search of food, while in a pen, sprawled out on filthy straw, is a large thick pig with a brutish face, panting through its snout as if revolted by its own stench. Battered cages with dark shapes inside them are stacked up against a medlar tree, while courtyard chickens run around screeching as they flee her footsteps. Seeing none of this, Elvira marches up to the front door and bangs on it with her fist. There is a pail at her feet that is half-full of pebbles, pebbles that are moving and shifting about. 'Snails! Ugh!' she cries, as Poldo appears around the side of the house. The old man is talking to himself, his small head shaking from side to side as if disagreeing with every word, while tucked under his arm are torn strips of newspaper, held close to his body, as his bent fingers fumble with the opening of his trousers. Momentarily discomfited by this scene, Elvira fixes her gaze to the cloth cap on Poldo's head, without which the gardener has never been seen, leading the villagers to jest that it had been nailed to his skull at birth. He comes closer, and as he does so Elvira catches the smell of old cloth impregnated with dirt, with plants, with straw and manure, and breath edged with the sourness of strong local tobacco.

'Poldo!' she begins loudly, for the old man is a little deaf. 'I have an urgent errand to attend to.'

'Oh aye?' he says, knotting the rope round his waist. If he is surprised to see her, he shows no sign of it.

'Yes. In the carriage … I need to find my husband. He's in Viareggio.'

The gardener runs a hand over his stubbled chin. He is paying attention now, weighing up the situation like the card player he is. He turns and spits on the ground.

Elvira tries again. 'I will, of course, make it worth your while …'

At this Poldo's eyes narrow into calculating slits. Waiting for him by the hearth is a small glass of grappa, distilled from grape skins and infused with juniper berries and lemon rind. It is his favourite, and at this hour he likes to drink a glass or two before having a snooze. *The last thing I want to do is go off with Signora Elvira on some wild goose chase. On the other hand, it wouldn't do to fall out with her. She could be a devil, she could. Some even say she has the malocchio, the evil eye, and put sprigs of rue around the house when she is coming to call,* he recalls. Poldo doesn't believe in that sort of thing himself, but he has noticed the nervous way she is scratching at her hands.

'Very much worth your while,' she adds, sounding out each word as if speaking to a small child. Poldo swipes away the wasp that is buzzing around the neck of his collarless shirt. 'A trip in the carriage, is it?' he agrees reluctantly. They drive up and down the promenade, with Elvira clambering in and out of the carriage to search behind walls and in alleyways for Giacomo's motorcar. She doesn't have much to go on, only the postmark on the green envelope and a nose for this sort of thing, born of previous experience. She presumes the little hussy is someone he met in Milan, a chorus girl most likely, swept off her feet by his attentions, and she is staying in a hotel, one of the better places at the northern end of the town, on the way to Lido di Camaiore. After a second sweep of the promenade with still no sign of the automobile, Elvira is beginning to despair. She can't ask Poldo to continue for much longer, yet she is certain Giacomo is here somewhere among the villas and the pine trees ... *Pine trees!* Her jaw drops. *Of course*! 'Poldo!' she cries, leaning forward and tapping him on the shoulder. 'We must go in the opposite direction, right along to the far end!'.

As the carriage swings around, Elvira thinks back to the chalet where she and Giacomo used to spend the summer holidays when the children were young; a shabby disagreeable place inhabited by spiders and prehistoric-looking lizards that jerked across the walls on their toe pads. What a sufferance! The heat, the insects, her skin turning red and blistering no matter what she did ... and the sand that got everywhere, even in the food! Oh God, how she loathed it, and how relieved she was to have an excuse to abandon it forever when that sly little maid started stealing from them. First it was food, then money from her purse, and finally a pair of pearl earrings that had belonged to Giacomo's mother. The *carabinieri* had been unable to trace them, and so it was Elvira's word against the girl's, and although it was obvious who was the liar, the vindictive little minx put it about that Giacomo had tried to kiss her, and after that no mother would let her daughter come to work for them. Only then did Giacomo concede defeat, and in the following years they took a house in the countryside with lovely views and a garden for the children to play in. Elvira had rarely worn the earrings, which Giacomo gave her to celebrate the birth of Antonio. Their insipid colour and overworked setting didn't suit her, not to mention the looks she got from Giacomo's sisters! All things considered, it was a small price to pay to escape from that suffocating beach-box. The chalet! What sort of woman would go there?

Poldo draws the carriage to a halt at the end of promenade, pulls a hand-rolled cigarette from his pocket, lights it, and rests his patched elbows on his knees. He knows what this is about: the Maestro has been stoking the fire in his *coglioni* again. Sucking in a mixture of burning tobacco and chestnut leaf, the gardener ruminates a little on his master, a man with not a drop of snobbery in him, just overheated blood that no woman seems able to cool. Certainly not one like Signora Elvira. You'd think he'd be more careful, what with her temper and all, but she always finds him out, and then there's shouting and throwing things, with Cook and that laundry girl tittle-tattling about it afterwards behind the washhouse. Mind you, there's not many men that would put up with her nonsense – Bruno, for one, who gives his wife the back of his hand every so often to remind her who's boss. Nobody liked it when Bruno sent one of her teeth flying, but a man can't let his wife have the run of him. It makes him look a fool. Like the time, after one of their rows, that the Maestro asked to be taken to the station, and then changed his mind halfway there! The shutters to the bedroom were closed after that, and the pair of them went around cooing at each other like turtledoves for a day or two. Not that Poldo would say a word about this to anyone. He knows his place, and that's to keep his nose clean and his mouth shut, even if Concetta does sometimes beg him for titbits of gossip to liven up her day.

Tired of his thoughts, the gardener flicks his cigarette to the ground and looks around. A taxicab approaches them along the promenade, swings around and pulls up by the path. The driver, a lithe fellow, thin as a whippet, hops down and opens the door, and a moment later, a doll woman appears on the path out of the woods and climbs up into her seat. After that, things happen so quickly Poldo can't for the life of him work out what's going on, but later, when he finally gets home to his chair by the hearth and his glass of grappa, he tries to fit the pieces together as best he can.

First there was a shriek, a sound to shatter glass, then Signora Elvira jumped down from the carriage, her weight rocking it from side to side. Still shrieking, she rushed at the taxicab. 'Leave my *husband* alone!' she shouted. 'How dare you, you little trollop! You puppet! You piece of rubbish! Leave him alone, do you hear me?' And with that, she threw herself at the cab and started beating at the girl with her fists.

Backed into a corner, the girl raised her arms to defend herself from the blows, then sang out in a voice not of these parts. 'My dear Signora, I don't know what you're talking about ... but are you sure the gentleman in question is your husband?' And then, with the speed of a snake, she struck Signora Elvira a blow with her parasol, sending the older woman stumbling back and falling to the ground with a scream. The young woman, cool as a cucumber, leaned forward and spoke to the driver, who lifted his whip and *whoosh*, they were off.

'Holy Mother of God!' Grabbing the rug, Poldo scrambled down as quickly as he could. 'Signora Elvira, are you hurt? Come on, now. Wrap yourself up in this ...' A hand rose limply from the dirt, and as he helped to haul his mistress back onto her feet, out of the corner of his eye he saw the taxicab disappearing into the distance.

Chapter 17
PUCCINI MAKES A PROMISE

Puccini is humming to himself as he swings his motorcar into the garage and saunters around to the back door. Why shouldn't he be happy? Life has never been better. The house is peaceful, his work is coming along apace, this morning he'd bagged a pheasant as well as his usual quota of coots and wild ducks, and Corinna … Here he hesitates, at a loss to describe the extraordinary young woman whose depths he is only just beginning to fathom, and whose lips have left his skin tingling like a thousand tiny starbursts. There is, however, one shadow crossing his moon: she will soon be returning home to Turin, a thought that makes him ache with misery. He cannot let her go, for although he doesn't realise it, she has become his muse, his compass rose, guiding him through the seas of his own creativity. And so, as his feet crunch along the path, he considers how their delightful liaison might continue, an idea that on the face of it seems impractical, for she has her studies at the university, he his home and life in the country. But a man of his means can make things happen. Turin is barely an hour away from Milan by train, there is his apartment, there are hotels and rooms to rent …

It takes Puccini surprisingly little time to formulate a plan (for he is rather good at this sort of thing), so that by the time he reaches the back door, having paused to gaze at the ripe tomatoes hanging like red stones from the plants in the vegetable patch, he has all but worked out what steps he needs to take. The door is locked, and remembering that Elvira had said something about going to fetch the honey, and being in no mood to work, he decides to fritter away the hours before supper at Club della Bohème, quaffing wine and chatting to his friends.

Ferruccio is there under the awning, drunk as usual, and with him are some other artists who visit the village from time to time: Angiolo Tommasi, recently returned from Patagonia, his younger brother, Ludovico (who plays the violin, but a little too heavily on the bow for Puccini's taste), Francesco Fanelli, a serious young man in a black coat with hair falling across his face like a Russian poet, Raffaello Gambogi, smoking nervously, and Plinio Nomellini, author of the frescoes on Puccini's studio walls that have faded disastrously in the humid lake air. And with them is Don Zeno, who claims his presence among these godless men is an act of Christian charity yet in truth he far prefers their conversation to the petty, often self-righteous concerns of his parishioners.

'Boys!' Puccini cries expansively. 'Wonderful to see you all! Good afternoon, Father. How's business?'

The priest runs a hand across his brow, which is gleaming as if coated in oil. 'Fine, thank you, Giacomo. In fact, I should say booming.'

'Pleased to hear it!' the composer says, lowering himself onto a seat.

There is hearty laughter in which the priest joins in, slapping his hands on his tunic and leaving behind marks like continents on a map. Don Zeno is a great lover of pasta, and his housekeeper, Rosaria, believes that feeding him well will earn her a place in paradise. For years the effect on his waistline has been negligible, but recently the priest has been having trouble with a hip, which has seriously impeded his ability to get about. The ensuing inactivity has caused his girth to expand like a slowly inflating balloon; his jowls, too, have puffed up to the point where he reminds Puccini of the pet hamster Antonio had as a boy, which ended up between the jaws of one of the dogs.

'Andrea! Bring us a couple of bottles of something decent, will you?' the composer calls. Blackbird Legs is behind the bar, his hands spread flat on his newspaper, his eyes riveted to the article he is reading. 'Hey … did you hear me?'

The response, something to do with money and a wallet, is lost because at that moment Mingo, the postman, appears in the doorway and stares at Puccini in a sort of terrified awe, as if seeing a holy apparition. Then he lowers his head and scurries off down the path. 'Did you see that?' Puccini asks Nomellini, whose shrewd eyes are facing the same way as his.

'No, what?'

'Mingo, acting strangely.'

'Mingo is strange,' Nomellini says dismissively. 'He's probably lost your letters again. If I remember correctly, the last time you threatened to shoot him with one of your hunting rifles ... Now then, before I forget, what's happening about the frescoes?'

Forgetting about the postman, Puccini turns his attention to the question. 'It's no good, Plinio,' he says with a sigh. 'I've consulted Puccinelli and he says there's nothing to be done. It's back to whitewash, I'm afraid.'

'Whitewash?' Andrea plonks two flasks of cheap wine on the table. 'While we're on that subject, you still owe me for last time.'

'Do I?' Puccini says, genuinely surprised. 'You'd better remind me to pay up before I leave.'

'I can't be expected to do everything!' Andrea barks. 'You know where I am. Come and find me!'

'But I don't like to disturb you,' Puccini parries, beginning to enjoy himself, 'not when you've got your nose stuck in the newspaper.'

'I'm reading about the siege of Peking,' Andrea says, unaware he is being teased. 'The government's sent in troops against those Boxer fellows. It's a wretched disgrace, it is!'

Puccini's eyes meet Don Zeno's in a moment of shared dismay. If this lot get going on the rights and wrongs of the Boxer Rebellion, there will be no end to it, and sooner or later it will turn nasty. His position, which he will be keeping to himself, is that he couldn't care less about events in China because all his thoughts are concentrated on her diminutive neighbour, and the only warship that interests him is Pinkerton's.

Fanelli, his youthful face shining with idealism, is intent on having his say. 'I'm not surprised they call us foreign devils,' he says, earnestly. 'We go there and take, take, take and put nothing back, while at the same time despising the people, their ways and traditions. We even try and foist our religion on them!'

Don Zeno flinches. 'That may be so,' he says, in spite of himself, 'but one can hardly condone setting on the German ambassador and gouging the poor man's eyes out.'

This is too much for Puccini. 'I'm off,' he says, standing up. 'Elvira will be home by now.' He gives them all a wave. 'Bye fellows, Father ...' And a minute later, having paused to listen to the pretty *ci- ci-ci* of the green and yellow tit that is singing its heart out in the lower branches of the oak tree, he hears a roar coming from Andrea's shack. Back home, he's given no warning. One minute he is stepping through the back door, a whistle playing on his lips, the next a shadow has loomed across the corridor and Elvira is standing in front him, her arms crossed, blocking his path.

'Hello, Elvira,' he says. 'Did you get the honey?' It is then, in that moment of excruciating silence, that he realises something has gone wrong, and that there will be nothing sweet about this encounter.

She doesn't waste words. She jumps at him like a cat in the night, ripping his cheeks with her fingernails. 'You bastard,' she hisses. 'You double-crossing liar!'

Puccini's heart stops ... then starts again. He catches her wrists, holding them away from his face. He wants to strike her, call her all the terrible names he can think of, but he cannot bring himself to do so. 'Elvira! What's got into you? Stop it this instant, do you hear me?'

But she cannot hear him, for her head is full of rage, and so she wrestles with him, flailing her arms, trying to break free.

'You're insane, Elvira, mad ...'

'Mad? Yes, I must be, to put up with you!'

He holds her tightly, using all his force to keep her fingernails from his cheeks, and in those seconds, wondrously, the years melt away, and it is another Elvira he is holding in his arms, a beautiful young woman with passionate eyes – his very own Tosca – the woman who made him cry out with longing and ripped at his heart till it bled. He shakes his head, but the image won't leave him. 'Elvira, please, see sense!' *Oh Christ, my eyes are filling with tears,* he thinks, loosening his grip to step back. 'You know I'll never leave you.'

'Promise me you won't see her again!'

He can't take his eyes off her, for she is like a wild animal, and quite quite beautiful. 'It doesn't mean anything, really, you know me ...'

'Promise me!'

There is a silence, then something inside him gives. 'All right.'

'On the soul of your mother ... your brother, Michele ... swear to me!'

Tears are dripping onto his cheeks like sap from a cut vine. 'All right,' he whispers, 'I swear.'

'Say it properly!'

He swallows, the words choking him. 'I swear I won't see her again.'

Chapter 18
GIULIO RICORDI
MAKES A DECISION

No one in the village knows how Poldo came to be so canny at playing cards, but his skill is as legendary as the cloth cap on his head. Some say it is a talent passed down from his grandfather, a small man with the darting eyes of a mole who, like his grandson, kept to himself. Others claim that there is some special ingredient, a herb or a berry, in the grappa he drinks each day. Poldo's deafness, along with a notable lack of interest in others, makes him immune to the speculation that surrounds him, but had he been asked, he would have stared silently into the distance, wondering why something so obvious to him was not clear to others. For surely any fool could see that it wasn't the value of the cards in your hand that mattered, it was the careful choice of when to play them.

In the autumn of 1903 with winter approaching, in Milan, which is about two hundred and sixty kilometres north of the village, a person with an equally deadly finesse is sitting in his office in a sandstone building in Via Bagli, not far from the theatre of La Scala. He, too, is a small man, renowned for his skill at the card table, who learned much from his grandfather, but here the comparison must end, for he is wearing an immaculately cut suit with a handkerchief forming a neat angle in his breast pocket, and his silk tie is pinned into place by a five-carat diamond. He has a straight hairline, an intelligent forehead, grey eyes to match his suit, and the pointed ears of a wizard, which in some respects he is. He is also a man of great power and enterprise, qualities inherited from his grandfather, Nonno Giovanni, founder of the company, who, flanked by a pair of candelabra, is staring impassively down at him from the wall above the fireplace.

Giulio Ricordi rests his pen on its stand, picks up the sheet of dazzling white vellum and presses it carefully to the blotter, waiting for the ink to dry. He has a problem, one of those knotty problems with far-reaching consequences. As ever when faced with such a situation, he thinks of his grandfather, who had died during Giulio's final school year at his *liceo*, but not before instilling in him the dictum by which he himself had lived: use your brain, use your imagination, and never give up. Nonno Giovanni, an energetic man with a penchant for fat cigars that filled the drawing room with a rich manly aroma, had followed his own advice to the letter. As a young orchestra leader, he noticed that the carpenters and set builders at La Scala wore paper hats made of discarded sheet music to protect themselves from the dust. Further investigation revealed that valuable scores and orchestra parts lay abandoned in the cellar, there for the taking. Giovanni offered to buy them up, established himself as a copyist, and in a stroke of genius that laid the foundations for the House of Ricordi's success, stipulated that any music he produced should remain his property after the performance.

Giulio adored his grandfather (his own father had been away much of the time, setting up offices in Rome, Naples, London, Palermo and Paris). Giulio saw his grandfather as a man who treated him as an equal, taking him to dine in fine restaurants, eliciting his opinion on everything (especially the piano music he was studying), and never once chiding him for views that were unformed or naive. When he died, Giulio wept openly, and then, deciding that Nonno Giovanni would not approve of such a show, vowed to build an empire that would have made the old man truly proud of him. Ricordi, overcome by a rush of emotion at these reminiscences, looks around his office, at the bookcase that runs the length of one wall, the Murano chandelier, pale arms curving gracefully towards the ceiling like those of a ballerina, the chaise longue, the hand-carved coffee table, silk rug, leather armchairs, antique lamps and his beautifully inlaid desk. Lifting the white vellum from the blotter, Ricordi turns it over and sees black words crossing the surface like footsteps in snow: *What is to be done about Giacomo*?

His protégé, a man who in many respects is more of a son to him than an artist under contract, is going through one of his awkward spells, changing his mind on every detail of Madama Butterfly (even the number of acts, which he now wants to reduce from three to two!), and blaming the delays on poor old Giacosa, sometimes even Illica – in fact anyone but himself. Meanwhile Elvira tells Ricordi that he is either out hunting (and getting himself arrested for trespass and not having a licence for his gun), carousing with his pals in that shed, or attending 'meetings' in Milan that are clearly of his own invention. Ricordi runs a hand down his carefully trimmed beard. It isn't the first time that Puccini has been sidetracked in the pursuit of pleasure rather than getting on with his work. Nor is it the first time he's had to speak to him about it …

There is a knock on the door. 'Come!'

An elderly clerk steps into the room, a man in a stiff-collared shirt and the suit of an undertaker, his spine as straight as a mast and his eyes the startling blue eyes of his Austrian forebears, one-time rulers of the city. 'Shall I stoke the fire, Signor Giulio?' he offers.

Ricordi glances at the grate. 'Not just yet, Carlo. I can't abide an overheated room, it makes one drowsy. But you could ask Signor Tito to come in, and bring us some coffee, please.'

The clerk bows, showing a scalp of thin, snow-white hair. 'Yes, Signor Giulio, right away.' While waiting for his son to join him, Ricordi crosses to the window and looks out over the balcony at the street below. He takes in the leafless trees, their stark branches warmed by a milky sun, the telegraph boy bumping by on his bicycle, the carter, a tool-bag in his hand, the motorcar slowly rounding the corner, preceded by a youth waving a red flag, and the horse-drawn tram rattling towards the opera house, a conductor on the platform waiting to help the ladies alight. This is what he likes to see, a civilised world in good working order.

Seized by a sudden impulse, Ricordi turns and heads across to the bookcase, twists the key and pulls out a large leather-bound, gilt-edged volume. *Le Villi*, Puccini's first opera, had earned six thousand lire, not a bad sum for a young musician just starting out …

There is another knock at the door. This time a fellow in his thirties appears on the threshold, a man as thin as Ricordi himself, with an open face, intelligent eyes, oiled hair that is receding, and the confident air of one who knows that his place in life is secure. Yet still the young man hesitates before entering the room, as one does before stepping into the inner sanctum of a church.

'Tito! Come in, come in!' Ricordi says warmly, replacing the volume to the bookcase. 'I've asked Carlo to bring us some coffee. Let's sit over there, where it's more comfortable.' Settling himself in one of the matching leather armchairs arranged next to a small table, Ricordi leans back and laces his fingers under his chin.

'We've got a problem, Tito.'

'What sort of problem, Papa?'

'It's Puccini. He's dried up again.'

Tito screws up his eyes and groans. 'Oh no! And the premiere of *Madama Butterfly* is booked for …?'

'Next February, in a little over three months.'

Tito does a quick calculation. 'He's not going to make it, is he? Have you spoken to him?'

'Of course I have,' Ricordi says, his tone letting slip the anger simmering away not far beneath the surface. 'I'm getting all the usual excuses and vacillations, as well as endless criticisms of poor old Giacosa.'

'He's good at that.'

'Better than good, he's a master.'

Tito crosses his legs and looks down at the ribbing of his sock. 'If *Madama Butterfly* has to be postponed …' he begins, then stops, allowing for one of those pauses when someone decides not to raise a difficult subject.

'… Sonzogno will make mincemeat of us!' Ricordi finishes for him. The mention of this name, uttered with an icy sibilance, is followed by a silence in which Ricordi finds himself plunged into an unwelcome consideration of his sworn rival, Edoardo Sonzogno, the only man in the world he truly detests. Some thirty years earlier, Sonzogno, who Ricordi considers a low-bred creature, had inherited a printing press, using it to churn out cheap editions of early music that earned him a fortune. Driven by an ambition that had the House of Ricordi firmly in its sights, he inaugurated a competition to draw talented young composers into his net with the promise of showcasing their works at the Teatro Lirico, which he had restored for the purpose at his own expense. But it didn't stop there. He then arranged for groups of thugs, paid by himself, to attend first nights at La Scala, the theatre under Ricordi's control, to boo and disrupt performances.

Tap, tap ...

'Come in!'

It is Carlo with a tray, which he places on the table between them.

There are specks of sugar on the curve of Ricordi's spoon, which he wipes away with his napkin before pouring a splash of steaming milk into his cup. 'We need to consider this carefully, Tito,' he says. 'It's not like the old days when we had dear old Verdi to coax out of retirement.'

'It's true, Papa. The old ones have gone and Sonzogno has poached the rest. Not that he has anyone the calibre of Puccini.'

'Indeed! It was a stroke of luck for us when the judges in his wretched competition couldn't decipher Giacomo's handwriting.'

Tito uncrosses his legs and reaches for his coffee. 'A nice irony, but what use is a genius if he won't finish a work?'

'Indeed!' Ricordi repeats, stirring his spoon slowly round his cup, his eyes reflecting the slightly glazed look of one whose thoughts are going back in time. 'You know, Tito, all this has the familiar ring of *Edgar*, Giacomo's second opera. What a nightmare that was! The writing dragged on for years, and when it was finally performed, both audiences and critics hated it, and it sank without trace. He wrote to me you know, the letter's still in the file somewhere, begging me not to terminate his contract. He said if I still had faith in him and wanted an opera from his pen, he had found the perfect subject ...'

'Manon Lescaut ...'

Ricordi nods. 'The other directors wanted to get rid of him then and there, but I insisted we keep him on. Giacomo thinks it was his letter that swayed me, but it wasn't. It was something I heard in his music, a quality that almost moved me to tears …'

'And you were rewarded with La Bohème and Tosca.'

The older man sighs. 'And Puccini gained fame and fortune, both of which have gone to his head.' A milky skin has formed on the surface of Ricordi's coffee. He skims it to one side then raises his cup and sips carefully.

'There is another possibility,' Tito says, crossing his legs again.

'And what might that be?'

'While I was chatting to Luigi Illica recently, he hinted – only hinted, mind – that Puccini is seeing another woman.'

Ricordi's cup clinks down on his saucer, making the spoon rattle. 'Oh no, not again! Not after that other little gold-digger – what was her name? Catrina, Carina … something like that. Poor Elvira! What she's had to put up with.'

Tito gives a wry smile. 'He's an artist, Papa. You know what they're like, always searching for inspiration, for that special –'

'No, no, no!' Ricordi cuts him off. 'Don't try and dignify Giacomo's behaviour with any of that nonsense. He isn't an aesthete, he's a child, a spoilt little boy driven by an untamed appetite. He uses women, pure and simple, ruining their reputations and breaking their hearts in the process, while he continues to enjoy the best of both worlds.' Rising to his feet, Ricordi starts to pace to and fro, his hands clasped tightly behind his back. 'Worse still,' he goes on, 'he doesn't know his own character. He likes to think of himself as a great romantic lover, but the fact is he'd be lost without Elvira and the stability she provides for him, without his villa and those soggy marshes.' Ricordi turns to face his son, his voice ragged with emotion. 'I can promise you this, Tito, if he leaves her for some young upstart, we won't get another note of music out of him!'

'Look, Papa,' Tito says earnestly, 'you may well be right, but it isn't getting us very far. If Sonzongo discovers Puccini has a mistress, just think of the scandal he'll whip up! It's bad enough that he's living with a woman who isn't his wife.'

Ricordi sinks into his chair and covers his face with his hands. 'Oh God, I can see it all! Giacomo mobbed in the street … *Madama Butterfly* booed off the stage …'

'You mustn't allow it, Papa.'

'And how do you propose I stop it?'

'Make him marry Elvira. It's the only solution.'

Ricordi raises an eyebrow. 'You imagine I hadn't already thought of that? Elvira's husband won't hear of an annulment.'

'Why not?'

'Partly revenge and partly because it suits his purposes.'

'You mean he's a womaniser?'

'And a gambler, a perfect wretch of a man.'

'A gambler?' Tito leans forward. 'Papa, if he's a betting man, he'll have a price.'

'He may well do,' Ricordi says stiffly, 'but I'm not in the habit of bribing people.'

'No, but Sonzogno is! Are you just going to sit back and let him destroy us?'

There is a silence in which Ricordi avoids his son's eyes by looking down and examining his hands: the raised blue veins, the blemishes that mark out his years, years that recently seem to have slipped by without his even noticing. He thinks of Nonno Giovanni, of his father, and of his son. He owes it to them to do everything he can to save the enterprise that bears their name – but this? 'How much?' he asks, finally looking up.

Tito shrugs. 'Six thousand lire should do it.'

'That much?'

'We have to make it worth his while.'

'All right,' Ricordi says wearily. 'Tell Carlo to get Elvira on the telephone ... and Tito, make sure she's alone.'

Chapter 19
DORIA ALONE IN THE VILLA

Early that same evening, Doria is standing at the stove preparing her supper, the table already set with a basket of bread, the parmesan and grater, a flask of oil, salt and pepper, and a glass of water with a splash of wine in it. To one side, on a saucer so it won't get dirty, is her little picture of Santa Zita, which she glances at while stirring the wild boar sauce to go on the thick strands of pappardelle. Outside the night is as black as pitch, the icy wind howling down from the north ploughing the lake into furrows, swaying the trees, and rattling the window like the maid's own chattering teeth. Doria is here alone, and she doesn't like it. Not one bit. And it all happened so quickly there wasn't time to go and fetch Paolo or Lucia to keep her company. All she has is the Maestro's brown and white dog, curled up in a basket by her feet. And she nearly didn't get him.

'I simply don't understand you, Elvira,' the Maestro had said over lunch. 'This morning when I told you I was going to the throat specialist and asked if you wanted to come with me, you said nothing on God's earth would drag you out on such a cold day.'

'Yes, Giacomo,' Signora Elvira replied, 'but that was before I remembered I'd promised to look at baby clothes for Fosca. The wedding was such a success, and Fosca is now assured of a happy prosperous life. But we must continue to support her through this next phase as motherhood approaches.'

'Baby clothes? But the child isn't due for months!'

'Hmm! I wouldn't expect a man to understand.'

The Maestro paused, then said, 'All right then, but what about

Doria? Are you going to leave her here on her own?'

Signora Elvira thought for a moment. 'She can go home for the night.'

'Elvira, we can't just pack her off like that! What will her mother say? At least let the dogs come into the house. She'll be safe with them to guard her.'

'The dogs? Well, I suppose if it were just Nello ...' Doria fishes a strand of pasta from the bubbling water and bites into it, feeling its chewy resistance against her teeth. Signora Elvira's change of mind had nothing to do with Miss Fosca's baby. It had to do with the telephone call she received. The girl carrying the steaming pot from the stove to the sink is taller than the one who came to work here over two years ago, rounder too, thanks to the generous helpings of nourishing food. And she's looking quite pretty in a brown dress with a white collar and matching cardigan (Miss Fosca's cast-offs), with her hair worn loose, held off her face by a tortoiseshell Alice band. These improvements can be put down to the good efforts of Signora Elvira who, true to her word, has helped and encouraged Doria in all manner of ways, not least her education, so that now she can make out the words printed under the image of her favourite saint. There are other differences, too. Doria has lost some of her shyness, and although she still stares at things, her mind drifting off goodness knows where, the spells don't last as long, and are less noticeable than before.

Grating cheese onto her pasta, Doria lifts her fork, plunges it into the ribbons, twists, then sticks it into her mouth, flicking up a straggling strand with her tongue. She chews quickly, her eyes moving back and forth from the rattling window to Santa Zita, who is protecting her from who knows what terrors of the night. *If only Signora Elvira was here!* she tells herself.

Earlier, before darkness fell, Doria had roamed the house, switching on lights in an effort to ward off the sudden noises, the creeping shadows, the groaning radiators. Round she went from room to room, pausing to look at herself in the Maestro's shaving mirror and run his comb through her hair, to sniff the bottles on Signora Elvira's dressing table and open the drawers, where she found an old photo of Master Antonio in a sailor suit. Then downstairs to the studio, to pop sugar cubes from the drinks tray into her mouth, and suck on the Maestro's shiny black pipe, which tasted nasty and bitter. The window frame rattles, stills, then rattles again, buffeted by a fierce gust of wind. Laying down her fork, Doria goes over and peeps through the frosted glass, seeing nothing but blackness in the garden outside. Reaching out her hand, she touches the window's icy surface, tracing the outline of the fern leaf that has formed there, following its jagged edges with her finger. The kitchen light flickers and fades, then comes back on again, brighter than ever. Doria holds her breath, not daring to imagine what could happen next, and as she stands there, her insides as chilled as the frosted glass, she remembers stories she has heard about when electricity was hooked up to the villa so many years ago.

First came poles as high as haystacks, dug in along the road, and then the wires that joined them up – 'the devil's washing line', the villagers called it. And that's not all they said: the harvests would fail, leaving them all to starve, and the birds would die too, their charred little bodies falling to the ground like stones. The mood turned nasty as tempers began to fray. Don Zeno, fearing that it could turn violent, called a town square meeting to which everyone came, even the old folk who liked to stay close to their hearths. There a man in a black hat addressed them from a wooden box, only nobody could hear what he was saying, what with all the shouting and the dogs barking. Even Renzo joined in, limping up and down with his hands over his ears, wailing as if his grandmother had just died.

The next morning, the villagers woke up to find the poles had gone, axed to the ground while they slept, leaving nothing but stumps for the children to jump on. Nobody seemed to know who had done it, but Beppino, the blacksmith, went around laughing and shaking everyone's hand, and later his forge gave off a strange grey smoke …

There is a yelp from the foot of the stove. Nello is hanging his head over the side of his basket, watching her as if to say, *why are you just standing there*? Doria gives him a look. 'The Maestro said I'd be fine with you to look after me,' she says, her tone accusing, 'but all you do is sleep!' As if to order, Nello slumps down and closes his eyes, and within seconds his chest is heaving in and out like a small pair of bellows. The maid sighs, and deciding not to finish her supper, which by now will be cold, she takes her dish over to the sink, turns on the tap and lets it run. What could be wrong with having hot water to do the washing up, and a humming radiator next to her bed, to warm her tired, aching legs, she wonders?

In the pantry, stored in a tin with a crown on the lid, is the polenta cake that Cook baked for the Maestro, and it is to this that Doria's attention now turns as she soaps and rinses her dirty plate. She isn't supposed to have any, she knows this because when Cook caught her looking at it, she said in her cross voice, 'Who do you think you are, my girl, the Queen of Sheba? That cake isn't for the likes of you!' But if Doria takes a very small piece, 'a sliver' Signora Elvira calls it, Cook might not notice …

Doria is still thinking about this as she pulls out the plug and waits for the water to drain away. But it doesn't, it just stays there, a murky pond with slicks of oil floating about on its scummy surface. She stares at it, willing it to disappear, then dives her hand in and pokes around, feeling a lump wedged into the plughole, too far down for her to reach. 'Hmmm …' Unsure what to do, she takes a fork and digs around, and when that doesn't work, she jabs at the hole again with her finger. 'Hah!' she cries as the lump gives way and drops into the downpipe. 'That's got it!' And it has. Doria's finger is stuck in the plughole.

She tries to ease it out, gently at first and then with more force, feeling a sickening drag on her knuckle but no movement. Next, she twists her hand back and forth like a screwdriver, tugging all the while. Nothing. Her head is going funny inside, and she thinks she might faint. The prospect of this frightens her into one last, desperate yank. But her finger is as tight and swollen as a sausage shoved deep into the mouth of a bottle.

'Help me, Santa Zita!' she wails, turning her head towards the table, and the small card on the saucer. 'Please help me!' But no one hears her, not even the dog.

Later, much much later, when the night is even darker and Doria's hope has been completely lost in exhausted sleep …

'Doria, what on earth are you doing there?' The question makes no sense, not until she comes to and realises that her head is resting on the cold hard draining board of the sink, her arm frozen with pins and needles, her hand drowning in cold disgusting water, trapped there by the plughole that has sucked away her finger and her pride.

'Filippo!' she wails.

'Shh, shh …' he says, putting a comforting arm around her.

'My finger's stuck!'

'I can see that. But don't worry, we'll soon have you out of there. Where's the oil?'

'The oil? It's on the table.'

'Righto. Now keep still while I pour some onto your hand … good. Now wriggle your finger slowly … Slide it, don't jerk it …'

Doria focuses all her attention onto her finger, moving it carefully, willing it to come free. At last it eases out of the trap. Then suddenly she is aware of another sensation, the warmth of Filippo's body all around her, his breath on her neck like a sun-warmed breeze, sending a delightful shiver through her. And now he's touching her hair, combing it with his fingers … His breathing is getting faster, coming in waves … What is he doing? He's gasping like Poldo with the milk churn on his back. *Oh God! But this is a sin! He'll go to hell! She'll go to hell! They'll both go to hell! O Santa Zita, make him stop …. Please make him stop …'*

Chapter 20
PUCCINI VISITS
A THROAT SPECIALIST

Up a winding pass, about fifteen kilometres east of the villa is the walled medieval city, Lucca, that had been scandalised to its provincial core by Puccini's elopement with Elvira. And here, in the rooms of Doctor Bianchi, the composer is lying on a surgical chair, his arms by his side, his head tilted back at an unnatural angle while he undergoes an examination for the sore throat that has been bothering him since Christmas.

'A little wider, if you please!' Doctor Bianchi says, shining a torch into his mouth. Puccini extends his jaw as far as he can and thinks of something pleasant, like the dinner that is waiting for him at Rebecchino's, the town's finest restaurant, which is where he'll go as soon as this disagreeable procedure is all over.

'This won't hurt a bit,' Bianchi says, sliding an instrument between his teeth. But the doctor, like most medical men, is a liar, a fact confirmed when Puccini feels a sharp jab followed by a pain as if a piece of lead pipe is being shoved down his gullet, causing a wave of stomach acid to spurt up the back of his throat.

'Aaah!' he gags.

'Nearly finished ...' Another lie. Now Bianchi is introducing a second instrument, a device that looks – and feels – like a miniature version of the cage Elvira keeps her finches in. Puccini closes his eyes and pictures a bowl of thick minestrone, chunks of succulent beef, braised artichokes, and soft, creamy potatoes ...

'Righto!' the doctor says. 'Keep still ... that's it ...' There is a silence and then a scratching sensation as the birdcage is pulled from his mouth and dropped into a basin with the ping of a bullet landing in a silver dish. 'Everything looks fine,' Bianchi says. 'The larynx is a little red, nothing more. I'll give you a solution to gargle that should clear it up in no time.'

And so it is a relieved Puccini who, a few minutes later, is turning up the collar of his overcoat, pulling his hat over his temples and stepping out into the sharp night air. From the corner he hears the whirr and bang of shutters being yanked down and bolted into place. Eight o'clock, time to meet Elvira and his old friend Alfredo Caselli, proprietor of the cafe in Via Fillungo, where programs of his operas are displayed in the window alongside trays of glossy chestnuts and squares of honey cake. The thought of food makes the composer swallow, and then again. His throat feels like a nutmeg that has been finely grated, leaving him with the peculiar sensation that something is now lodged in it. But for all that, he pulls out a cigarette, lights it, and puffs furiously before throwing it down and grinding it under his foot. Thrusting his hands in his pockets, he sets off down Via San Paolino, his gait surprisingly light for a man of solid build, and after a hundred paces he turns left into Via di Pioggio, pausing in front of the house where he was born and brought up, like his father and grandfather before him.

A lamp is glowing in the first-floor window of the bedroom he once shared with his brother, Michele, calling up memories of himself sitting there gazing out onto the heads of the passersby when he should have been doing his homework, or hanging out as far as he dared to puff on a forbidden cigarette. As boys, he and Michele were spared the duties that fell to their sisters, and instead roamed the labyrinth of narrow streets, or took an old cart up onto the ramparts of the walls and spent carefree hours pulling each other along, or screaming down the steep paths and falling off into the grass.

The next window, black as night, is the room where his mother gave birth to nine children, seeing six of them safely into adulthood. She was a saint, his mother, a woman sustained by her unfailing faith in God, a faith that gave her the strength to raise her family on the meagrest of widow's pensions while ensuring they all had a good education. But it was for him, her first son, that she nursed a particular ambition: that he should follow in the footsteps of his father, grandfather, and three generations of Puccinis before him, by becoming the town's foremost musician. And so she had arranged for him to have piano lessons with her uncle, old Cepu, a thin man with wheezing lungs and spittle pooled in the corners of his mouth, who kicked him in the shins whenever he played a wrong note.

Puccini remembers them all now as he stands looking up at his family home. Uncle Cepu, who reported back that his pupil had no talent at all, Mamma, with her weekly letters and parcels of beans and olive oil to his digs in Milan, his daredevil brother Michele, and his father, the cathedral organist, a figure he only vaguely remembers for his gentle laugh, breath that smelled of strong mints, and a soft beard infused with tobacco. Sensing that he is sailing perilously close to the sort of uncharted reefs of memory that are best left to others, Puccini reaches into his pocket, pulls out his cigarette case, strikes a match and draws in a long breath, counting to five before turning and striding to the end of the lane.

There is a church in the small square in front of him with a spire that reaches up to the moonless sky, and two angels and an archangel perched high up on its gable end, frozen for all time. This is where his career began, singing Mass twice on Sundays, and stealing candle stubs when the priest's back was turned, to melt down and sell for pocket money. The composer hesitates before turning the corner, struck by the curious idea that he can hear a heavenly tut-tut coming from his marble friends, when it is only the echo of footsteps, muffled by swirls of mist.

Women hurry past, their heads bowed against the cold, their chilblained fingers clutching baskets containing items wrapped in paper. Finding nothing to feast on in these worn housewives, Puccini's thoughts turn to another woman, one with almond eyes and glowing skin, and as ever when he contemplates this divine creature, his face softens into a smile.

The composer has arrived at Piazza Napoleone, and stepping into the square, he is buffeted by a gust of wind sweeping through the branches of the plane trees, making them whistle as they sway restlessly overhead. Drawing his scarf closer around his neck, he continues on towards Teatro del Giglio, past the palace that Emperor Napoleon built for his sister, Elisa, a woman both hideous and insatiable, according to Puccini's grandfather, who was director of court music at the time. Thanking heaven he has never been called on to service such a creature, he arrives at the restaurant, stamps out his cigarette and opens the door. A current of warm air greets him as he steps inside, a current that carries on it the flavours of prosciutto, roast beef and seasoned parmesan, a smell that makes him ridiculously happy. Although it is still early, the restaurant is buzzing with voices, broken by the occasional laugh.

'Good evening, Maestro!' The waiter, a trim man with sparse hair rising in curls from his temples, reaches out to take his coat.

'Good evening, Ernesto. My usual table?'

'Certainly,' the waiter says, indicating an alcove at the back of the room with a table that looks as if it wants to disappear.

Puccini turns, and seeing no one there, his happiness turns a notch closer to irritation. Alfredo will be locking up his cafe, but where is Elvira? She should be here by now. Threading his way across the room, smiling and nodding at the other diners, he considers Elvira's strange behaviour earlier in the day. Why had she changed her mind and insisted on coming with him when earlier she had so adamantly refused? And why had she now disappeared? Could it be her time of life making her more unpredictable than usual? Women! He would never understand them.

Reaching his table, he sits down, slides his silver cigarette case onto the starched white cloth and flicks it open. Elvira isn't the only one upsetting him at the moment; the honour is shared with the man who considers himself his boss.

'Too slow, Signor Giulio? I'm going as fast as I can ...'

'Verdi? But he fired them off like bullets ...'

Leaning forward to the candle, he puffs a cigarette quickly alight and plumes smoke sideways from the corner of his mouth. He's tired of Ricordi treating him like a schoolboy, as if such a person, a mix of foxy entrepreneur and faux musician, could ever truly understand what went into creating an opera – the effort, the concentration, the wringing oneself out for every last drop of inspiration, the sheer, relentless grind of it …

Puccini feels the bitter taste of bile rising in his throat, and not wanting to spoil his dinner, he swallows it down, sucks in a mouthful of cigarette smoke and looks around the room at waiters who are tending to their clients as if nothing could be more important than putting exquisite food before people who will later be sinking their heads into soft goose-down pillows.

There is a woman at the next table wearing a blue evening gown that ripples like water whenever she moves, a beautiful woman with a pale freckled face, reddish-brown hair held in a loose bun and diamonds the size of small coins on her earlobes. Puccini gazes at her from the dimly lit safety of his alcove, taken by her soft beauty, the roll of her bosom, her slightly reticent air, as if she knows a secret she may or may not share with her companion, a man his own age who could be a doctor or a banker. And suddenly, amazingly, he is back in the chalet in the pinewood, and there is Corinna curled up in the chair in front of the window, a rug round her shoulders, her pretty face creased in misery as she reads the note he has just thrust in her hand.

My dear, these words will pain you as much as they do me, but for reasons too complicated to explain, our delightful arrangement must come to end …

She had looked at him, and in her eyes he saw no accusation, no bitterness, only pain, a pain so raw, so elemental, so utterly unbearable, that he had snatched the note from her hand and ripped it to shreds. But the extraordinary thing, the thing that even now he cannot believe ever really happened, is that as his fingers worked furiously to destroy the offending words, the strains of an oriental folk tune started up in his head, and the strips of paper, as if by a miracle, turned into strands of silky black hair.

'Corinna!' he sighs, tasting the word in his mouth. Tomorrow he will take the early train to Milan and be on the platform to greet her when she arrives from Turin. The composer leans back in his chair and lowers his eyelids, allowing himself a few moments to savour the thought of his young lover. But it is hunger of a different kind that makes him open them again, pull out his watch and study it. Twenty past eight! What on earth is keeping Elvira? The question has barely formed in his mind when there is a blast of chill air from the doorway. Puccini looks up and sees a beggar woman standing there, a straggly creature whose shawl is falling off her shoulders, with her hat skewed to one side, revealing hair like an untidy bird's nest. She steps into the room and looks around, her eyes moving about until, with a fearsome stare, they fix on him.

'Oh Christ!' An icicle stabs him in the heart. 'Elvira!'

The room falls silent as Puccini struggles to his feet, preparing to defend himself from the woman who is striding towards him, her chin thrust out, a sense of deadly purpose etched on her furious face.

CHAPTER 21
ELVIRA HAS AN UNFORESEEN ENCOUNTER

Elvira's heels hammer their way along the cobblestones of Via Fillungo, heading towards the house that twenty years ago she had sworn never to set foot in again. And if not for Signor Giulio's telephone call earlier in the day, she would have kept her promise, for only a request from a man whose kindness to her has been unstinting over the years could drag her back to that frigid place with its cold hypocritical heart, the place that harboured those who stole her son from her. And even then, had it not been for Ricordi's assurance that his plan could not fail, she might have refused. For although more than two years have passed, she has no desire to be reminded of that painful and humiliating encounter with Renato.

On Elvira goes, past hissing gas lamps that are casting long shadows on the frosty surface of the lane, ignoring the brightly lit shops offering her funghi porcini and wild boar salami, holy pictures and alabaster statutes of the Virgin, pipes and pipe-cleaners, on and on, every step daring her to believe that this time she really will achieve her goal, and with it the peace of mind that has eluded her for so long. Slowing down to avoid the huddle of fur-wrapped men and women leaving the warmth of Alfredo Caselli's cafe, she catches sight in the window of the telegram sent to Giacomo by the old King for the premiere of Tosca. 'Vultures,' she snorts, pushing past, 'feeding off his glory now that he's famous!' An old biddy gives her a look, a woman with a wrinkled face that has had all the kindness sucked out of it. Nodding curtly, Elvira moves on, heading to-wards the end of the lane. On the corner is a baby boutique, and here Elvira pauses for a moment to gaze wistfully at the tiny smocked dresses, matinee jackets, bootees and cradle blankets, light as froth, draped across a navy blue perambulator. How she longs to hold the tiny garments in her hands, to feel their softness against her cheek and breathe in their promise of a pure and blissful joy. But now is not the moment. Pulling her shawl tightly round her, she edges past two young women who are peering into the fashion shop next door, where a sequined gown is shining like a thousand tiny fireflies.

'Hey, watch out!'

Elvira steps back as a pack of urchins in pursuit of a ball dash out from one of those crannies that lead to thick walls and secret doorways. 'You've dropped something!' she shouts after them, her voice melting in the thick night air. Bending down, she picks up a shabby peaked cap, and then, from habit long since unnecessary, turns it inside out and inspects the seams. And in that gesture, her mind slips back to those early years with Giacomo, when he was just starting out as a musician, and one lira had to do the work of three.

She, pregnant and cut off from his family, had taken Fosca and gone to live with Ida in Florence, while Giacomo stayed in Milan, coming to see her when he could, or more often sending money to pay for his absence. When he did visit, he always brought with him a bunch of orange lilies, the strongly perfumed kind, purchased from the barrow boy outside the station. They were a consolation, the lilies, and after he had gone, Elvira would sit in the parlour taking in their smell, his smell, while writing his name with her fingertip in the pollen that had settled round the base of the vase, praying that he missed her as much as she was missing him …

'Signora!' There is a tug at Elvira's skirt, and looking down she sees a small boy, about five or six years old, with dark eyes and a dirty, angelic face.

'Renato!' she cries, reaching out to him.

The child steps back and looks at her suspiciously. 'Where is it?' he says.

'Where is what?'

'My cap. Mamma will kill me if I lose it.'

'Oh … here.' Handing it over, Elvira watches him tug it on his head and scamper off, an outcast in his own town. Like her. She looks around, her eyes clouded by so many memories that she cannot quite recall where she is, and then she sees the lane widening out into Piazza Bernardini, and it all comes flooding back.

There is a couple standing outside the jeweller's shop, a blousy woman in a fur wrap and a diminutive man with a small bushy moustache, wearing a coat with an astrakhan collar and matching hat. He, the puppet man, is holding the woman's arm in a proprietorial manner, anchoring himself to her, while she peers through the glass, weighing up her value in gold, emeralds and pearls. With barely a glance in their direction, Elvira crosses to the house where she once lived, mounts steps worn down by the shoes of generations of people who have lived here, and presses the bell.

A coarse greedy laugh ripples across the square. Elvira glances around and sees the blousy woman pop a red kiss onto the lips of her consort. Turning back, she presses the bell again, this time pushing her finger to the wall. At this hour, Renato and his grandmother will still be in the shop, but Narciso should be home. Sure enough, there is a buzz, the door opens, and Elvira steps into the entrance hall and begins to climb.

The door on the top landing is ajar, and Elvira, about to knock, finds her hand stranded in midair as the door is suddenly yanked open from the other side by a stout woman in a floral overall, a woman in her sixties with horse-mane hair, plaited and pinned to the top of her head, charcoal line eyebrows, a curved, downward pointing nose, and a top lip sprouting the whiskers of an adolescent youth. Peering out through small, suspicious eyes, her expression reveals everything that she is: a hard, mean person, unbending in all matters except the love she lavishes on her dolt of a son.

'Good evening,' Elvira says. 'I have come to pay a visit to Narciso.' Old Ma Gemignani moves to block the entrance, her hands planted defiantly on her hips. A lesser woman might have fled, but cowardice is no part of Elvira's make-up. 'Let me pass,' she insists, 'I need to speak to Narciso.'

'Narciso?' the old woman repeats, as if the name means nothing to her. 'Oh ... you mean Narciso, your husband.'

Elvira sighs impatiently, 'As you wish. Could you tell him I want a word with him?'

Signora Gemignani steps forward, her bulk shifting like grain in a sack. 'No, I couldn't! How dare you turn up here! This is my house, Signora Elvira, and you are no longer welcome in it!'

'It will only take a minute.'

'Oh yes?' the old woman sneers. 'How can you be so sure? You want him to agree to an annulment, don't you? Well, you can forget that. Over my dead body! You married my son in the eyes of God, and married to him you will stay!'

'And why, pray,' Elvira retorts, knowing she is making a dreadful mistake, 'must I remain married to a man who courts women all over town?'

Signora Gemignani rocks back on her heels, her face glowing like embers. 'All over town? All over town, do you say? Well, Signora Elvira, that's grand coming from you! My son, since you had the audacity to leave him, may suit himself. But Signor Giacomo, may he suit himself? Because that's exactly what he has been doing. Oh yes, he's a fine example! And if you ask me ...'

'I'm not asking you, you old witch! You'd say anything to hurt me!'

There is a cackle like the smashing of a plate. 'Oh no, Elvira, I'm simply telling the truth. She's a pretty little thing, apparently ... comes to visit him on the train. And there's talk of marriage. I'm surprised you don't seem to know anything about it.'

Elvira gasps and clutches her throat, where a fireball has exploded, filling her lungs with a deadly choking heat. She wants to fly at the old woman, grab her by the hair and drive her smug face into the wall. But all she can do is let out a cry, grasp the banister rail and stumble down the stairs.

Signora Gemignani, emboldened by the first truly heartfelt exchange she's ever had with Elvira, waddles after her. 'Why don't you ask him?' she calls down the stairwell. 'I'm sure he'll be only too happy to enlighten you!'

The answer comes in Elvira slamming the front door.

Chapter 22
THE JOURNEY HOME

Elvira raises her head, surprised to see her hands around a tumbler of water with a slice of lemon in it. Around her, the diners have resumed their chatter, droning away like so many insects; the waiters, too, are gliding in and out of the kitchen as if nothing has happened. She lifts the glass and takes a sip. There is a loose thread hanging from the button of her glove which she wants to bite off but does not.

'We're going home,' Giacomo says, his voice edged with steel.

'What about Alfredo?'

'I'll leave him a message.'

Elvira glances towards the door, where wisps of spun wool fog are curling against the glass. 'Is it safe to drive in this weather?' His eyes are fixed on the cigarette case in his hand. 'You should have thought of that before you made such a diabolical scene. The evening's ruined.' Elvira lowers her head. 'Wait here,' he says, scraping back his chair. 'I'm going to fetch the motor.'

The vehicle splutters to the end of the lane, turns left beside the culvert, under Porta Elisa, then skirts the city walls before heading out into the countryside, making its way, ghost-like, through olive groves and fields of frosty winter vegetables. Despite the rug wrapped around her, Elvira finds the cold astonishing; it seems to flay the skin right off her face. She stares at the road, at the beams from the lanterns that are projecting shivery ellipses onto its black surface. How she longs for the warmth of her bed!

They journey along in silence, each sensing the danger of the other's thoughts, until finally Giacomo says, 'I'm going to Milan tomorrow. I won't be back for a few days.'

'Are you sure?'

'Am I sure of what?'

'That you'll be coming back?'

'Don't start, Elvira!'

Now she turns to look at him, studying his profile as if it is new to her. 'Don't start what, Giacomo? Asking questions you don't want to answer? How about the truth for a change?'

'The truth?' The word swings between them like a blade. 'If it's the truth you want –'

Elvira cuts him off, her voice low and thick, like slurry in a pit. 'After all I've been through! The gossip, the humiliation – years of it – and now you intend to make a fool of me!'

He snorts. 'Nobody is making a fool of you, Elvira. You're doing it all by yourself!'

'Really?' she says, and then mimics a false, high-pitched voice with an accent from the north: 'My dear Signora, I don't know what you're talking about ... but are you sure the gentleman in question is your husband?'

'Stop it, Elvira! You're being ridiculous.'

Her response is to hit out at him with her fist, landing a blow on his shoulder with such force that it knocks the steering wheel clean from his grip.

'What's happening?'

The motorcar lurches to one side and veers across the road, heading for the line of trees along the embankment and a drop down into the gully. Grabbing the wheel, Puccini twists it and pulls on the brake. There is a hideous screech, the motor slews round, and the tyres, finding nothing to grip onto, skid sideways, hurtling towards the trunk of an overhanging willow.

'Oddio!' Elvira screams. 'Help us, help us!'

The car hits the tree causing a massive jolt, spirals, teeters on the edge for a moment, then tips them over the ridge into the blackness below.

Chapter 23
CORINNA GOES TO THE POST OFFICE

The city of Turin lies on the banks of the river Po at the foot of the Alps in the north-west of the country. It is the seat of the House of Savoy, the Italian royal family, and from 1861–65 was the capital of the newly proclaimed United Kingdom of Italy ... These are the words that Corinna, now standing in the queue at the post office, had inscribed on the blackboard in her classroom earlier that morning, before strolling up and down between the banks of desks, ensuring that the twelve-year-olds copied the information neatly and accurately into their exercise books.

Life at least in that respect has gone as predicted, she thinks, as she edges forward towards the brass grille. Here she is dressed in a plain coat and hat, her legs forced, salami-like, into thick woollen stockings, in turn wedged into sensible shoes. Her weekdays, as uniform as her clothes, consist of preparing lessons and marking homework, reading to her mother, dining with Papa when he is at home, and always seeking to avoid the nurse, a thin woman with pinched lips and a large cross round her neck, whose questions about where she goes at the weekends distress and unsettle her. There is suspicion in the woman's eyes, and something else, dark and unforgiving. Can she sense that Corinna has known a man, really known him in every fibre of her being? When she returns on Sunday evenings, does Giacomo's smell remain on her, or exude animal-like from her pores, despite her careful bathing in lily-of-the-valley scented water? Or perhaps her thoughts leak from her mind like her mother's strange mumblings, to be deciphered by those with especially acute hearing? It seems unlikely, but surely the nurse suspects something of her double existence.

Today being Friday, when she has completed her task at the post office, Corinna will hurry to the station at Porta Susa, each step taking her further away from the chalkdust and ink. Not that she dislikes teaching. In fact, since taking up her post last September, she has become fond of the twenty-one children in her care, the untidy boys in short trousers and laced-up boots, the girls with hair-ribbons and eyes that shine, like hers once did, with ambition beyond their reach. But she doesn't intend doing it for long: only until Giacomo has finished his opera, when she will be embarking on an altogether different kind of life. It is not the future, though, that Corinna is contemplating as she taps the toe of her shoe on the cold stone floor, watching a frown appear on the brow of the clerk behind the grille.

Two years have passed since Corinna's brief but unforgettable meeting with Elvira, an encounter that had left her shocked by its precipitous nature, by the vicious way Elvira had lashed out at her, as if her life depended on it. But it was not that which had made her retaliate so decisively; it was the look of madness in those black eyes. In the minutes that followed, as the taxicab jostled back along the promenade, an image of Elvira slumped on the ground howling like a wounded beast stayed with her, and so did a startling revelation. Giacomo's companion was not, as she had imagined, a sophisticated woman, but rather a provincial type with the instincts of a fishwife, not the sort he could squire around the capitals of Europe, and certainly not the sort he could ever marry. And with that knowledge, something inside her shifted, so that by the time the taxicab came to a halt at the square near the church, and she alighted on the footpath that would take her to the lane at the side of the house, her footsteps were quite certain and sure.

The toe of Corinna's shoe continues its rhythmic beat. The queue in the post office is always slow at this time of day because of the rush of secretaries consigning their morning's work to the counter before it closes at one-thirty sharp. This clerk though, an older woman with a pointed nose, seems to delight in taking her time. The nose looks up, and the eyes identifying Corinna as the culprit of the *tip-tap, tip-tap,* the clerk glares at her over the top of a pair of half-moon lenses. Corinna calmly meets her stare. The grille is casting shadows like tramlines down the woman's cheeks, reminding her of that final day at the chalet.

It was September, the days were getting shorter, the afternoons cooler, and through the window Corinna could see clusters of perfect pale mushrooms growing in the thicket, like an illustration from a book. The summer birds had headed south, leaving the rooks and woodpigeons behind, the tortoise no longer came for her *passeggiata*, and Corinna, instead of sipping cool glasses of cordial, snuggled in the chair with a rug around her shoulders. She had continued reading *Madame Bovary*, but only in the hope that Emma would come to her senses. Every page she turned, though, brought with it a sigh of exasperation. Emma had fallen in love with a young law student, Léon, but instead of revealing her true feelings for him, she had hidden them behind the pretence of being a devoted wife and mother. When he gave up all hope and left for Paris, she, lonelier than ever, allowed herself to be courted by a wealthy landowner, a man well-versed in the art of seduction. It was then, at the beginning of chapter nine (as Rodolphe, the landowner, reappeared after an absence of weeks, an absence designed to weaken Emma against his advances), that Corinna heard footsteps climbing the front steps.

'Come in! Come in!' she called, her face brightening.

But Giacomo did not come in. Instead, he stood in the doorway, his eyes not meeting hers, the dark spread of a beard unable to hide the livid red scratch marks on his cheeks. She remembers the strangeness of it, and the chill that ran through her.

'What is it?'

He did not reply, but instead crossed the room, plucked the book from her hand and replaced it with a note that she, rising, unfolded and read. Then she looked in his eyes, seeing ... what? Guilt? ... sorrow? ... anguish? Whatever it was, it faded in that moment, overtaken by an emotion she did recognise, one that was certain and true. With a sob, he threw himself on her, crushing her in his arms and covering her face with his kisses.

Corinna did not question him about the note, the scratches or his tears. This had to do with Elvira, and in the fervour of his caresses, the whispering of her name as he begged her forgiveness, she knew she had won.

Tip-tap, tip-tap ...

'Signorina, please!'

Corinna shrugs, feigning innocence. She knows the sound of her shoe is driving the clerk mad, just as surely as she knows that this is the woman who examines the letters Giacomo sends to her *poste restante*, picking at the flaps and holding them up to the light to see if any titbits can be gleaned from their contents. Today, though, Corinna is in a hurry. There is a train to catch … She has reached the head of the queue.

'Yes?' the woman snaps, not looking up.

Corinna slides a form under the grille, together with a coin. 'I wish to send a telegram,' she says. The clerk hesitates then lifts the paper gingerly by the corners, as if it might scald her. On train as usual. C. She sniffs and sweeps the money into the till then reaches for a rubber stamp, which she inks and thumps down. 'Next!' she calls. A few minutes later, Corinna is hurrying along Via Garibaldi towards the station, the icy wind swirling snowflakes around in the sharp air. The shops have closed for lunch, and upstairs families sit down to bowls of warming soup. Corinna, though, has no time to think about food. Before her train leaves, she must retrieve a suitcase and hatbox from the left luggage office and take them to the ladies cloakroom. There she will roll off the thick stockings and replace them with gossamer silk, slide her feet into shoes secured with a button and strap, don a skirt and matching bolero jacket, then an empire-line coat, and top it off with a hat with silk poppies on the brim.

Increasing her pace, Corinna overtakes a beggar, a dirty sour-smelling creature shuffling from his usual position outside the church to the back door of a nearby trattoria, hoping for crusts of leftover bread. *Hurry up! Hurry up!* In a little over an hour, she is due to meet Giacomo at Milan railway station, and from there travel back to his apartment where, after a light lunch washed down with champagne, they will withdraw to the bedroom and spend the afternoon delighting each other in ways she had never imagined possible. This will be the twenty-fifth weekend that Corinna has spent with the composer, a fact she hasn't noted in the diary she keeps locked away in her desk drawer (along with the pearl earrings in the crystal jar), but in her memory, where it is safe. Twenty-five weekends of passion and bliss, of companionship that has had none of the little tensions that can build up when a couple spend time in each other's company. Corinna has made quite sure of that. Puccini enjoys his food, and becomes grumpy when he is hungry, so Corinna has learned to cook, becoming rather proficient in the kitchen, although early on she curdled the béchamel sauce for the lasagne, and on another occasion overcooked the pumpkin, creating gnocchi that collapsed in a fibrous orange heap. Instead of complaining, as most men would, he tucked into those early disasters with exaggerated gusto, showering her with compliments, and presenting her a discreet while later with a beautifully wrapped recipe book.

On fine days, they motor out to a little tavern on Lake Lugano where the people speak German, and in the cool manner of the Swiss, show little interest in their guests. Recently, when Corinna suggested they dine closer to home, served by people in their own tongue, Giacomo cautioned her to be patient, for it was still too early for them to be seen together in public. She has learned, too, not to disturb him when he is working, his fingers flying over the piano keys with sparks coming from their tips, or at his desk firing off letters to his librettists, his sisters and his friends. No, she must not impose herself on him, for it is something he cannot abide. While he is busy she explores the apartment, opening wardrobes and pulling out garments that would go around her twice, or rummaging through drawers containing scraps of lace and dyed feathers that smell of patchouli, a scent worn by women her grandmother's age. In the evenings, they listen to disc recordings on Giacomo's gramophone while he browses through the newspaper or skip-reads his way through novels, seeking inspiration for his operas. Presently he is reading Maxim Gorky's *Scenes from Russian Life*, which he will look at after supper, relaxing in his smoking jacket in the armchair in front of the gilt mirror, one leg crossed over the other, thumbing through the sections that do not hold his interest, frowning from time to time, a cigarette smouldering in his hand. Then he will rest the book in his lap and say, 'And what does my little schoolteacher think?' And she will offer her views on the people in that vast, freezing land while he listens, his hand stroking his chin, his eyes betraying thoughts that may not entirely be focused on the opinions she is advancing.

Sometimes, when he is too tired to read, he pours himself a

whisky and amuses her with tales of people she one day hopes to meet: Pietro Mascagni, a baker's son from Livorno, who shared lodgings with him in Milan; Ruggiero Leoncavallo, whose ideas for his operas come from cases described to him by his magistrate father; Enrico Caruso, with his red handkerchief and white-tipped shoes; and Giacomo's librettist, Luigi Illica, known as Mr Perpetual Motion, a wild character who spent four years at sea, and later had an ear shot off in a duel over a woman.

Corinna has arrived opposite the station, where she waits at the kerb for an old man in a conifer-green cape to wobble past on his bicycle, then a fellow pushing a cart. A girl huddled among the sacks gives her a friendly wave as she passes and Corinna waves back, seeing something of Giacomo's stepdaughter in the pale, open face and fair hair. Not that she has ever met Fosca, but there is a portrait of her in the hallway, and photographs in the albums in the dresser. He doesn't mention her very often, but when he does, his face lights up, revealing in his loving expression a sense of the type of father he could once again become.

Now a taxi carriage clatters by, its passenger looking nervously around, as if lost. It is Father Masetti, the young priest who comes to visit her mother. Two and a half years have passed since he took over from old Father Gervasi, and still he won't look Corinna in the eye. Not only that, but when he calls at the house to deliver a book for Mamma (from his endless collection on the lives of the saints), he places it on the back of a chair rather than into her outstretched hand. Corinna imagines that the thin-lipped nurse has whispered her suspicions to him in the dim sanctity of the confessional, but when she told Giacomo this, he just laughed and said the fellow was more likely terrified of her.

The street is now clear. Corinna steps down and hurries across, stepping up again in front of the newspaper kiosk where the vendor, a youth in a flap-eared cap, is stamping the ground, trying to bring life back to his frozen feet. 'Good afternoon, Miss,' he chirps.

At that moment, she sees his billboard displaying the front page of the evening newspaper. Half the page is taken up with a photograph of a motorcar lying upside down in a field, its chassis buckled and twisted, its mudguards ripped off, its wheels pointing skywards. Blazoned above are words so terrible that Corinna is struggling to take them in: *Puccini in horrific accident!* A block of ice slams into her middle, doubling her over and forcing the air from her lungs.

'Hey, Miss!' the newsvendor calls, alarmed at what he sees. 'Are you alright?'

Chapter 24
PUCCINI WAKES UP IN HIS STUDIO

With no recollection of how he got there, Puccini comes to – in 'hell', or so it seems to him, for he is lying on a hard, flat surface, his head slightly elevated, his arms by his sides, racked from head to foot by the most atrocious pain. Not only that, but the devil himself has plunged a fiery pitchfork into the calf of his right leg, searing the flesh to the bone. He moves his eyes, seeing an eerie red glow, the furnace where the instruments are being prepared, and a figure, dark and menacing, floating away from him. *Clank*! It is the sound of a bolt being driven home.

'No more!' he moans. 'For God's sake, have pity!' He tries to sit up, finds no strength and slumps back onto the unforgiving slab. Then a dagger slashes down his side in a sensation so shocking it makes him cry out.

The dark figure turns. 'Ah,' it says, 'so you're awake at last!'

'*Elvira*? … Elvira! Where am I?'

'At home, Giacomo, in your studio.'

What is she saying? Puccini closes his eyes and searches for clues that might help him understand what is going on, but there is nothing, just Elvira's words, and himself in a nightshirt that smells of soap and fresh air. He wriggles his toes, they seem to be working, and flexes the muscles in his leg. This time the dagger rips into the tendon, shredding it like a piece of old rope. 'Mary, Joseph and Jesus!' he gasps, the bitter taste of fear spilling into his mouth. *No, this is hell,* all right, and he is right in it!

'Don't move, Giacomo!' Elvira says anxiously, coming to

stand by his side. 'The doctors say you must lie perfectly still until all the swelling has gone down.' *Doctors? Swelling?* Elvira clicks on a lamp. 'Look!' she says. 'It's past eight o'clock. You've been asleep all day. You must be hungry. Would you like a little *brodo*?'

A plate of broth is the last thing on his mind. 'Yes,' he says, from habit. 'Thank you ...' She moves towards the door. 'Elvira!' he calls after her. 'What happened?'

She doesn't look around. 'There was an accident ... We'll talk about it in the morning.' There is a moth fluttering about inside the lampshade, drawn to the light only to be repelled by the heat, caught up in one of nature's bad jokes. Puccini listens to the muffled sound of its futile dance, feeling sorry for it. Then he is distracted by the smell of broth fumes coming through the doorway; shinbone and onion, carrot, celery and cobblestone tomato, covered with stock and left to simmer on the hob. The smell brings back memories of his childhood illnesses, and of being tucked up in bed by his mother, the window firmly closed no matter what the season, while one of his sisters, usually Otilia or Tomaide, brings him helpings of nutritious soup. The recollection is so powerful, so imminent, that when Elvira reappears with a tray, he wants to snatch the bowl from her and gulp it down at once.

'Good!' she says, resting the tray on the bridge that arches mysteriously over his legs. 'Poldo's device works very well!' *Poldo? Device? What is she talking about now? And why doesn't she put the broth where he can get at it?* Perching beside him, she dips the spoon into the liquid and draws it to his mouth. 'Here ...' she says.

Madonna! He is to be fed like a baby! But after the first few sips, which slide down his throat like nectar from the gods, he submits less grudgingly to his fate.

'Your sisters have called,' Elvira says, picking a stalk of parsley from his spoon, 'all except Iginia, of course.'

His mind conjures up an image of a nun with a long serious face. 'I'm sure God will find a way of letting her know.'

'I daresay he will. Speaking of which, Alfredo put up a notice in his cafe window. The response has been incredible, the telegrams and the telephone calls. Thank goodness Ida is coming tomorrow!' She lifts the spoon and he opens his mouth like a newborn bird.

'In fact,' she continues, 'everyone is being very helpful, except Cook, of course! She insisted on putting garlic in the *brodo*. Garlic! I ask you! She said it would help the bone to knit, or some such nonsense. When I told her you never put garlic in clear soups, she turned on me ...'

There is a weight pressing on his eyelids ... the food, the warmth, the drone of Elvira's voice ...

'Oh, and I nearly forgot! Signor Ricordi rang. He was most distressed to hear of the accident.'

Ricordi ... The name floats towards him on gossamer wings, followed by another ... *Butterfly* ... and a third ... *Corinna*! His eyes shoot open. He was due to meet her – when? Today – this afternoon! 'Oh God!' he groans, his hands finding his face. Elvira stares at him. 'You've gone very pale, Giacomo. I think you need to rest.' She sets the bowl down and crosses to the fireplace, takes a log in each hand and adds them to the grate, sending showers of bright sparks up the chimney. 'The pot is on the table next to you, and the bell. I'll be in the drawing room if you need me.'

And Puccini, having exhausted what little strength remained to him, sinks back into his pillow and drifts off into the void.

It isn't sleep. It's a realm without definition or dimension, where obscure, deformed objects swim around him in an ocean with no light, merging and coalescing in a kaleidoscope of images that can only momentarily be understood: the number-plate of his motorcar shimmering in the beam of a severed lantern, the steering wheel twisted around his neck like a noose, Elvira's hat, smeared with icy slime. And the noise! He cannot block out the noise: the tearing metal, the shattering glass, the screams that pierce the night sky. But worse still, if anything could be worse, are the fumes that sear his eyes, his mouth and his nostrils, and the leather wedged against his face, suffocating him ... He cannot breathe! He's going to die!

'Don't worry ... you'll soon be out of there!' It's the voice of a young man ... or perhaps an older woman, one of those large, comforting types with the skin of a peach. A pair of arms encircles him, dragging him, lifting him, wrapping him in something warm and soft. He turns to his rescuer, whispering silently of his love, his gratitude. But there is no one there.

Chapter 25
CORINNA SEEKS HELP

'Don't push!' A woman is addressing Corinna, a middle-aged woman with sharp elbows and an organza peony pinned to her collar.

'I need to buy a newspaper,' Corinna says, distractedly. 'I'm in a hurry ...'

'We're all in a hurry!' the woman replies crossly. 'Wait your turn.'

And now she has it, folded in her hand, the grainy dots of Giacomo's motorcar leering at her from under the shocking headline. Something has worked loose inside her and she thinks she might vomit. She needs to sit down. But where? Fumbling the paper into her bag, she looks around and sees a bar a little further up, on the other side of the road.

It is a dingy place, the entrance down a side alley, and Corinna hesitates before turning the doorhandle and entering. Inside the air is a thick cloud of swirling smoke that stings her eyes.

'Corinna! What are you doing here?'

'Aurelia!'

A red halo appears through the fog and takes her arm, letting out a loud, screechy laugh. 'Well, well, what a surprise! Have you come to join the meeting?'

'The meeting?' Only now, as Corinna glances round at the sawdust floor, the phlegm-filled spittoon, the dusty mirror, does it dawn on her that she's been here before. 'No, no ...'

'My God, dear thing, but you're shaking! Let me look at you. Heavens above, you're paler than a saint! Franco, a brandy over here, if you please.' And taking her arm, Aurelia guides her to the table in the corner by the fire. The brandy trickles down in scalding rivulets that paralyse Corinna's throat. Unable to speak, she pulls the newspaper from her bag and unfolds it on the table.

Aurelia looks at the headline and then at her, her face stricken. 'Of course, it's Friday … you were going to see him … But he's still alive, isn't he? What does it say?'

'I don't know,' Corinna whispers. 'Aurelia, please, you read it … I don't think I can …'

Her friend hesitates, then picks up the newspaper, which rustles like a dead leaf. 'It was last night, on their way home … the car skidded into a gully. He was trapped underneath, unconscious. There's not much else …'

'And Elvira?'

Was there an edge to the question, a pinch of wickedness? If there was, Aurelia missed it. 'She was thrown clear, unharmed.'

'I see.'

Aurelia is rubbing the side of her mouth. 'Listen,' she says, 'you can't go home, not in the state you're in. Come to my house. It's where they all think you are anyway.'

'But Giacomo!' The name cracks open like a nut. 'I must see him!'

Aurelia's hand covers hers. 'You can't, dear thing, not yet.'

Chapter 26
IDA ARRIVES AT VILLA PUCCINI

Ida lowers herself into one of the red armchairs, tucks a strand of ash-blond hair into the coil on top of her head and smooths the imaginary creases from her skirt. It is twenty-four hours since Elvira's breathless telephone call requesting help, and this morning, having made arrangements for Giuseppe and the children, she has taken the train from Florence to Pisa, and a taxicab for the final stretch to the villa.

The journey was not pleasant. The cab driver, one of those sullen thickset types that are bred in these parts, was going too fast, bouncing her around like an infant on its grandfather's knee, but when she shouted for him to slow down, the fellow ignored her. So, to distract herself she looked out of the window at the grey scrubland dotted with shacks and stone houses, at the dirty smoke billowing from chimneys, at the stunted trees and water-logged fields.

There is a rap on the door. 'Come in!' It is Doria, bringing with her a reviving pot of coffee, a plate of biscuits and a draught from the hall. 'Put the tray there, Doria, on the side table ... thank you.' The maid does as she is bidden, bobs a quick nod, and is gone. Ida chooses a buttery shortbread and lifts it to her lips, noting that Doria has become more womanly since she last saw her. In fact, she might even be considered bonny, especially with that hair – such a waste on a servant! Yes, almost bonny if not for those staring eyes and her unnerving silences. How grim it would be to have a girl like her padding, nun-like, around the house ... although at least she posed no temptation to Giacomo, poor man. Ida shudders, thinking of her brother-in-law's recent narrow escape. Nibbling the edge of her biscuit, she redirects her thoughts to the maid for a few minutes.

Ida thinks that despite Doria's low expectations, she has settled well into her new role, rubbing along smoothly with everyone, even Elvira's bad-tempered Cook. Rather, Ida feels that it is in her sister that she has detected something a little unbalanced, disturbing even, a subject she had broached with her last summer. She raises the matter tangentially once Elvira comes in from attending to Giacomo to welcome her sister and share a morning coffee with her.

'Elvira, dear, Doria is a good, hard-working girl, but you must take care not to become over-friendly with her.'

Elvira's expression has shifted to wary. 'What do you mean, "over-friendly"?'

'I mean having supper with her in the kitchen when Giacomo is away and taking her with you on shopping trips.'

Elvira frowns. 'So I am to do *everything* on my own, am I, now that Fosca has left home?'

'No, of course not, dear! I'm just saying that it's not a good idea to get too close to the servants. Sooner or later, they'll take advantage of you by asking for favours or becoming insolent.'

At this Elvira gives a little smile edged with triumph. 'Oh no, Ida, I assure you, Doria isn't that type of girl at all. She may seem like a country bumpkin to you, but in fact she is quite different.'

'Oh really, in what way?'

Elvira thinks for a moment then explains. 'She never curses or speaks ill of anyone, and she's most particular in the way she carries out her tasks ... and her memory is nothing short of extraordinary. Do you know, she can remember at least twenty items on a shopping list! And I've taught her to read ... No, Ida, don't look at me like that. It's true, I swear it. She soaks up words like blotting paper.'

Elvira doesn't have time for further explanations, as she jumps up to check whether the mail and newspapers have been delivered.

Ida puts a sugary finger to her mouth and licks it, her mind clicking logically to the next thought. If Doria has the sort of memory

Elvira claims for her, how come, on the evening of the accident, she forgot about the blocked sink in the kitchen that Poldo had neglected to clear? Imagine what would have happened if Filippo, the postmaster's son, hadn't insisted on cycling down to the villa when no one answered the telephone? Doria and her finger would have been stuck there until morning! No, Elvira's little exaggerations were a way of justifying her fondness for the girl, as well as glossing over Doria's all too obvious shortcomings. Having reached her conclusion, Ida is pleased to hear the door open; a little less pleased, however, to see the way her sister spins into the room, her eyes flashing feverishly.

'Truly, Ida, the world has gone mad!' she begins, the words tumbling from her mouth. 'The accident is in all the newspapers: *Il Corriere della Sera*, *La Stampa*, even *Il Mattino* of Naples … the telephone and doorbell haven't stopped ringing … and the telegrams!' Throwing herself into a chair, she points at the pile of papers on a tray, anchored down by a crystal paperweight. 'Just look at them all!' Ida looks instead at her sister, seeing something loose in those black eyes. 'There's even one from the young King …'

'Gracious!' Ida says, in spite of herself.

'I know! Giacomo would be loving this if he weren't in so much pain.'

The vulgarity of Elvira's comment makes Ida look away so that she can collect her thoughts. For despite her sister's pallor and the dark panda-like circles round her eyes, she seems to have been strangely energised by the recent shocking events.

'Shhh!' Elvira hisses.

Ida looks back and sees her on the edge of her seat, a finger raised to her lips.

'What is it, dear?'

'Someone's listening at the door!'

'I didn't hear anything.'

Ignoring her, Elvira slides off her chair, tiptoes across to the door and flings it open with a theatrical sweep of her arm. The hall is quite empty.

'It was probably Doria on her way to kitchen,' Ida says, making light of the situation.

Elvira looks doubtful. 'Perhaps so,' she says.

Ida glances towards the window, and the orange lilies that are doing little to break up the dark gloomy light. How she longs to be at home again, in the noisy, cheerful presence of her children. 'Ida ...' Elvira, now seated, is reaching for the coffeepot. 'You remember I told you that Giacomo was having an affair?'

'I'm sorry ...?'

Elvira turns to look at her. 'An affair – surely you haven't forgotten?'

'Of course I haven't, but that was years ago.'

'Nearly three. Anyhow, Narciso's mother says he's going to marry her.'

Ida's mind goes blank. 'Wait a minute, Elvira. You've lost me. Who is marrying whom? And what has old Ma Gemignani got to do with it?'

Elvira's voice drops to a whisper. 'It was she who told me that Giacomo intends to marry his amante.'

'Giacomo! But he can't! He's married to you, as good as. Elvira, please, explain what's going on!' The reply, if there is one, is drowned out by the doorbell. 'Oh really!' Ida throws herself back in her chair and fans herself with her hands. Elvira runs to open the front door then gives a startled cry, for there on the doorstep is a short squat figure dressed in the black-and-red uniform of a marshal of the carabinieri. She glances down, seeing a pair of boots as black and shiny as ebony bowls. Oddio! He's come to arrest me!

'If you take me away, who will look after Giacomo?' she whispers. 'Please, I beg you, don't do it!'

The portly figure, unaware of the distress he is causing, clicks his heels and swirls his cloak like a bullfighter. '*Buongiorno*, Signora Elvira,' he says. 'How is the Maestro faring?'

Elvira's stomach heaves into her gullet. 'For pity's sake, just get on with it!'

The officer gives her a curious look and says, 'As you wish!' Pulling himself up to his full height, he clears his throat and declares in a pompous voice. 'It is my official duty to pass on good wishes to Maestro Puccini and his family at this difficult time –'

'*What?*'

He starts again. 'It is my official duty –'

'No, no ... I heard all that, but what are you doing here?'

Blood rushes to the officer's cheeks, matching them nicely to the plume of his hat. 'I would describe it,' he says, clearing his throat again, 'as an act of solidarity with Giacomo.'

'Giacomo?' Now Elvira peers closer, taking in the fleshy lips, the waxed moustache, the large, confused eyes. Of course! This is Massimo, one of *Giacomo*'s hunting pals! 'Massimo!' she cries, laughing with relief. 'I didn't recognise you! Do come in.'

'No thank you,' he says, shrinking back from her outstretched hand. 'I'm a little pressed for time. But tell me, how is he?'

'Giacomo? Yes, well the right leg – the tibia – is badly broken, and he's covered in cuts and bruises. It would have been a lot worse if that doctor hadn't come to our rescue.'

Massimo nods solemnly. 'Indeed,' he says. 'They say he would have suffocated.'

Elvira cannot respond to this, and so she gazes past Massimo to the gate and the road beyond, an unfathomable expression on her face.

'I'll wish you good day, then,' he says.

'Oh … yes …' Elvira says, pulling herself together.

But the marshal has already turned on his heel and is striding down the path. Ida's hand is hovering over the biscuit plate when the door opens and Elvira reappears, a handkerchief pressed to her mouth.

'Elvira dear,' she says, rising to her feet, 'I think we should call Doctor Falli.'

'Falli?' Elvira lets out a hoot. 'It isn't a doctor I need, Ida, it's a priest.'

The doorbell rings again. 'For goodness sake!' Ida snaps. 'Let Doria get it!' But it is too late. Elvira has gone, returning a minute later with a handful of telegrams.

'Open these, would you, Ida? Cook needs me in the kitchen.' And with a roll of her eyes, she is gone again.

Ida shuffles the telegrams with exasperated little flicks, wondering if she will ever get to the bottom of Elvira's extraordinary declaration. Giacomo getting married – what can it mean? Is the shock of the accident playing tricks with Elvira's mind? Or has something happened that she didn't yet know about? Pondering these questions, she starts ripping open the telegrams, finding the same banal sequence of words time and again. We wish you a speedy recovery … 'Really! People are becoming so common!' It is at the eighth telegram that Ida's fingers come to an abrupt halt, for this time, as she unfolds the message written out in the postmaster's careful hand, she discovers words of an entirely different hue, words so unexpected and shocking that she reads them twice to make quite sure that her eyes aren't deceiving her. Then her hand flies to her mouth, launching the papers into the air, where they flutter like windblown petals before scattering all over the floor.

Madam, we regret to inform you of the death of your husband, Narciso Gemignani. Signed: Giorgio Gambetti, Medical Officer, Comune di Lucca.

'Narciso dead!!' Her words are met by a moment's silence, and then the most extraordinary sight of Wagner, Verdi and Donizetti, the trio lined up on the mantelpiece, as their tiny statuette mouths drop open in perfect unison.

Chapter 27
DON ZENO IS SUMMONED TO THE VILLA

Five days have passed since the accident, five days in which Don Zeno has been confined to bed with a nasty bout of influenza, making it impossible for him to respond to Signora Elvira's request that he should present himself immediately at the villa. Now that the fever has abated, even though he is still a little wobbly on his feet, the priest wraps himself in his cloak, pulls on his beret and clambers onto his New Turner bicycle (a gift from the Maestro himself), ready to pedal the mile and a half down the road to the lake.

Bumping along on this chill morning, a breeze lifting his thinning hair, the priest finds himself thanking God for the bicycle's solid construction and anti-slip tyres, a thought that is interrupted when he sees the unmistakably large head of Filippo pedaling towards him. 'Hello, Filippo!' he calls, happy to have the excuse for a pause. 'Not working today?'

'Good morning, Father. And yes, I've just finished at the aia.'

Don Zeno thinks for a moment. 'Of course, it's Monday! I seem to have lost a day or two.'

A dog is yapping somewhere out in the patch of ground behind them. Filippo turns towards the sound. 'I have to go,' he says, urgently. 'The wretched dog's got out again ...'

'Of course, and I must get on to the villa.'

'The villa?' There's a glint in Filippo's eye. 'If you see Doria, tell her I was asking about her finger.'

'Her finger?'

But Filippo has already taken off in the direction of the barking dog.

Hah! the priest thinks, watching him go, *love is in the air!* His pleasure fades a little, though, when he considers its object, a girl he considers to be one of God's more enigmatic souls, a sort of mystic, saint and dimwit rolled into one. *But a wife?* Deciding that this is not the moment to ponder the mysterious ways of the Almighty, Don Zeno sets off again, but as he approaches the villa, he is overwhelmed by the desire for a restorative glass of red wine, and gliding past, he forks off onto the path to Club della Bohème. Andrea is alone, perched on a stool in front of a copy of *La Nazione*, a nasty-smelling cigar smouldering away in the ashtray.

'Good day, Andrea.'

The proprietor glances up to see the familiar corpulent figure of one of the club's regular visitors. 'Good day, Father.' The tone is morose.

'You sound a bit glum,' the priest says. 'What's that you're reading?'

Andrea shrugs and indicates a photograph of an upturned motorcar under the headline, *Puccini saved by a miracle.*

Don Zeno, who has already seen the article, is uplifted by a surge of joy. 'Yes, isn't it wonderful! The grace of God –'

Andrea, with none of the respect he usually accords the priest, interrupts him. 'No, Father, it *isn't* wonderful, it's a bloody disaster.'

'Ah, you mean the leg. Well, yes … but that's only a question of time.'

Andrea gives the sort of scowl he usually reserves for Ferruccio and other such imbeciles. 'Look!' he says, picking up the newspaper and jabbing it with his finger. 'It says here that Puccini has serious leg injuries and won't be walking for months!' He slaps the paper down and jiggles his hands in circles of frustration. 'Who's going to play the piano? And more importantly, who's going to foot the bill for all those drinking sessions he's had with his friends? *The evening's on me, Blackbird Legs. I'll fix you up later,'* he intones, mimicking the familiar, rich velvety voice made husky by too many cigarettes. 'I've lost count of the evenings, Father, but he sure as hell has fixed me!'

'Now, now, you mustn't carry on like that,' the priest says, softening his tone to the one he uses in the confessional. 'I'm sure you'll get paid in time.'

'Time?' Andrea fires back. 'I haven't got any time! God, I'm broke! The trouble with that lot is they all feel so at home here they don't want to pay!'

Don Zeno, himself a frequent nonpayer, stifles a cough and gazes at the smudgy landscape painting above the bar (a gift from Ferruccio in exchange for wine), searching for something suitable to say. 'Well, at least Puccini isn't dead,' he says.

'Yes,' Andrea shrugs. 'I'm sure we're all very grateful for that, especially Signora Elvira.'

'Signora Elvira!' The priest pulls out his watch. 'I have to go. I'm late for the villa!'

'The villa? In that case, Father ...' the proprietor levers himself off his stool and squats down behind the bar. 'Would you mind? I've a letter here for Puccini. I'd deliver it myself, but in the circumstances ... I know it's here somewhere ...'

The priest waits for Andrea to rummage through a pile of old newspapers, his attention caught by the slate board propped up against the wall, where the rules of the club are scrawled in untidy letters, slanted to the right:

No 1. The members of Club della Bohème pledge under oath to eat well and drink better. No 2. Grouches, pedants, those of weak stomach, idiots, puritans, and other wretches of the species are not admitted and will be chased away. No 3. The Treasurer is empowered to abscond with the money.
No 4. The premises are to be lit by an oil lamp, failing which, members are obliged to set fire to their own wicks ...

'Ah, here it is!' Andrea hands him a pale green envelope, which smells of flowers, and sin.

'Ah ... quite ... jolly good,' he says. 'I'll be off then ...' And pushing the letter into his cape pocket, the priest hobbles outside, mounts his bicycle and pedals off.

Chapter 28
ELVIRA'S CONFESSION

While Don Zeno is puffing his way to her front door, Elvira is lying on her bed, gazing at the canopy that surrounds her like a great yellow womb. Since the accident she has barely slept at all, despite the sedative prescribed by Doctor Falli, and the lime-flower infusion that Ida insists she drink morning and night. She is in purgatory, or a place so like it that it makes no odds, weighed down by the thoughts of the accident and the astonishing news of Narciso's death.

When Ida had called her back into the drawing room and showed her the telegram, Elvira found herself sliding onto a chair from which she seemed unable to rise. 'But he can't be dead … he was alive and well just a couple of days ago.'

'Elvira, how can you possibly know that?'

'I just do. How did he die, Ida?'

'I don't know, dear … Look, let me get you a little cognac.'

'Cognac? I don't need cognac, Ida! Please send for Don Zeno.' But the priest had a fever and was unable to come. In her desperation, Elvira had thought to send for Father Pieri from across the lake, a thin man with a pointed chin and a great love of children, But she decided against it when she considered how this would set the villagers' tongues wagging in her seeking solace beyond her local priest; not to mention the offence it might cause to her Don Zeno.

Narciso dead! A needle stabs her between the eyes. Elvira draws her knees up close against her body, rolling herself up in a ball of misery, misery with guilt heaped upon it, one more terrible than the other. She dare not speak of the turmoil she is in, not even to Ida, even though when they are sitting together in the drawing room she feels the words forming in her mouth, jostling to get out. No, she cannot tell anyone but a priest, not even the sister who has supported her through thick and thin; her immortal soul depends on it. For when she stormed away from Piazza Bernardini that dreadful evening, she had only one thought in mind – wishing that Narciso should die. And now she is convinced that in the fury of her imprecations, her pleadings for fairness and justice, she has killed him just as surely as if she had plunged a knife into his guileful heart.

On the wall beyond the dressing table is a portrait of Giacomo, his face lit up by a shaft of pale wavering light from the unshuttered window. It was commissioned after the premiere of *Manon Lescaut,* the success of his opera reflected in his shining eyes, the confident jut of his chin, the shoulders pulled back as he bares his heart to the world.

And Giacomo! Elvira turns and buries her head in the pillow, and as the tears break through to the surface, her mind goes back to that freezing cold night, to the motor spluttering towards the pass, and to Giacomo's voice taunting her with his evasions and lies. She stuffs her handkerchief to her mouth, trying to stem her despairing sobs. For those few seconds, blinded by rage, God help her, she had wished him dead, too.   It is Signora Ida with her blushing cheeks and pink lips who opens the door to the priest, taking his cloak and showing him into the drawing room. Her sister, she informs him politely, will be with him shortly. Don Zeno lowers himself onto a high-backed chair rather than one of the armchairs that would swallow him into its soft luxury, and from which he would have difficulty rising. While he waits, he rehearses what he will say to Elvira, but before he has formulated the first sentence, the door opens and the lady herself appears.

'Thank you so much for coming, Father,' she says, offering him her hand. 'Can I get you something to drink?' Elvira is avoiding his eyes.

'A glass of wine would be much appreciated,' he says, running his tongue around his parched mouth, 'perhaps with a splash of water?' The priest has all but drained his glass before realising that Elvira's discourse is not following the trajectory he'd imagined. Having shunned any mention of the accident itself, she launched into a description of the earlier visit of the bone surgeons, the injection of morphine and the setting of the leg in plaster, and now seems intent on going over old personal matters, best left forgotten. Yes, he is fully aware of her circumstances, and no, the church does not condone a man and woman living together without the holy sacrament of marriage, but why is she raking all this up now?

The answer comes in the form of the telegram about Gemignani's death, which Elvira thrusts into his large hands. He reads it quickly. 'Good Lord!' Despite years of hearing confessions, Don Zeno is genuinely surprised. 'This means your husband ... ahem ... Signor Gemignani died soon after the accident.'

Elvira nods. 'The following day, while we were coming home in the ambulance.'

'Well, well,' he says. Then, trying to get a better measure of the situation, 'Have you shown this to Giacomo?'

She glances down. 'No, not yet. I wanted to speak to you first.'

'Ah ... I see.' Don Zeno taps his leg, sending a jolt down the nerve and into his foot. He knows Elvira's unmarried status weighs heavily on her, a situation he would dearly love to resolve. For why shouldn't a mother who has devoted herself to her family, as exemplified by the blessed Virgin Mary, have the respect she deserves? His office, though, is not governed by his own instincts but by the statutes of canonical law, and the woman in front of him, anxiously wringing her hands, is not going to like what he has to say.

'Elvira,' he sighs sadly, 'I'm afraid there's nothing I can do. You will have to wait the full ten months before marrying Giacomo.'

'Marry Giacomo?' she says, as if the idea has never occurred to her. 'This isn't about marrying anyone, Father! It's about saving my soul!' And with that, she buries her head in her hands and begins to howl.

Don Zeno rises from his chair as quickly as he can and places a kindly hand on her shoulder. 'Now, now, my dear, please don't distress yourself. I'm sure we can sort all this out.'

Elvira looks at him through desperate eyes. 'I killed Narciso,

Father,' she blurts out, 'and if you don't do something, Giacomo will die, too!'

Puccini, meanwhile, is lying back on a crisp, monogrammed pillowslip, his eyes closed, his breath rasping from his half-open mouth in a way that suggests a deeply unnatural sleep. His leg, its full length now encased in plaster, is protruding from his torso like the barrel of a cannon, but with his face recently shaved and his hair brushed back in shining waves, he looks almost angelic from the neck up. The dream he is having, though, most decidedly is not about the soul. It features a young woman with dark hair, a sinuous body, pert little breasts, and lips formed into a willing pout. Circling her in his arms, he burrows his face into her neck and licks its surface, which tastes musty and quite delicious, while at the same time his hands move to stroke her, slowly, rhythmically. The woman lets out a dreamy sigh and starts singing in a voice as soft as a feather. *Ah, sweet night! Look at the stars! They've never seemed so beautiful* ... Brilliant sparks of fire trembling like the glint of an eye … He recognises the tune, knows it to be a song about love and surrender, but try as he might, he cannot place it.

Suddenly the woman pulls away from him and sits up. In the distance a train is tooting, coming closer and closer, and then, *clunk, whish*, a door slides open, and there, standing over him, is a railway guard dressed in black. 'Aaaah!' he cries.

'It's all right, dear fellow,' the guard says, 'it's me, Don Zeno. You must have been dreaming.' Puccini's eyes refuse to focus. 'How are we, then, hey?' the blurry figure continues. 'What a business! Everyone sends their greetings – Andrea, Ferruccio, Giorgio, all the lads from the club. They're waiting for me to report back to them.'

Madonna! It's Don Zeno! He isn't going to die, is he?

'… and the doctors say you'll be up and about in no time!'

Thank God! But how long has the priest been standing there? Puccini's mind veers off in search of an answer but finds instead Doctor Colzi, a weaselly man with gold-rimmed spectacles, and with him his assistant, a sandy-haired youth of about twenty-five. *Sadistic butchers the pair of them, he thinks. Earlier they stabbed me with a needle the size of a fork prong, then tortured me until I passed out.*

'... so nearly asphyxiated ... the good Lord had his eye on you ...' The priest's words are jumping around like notes on a score, a score with no music to it. Giving up trying to follow them, Puccini floats off to another realm, one where he is being bounced around in a vehicle that smells of antiseptic and death ... and there is Elvira, holding his hand. 'We're just coming to the hill down to the Minutoli farm,' she says. 'Try and relax. It's going to be a bit bumpy.'

'Aiyee!' A grey shape, murky and indistinct, has appeared on his horizon, its bulky mass taking on the form of an animal as it races quickly towards him. It's a pig or a hog ... No, no, it has tusks, it must be a boar, a wild boar and – dear God – it's charging straight at him! 'No, no, no!' he howls, thrashing his arms in the air.

Don Zeno, taken by surprise, takes a step back and crosses himself. 'Giacomo, dear fellow, what is it? Shall I fetch Elvira?'

Puccini slumps back onto his pillow. 'No, no,' he pants. 'Sorry, Father, I'm not at all myself. It's the morphine. I thought I was being charged by a – oh my God!' He stops and stares at the ceiling, momentarily paralysed by something the doctors had told him.

'You were lucky you landed under the motorcar. If you'd fallen into the gully, you would have drowned.' This was from Colzi as he wiped the chalky plaster from his hands. 'Or the wild boars would have got you,' added Colzi's thatch-haired assistant. Wild boars? Surely he'd misheard? 'Oh no,' Colzi confirmed in that matter-of-fact tone favoured by the medical profession. 'There are hordes of them in that area. They'll eat anything, dead or alive. They're worse than pigs!'

'Father, may I ask you something?'

'Of course, Giacomo,' the priest says cautiously, 'anything you like.'

'Is it possible to ascend to heaven from inside an animal?'

Don Zeno's eyes widen. 'I'm sorry, Giacomo, I'm not sure I follow you.'

'Well, say you'd been eaten by a boar, you'd be in its intestines, wouldn't you?'

The priest reaches across and tugs the bellpull. 'We can talk about that sort of thing later,' he says hurriedly. 'For now, you must rest. I'll come and see you again in a day or two.' The priest pauses by the box hedge on the path leading to the front gate (a hedge that Poldo keeps trimmed with geometric precision), his gaze drawn to the mountains beyond the lake where a mist lies over the tops, obscuring them from his view. Like God, he thinks, whose profound presence in his life promises so much, yet whose being is hidden from him, folded in on its own deep mystery. It is this faith that has sustained Don Zeno through the trials and tribulations of his ministry, the mothers and the babies dying in childbirth, the children cut down by typhoid and malaria, the old folk lost to dementia or writhing in agony from tumours or crumbling bones, earning their place in paradise. It wearies him, sometimes, his priestly burden, the suffering he sees around him, the weight of the words whispered to him in the cramped gloom of the confessional, a weight made even heavier by Elvira's extraordinary confession.

A ray of sunlight strikes through a rift in the clouds, offering him a glimpse of the village across the lake, the houses and chapel of the Minutoli estate surrounded by trees like eggs in a nest; the quarry, a great white gash where the mountain has been hacked away; the spire of the church where his colleague, Father Pieri, preaches. If only Elvira had called on him, a younger man with a sharp mind to counsel her, not an old priest like himself whose grasp of theology has dimmed with the passage of time to little more than a faint glow. The *malocchio*, the evil eye! When Elvira sobbed out that terrible word, he thought his heart would fail. How had she come to be in the grip of such dangerous nonsense? And Giacomo's questions on transmutation of the flesh! *No! No! This will never do! The devil has insinuated his way into the villa, and it is time to cast him out,* he thinks.

Don Zeno reaches into the pocket of his cape and pulls out the pale green envelope, catching once again its floral perfume, its call to sin. Gripping it firmly, he tears once, then again, and crushes the pieces into a tight little ball in his fist. Giacomo would be receiving no more of these, not if he got to them first.

And with the composer housebound, there would be plenty of opportunities to impress on him his duty as a man and a father, and with the good Lord's help, convince him to marry Elvira. A wave of sudden tiredness washes over the priest, a wave that brings with it a longing for the peace of his presbytery, for the comfort of his armchair by the fire, for Rosaria's dependable presence and for the plate of piping hot pasta she will be putting on the table at one o'clock sharp. And with these worldly matters in mind, Don Zeno limps to the gate, clambers aboard his bicycle and pedals off up the road.

Chapter 29
THE BARBER CALLS

Puccini rips the page from his notebook and hurls it to the floor where it joins the others in a long tapering pattern reminiscent of Gustave Eiffel's iconic tower, the one depicted on the postcard that Antonio had sent in happier times.

Oh Corinna, why haven't you written? The silence is killing me! Then he stops, knowing he is being disingenuous, for she surely has written and her letters are piling up behind the bar of Andrea's shack, where he cannot reach them. Today, though, he is feeling more than a little sorry for himself. Over four weeks have passed since the composer and his life were thrown up in the air. Four weeks of pain and discomfort, of Elvira and her cohort of chattering females fussing over him day and night, of visitors reminding him what he is missing in the world outside, and endless hours of boredom. Oh God, the boredom! It weighs on him like a mortification for his sins, draining his life force from him, drop by tedious drop. He doesn't want any of this: he wants *Butterfly*, and he wants Corinna … to touch her, to feel her skin next to his, to hear her sighs as he retraces his steps along the pathways of her body like a lost pilgrim.

Looking down, he sees the empty pages of his notebook staring blankly back at him, waiting for inspiration. Like him, endlessly waiting. *Oh Corinna!* He stills his breath and tries to bring her back … and suddenly there she is, stepping down from the train, looking gorgeous in a red coat and matching hat, a scarf thrown loosely round her shoulders like a cape, her lively gold-flecked eyes looking around, seeking him. It was her first visit to meet him in Milan, and an unseasonably cold day with a wind that cut through the city like a knife, whirling dry leaves around in the gutters and piling them into doorways. He had thought to suggest a stroll or an *aperitivo* and a little window-shopping, but instead of mingling with the crowds in the Galleria, gazing at windows draped with silk and organza, or throwing coins to accordion players squeezing out tunes of sunshine and love, they had caught a cab back to his flat, stopping to buy chestnuts from the street vendor on the corner, then taken them upstairs to his kitchen where they had peeled and fed them to each other, sucking and biting the oily flesh. Before they repaired to the bedroom.

'Do you love me, Giacomo?' He remembers turning to her, seeing the flush of her skin. 'Well, do you?'

How many times had he been asked that question! 'Um-hum ...' She pulled the blanket over her head, burying herself until all he could see was a few strands of black hair, which he took in his hand and stroked, enjoying the silky feel against his fingers. And all the while he was fighting off an impulse to tear the bedcovers from her, take her in his arms and start all over again.

'Is that um-hum, yes? Or um-hum, no?'

The pipes gurgled, and the radiator under the window gave an answering shudder. There were other sounds too, the murmuring of voices in the street below, the cries of a chestnut seller, the horses pulling away from the tram stop on their way to La Scala.

'You are so beautiful,' he said, kissing the long strands before letting them go, 'and always asking questions.'

Now, confined to his bed, Puccini knows he is lucky to be alive. He knows this because everyone keeps telling him so (except Elvira, who turns pale and leaves the room at the slightest mention of that evening). His sisters endorse his good fortune: Otilia, the eldest (along with her husband, Del Carlo, a prig of a man; Tomaide, who brings him bags of the strong mints favoured by their father; Nitteti, a widow with two young children who lives in Pisa; and Ramelde, the youngest and closest, whose penchant for puns and silly verse does little to cheer him up. It appears he must throw his hat in the air and give three hearty cheers for being stuck here, deprived of everything that makes his life worth living. Don Zeno, too, comes to play a game or two of draughts, but instead of amusing him with talk of Blackbird Legs and his friends from the club, the priest has taken to banging on about the sanctity of marriage and other such claptrap, making him feel even more of a prisoner to a malign and capricious fate. Corinna, the only person he truly longs to see, is denied him, as is Giulio Ricordi, who sends messages via Elvira. As for the rest of his friends, they come nowhere near him, a circumstance he finds upsetting because it is out of character, but there must be a reason for it, probably that Elvira will not allow them in the house. Puccini's mother used to say that troubles never arrive when you want them, a maxim he was reminded of during the recent visit of Doctor Colzi and his assistant. The bone in his leg is not knitting together as it should and must be broken and reset. As well as this, the gashes, cuts and abrasions that cover his body in oozing purple sores show no sign of healing, despite being bathed in iodine and carefully bandaged. Colzi can offer no explanation and has asked the local doctor to arrange for a series of blood tests, the results of which will not be known for two weeks.

It is this latest blow, bringing with it an unquantifiable measure of fear and uncertainty, that has driven the composer's mind into dark and unfamiliar places. How is Corinna faring without him? She is young and pretty, and now, thanks to his influence, quite worldly. How long will she wait for him? He has seen the way other men look at her, knows that time, his enemy, will slowly chip away at her resistance, weakening her to their glances.

A knock on the door interrupts his thoughts. It is Doria, who bobs one of her clumsy curtsies. 'Excuse me, Maestro,' she says, 'the barber is here.'

'Thank you, Doria,' he says, his tone short on enthusiasm. 'Show him in.'

The doors swing open onto a tableau that previously would have impressed Puccini with its theatrical qualities. A fat little man with immaculately oiled hair, his body tapering to his feet like a penguin, is making an exaggerated bow to Elvira, his moustache hovering only inches from her bosom. But this is not theatre, and on seeing the leer in the barber's close-set eyes, Puccini dispenses with any attempt at a civil greeting.

'Ah, Settimelli,' he calls, 'I suppose you've come to cut my throat!' Arturo Settimelli has been the village barber for more than twenty years, although never summoned to the villa before. From Tuesdays to Saturdays, he works in his salon, shaving the jowls and trimming the moustaches of those rich enough to afford his services, while on Mondays, his day off, he sends his assistant, Filippo, around the area, seeing to those too poor or wretched to visit his premises. Settimelli, a man with an ambitious nature, would like nothing better than a permanent appointment to the Puccini household, not only so that he might rub shoulders with a better class of person (having grown up in poverty, he feels nothing but revulsion for head-lice and dirt), but also to wheedle his way into the affections of Signora Elvira, a woman he has long admired from afar. His own wife, pretty enough in her day, has dried up like a stick, a stick with a list of ailments pinned to it. His thoughts wander: *Signora Elvira, now there's a fine figure of a woman, a Brünn-hilde, and surely not averse to a little attention now that the Maestro has been out of action for a few weeks.*

The barber gives a sycophantic little laugh, which he lets fade as soon as he realises his client isn't joining in.

'It's no laughing matter,' Puccini snaps. Settimelli, not liking the tone, is grateful to see Filippo coming from the kitchen with a jug, bowl and fluffy white towel. Clicking open his bag, he unrolls a felt strip containing combs, razors and scissors.

'Look at that!' Puccini says, raising his hand and pointing at the piano. Settimelli turns his head, seeing nothing out of place. What is he supposed to be looking at? The writing table covered in papers, or the revolving chair with a battered hat on its leather cushion?

'Hmm … yes,' he says, picking up a comb and doing a little ritual flicking and fawning.

Puccini, who can't at this moment lift his head, raises his voice instead. '*Just look at it!*' The barber jumps. 'It's been weeks,' the composer goes on, 'and I can't get near the damn thing!'

'Hmm. I'm sorry, Maestro,' Settimelli says, adopting a tone

which he hopes expresses the right degree of sympathy, although he has no idea what for.

'Can you believe it?' Puccini says. 'Three bloody years! And as usual, those scribblers and I have come to blows over just about everything.'

Drops of sweat are forming at the nape of Settimelli's neck. What is the man talking about?

'It's like being in prison! It's terrible – terrible!'

The barber can feign comprehension no longer. 'What exactly is the problem, Maestro, apart from the broken leg?'

Puccini gives him a derisive look. 'The problem, man? My work, that's the problem! I'm sitting here like some forgotten Buddha, when I should be over there –' he jabs his finger at the piano, 'getting on with my opera!'

Settimelli lowers his scissors. 'So why don't you go over there?' he asks, cautiously.

'Yes?' The word resonates with sarcasm. 'And how do you propose I get this –' Puccini points to his plastered leg, 'under that?' he jabs at the piano again. 'Unless, of course, you'd like to hack it off with one of your damn razors!'

There is an awkward silence then a huh-hum from Filippo, who is standing tactfully to one side. 'Perhaps,' he says slowly, 'the Maestro might consider one of those large pianos, the ones with a curved end?'

Puccini twists his neck and stares at the hapless youth. Settimelli holds his breath. *O merda! All hell's going to break loose ...*

Then amazingly, the composer throws back his head and gives a throaty laugh. 'Of course! A grand piano! Why didn't I think of it myself? Thank you! Thank you! Er ... what did you say your name was?'

'Filippo,' Settimelli cuts in quickly, grabbing the credit. 'At your service, Maestro!'

Doria is in the kitchen with a mixing bowl in her hands, the one that Cook had used earlier for making a cake. She is supposed to be washing it up, but every time she goes to plunge it into the hot, soapy water, she remembers the night of the accident, and Filippo shaking her to wake her up. 'Doria, what on earth are you doing at the sink?' The mixing bowl is smeared with creamy cake batter like swirls of thick paint. Unable to resist, Doria sweeps her finger around the bowl and pops it into her mouth. 'Mmmn ...' she breathes as the sweet eggy mixture dissolves on her tongue, 'and there's still some more to go ...'

Before Cook went out to fetch the vegetables, she said, 'When you've finished that bit of washing up, girl, you can get the refreshments ready for Settimelli and that lad of his – your knight in shining armour!' Then she rocked back on her heels and made the noise of a coffeepot bubbling up.

Doria doesn't understand half of what Cook says, which is why she likes it when she goes outside. And because there's no one then to scold her – or to stop her scraping the crispy bits from the baking trays or looking at herself in the pans on the wall that make her skin go all gold and lumpy like she's got some funny disease – Doria hooks a blob of cake mix into her mouth. Sometimes when she's on her own, she pretends she's mistress of the kitchen, bustling around like Signora Elvira and talking about all those fancy dishes for the Maestro. *He likes his food, that one does. You should see the way his face lights up when he sees what's on his tray ...* Doria gives her finger a final lick ... *The doctors say he won't be walking for two whole months! It can't be much fun stuck in that bed all day, even if he does have his music machine to listen to.*

Doria slides the mixing bowl into the water and watches it fill up to the top. Cook is taking a really long time, which means she's likely lost again among all the rows of beans and peas and purple sprouting broccoli. Like yesterday, and the day before, when she came back without the turnip tops, wiped her feet on the mat, and said, 'Well, I never! You mark my words ... one day he'll take off with one of those floozies.'

'What's a floozy?' Doria remembers asking her.

'One of those loose types what gets all dolled up in fancy clothes and steals men, if you know what I mean.'

Doria didn't know what she meant. 'Steals men? How?'

'Takes them away to live in sin.'

'Sin! What sort of sin?'

Cook looked at her crossly. 'Get on with those potatoes, girl, and don't meddle in things that don't concern you!' Doria runs the dishcloth around the bowl then upends it on the rack. Now for the visitors' refreshments … Going to the pantry, she lifts a cake from the crown-lid tin and takes it over to the table, picks up a knife and thrusts it into the centre, feeling the soft sponge give way under the blade. Then she cuts again and eases the wedge out and onto a plate for Settimelli. She lifts the plate to her nose to sniff the sugary smell edged with aniseed.

Doria cuts a second slice, for Filippo, bigger than the first, but as she lifts the yellow wedge, an all too familiar longing wells up inside her, telling her to sink her teeth into the moist sponge and let its sweetness crumble on her tongue. She knows she shouldn't – *Ooooh!* – but it's no use. Quickly, her fingers break off a corner and stuff it into her mouth, as she hopes Cook won't come back and discover her.

'*Arrivederci,* Maestro. Until the next time …'

'The barber!' Doria swallows, but the cake doesn't go down, instead lodging itself in her throat like a lump of wet sand. Through the doorway she can see the barber shuffling towards her as he bows out of the studio, with Filippo behind him, carrying his bag. He grins at her, Filippo does, and winks one eye, which makes her swallow again.

'Ah, Doria,' Settimelli says, raising his head. 'Thank goodness it's you! I am in the most desperate need of a good strong cup of coffee.'

Doria nods, and as Filippo slides past her to take his place at the kitchen table, he leans over, blows a kiss in her ear and whispers, 'Nice cake?'

Doria flushes the colour of mulberries.

Chapter 30
ELVIRA SHOWS GIACOMO
A TELEGRAM

While Doria is serving coffee to Settimelli and his lad, Elvira is upstairs sitting at her dressing table, a mask of perfumed clay spread on her face and a slice of cucumber pressed to each eye, giving her the startled look of a circus clown. Under her protective cape is a cream blouse cut into an enticing V, the same garment that a short while ago had electrified that funny little barber man. Elvira had not immediately understood the significance of the look in his eyes, the heat of his breath on her skin, but now, having had time to reflect, the incident begins to make more sense. Giacomo has been immobile for weeks, and she is wearing French perfume and a revealing blouse. To a man like Settimelli, this could mean only one thing, to which he was only too eager to respond. Peeling away the cucumber, Elvira takes a flannel and dabs at the clay sludge, an amused smile playing on her lips. *Well, well! And the look on Giacomo's face! You'd almost think he was jealous.*

Elvira is paying particular attention to her grooming today because after a lunch of asparagus risotto, roast pheasant in white sauce and *crema fritta*, she is going to show Giacomo the telegram concerning Narciso's death. It's a prospect which, until recently, would have kept her awake half the night and set off one of her headaches. How will he take it? Will he declare his intention to leave her, even though there has been no sign of the other woman, no letters, no telegrams or telephone calls, she is certain of that. Yet it is not the silence of her rival that has led to this change in Elvira, which she experiences as a shift in mood, in perspective, making her calmer, more accepting of her fate. As if the raw sensitive parts of her, the parts that have given her so much pain in the past, have finally begun to heal over. Nor can it be wholly attributed to her confession to the old priest, although this has certainly lifted a great burden from her. Rather, she is beginning to see Giacomo in a new and not very flattering light.

Reaching for the hairbrush, Elvira tugs it through her hair, counting the strokes as she goes. Since the accident, she has devoted herself unstintingly to his needs, dispensing medicines, helping him shave and dress, organising his meals, and generally running around responding to his every little whim. And what whims they are, the notebooks and score sheets to be ordered (despite the fact that he is doing no work at all), recordings for his gramophone, chocolates and cigars, but only the very best. Not to mention the visitors! On some days it seems as if half the country has traipsed through the house, obliging her to smile at people who have been perfectly horrid to her in the past, and all of whom require refreshments, lifts to the station, or even a bed for the night. While there he sits, reading his newspaper or browsing through his articles, scooping chocolates into his mouth and smoking his cigarettes, civil to her one moment, flaring up the next.

Her brushing continues … *Fifty, fifty-one, fifty-two, fifty-three* … Elvira wants to shake him, to tell him that he should be grateful for her efforts, and rather than indulging his moods, he should be plying her with smiles and compliments like any proper man would surely do (that barber fellow, for one). She turns her thoughts instead to Fosca and the new baby. It is only a matter of weeks now until she will become a grandmother, the prospect of which fills her with such a fierce excitement that at times her insides hurt. How she longs to hold the dear little new life in her arms, breathing in its milky smell, its warmth, its helplessness; and the pleasure, too, of sharing the experience with Fosca, who will be grateful for her efforts, and not complain.

Ninety-eight, ninety-nine, one hundred. Elvira sets down the hairbrush and unties the strings of her cape, the thought of escaping from Giacomo and his demands making her almost giddy with relief. 'A bear, that's what he's become, a big, brown grizzly bear.'

The subject of Elvira's thoughts, her errant husband, runs a hand down his recently shaved jaw and sniffs his skin, which has about it the whiff of a wet, smelly dog. 'Bloody barber!' he says, picking up his pen and dating a sheet of notepaper. If he can get the order in the afternoon post, the piano could be delivered before Easter, a thought which makes him almost smile. And in the wake of this, he closes his eyes and drifts off to find Corinna.

'So we could get married?' she asks him.

They are in a set of rented rooms in Viareggio, and it is summer again, a full year after their first meeting on the train.

'Uh hum …' He is standing in a strip of scorching light where the shutters don't quite meet, a towel around his middle, a recently lit cigarette in his fingers.

'Would it make you happy?' she asks.

Through the gap he can see the roof of the station, hear the *chug-chug* of a train. 'Would what make me happy?'

'To be married …'

He gazes up at the light fitting, its opaque surface settled with layers of thick dust. Would it? He had never really given the matter any thought but supposed it could be pleasant. After all, Corinna wasn't like other women; she didn't nag or make demands or have headaches.

'Well …?'

He turns to look at her, the smile on her lips, the twisted sheet, her clear eyes directed at his.

'Yes, of course,' he says, as if his words are airy things of no consequence, to drift away like puffs of his cigarette smoke.

'Then perhaps we should plan a wedding?'

'A wedding?' He has been thinking of little else. Madama Butterfly's bridesmaids, her relatives, her uncle the priest, storming in and denouncing her for marrying a foreigner, and Pinkerton hurriedly shooing them all away … There is a cry from the station like a wolf howling in the night. The train for La Spezia is about to depart, the signal for Corinna to start dressing in order to be ready for the taxicab that will drive her back to her grandmother and great aunt. But there is still time for one little caress.

'Here you are, Giacomo. You must be hungry!' Puccini's eyes blink open, and there is Elvira with a tray. 'What makes you say that?' he asks, buying himself a moment to realign his thoughts.

'You were licking your lips.'

He gives an amused smile to which Elvira responds, smiling back. 'Look at all those letters!' she says, indicating the stacks of envelopes on the floor.

He follows the direction of her finger. 'Over three hundred ...' he says.

'Really? So many?'

'Yes, I counted them, seeing as I don't have much else to do with my time. I can tell you this, Elvira, a brush with death certainly sends people running for their pens ...' And here he stops, for he has just seen what is on his tray. 'My goodness, what a feast!' Elvira smiles again.

Reaching for the carafe, he splashes red wine into his glass, quaffs it and gives a satisfied grunt. He stabs a spear of asparagus with his fork and lifts it to his mouth. 'Delicious!' Elvira, meanwhile, has turned to gaze through the French window, her fingers straightening the cuff of her blouse.

'Are you not having lunch?' he asks, wiping his mouth with the back of his hand.

'Later, perhaps.'

He dives back into his food, forking it into his mouth and chewing with such concentration that he doesn't see Elvira's hand reaching towards him, not until its shadow passes in front of his eyes. Then he moves his head, believing she is about to touch his cheek. But no, she is holding something – a telegram – which she drops on the tray.

'I'm a little tired,' she says. 'I think I'll go upstairs.'

He watches her move towards the door, her hips swaying in time with her footsteps, the train of her skirt following her like a peacock's tail. Elvira could still turn a head or two, he thinks, as he lays down his fork and picks up the telegram.

Chapter 31
DORIA IS SENT HOME

March has slipped quietly into April, the month that warms the most hardened of hearts with its perfumed breezes and promise of new life, the month when the peasants, instead of cursing their fate, welcome the early sun on their backs. Poldo can be heard humming as he goes about collecting the herbs and flowers to distil for his infusions and pastes; *sambuco* to settle the stomach, *rovo* to dry up acne and pockmarked skin, the spindly yellow-flowered *trifoglio* to heal cuts, and *passiflora*, whose ingested fruit promotes a deep dreamless sleep. It is a time to stroll in an orchard in the leafy shade of the sweet-scented orange trees, listening to the happy chirping of the birds, or go for a spin to the coast for a glass of lemonade or chilled prosecco, before driving home into a lingering pink and gold sunset. But not for the inhabitants of Villa Puccini.

Doria, as on every other morning, jumps out of bed as the church bell strikes six, runs a damp cloth over her face, dresses quickly and twists her hair to the crown of her head, then drops to her knees and makes a hurried sign of the cross. 'Holy Zita, bless this house and all who live here.'

Doria's prayers will have to be quick this morning because after breakfast the doctors are coming (the bone surgeons as well as Doctor Falli from the village), and then Don Zeno, not to play board games with the Maestro, but to bless the house, a ceremony performed in all Christian homes during Lent. But before holy water can be sprinkled around the rooms, they must be aired and dusted, the floors swept and the windows cleaned. Later, after her rest, she will take the dogs for a walk, now that the Maestro is laid up. And as it's Friday, Filippo will be waiting for her on the path by the oak tree. He's good with the dogs, especially Nello who jumps on Schaunard and tries to bite him on the neck. She takes the females, Bruna and Lea, and he takes the other two, the 'sniffing sacks', he calls them; then he laughs out loud, like he's won a prize at the fair. Sometimes when they're walking through the woods Filippo reaches out and touches her hair, his eyes going as damp as dew, and once he bent down with his lips pushed out, waiting for a kiss. Doria knew what he wanted, but pretended she didn't because the grasshoppers had started up inside her. Not the grasshoppers she gets from Rodolfo and Bruno the wife-beater, but a different sort, ones with wings that flutter against her heart and make her go tingly all over. Like she did the night Filippo rescued her from the sink.

It is five minutes to nine when Doctor Francesco Falli appears. He's a slight man, looking older than his fifty years, with prematurely curved shoulders, a grey tinge to his skin, and deep lines, like brackets, enclosing his mouth. Today he's wearing a cream linen jacket and a hat with a brown hatband. He brings his mare to a halt outside the villa, dismounts and fastens the reins to the railings. Glancing towards the garage, where swallows are feverishly building nests under the eaves, he opens the gate and walks down the path, surprised to see that Signora Elvira is not waiting for him on the doorstep, as usual, for her family's various ailments and fevers: when Fosca was bitten by a dog, when Antonio sustained a nasty cut on his forehead falling off his bicycle, and during the Maestro's recent bout of throat trouble. Falli admires Elvira's strong attachment to her family, while at the same time wishing it were not coupled with a nervous response at the least sign of trouble. He has tried suggesting that she trust a little more in the healing power of nature, but she just scoffs at this, pointing out villagers who have various dreadful afflictions. There is no comparison, of course, because most of the local folk live in conditions more suited to their animals, and suffer, at least to some degree, from malnutrition. Anyway, he supposes he should be grateful that she calls on him at all, as the other well-to-do families wouldn't dream of consulting a state-appointed medical officer such as himself for fear of being seen to support the socialist initiatives taking over their country.

Yet it was these very initiatives that inspired young Francesco to become a doctor in the first place, and his belief in a better fairer society has never wavered, not even when faced, day in, day out, with illiterate peasants too poor to afford his services, and masters too rich to give a damn. He has always refused to compromise, refused to rush off to become the simpering assistant of some fine greedy surgeon in smart rooms in a city. These local people need him, and he will use his skills however he can to help them, even if it does mean extracting rotten teeth and treating pigs struck down by swine fever. The good doctor's approach does bear fruit of a certain kind: not only the esteem in which he is generally held, but also the continuous supply of eggs, oil, fish, game and vegetables that finds its way to his doorstep. If Falli has one regret, it is that he has never married, doubting that a doctor's wife could thrive in a place such as this, and reluctant to renounce his passion for reading (history of the Roman Empire, especially the rule of the enlightened Antoninus Pius), a condition that any bride would surely impose on him.

Doctor Falli steps away from the front door and peers through the window into the drawing room, seeing a vase of orange flowers but no Signora Elvira. She does, however, arrive promptly at the first ring of the doorbell.

'Good morning, Doctor,' she says, looking flustered. 'I'm so sorry I wasn't here to welcome you. My husband needed me to find a journal for him. Please come in, this way ...' She leads him into the drawing room where he chooses the same high-backed chair as the priest and waits for her to sit down before doing so himself.

Taking his pince-nez from his waistcoat pocket to place on his nose, he says, 'Now then, I have the results of the blood tests.' Elvira is squeezing the palms of her hands together as if trying to crush a nut. 'I can assure you there is nothing to be overly concerned about,' he says gently.

'Whatever do you mean?'

'The Maestro has diabetes, which is why the cuts and abrasions are not healing.'

Her face blanches. 'Oh dear! He's been eating puddings every day, not to mention caramels and chocolates!'

'All that will have to stop, I'm afraid, and he'll also have to cut down on fruit and wine ...'

'Wine?' She squeezes her hands again. 'He won't like that!'

'I daresay not, but fortunately his condition is mild so we should be able to control it with a diet of small meals, five times a day.'

'Five! Like the British?'

'Exactly like the British.'

'But all that extra work! Cook will have a fit!'

Doctor Falli gives her a rueful smile and tucks his pince-nez back into his waistcoat pocket. 'Indeed!' he says. 'Now, if I may have a quick word with the patient before Doctor Colzi arrives.' Doria spoons finely ground coffee into the *caffettiera*, screws the top to the bottom, takes it over to the hob then goes to the pantry to fetch biscuits, lemon with a marmalade glaze, which are cooling on the rack. When she emerges, Signora Elvira is standing in the doorway, looking nervous.

'Where's Cook?' she asks.

'Outside, Signora.'

Her mistress makes a face like she's swallowed a frog. 'Gossiping again, I suppose! Well, when she comes back, tell her the Maestro won't be having the zuppa inglese for lunch, not with all that fruit and custard. And Doria, when you have a minute, bring the chocolates from the studio in here ... and you can leave those biscuits in the pantry. Better not put temptation his way.'

Doria can make no sense of this. 'But Signora, the Maestro loves his sweet treats!'

'Not any more, I'm afraid. He's been diagnosed with diabetes, the sugar disease ... Ah, there's the doorbell. That will be Doctor Colzi.'

Doria unhooks the latch of the stove and shovels lumps of silver-grey coke onto the dying embers, her mouth filling up with strands of thick hungry saliva. She is thinking of the glass bowl in the pantry, the one with layers of red and yellow pudding topped off with grated chocolate and cream. If the Maestro can't eat it, perhaps she'll get a double helping before the day's out … and the sugar jellies … and the pink and green squares that taste like almonds, only sweeter. She knows this because when she goes into the studio to tidy up, and Signor Giacomo is sitting there listening to his music, he looks at her with his big eyes and says, 'Thank you, my dear. You're an angel. Now, I expect you'd like one of these – they're from Switzerland, you know – the very best in the world.'

A length of spittle oozes from the corner of Doria's mouth. She wipes it away with her cuff. If the red chocolate box is to be kept in the kitchen, she can help herself whenever Cook goes outside!

The caffettiera is bubbling up. Doria lifts it from the heat and upends it and while the water is dripping through, she arranges four small cups and saucers on a tray, then the teaspoons, all facing the same way. And the sugar … *Sugar!* Doria's eyes fix on the little white bales stacked up in the sugar bowl. *But the Maestro mustn't have sugar!* She thinks for a moment, then picks up the tongs and drops a cube into three of the cups, pours in the steaming coffee and heads across the hall to the studio. The door is closed, so Doria edges sideways, bends her knees and presses the handle down with her rump. It swings open, and what she sees gives her such a fright that the tray pitches forward, sending a teaspoon tumbling to the floor.

The Maestro is lying on his back, a towel around his middle, his legs there for all the world to see. But they're not legs, they're sticks the colour of milk, one bent up like an elbow, the other smeared in dark, sticky jam. The bone surgeons are standing on either side of him, but instead of their normal suits, they're wearing large white aprons like Enzo, the butcher. The younger man with the sandy hair has a towel in his hand, while the old bald fellow has a mallet which is swinging like the pendulum of the clock in the hall. He stares at her through his glasses, the old one, then at the teaspoon on the floor.

'Doria!' the Maestro gasps. 'You've saved me, at least for the time being.' Doria looks at him, and then at Doctor Falli, who is sitting by his side, holding a handkerchief to his brow.

'It's all right, my dear,' the doctor says, with a kindly smile. 'We're just straightening the bone.' Doria's eyes move to the small metal coffin on the wheelchair at the end of the bed.

'And that,' he continues, following her terrified gaze, 'is to make sure that when we've finished the Maestro won't be able to move it, not even an inch.'

'Oh!' Doctor Falli has begun shimmering at the edges like the picture of Santa Zita in her missal … and now the lampshade behind his head is glowing … and everything in the room has blurred into funny shapes … 'Oooh!' Setting down the tray, Doria turns and stumbles back to the kitchen. Elvira is in the drawing room when she hears the first of Giacomo's screams, a sound so chilling that at first she believes the sound to be false, like the cries of mourners paid to wail over the coffins of important people. Her immediate concern though, somewhat surprisingly, is not for him, but for Doria. 'Oddio! She'll be scared to death. I must find her …' Which she eventually does, crouched down in a corner of the pantry, her hands over her ears, her eyes screwed tightly shut. 'Doria,' she says, resting a hand on her shoulder. The maid shrinks back against the wall. 'Doria!' she repeats loudly. This time the eyelids roll up, revealing terrified orbs that no words will console. 'Go home, my dear,' Elvira says gently. 'We can manage without you until Monday.'

Doria struggles to her feet. 'But the dusting … the windows …'

'I'll get Silvia to give me a hand. You run along now, and take the biscuits with you. Oh gracious, they've nearly all gone!'

A seagull pecking at a clump of weed on the lake foreshore looks up and sees a girl coming out through the gate of the big house with one of those biscuit boxes in her hands. Waaw! he squawks, flapping excitedly towards her. Slimy lakeweed might be all right for some, but he has more refined tastes cultivated during his summers at the seaside. The happy season, though, has not yet begun, and as usual he is hungry. The girl scuttles on up the road, her head bowed, paying no attention to anything.

Good … this one's going to be easy! Spreading his wings, he takes to the air and circles around, gaining height as he goes. Then, when she is near the well, he swoops down, aiming at her back. Eeaaw! he screams, missing her by a fraction as he veers off over the footpath. The girl lets out a shriek and, as he'd hoped, drops the box onto the road, where it bursts open. *Whoa … yippee! Look at that!* Now all he has to do is scare her off for good. Swinging around, he soars upwards, circles again and dives. But this time she's waiting for him.

Whoom! She whacks him with the flat of her hand, a blow that sends him spinning into a clump of stinging nettles. *Aaargh! She's winged me!* The girl, without as much as a glance in his direction, crouches down, scoops his prize back into the box and sets off again along the path. The gull rolls onto his good side and pushes himself up – *Ouch! Ouch! Ouch!* – then waddles slowly over to where the box fell. There isn't a crumb left on the ground, not a single one!

Clutching the biscuit box to her chest, Doria hurries along, the squawks of the gull and the Maestro's screams reverberating in her head like church bells on a frosty morning. And with them, from across the fields, drifts a sweeter sound, one that Doria does not hear, of voices singing. The peasants are out gathering clover, which they will dry and store as winter fodder for their animals.

Each month has a rhythm of its own, as well known as the days of the saints. May for cherries, wheat and hay in June; July brings apricots, peaches and the tomatoes that will be bottled and eaten over the winter. In August there is corn and the early plums; in September, figs, grapes and chestnuts, to be roasted or ground into flour. The late corn ripens in October, and the following month olives are shaken from the trees and crushed for oil. All the produce, God willing, will provide enough to pay the mezzadria, half going to the estate in lieu of rent, and keep the family going until springtime, when the cycle begins all over again. But that is not all. In winter, there is hunting and trapping, the crafting of fishing rods and the repairing of boats, while the women gather cane from the lake to weave baskets and mend chairs. Like the bees in Bernardo's hives, the people here devote every moment of the day to a relentless God-ordained plan of survival.

Signora Cioni's cat is curled up on its doorstep, but Doria doesn't see it as she hurries to her own front door, presses her hand to the splintery wood and pushes, listening for the familiar creak. She is home! She is safe! Through the dim light she sees her mother at the bread trough in the corner, her back turned, her shoulders heaving up and down. Doria's siblings are nowhere to be seen, no doubt off with their friends for the afternoon.

'Mamma,' Doria calls, dropping the biscuit box onto the table. 'It's me ...'

Signora Manfredi's head jerks round. 'Doria! What are you doing here?'

'I've come home.'

'I can see that, but why?'

'Because ...' Doria's lip starts to tremble.

'Dear girl, what's the matter?' Fighting back tears, Doria closes her eyes, waiting for the warmth of her mother's arms, the scratch of cheap cotton, the smell of smoke on her hair. 'You're very pale,' Mamma says, placing a floury hand on her forehead. 'You're not sick, are you?' Doria opens her eyes. 'No, no. It's the Maestro ...'

'The Maestro!' Mamma stiffens and Doria watches a vein pulse in her neck. 'He didn't try ... you know, want to ...'

'Want to what?'

'Oh, never mind ... So what is the matter?'

'They're going to put his leg in a coffin, so that means it's dead, doesn't it ... like Papi?'

'Oh my dear,' Mamma says, squeezing her, 'it's just their way of mending it.'

Doria sniffs, beginning to feel better. Then she remembers the seagull. 'And a gull tried to steal the biscuits!'

'What biscuits?'

'These,' she says, pointing to the table. 'They're from Signora Elvira.'

'Heavens!' Mamma says, 'Don't they give up sweet things in the villa for Lent?'

'They don't give up anything.'

Mamma shakes her head. 'Well, I never!'

'I dropped them,' Doria goes on, 'but then I picked them up again.'

'But Doria, we can't eat ... Oh, never mind! How long are you here for?'

'Until Monday.'

'Monday?' Mamma says. 'But that's grand! If the weather stays fine, we can do a wash. Now, where was I? ... Ah yes, the bread. You put your things away, Doria, while I finish it off. There's some focaccia and milk if you're hungry.' Doria takes the jug from the cool chest and half-fills a beaker, breaks off a piece of focaccia and takes them over to the table. Sliding onto a stool, she sips the foamy milk and watches her mother kneading the dough in the corner, her shoulders moving slowly up and down as if weights have been strapped to her arms. A tear squeezes out into the corner of Doria's eye. If only Papi were still here! She bites into the focaccia and begins to chew – then stops. *Ugh, it's stale! How long has it been in that tin?* About to spit it into her hand, Doria suddenly remembers where she is: not in the villa but at home, where every scrap is eaten up, and grateful thanks given for what little they have.

To take her mind off the sour taste, Doria scuffs her feet on the dry earth floor and stares into the embers of the fire, where two flasks of beans in water flavoured with sage leaves and a little oil are beginning their slow journey into the soft, plump fagioli that bulk out every soup and stew. Then she looks around at the grimy walls and smoke-blackened ceiling. How dirty it all is – and how small! Why, everything in the house would fit into just the dining room of the villa. Ha! Imagine her brothers and sisters clambering onto the red and gold chairs, leaving their sticky fingermarks all over the polished table!

A sound like the banging of a shutter in a gale brings Doria back to her mother, who is bent double over the trough, hacking out coughs from deep inside her chest. Doria mutters a quick prayer and directs it to the splayed figure on the cross above the fireplace, remembering what Mamma says to her each Sunday before she sets off for the villa.

'Never forget, Doria, we live in our world and the likes of Puccini and Signora Elvira live in theirs. They don't mix, so don't go getting ideas into your head!'

Doria's gaze slips from the crucifix to the photograph on the shelf underneath, which has been there for as long as she can remember, of Mamma in her wedding dress, smiling shyly at the camera, with Papi in his Sunday best, holding her arm. Over the years the heat and smoke have roasted them both to the colour of acorns, yet Doria can still see that special look in her father's eyes, a look that reminds her of something Cook had said.

'Mamma, what's "living in sin"?'

Her mother turns, her cheeks red, although whether from coughing or alarm is impossible to say. 'Who's been telling you about such things?'

'Cook,' Doria says innocently. 'Why? Is it something bad?'

Mamma wipes her mouth on her apron. 'Yes, Doria, it's very bad.'

'But what is it?'

Mamma hesitates then says, 'I suppose you're old enough to know. It's when a man and woman live together without the blessing of the priest.'

'Oh ... and what happens to them?'

'They go to hell, my girl, that's what happens!' Doria looks down and shuffles her feet. 'Yes,' Mamma goes on, 'the Devil himself throws them into the flames where they burn for all eternity.'

O Santa Zita! Doria's hand is shaking as she lifts the beaker to her mouth and pours in the last drops of creamy milk. When the dough is ready, Mamma brings it over to the table, slices it through with the wire, rounds off the quarters and arranges them on a floury board, then carves a small cross on the top of each one and says a quick blessing. But instead of the usual pause after the *Amen*, she blurts out, 'I nearly forgot to tell you, Doria, your sister is getting married!'

'Alice?' Doria says, not quite taking this in ... 'but who to?'

'Marco Pucci from Quiesa, over on the other side. I've spoken to his family and it's all arranged.'

'That's good,' Doria says uncertainly.

'It certainly is,' Mamma agrees. 'He's a strong fellow, sober and hardworking ...' She lifts the board and bends down to slide it near the smouldering embers. Specks of flour are falling from the loaves like flakes of winter snow. 'You'll be next!' she says over her shoulder.

A leftover breadcrumb catches in Doria's throat. 'What about Rodolfo?' she splutters. 'He's older than me ...'

'Boys marry later than girls,' Mamma says, pushing herself up. 'I was seventeen when I married your father, and he was nearly twenty-five.'

'Seventeen? But I'm almost seventeen!'

'I know you are,' Mamma says, giving her a look.

The edge of the stool is cutting into Doria's thighs. 'What shall I do now?' she says, sliding off.

'You can put your things away and then make the polenta. I've got a bit of weaving to get on with before the children come in. It's a set of sheets. If there's a wedding in the air …' Doria crouches down in front of the pot of boiling water on the fire, upends the bag and watches a stream of yellow cornmeal flow into the bubbling water. She takes the wooden spoon and beats the mixture until it is smooth, settles back on her haunches and begins to stir, waiting for the grain to thicken into the polenta that will be cut into squares, fried, and eaten with a little fish or rabbit, bottled tomato, or herbs and a splash of oil. Her spoon moves slowly, inscribing wide circles and figures of eight, and as she follows it with her eyes, she thinks of her sister, Alice. And of growing up in this house where there had been no sliced-in-half dolls house, or wind-up horses, or chariots marked Lehmann and made in Germany. Instead, they had built castles from mud or played 'hit the wall', pulling buttons off their blouses to use in place of pebbles. There were airless evenings in the aia jumping over rows of drying corn, and long winter nights huddled round the fire, while chestnuts popped open on the grate and Papi played tunes on his mouth organ.

'You'll be next!' Doria closes her eyes and soon she is drifting off to that warm, dreamy place where anything is possible … And there, waiting for her, is Filippo …

Chapter 32
KEEP HOLY THE SABBATH

As the first streak of sunlight shows on the blue-black horizon, Signora Manfredi slips her feet onto the floor and treads quietly through to the main room. She opens the front door and shoos the chickens back out into the aia, pausing for a moment to breathe in the gentle dawn air. Towards the lake soft threads of sunshine are glowing over the mountain tops, while from the village the church bell is calling early risers to Matins, answered by bells from across the lake in Quiesa, Massarosa and Massaciuccoli. Emilia, struck by a sense of God's presence all around her, watches the light eke through the gaps in the clouds, then returns inside the house. God may have rested on this, his holy day, but there will be no respite for her. Yesterday evening, she had filled up the tub in front of the fire and first the boys, then the girls, had a bath while she busied herself with the Sunday clothes, taking them out of the wardrobe to air.

Everyone has one good outfit, made up in return for eggs, tomatoes, rabbit skins or whatever could be spared at the time, and each garment tells its own story as surely as any written account: the shawl that had warmed the shoulders of her own dear Mamma when she had taken to her bed, thin and listless from days of coughing up thick, black blood; the yellow dress, now more grey than yellow, that had passed from Alice to Doria; the white one, worn by the older girls for their first communion and which, with the addition of a check collar, now belongs to Lucia; Paolo's grey shorts, passed on from his brother; Rodolfo's suit, in which he will be married and buried, like her own dear husband; and finally her recently sewn black dress, her widow's uniform, its shoulders speckled with confetti-like dust.

Doria is lying awake next to Lucia listening to the crackle of corn husks in the mattress under her, home to the bugs that have feasted on her overnight, leaving her skin a mass of red, itchy bumps. Through the doorway she can hear her mother raking the fire then setting the table with just one plate and mug. Only Eva, the youngest, who hasn't yet taken first communion, will be sinking her teeth into the crusty new bread. Everyone else will have to wait until lunchtime.

Shifting onto her side, Doria's mind conjures up a warm buttery brioche dunked into sweet milky coffee. What she wouldn't give to be at the villa instead of bundled up beside Lucia, who had kicked and fidgeted the whole night long, but now is lying as still as baby Jesus in his manger. In the next bed are Paolo and Eva, their arms thrown open like a pair of swans in flight. Beyond them, next to the mirror, the Sunday clothes are hanging on the wall, her mother's black dress, a grim reminder of Doria's first day at the villa, when she'd mistaken the Befana for a real witch, and her own grey cotton, the colour of a storm-tossed sky. She thinks of the gowns in Miss Fosca's wardrobe, the purple satin trimmed with lace, the white muslin with puffed sleeves, the red chiffon with the matching jacket that sparkles. Oh, to wear one of those, if only for a few minutes!

The front door lets out a mournful creak. Mamma has gone outside to feed the chickens, but still Doria doesn't get out of bed. Instead, she lets her mind drift off to the villa, and the Maestro with his leg shut up in a coffin, his eyes full of sadness, a pretend smile on his face when he asks her to fetch a drop of whisky or turn the handle of his music machine. And now he can't even have the chocolates in the red box! If only she could do something to help him ...

'Doria, are you awake yet?'

'Coming, Mamma!' she calls, giving her itchy arm a quick rub. The dried cod, made fleshy by soaking in water overnight, slips through Doria's fingers and sizzles into the smoking hot oil. She adds garlic, bottled tomatoes and a sprig of rosemary, pops on the lid and slides the pan to the edge of the grate. By lunchtime, it will have turned into *stoccafisso*, chunks of succulent fish coated in a thick red sauce, to be eaten with polenta and the new bread.

'Come on everyone!' Mamma calls, steering her brood towards the door. 'Hurry up or we'll be late for Mass.'

Rinsing her hands, Doria pulls off her apron and runs after them. The path swerves left before opening out onto a track that runs towards the village, a track bearing other families ambling along in the warm spring air, the men in badly fitting suits, the women in dresses and headscarves, the adolescent girls turning to steal glances at their sweethearts, who wink and smile back. Mothers hold the hands of small children with scrubbed faces, stumbling along in shoes they are not used to having on their feet, while widows bring up the rear, mumbling Hail Marys and fingering their rosary beads. Along with their lives ground down by poverty, there is one element uniting this ever-growing group as it winds towards the church: not one of the adults is wearing shoes, which are strung around their necks like halters to preserve the soles.

The service over, Don Zeno is standing at the church door greeting his parishioners as they file out into the sun, his hands clasped in front of him in the same pose as the statue of Saint Joseph, the patron saint of his church, who stares lovingly into space from a plinth in the sacristy.

'Signor Gambogi, good day to you! ... Tommaso ... Concetta, Poldo, thank you for the tonic, those caper buds work miracles, don't they? ... Emilia, how are you? And the children, all fine? ... Good, good ...'

The priest's smile is hiding a pain in his lower back that is sending sharp twinges down one leg, as if his buttock is being prodded with a spike. He eases his shoulders back and looks out over the square, which during Mass has been transformed into a fairground of stalls selling pastries, cakes and fizzy drinks, brightly coloured balls, streamers, and balloons on sticks. The buzz of activity is accompanied by the sound of an unseen and out of tune accordion. Gypsy women in red skirts and matching lipstick mingle with the crowd, plying the weak-minded with charms and bracelets promising good luck. 'Look at them all!' the priest mutters. 'They're worse than Protestants!'

A group of women are chatting in the shady corner by the step, their voices coming to him like a plague of busy locusts. *Did you hear Signora Grassi has sprained her ankle? It's swollen up like a grapefruit ... That artist fellow has been hanging round the widow Rossi again ... No! You don't say! ... How are you today, Signora Manfredi? That's good, that's good ... Alice has a findanzato? Marco Pucci from the estate? Well, he's a hardworking lad ... Paolo Dardi has got a job in Corsica? They say the pay's nearly double ...'*

The priest knows that these conversations in which no detail, however trivial, is omitted, weave the fabric of life for people who can neither read nor write. But today he is not feeling as charitable as he should. *I suppose it gives them the chance to air their teeth!* he thinks, turning and hobbling onto the porch, then he locks the door behind him and carries on down the aisle to the sacristy. Signora Manfredi is looking around for her girls while half-listening to the tale of Signora Pezzi, who went to Doctor Falli for gastric flu, only to discover that she was expecting a baby after twenty years of childless marriage. *Ah! There they are, over by the bench in the shade. But who's that talking to Doria?* She strains forward, making out a tall figure with a pumpkin head. *Filippo!*

Mindful of her daughter's reputation, her first instinct is to rush over and put a stop to it, but then she pauses to consider another possibility. With Alice now engaged, there is nothing to stop Doria following in her footsteps, an idea she warms to the more she thinks about it. After all, Filippo is a good-natured lad who would put up with Doria's funny little ways, and with his father as the postmaster (a job with a pension as well as a steady wage), they would never go hungry. The strongest argument, though, and the one that sweeps away any doubts that might have been lingering in Emilia's mind is that by marrying, Doria would have to leave the villa, a place where no God-fearing girl should be expected to work. But things still had to be done properly.

Excusing herself, Doria's mother walks purposefully across the square. 'Doria, Lucia, Eva – it's time to go home. Ah, Filippo! *Buongiorno*, I didn't see you there. How's your mother? I heard she'd hurt her hand. The dog bit it? I see … Well, ask her to call on me and I'll make her one of my poultices. Now then, come on everyone. At this rate we won't be eating until suppertime!'

'But Mamma,' Lucia pipes up, 'Doria said she'd buy us a *buccellato!*'

'Don't be silly, Lucia! Doria doesn't have money to waste.'

'But she promised!' Lucia wails.

'That'll do, Missy. You know we don't eat sweet things in Lent. Now, where are the boys? Never mind. They can catch us up later.' Doria dawdles slowly behind her mother and sisters, her feet dragging along in the fine dust on the track. The border of the pathway is teeming with poppies, celandine, coltsfoot and daisies in brilliant hues of red, yellow and white, like the colours of Signora Elvira's paint palette, she observes. *Why shouldn't I spend a few soldi on raisin cake for Lucia and Eva if I want to? she thinks. It's my money, and I've worked hard for it! And how come Rodolfo and Paolo are allowed to stay on at the fair while I have to go home? And ... what was Mamma thinking of, asking Filippo's mother to call when she doesn't even like her. Not unless ...*

'Aiyee!' Doria's foot swipes a clump of stinging nettles, adding more bumps to her skin. Crouching down, she plucks a dock leaf from among the wildflowers and rubs it on the offending patch. A weekend at home is beginning to seem like a very, very long time. The table is set, the wine poured and water added, Mamma says grace, and suddenly the room is filled with the clatter of forks scraping up polenta and fish from the tin plates, followed by the sound of chewing, grinding and swallowing. Then, like birds at dawn, everyone starts chattering at once. *Did you see Signora Bianchi's hat? She needs two heads for that thing! ... Giorgio went to Doctor Falli and had all his teeth pulled out with the pliers ... Aiyee!*

Through the clamour, Rodolfo catches Doria's eye. 'Was that Filippo I saw you talking to in the *piazza*?' he asks, his tone accusing. A grasshopper jumps clean up Doria's windpipe, making her cough. Rodolfo tears off a piece of bread and squeezes it in his fingers, his eyes not blinking. 'If I see you with him again, you'll have my hand to answer to!'

'But I wasn't on my own!' Doria says quickly. 'Lucia and Eva were with me!'

Rodolfo's fist slams onto the table, making the glasses jump. 'Don't answer back!'

Doria turns to her mother for help.

'He's right, dear,' Mamma says sadly.

Doria looks down and shuffles her feet. Then, before she can stop herself, she jumps up and faces him. 'You think you've taken over from Papi, but you haven't – and you never will!' Then she turns and bolts through the front door, across the aia and onto the path, every step distancing her from Rodolfo, from the filth and grime, bringing with it a sense of relief, of happiness almost, so that by the time she reaches the lake and sees the jetty sticking out into the water like her own thirsty tongue, Doria has all but forgotten why she is there. The path is deserted, and there is no one by the shallows where Papi showed her how to catch tadpoles in a jar, crouching down to scoop the black-tailed dots from the water. She wanders aimlessly along, past Andrea's shack, looking around at the sky, the mountains, the patch of dark green on the other side of the lake that is the estate where Alice works. Alice who's getting married … *You'll be next!* Doria pushes her mother's voice away and continues until she reaches the rocky point, where she stops to gaze at the lake. Then, with an idea in mind, she turns and clambers over the boulders, avoiding the sharp edges that will cut her feet, until she comes to a low overhanging ledge, and here she sits down, leans her shoulders against the cool rock and dangles her toes in the water.

A clump of weed floats past, rippling like a jellyfish. Doria watches it drift out towards the fishermen's huts, and then, seized by an impulse, she scrambles up, slides her dress from her shoulders and lowers herself into the water, inch by freezing inch. Her feet find the silty slimy bottom of the lake, and she winces as it squelches up between her toes. Her bloomers have filled with air, buoying her up like a balloon. As they slowly deflate she edges around and wades out towards the huts, the icy water gripping her legs, her stomach, her breasts, until it is just below her chin.

The sun is high above her, pouring its gold onto the surface of the lake, and from the woods behind her Doria can hear the song of a nightingale courting his love, the short notes gathering in intensity as it trills, whistles, trills the melody to the sky. Doria stops to listen, entranced by sounds that seem to touch her very soul. And as she stands there, the water swirling around her, she thinks of Filippo, and she trembles. For she cannot swim, and if she stumbles and falls under the water, she fears she might drown.

Chapter 33
RETURNING TO LIFE

It is nearly the end of May, and Puccini is sitting in the shade of the oak tree in his wheelchair, which he calls his 'automobile without gas', waiting for Don Zeno to join him. Until a week or so ago, they would have met up at Club della Bohème, to play draughts and take a small glass of mid-morning wine. But Blackbird Legs, pushed into impecunity by his nonpaying guests (and tempted by a shifty-eyed agent who promised him a better life in a country he had never set foot in himself) has nailed up his shutters, packed his bags and set off for America, leaving nowhere for the lakeside friends to congregate. In fact, in the ten minutes or so since Poldo parked him here with his faithful hound, Nello, for company, the composer hasn't seen a single soul to greet, let alone to have a drink and chat with.

Straightening his rug, Puccini manoeuvres the wheelchair to the right, trying to get a better view of the bird stalking along the shoreline, which is surely a plover with its red feet, wispy crest, and habit of pausing before it jabs the mud. When it disappears behind a sandbank, he leans back and sucks in the heady fragrance of the white-starred jasmine behind him, where the villa railings are woven with glossy green foliage, the new shoots spiralling out like toddlers venturing away from their mothers for the first time.

A few weeks have passed since Puccini learned of Narciso Gemignani's death, weeks in which he has been the unwilling recipient of pressure so finely orchestrated that, were he not its target, he would have found himself quietly impressed. There

227

have been letters from Antonio and Fosca begging him not to distress their mother any further, a note from Iginia in her convent telling him that his soul is in peril, and that their own dear Mamma is watching him from heaven (for God's sake!). And comments left and right from his other sisters who, choosing to forget those early years when they had reviled Elvira, now feel emboldened to insist he should marry her. Don Zeno, too, makes his position clear, although the priest is a good old stick who doesn't need to be taken too seriously. Elvira, on the other hand, the one person from whom he would have expected a head-on assault, has said nothing, a circumstance that puzzles him, as does her demeanour, which is vague and distracted, unless the matter concerns Fosca and her soon to be born baby. *In any event, it makes no matter*, he thinks. His mind is made up, and it will take more than entreaties from his nearest and dearest to change it. *But I don't need to reveal my hand just yet, not while I'm still in this damn wheelchair.*

A whine from the shady spot by his side distracts Puccini from his thoughts. Nello is looking up at him, his tail wagging hopefully from side to side. 'All right, old fellow, you've waited long enough.' Reaching under the rug, he produces a paper bag, and from it a biscuit, which he tosses to the ground. The dog crunches it between his teeth. When he has swallowed every last bit, he looks up again, but the paper bag has disappeared, so he slumps down, rests his head on his paws and shuts his eyes.

Watching him, the composer draws a cigar from his pocket and rattles it against his ear, listening for the quality of the tobacco. A dragonfly agitated in the clear spring air darts this way and that, its wings shimmering red as it heads towards the water. Nello raises his head, gives a halfhearted growl then gives up. There will be hundreds of them before the day is out, and as Puccini strikes a match and rotates the aromatic cylinder in his mouth, he feels a momentary sadness for the beautiful insects that survive for just one day. Confoundedly, it is a thought that leads him to Corinna.

Although he has heard nothing from her since the accident, he knows she is waiting for him. She must be, for she is never far from his mind, sharing his daytime thoughts and suffusing some of his nights with the most passionate of dreams. Not only that. When he wheels himself to the piano, the music that flows from him is not his but hers; the notes of longing and pain, her longing and pain, as if her spirit is inhabiting his body. And today, at long last, his dreadful wait has come to an end. This morning Elvira left for Milan to be with Fosca for the birth, leaving him in the care of Doria and his widowed sister, Nitteti, who will go home each day after lunch. It is the opportunity he has been waiting for. But first he must send Corinna a note (brief, in case it falls into the wrong hands), and inveigle Doria into taking it to the post office for him.

Puccini's thoughts are interrupted by a scuffling at his feet, where Nello is worrying over a small pebble-like object in the dirt, rolling it back and forth with his paw. It is a dung beetle, curled up into a shiny black marble. 'Leave it alone, Nello!' The dog looks at him, then turns his head towards the road, distracted by the sound of a horse clopping along the path.

'Doctor Falli,' Puccini calls out, seeing a small figure in a brown hat astride a dappled grey. 'Hello! Good morning to you!' The doctor brings his horse to a halt, swings his leg over and slides to the ground. 'I was expecting Don Zeno,' Puccini says.

'You'll have a long wait,' the doctor replies. 'He's in church saying Mass. It's the feast of Sant' Emilio.'

'Good grief! Is it really? I'd quite forgotten. In my condition, one day is very much like another.'

'Mine, too,' Falli says. 'Anyway, I'm pleased I found you because I've had a letter from Doctor Colzi. He's coming to take the leg-iron off next Monday, but says you'll need a brace and walking stick for a good while longer.'

Puccini's face drops. 'A brace? And how am I supposed to …' Then he stops, remembering that the doctor is one of those intellectual types who seem to manage perfectly well without the pleasures of the flesh.

Falli, though, perceptive enough not to miss the point, assumes the wrong target. 'Don't worry, Maestro,' he says, with a quick, professional throat-clear, 'you and Signora Elvira will be waltzing again before the year is out.'

A cursory glance at Puccini's face would have told the doctor that he was off track, but at that moment Nello decides to take a run at his horse, snapping and jumping up at the animal's hind legs, causing it to whinny and rear up. Doctor Falli throws himself onto its neck and hauls himself into the saddle. Soothing the mare with calming words, he gives a parting wave and trots off, leaving Puccini to digest this new and unwelcome information.

A brace! A walking stick! Thrusting the cigar in his mouth, he sucks on it with quick little bursts, but the wretched thing has gone out, leaving a cold, bitter taste in his mouth. He spits it out and looks at it, and that is when he hears the grey, toneless voice that comes to him in unsuspecting moments.

Shame on you! it whispers. Shame!

After a lunch of fillet steak and zucchini flowers fried in batter, followed by pecorino cheese with a drizzle of oil and lots of black pepper, Puccini takes up his position near the studio door. First, there is Cook, who pulls her hat over her ears without bothering to look in the mirror before thumping down the corridor to the back door, then his sister, Nitteti, in a rush for Poldo to take her to the station. A few minutes later, he hears lighter footsteps.

'Doria,' he calls, 'can you spare a minute? Sit down, my dear. Here … where I can see you.'

Doria lowers herself carefully onto the edge of a chair, her eyes frosted with confusion.

'You're going to miss Signora Elvira while she's away, aren't you?' he begins.

'Yes, sir.'

He can barely hear her. 'I thought so,' he smiles. 'So while she's in Milan, you must come in here and sit with me. A little company cheers the heart, isn't that what they say?' Doria rubs her hands on her apron, leaving behind a damp smear. 'My dear,' he nudges gently. 'You're a trustworthy girl, aren't you?'

'Oh yes, sir!' If she moves any further forward, Doria will fall on the floor.

He nods in encouragement. 'So if I asked you to post a letter for me, you'd do that, wouldn't you … without mentioning it to anyone?' Now her gaze has moved to the coin he is holding up between his thumb and forefinger. 'Of course,' he carries on smoothly, 'I don't expect you to do extra chores for nothing. But it must remain ...' he lowers his voice, 'our little secret.' His magic is working. The strands of his charm are weaving themselves into her imagination, binding it up with their sticky promise. Doria nods, her eyes still fixed on the coin. Then she slides them down to meet his and gives him a smile of such innocent gratitude that he is obliged to turn his head away.

Chapter 34
GIULIO RICORDI RECEIVES A VISITOR

Giulio Ricordi looks up from his desk to see a greenish-yellow leaf carrying seedpods, from the linden tree outside, drooping through the window that Carlo, his clerk, had latched open earlier to let in fresh air on this glorious mild June morning.

'Oh, no you don't!' he says, rising to catch the offending item. *'Achoo! Achoo!'* Plucking the handkerchief from his breast pocket, Ricordi holds it to his nose, then with his other hand he takes the bract leaf to the window and pushes it through the opening, watching it hover for a moment before falling towards the bowler hats of the men hurrying to start their day's work.

Milan, his beloved city, which had been shamed over recent years by strikes, marches and the food riots that led to the assassination of the King, is a *gran signora* once again. It is resplendent in industry, bejewelled with new banks and financial institutions, and perfumed by people from the south who have flocked there to build a new life for themselves.

There is nothing more despicable than a rich man's scorn for the ambitions of the poor. Ricordi knows this, yet still he can whip up little enthusiasm for the renewed prosperity that has allowed his son, Tito, to undertake research into the disc recordings being pioneered in Germany and England, which is where the future of their company surely lies. To tell the truth, now that he is well into his seventh decade, Ricordi finds himself more attached to the past than the future. His slowing heart is filled with nostalgia for the era of the House of Ricordi's finest composers, for Bellini, Donizetti and Verdi. And although he knows La Scala will never wear such a diamond-studded crown again, at least not in his lifetime, he still longs for one last grand opera to be staged at his theatre; not just staged, but playing to sell-out audiences and critical acclaim, the winning trump card to trounce his hated rival, Sonzogno.

'Achoo! Achoo!' *Ricordi* closes the window and turns to face the work piled up on his desk: correspondence to be answered; ledgers to be countersigned; the latest set of corrections to *Madama Butterfly*, painstakingly transcribed from Giacomo's notebooks by the clerks in the print room; and on the top, a report from a private detective by the name of Sergio Zipproni that he has already read.

Since the delivery of the grand piano, Giacomo has been working as never before, producing some of his finest music, a circumstance that should console Ricordi for all the delays and difficulties of the past few months. And so it would if not for a series of reports from the detective, Zipproni. He was the sort of person who knows how to sniff the air, catching things most people miss, to question doormen and waiters, to blend into the wallpaper, his presence only intuited by the reek of his breath – a disgusting mix of caries, tobacco and cheap wine. Ricordi imagines it to be the trademark of the bars and brothels where Zipproni's murky business takes him. Following his conversation with Tito, *before* the accident, Ricordi determined to discover the identity of Giacomo's lover, then discreetly inform her husband of the situation (for certainly she would have one). So he commissioned the services of the shadow-like Zipproni, the idea of which still makes him shudder, as surely it had his grandfather before him when obliged to investigate that other scoundrel, Donizetti, who had disintegrated into the cruel madness of syphilis.

Returning to his desk, Ricordi picks up Zipproni's latest report. *The clerk at the post office in Turin confirmed that a young lady comes each day to enquire for mail, and that the same person sends letters to an address in Tuscany …* Opening the top drawer, he drops the report in to join the others, his mouth pursed in distaste. He does not wish to be reminded of Puccini's myriad lies and deceits, nor the trail that led Zipproni from the post office in Turin to a drinking shed in Tuscany, where a bribe to the proprietor (a man going by the ridiculous name of Blackbird Legs who had now already moved to America) revealed that the young woman's letters were collected and passed on to Giacomo by the old priest. Not only that, the envelopes were the same pale green as those that had been arriving before the accident. Corinna! It had been that little gold-digger all along, the one that he understands Puccini had solemnly sworn to renounce! And she was being aided by a priest! What was the world coming to?'

No one likes to be made a fool of, especially not someone of the standing of Giulio Ricordi, but that is precisely what he does feel when he remembers his response to Elvira's telephone call telling him of Gemignani's death, and the old priest's subsequent visit.

Elvira, my dear, the ten-month wait is an obstacle, I grant you, but all you need is a promise. Speak to Giacomo's sisters. Get them on your side, and the children, too, if you think it will help. However, I do advise caution. Nowhere are the men so simple and yet so complex as in your own dear Tuscany, with common sense yet so easily deceived, so respectable yet so disreputable – in a word, so good and so bad. Tread carefully, and time will do the rest …

'Achoo! Achoo!' Ricordi swipes his handkerchief from his pocket and pinches it to his nostrils. He should have known better than to trust Fate, that most fickle of creatures. Corinna – a girl younger than Fosca! *Damn Giacomo! How dare he break his word! Does he think there will be no consequences? Or has he become so puffed up he doesn't care? Well then, let him be reminded that his works, every single one of them, belong to the House of Ricordi. We made him, and by God, we can destroy him, too! All it would take is a few strokes of my pen.*

It is well into the afternoon when Ricordi closes the final ledger and reaches for the corrections to *Madama Butterfly,* sliding them to the right of his blotter the more easily to turn the pages. He has pored over the work so often he can hum at will the energetic opening bars as the servants prepare the little love nest for the lieutenant and his bride; the strains of the American national anthem reflecting Pinkerton's cavalier attitude, his declaration to the consul that the arrangement is just for fun, and has no bearing on his desire for a proper, home-grown wife; the consul warning him that Butterfly is a sensitive girl with a loyal heart, not the sort to toy with; the change in mood as the bridal party is heard offstage, and Butterfly's breathtaking entrance. Despite his initial opposition, Ricordi has been won over by the power and subtlety of the music, by the poignant presence of Butterfly herself, and by the terrible fate that awaits her. So much so that his hand shakes a little as it turns over the pages to find the place in Giacosa's prose.

Pinkerton and his ship have long since sailed away and Goro, the marriage broker, has found Butterfly a new husband in the figure of the wealthy *Prince Yamadori. She, though, is contemptuous. She already has a husband.* Ricordi leans forward to study the music, his eyes following notes of anguish and rage. And if Pinkerton doesn't return? – I could become a geisha again, or better still, die … A roll of percussion booms out, easing off into a stunned silence. 'Masterful!' Ricordi breathes. 'Quite masterful!'

Tap, tap …

Oh no! Not now! 'Yes, Carlo, what is it?'

'Your visitor is here, Signor.'

'My visitor? Oh heavens, I'd quite forgotten! Give me a minute and then show her in.'

The woman in the pale lemon outfit who steps into the room seems at first glance to be someone other than Elvira, for her smile is radiating the warmth of a summer day, and her eyes have none of that dark broodiness that Ricordi has seen so much of in recent years. 'Elvira my dear,' he says, puckering his lips to her glove. 'How lovely to see you. You're looking remarkably well!'

'Thank you, Signor Giulio,' she says, returning his smile. 'I must say I feel in top form, even with all the running around to do for the new baby.'

'And how is your little granddaughter?'

Elvira barely pauses to draw breath. 'Heavenly! Really the sweetest little thing, with fair hair, masses of curls, and so good she hardly ever cries. But I mustn't go on. Men don't feel these things in the same way as women … Thank you, by the way, for the dear little bear.'

'It's a teddy,' he says, 'named after Roosevelt.'

Elvira isn't listening. She is looking around, twitching her nose like a cat. 'Are those lilies I can smell?'

'Yes, my dear,' he says, gratified. 'The orange ones. I know they're your favourite.'

A shadow crosses her face. 'Oh dear,' she says, 'I'm very sorry, but I think they might bring on a headache.'

Ricordi moves towards the bellpull. 'In that case, my dear, I shall have them taken out.' The lilies have gone, and Elvira is sitting opposite him, her handbag open on her lap while her hand pushes aside knitting needles, a small phial of smelling salts and a brown leather purse.

'Here you are!' she says, taking out a glass pot and sliding it onto the table.

'But my dear, you shouldn't have! May I?' Ricordi twists open the lid and holds the pot to his nose, inhaling the sweet fragrance of fruit with the tang of citrus. 'Ahh …' he sighs, 'your very own marmalade. Am I right?'

Elvira gives a satisfied nod. 'I know your wife likes it.'

'She certainly does! How very kind!' He sets the pot down with exaggerated care. 'Now then, can I offer you a little refreshment? A glass of lemonade, perhaps?'

'Thank you, no. I can't stay long.'

'Well then, I imagine you're wondering why I asked to see you?' She nods again. 'The reason is quite simple. I need to know what's happening with Giacomo.'

This seems to surprise her. 'Giacomo? What is there to say? He sits at his piano for hours …'

'I rather meant, my dear,' he says gently, 'on the subject of marriage.'

Elvira pushes a stray knitting needle back into her handbag and snaps it shut. 'He has said nothing to me.'

'What! Nothing at all?'

Her cheek twitches. 'Not a word.'

Ricordi pauses, sensing an unexpected obstacle, then decides to change tack. 'And has he asked why I haven't been to visit him?'

Elvira pushes her bag to one side and straightens her skirt. 'At first he seemed offended, and then he said you would have your reasons.'

Ricordi frowns. 'That's strange. In the past, he has always court-ed my good opinion.' Elvira gives a little sniff but says nothing. He presses on. 'And is he is planning to go anywhere?'

'Where can he go in a wheelchair?' she asks dismissively.

'Indeed, but on Monday the plaster is coming off.'

'Then I suppose he can limp off wherever he likes.'

Ricordi has had enough of this baffling conversation. 'My dear,' he says, leaning forward, 'I believe it's time for you to broach the subject of marriage.'

'Really?' she says huffily. 'I thought the man was supposed to do that.' Then her voice softens. 'Listen, Signor Giulio, I am grateful to you for all your support over the years, truly I am. But for my part, I have decided to spend more time with Fosca and the baby.'

'Here in Milan?'

'Certainly in Milan.'

'And Giacomo?'

She shrugs. 'He may please himself, just as he has always done.'

Ricordi raises his hands, showing her the palms. 'Elvira,' he says urgently, 'what on earth is going on?'

She looks into her lap and then at him. 'Signor Giulio,' she says, measuring out her words, 'you more than anyone know that I have stuck by Giacomo through thick and thin, despite insults from his family, his friends and society at large. What did I expect in return? A little love and respect, both of which he has chosen to deny me. Now I find myself the grandmother of an adorable little child, a circumstance which offers me an-other chance of happiness: a different sort, I grant you, but at least one that is freely given. Tell me, you who know Gi-acomo's character so well, why I shouldn't accept?' Elvira's heartfelt speech, delivered with an honesty that is rare outside the confines of a family, strikes Ricordi in a place where there are no words, and so he turns his head and looks at the portrait of his grandfather above the fireplace, while into the silence crashes a wave of anger towards Giacomo, whose cowardice has pushed this poor woman into wanting nothing more than to stay close to her daughter and gather her grandchild safely in her arms.

'So, if you'll excuse me,' Elvira says, standing up, 'I must get back.'

'Of course, my dear,' he says, rising himself.

'And you'll come to the christening?' she asks, heading towards the door.

'I wouldn't miss it for the world. Does the little girl have a name yet?'

'Renata.'

'Renata …' a faint memory arises, then fades. 'A lovely name,' he says. But Elvira has already swept out of the room. From the window Ricordi watches her climb into the taxicab, which moves off down the street. When it is out of sight, he returns to his desk, seats himself squarely to the blotter and pulls out a sheet of dazzling white vellum. Lifting his pen, he dips it into the black ink and drives it across the surface of the paper, his words forming an icy torrent that would chill the most hardened of hearts. Yet strangely, as his nib marks out the upstrokes and downstrokes of his fury, his mind conjures up the image of an eager young man with a strong sunburnt face, hat at a jaunty angle, hands in pockets, and a step that is swinging and rhythmical, a country fellow with a touch of rough shyness …

This time, Giacomo would be left in no doubt as to the extent of his displeasure.

Chapter 35
CORINNA DECIDES TO ACT

Feeling the need to change her routine, Corinna bounces into the post office early one morning, hoping for better luck. 'Good morning. Is there a letter for me? My name is …'

'I know what your name is,' Sharpnose interrupts. 'You've been coming here every day for months. Just a moment!'

And there it is, being pushed under the grille. Corinna looks at the familiar handwriting and feels her legs weaken. If there was a chair, she would sit down.

Not many minutes later, she is hoisting open the window of her classroom, pausing to gaze up at a sky that is suddenly the brightest of blue. How can she teach this morning when she has become as light as air and her feet are not heavy enough to keep her anchored to the ground? She pats the pocket of her skirt, feeling Giacomo's note through the lining. Two words and an exclamation mark. This is what she has been waiting for all these hours, days, weeks and months: just two words and an exclamation mark. *Telephone me!*

Corinna turns and breathes in the dry air of the classroom, the chalk and ink mingled with dust, the breaktime panini of cheese and salami, the musty smell left after the children go out to play. Shiny white inkwells, like a row of Cyclops eyes, stare up at her from the benches, while her own desk stands elevated like the bridge of a ship. Heading to it, she picks up her notes, finds a good length of chalk and begins to write on the board, her body swaying happily in time with her hand. In a minute the bell will ring, bringing her pupils in from the playground.

Since that first dreadful afternoon, Corinna has been sheltering under the wing of Aurelia and her family who, believing her visits to be a consequence of her mother's worsening condition, quietly offered handkerchiefs for her watery eyes and left her to the early roses and chirruping birdsong of the garden. Their kindness made her feel guilty, for it was being elicited on grounds that were less than honest. Aurelia, though, dismissed her concerns. 'Dear thing, how very bourgeois you are! I don't see that it should matter to them why you are suffering!'

Yet still she felt uneasy when Aurelia's mother brought her yet another glass of verbena tea, or Maurizio, now in the family practice, sought to cheer her up with tales of his more amusing cases, like the market stallholder who denounced a donkey for chewing up his vegetables. Only from Aurelia has there been the occasional glance with an equivocal edge. Corinna knows why this is, or believes she does. Her friend doesn't care for Giacomo, or rather, since she had never met him, she doesn't like what he represents – a public figure wasting his time on the elite when he should be devoting himself to the poor. And implicit in this is a criticism of Corinna herself: she should have chosen differently, chosen better. She has never found the words, or perhaps the courage, to explain that she has no desire to set the world to rights, that her palette is smaller, the colours paler and less well defined, brought to life only by her feelings for Giacomo.

Placing the chalk on the ledge, Corinna turns and runs her hands down her skirt, waiting for the bell, and for the onslaught of pushing, jostling children it will bring. And as she stands there, a wave of feeling suddenly hits her, bringing with it all the distress of the past few months when she had been lost in a tangle of endless days and sleepless nights. As an outcast (for this is what she had become), she had to face daily raids on her sensitivity, her father's unseeing indifference to her misery, the nurse's questioning stares, Aurelia's tacit criticism. The time in the classroom dragged by, the faces of the children that followed her like sunflowers becoming unbearable to her, their cheerful voices so jarring it seemed as if the noise would shake her to bits. Most days after school, she would trudge to the post office, to be met by Sharpnose's *Not today,* delivered with the contemptuous nod of one who really wanted to say, *There you are, Miss, you had it coming to you!* But there was worse still to come. As time passed, Giacomo began to slip away from her, his features to blur and his image to fade until all that was left in the haze of her consciousness was the sound of his fingers clicking in search of a lost word.

'Good morning children!'

Here they are, bundling into their places. 'Good morning, Miss,' they chant back.

'How wonderful to hear such happy voices! Now, settle down … quickly please …' She draws breath. 'Today we'll be studying Florence. Who can tell me exactly where it is?'

'Italy!' a lad suggests from the front row, his answer provoking giggles from around the room.

'Very good, Franchi, but can you be a *little* more precise?'

'Down south, Miss.'

'You're heading in the right direction, although it's more central than south … Tuscany, in fact.'

'Is that so, Miss?' The comment is followed by more giggles.

Corinna sweeps her gaze around the class, commanding silence with her eyes. 'Florence,' she begins, 'was founded in 59 BC as a retirement village for the troops of Julius Caesar's campaigns. Much later, in the fourteenth century, it grew into one of the largest cities in Europe, thanks to the silk and cloth trade, the wealth used by the lords of the city, the Medici family, to promote art and music as well as astronomy, mathematics and navigation.' She turns and points to the board. 'Now copy these notes into your exercise books. Neatly, mind!'

The children lift their desk lids to pull out exercise books and pencils, and as they settle to their task, Corinna reaches into her pocket for Giacomo's note.

Telephone me! How could two words bring such joy and relief while at the same time bury the terrible longing, the entranced state of being, her feeling more dead than alive? She looked back on the days of duty and nothingness, the sleepless nights when in her fear and loneliness she had clipped the pearl earrings to her ears, murmuring to herself, like poor deluded Emma Bovary, 'I have a lover! I have a lover!'

'Miss!'

Corinna looks up. 'Yes, Franchi, what is it?'

'Your eyes are watering, Miss. Do you want to borrow my hand-kerchief?'

After school Corinna takes the tram into the centre of the city and walks one block to the majestic five-storey building where Aurelia has an office in the family law firm. Inside the entrance is the janitor's booth, and as Corinna nears it, she sees a reflection in the glass of a nondescript man who had been sitting opposite her in the tram. She raps urgently on the door, where the janitor is reading a newspaper, a pipe hooked onto his lip.

'Yes?' he says, without removing his pipe.

'I'm being followed,' Corinna says, 'by a man with a birthmark on his neck.'

An ironic eyebrow arches up. 'Is that so, Miss?'

'Yes, he's out there …' She points behind her to the road.

The janitor strains forward. 'I can't see anyone.'

Corinna turns, and sure enough, the man has disappeared. 'He must have slipped into a doorway.'

'Perhaps so, Miss. Would you like me to call the *carabinieri?*' The question is designed to sound facetious.

'No thank you,' she says primly, 'that won't be necessary. I'm here to see Dottoressa Pilotti.'

'First floor,' the janitor says, sucking on his pipe and disappearing behind a haze of smoke. Upstairs, Corinna knocks firmly on the last door at the end of a long corridor.

'*Avanti!*'

She turns the doorknob and there, sitting at a large desk, is the familiar red halo attached to a telephone.

'Come in, come in!' Aurelia mouths, her face opening into a smile. 'One tick and I'll be with you …'

Corinna sits down opposite her and looks around, surprised to see a photograph on the desk of Luigi Galleani, the anarchist from the dingy bar who had appalled her with his revolutionary ideas.

'*Grazie … sì … grazie … arrivederci.*' Aurelia drops the receiver onto the stand and sprawls back in her chair. 'What an idiot! Honestly, sweetness, you're better off out of this game.'

'It would seem so!' Corinna agrees, nodding at the papers, notes and newspaper clippings littering the surface of the desk. 'But why are you working at this hour?'

Aurelia sighs. 'I wouldn't be if that fool hadn't lost the contract … Oh, you mean this?' She surveys the mess. 'Well, this isn't really work, is it?' Leaning forward, she lowers her voice. 'He's asked me to help him.'

'Who has?'

'Luigi Galleani, of course!'

'Really? Doing what?'

'Compiling a pamphlet. I've only got one page so far, but it's going to pack a punch.'

'I'm sure it will.'

'I'm planning a piece on free love,' Aurelia continues, caught up in her own excitement, 'and another against the tyranny of government and do-gooding socialists. Luigi himself is working on a manual called "Health is in you".'

'It sounds like something my pupils should read.'

Aurelia throws back her head and laughs. 'I don't think so. It's a bomb-making manual!'

Corinna's mouth drops. 'Aurelia, you're mad! You'll end up in prison!'

Her friend's tone switches from amused to deadly serious. 'Prison? And what do you imagine that is?' she says, sweeping her hand towards the window. 'Do you suppose the people out there have any more say in their lives than prisoners?'

Corinna knows better than to argue. 'Look!' she says brightly, sliding Giacomo's note across the desk. 'I haven't come to talk politics, I'm here to show you this!'

Aurelia glances down. 'Ah, so that's why you're looking so happy.'

Corinna, stung by the tone, snatches the note back. 'It's not what you think!'

Aurelia looks surprised. 'And what do I think?'

'That it's just a dalliance with an older man. It's not like that at all. We love each other. We really do …' And then to her horror, she bursts into tears.

Aurelia jumps up, comes around and hugs her. 'Dear thing, please don't cry! I'm not judging you. How could I when I don't believe in such things as morality? But I do care about you, and it would be very easy for a man like him to take advantage …'

Corinna doesn't let her finish. 'We're going to be married,' she sniffs, 'after the premiere of Madama Butterfly.'

Aurelia straightens up and gives an awkward little laugh. 'Gracious! You kept that one to yourself.'

'Yes, well,' she says, searching her pockets for a handkerchief, 'Giacomo made me promise not to tell anyone. But I don't see the need for secrecy now.'

'And his ...?'

'Elvira? That was over years ago.'

'I see ...' Aurelia rubs the side of her mouth, thinking. 'So if he wants to speak to you on the telephone, why not in person?'

Corinna stares at her. 'You mean just turn up at the villa?'

'Why not? It's perfect weather for a day out in the country. And I'll come with you, just in case you run into difficulties.'

Chapter 36
PUCCINI WAITS FOR
CORINNA'S CALL

Three years have passed since Pinkerton's ship sailed away, leaving Butterfly alone with Suzuki, her maid. By now, no one expects the lieutenant to return – no one, that is, except Butterfly.

One day we will see
There on the far horizon
One fine day, we'll see
a distant wisp of smoke
rising on the horizon.
Then the white ship
will appear in the harbour,
thundering out its signal.
You see? He's come back! ...

Puccini drops Giacosa's verse onto the score table and reaches for the silver box, lights a cigarette, inhales deeply and counts to five. Five! ... The number of days since Doria took his note to the post office ... the number of days in which he has not done a jot of work, for every time his fingers touch the ivory keys, his thoughts turn to Corinna. *Why hasn't she telephoned?* The waiting is driving him out of his mind! So much so that yesterday, after supper, he asked Doria to bring him a jug of ice, which he added to shot after shot of single malt whisky, gulped down while listening to the voice of his friend, Caruso. After that, instead of blissful unconsciousness, he lay on his bed tossing and turning, his stomach on fire, his skin exuding sweat as if he had been buried alive. This morning, unsurprisingly, he woke to a parched mouth and a splitting head that made it impossible for him to arrange his thoughts in any semblance of order; a condition which, despite a handful of aspirins, refused to abate, as did the churning in his guts that had him picking at his breakfast like a bird. Puccini rests his cigarette in the ashtray and picks up another folio.

Butterfly hears a siren, rushes outside and sees Pinkerton's warship approaching the harbour. He has come back! Beside herself with joy, she exhorts Suzuki to help her decorate the house with blossom, then prepare for the long night's wait ahead:

I'm not the same as I was!
This mouth has sighed too much,
and my eyes have gazed into the distance for too long ...

And suddenly Puccini is back in the velvet-lined theatre in London, his heart stilled by the strange and moving silence, his gaze fixed on an evening sky imperceptibly deepening to an inky purple, to a star twinkling in the black, leading to the gentle glow of a pink dawn ...

'Corinna! Oh Christ ...'

'Maestro ...' Doria is at the door. 'I knocked,' she says nervously.

He attempts a smile. 'Of course you did, my dear. I was off with the elves ... What is it?'

'A letter ...'

And now he sees the dazzling white envelope in her hand. 'Bring it here!' he says, his expression widening with joy.

Doria lifts the pillow from Miss Fosca's bed and slides it into the pillowslip, plumps it up and straightens the crisp, freshly ironed surface, then inspects the row of flat pearl buttons lying against the seam. Should she start from the outside and work in, or from the inside and work out? Or even go from edge to edge? She likes playing these little games as she goes about her tasks, standing on one foot and then the other as she dusts the banisters, or lining up the ornaments by colour, shape or size, depending on her mood. And now that Cook and Signora Nitteti have left for the day, and the Maestro is downstairs having his afternoon nap, she has all the time in the world to indulge her little fancies.

Laying the pillow back on the bed, Doria turns to face the chest of drawers by the window, where an assortment of decorative boxes is laid out on a lace cloth. Crossing over, she stands in front of them, taking them in with her eyes; the varnished rosewood, the white porcelain with painted fairies around the sides, the pink heart covered in speckled shells. This is the one she likes best! She reaches out and lifts the lid, enchanted as a ballet dancer the size of her fingernail begins twirling round to a faint, clinky tune. When it stops, she picks the trinket up, blows away the dust and pops it into her apron pocket. Stealing is a sin, but surely Miss Fosca wouldn't mind if she kept it in her room for a day or two?

Before Signora Elvira left for Milan, she gave Doria a shopping list. *This afternoon, Doria, you're to go to the village and fetch these things.* But after what happened in the morning, Doria forgot all about her errand, and the next day Silvia complained that they were out of soap flakes, and then Cook joined in, yelling, 'How am I supposed to make the pasta with no salt, you daft girl!' Luckily Signora Nitteti heard her shouting and came into the kitchen, giving her a look like a fox about to take a hen. She's nice, Signora Nitteti, with her funny little sparrow walk and her head held to one side. And she never shouts. Never. She's got brown eyes, smaller than the Maestro's, but just as sad. Cook says she doesn't have a lira to bless herself with and would starve if not for him.

Doria pulls the music box from her pocket and rests it on her palm, gazing at its prettiness and wondering whether to wind it up again. All the while, her head is invaded by thoughts of the incident that made her forget the shopping, and no matter how hard she tries, the thoughts just won't go away … Signora Elvira left instructions that all the bed linen should be washed while she was in Milan, and so on that first morning, instead of dusting, sweeping and polishing, Doria had given Silvia a hand in the laundry, piling the sheets into the copper and rinsing them in the tub. It was heavy work, but not as bad as at home where everything had to be carried down to the lake and back, and in the villa they didn't use ashes from the grate to bleach the whites, so there was no scum to scrape off.

When Doria had finished pegging out the last load, Cook told her to keep an eye on the beans on the stove while she went out to fetch the vegetables. And that's just what Doria had done, standing over the simmering saucepan with the lid in one hand and the wooden spoon in the other, stirring the sauce of tomatoes, onion and herbs. *Mmm* ... it smelled good. Just one little taste, then ... Lifting the spoon, she took a careful sip, and then another. Which is when she remembered the chocolate box tucked away on the top shelf of the pantry. But she'd have to be quick! Dragging a stool across, she clambered up, reached for the box and prised off the lid, but just as her fingers were digging out a sugar jelly, she heard footsteps behind her in the kitchen. *Oh no!* The stool began to wobble, then rock, then tip towards the ground. 'Help!'

A moment later, two strong arms grabbed her around the middle and slid her down to safety. 'That was close!' a familiar voice said.

'Filippo! What are you doing here?'

'It's Monday,' he said with a chuckle. 'I've come to make your boss look pretty!'

Then suddenly everything went dark, like the moon crossing in front of the sun. Cook was standing at the back door. 'Doria!' she thundered, stomping over to the stove. 'Where are you, you useless girl? I can smell the beans burning from outside!'

Doria peeped nervously around Filippo, and there was Cook, staring at them both, her cheeks the colour of a boiled ham. 'What the devil's going on?' she roared, grabbing the spoon from the pot. 'You scoundrel! You cur! Think you can make off with the maid under my eyes, do you? I'll teach you a thing or two!' Whirling the spoon in the air, at the same time launching a glob of beans, she lunged at Filippo, but he was too quick for her. With a shriek, he dived through the door into the garden and disappeared around the side of the laundry.

'That's got rid of him!' Cook said with a satisfied grunt. Then pointing at the floor, 'You, girl, you'd better get on and clean up that mess. Your intended won't be showing his face around here again for a while!'

'*Intended?*' The word slipped from the corner of Doria's mouth.

Cook gave one of her cruel laughs. 'Are you stupid, girl? It's all round the village that you and him are going to married before the year's out, although I can't say I know why. Men! They're all the same, animals, the whole ruddy lot of them. Now you get on and clean up!' And with that she turned and stomped back outside.

Doria stared at the red streaked beans lying on the floor like pieces of bloodied flesh. Was it true, what Cook said? And was that why Mamma had asked Filippo's mother to call at the house? Was she to marry him and go and live in a cottage somewhere, where nothing would ever gleam or shine no matter how hard she scrubbed or polished – a place with no nice food, or clothes, or things to look at? Doria bit down into the sugar jelly, releasing its juicy sweetness. '*O Santa Zita,* don't let it happen! Please!' Determined to push all thoughts of this incident far from her mind, Doria tucks the music box into her pocket, picks up the feather duster and starts busily dusting the dolls on Miss Fosca's shelf, flicking at the shiny ringlets, the new moon tiaras and the strange foreign clothes. Then with another idea in mind, she crosses to the wardrobe and takes out the purple gown trimmed with lace, holds it up against her and runs her hand down the material, feeling its smoothness under her fingers. A tune has started up in her head, a tune that has her jigging from side to side. Pulling off her cap, she unpins her hair, enjoying the feel of its weight uncurling onto her shoulders and down her back. There is music everywhere, outside her and within, music that has her swaying like a milk thistle in a breezy field, her arms, her legs, her fingers and toes. And now she is twirling around, going faster and faster as she trips across a dance floor in the arms of a man.

So full of music is Doria that she doesn't hear the doorbell at the first ring. It is only the second peal, long and insistent, that breaks into her reverie. 'Oh heavens!' Dropping the gown on the bed, she rushes along the corridor and down the stair to answer the front door.

There are two women on the doorstep, one tiny, with pale skin and eyes like one of Miss Fosca's dolls, and the other with hair flaming red like fire who is so tall she is blocking the sun. 'We have come to see Maestro Puccini,' the tall one says, not blinking.

Doria looks at her, seeing no features, only hair. There is something tapping against the doorstep. She looks down and sees a pink parasol with a ruffle like a meringue. 'Ooh ...' she sighs.

'Giacomo,' the small one insists, 'is he at home?'

Giacomo? Doria steps back, misses her footing and bangs into the door. *That woman said the Maestro's name like she had a sugar jelly in her mouth!* She looks once more at the parasol, trying to collect her thoughts. *What do they want, these strange women, with their fancy clothes and funny voices? ...* And then she has it! *O Santa Zita! These are the floozies Cook was talking about, the devil women who come and take men away to live in sin! And they're here for the Maestro, now that Signora Elvira has gone to Milan!*

Understanding everything and nothing, Doria draws a breath, about to tell the biggest lie of her life. 'No!' she says, firmly.

There is an awkward silence, then the red-haired one says, 'Are you sure the Maestro isn't in?'

Doria looks down and shuffles her feet.

'Then what about the Signora?'

'Signora Elvira?' Doria says uncertainly, looking up.

'Yes, who else but Signora Elvira?' Flamehead says sharply.

Doria looks from one to the other. Curls of thick mist have filled her brain, fogging up her thoughts ... and then suddenly her mind clears. 'Yes,' she says, looking the tall one in the eye, 'Signora Elvira is at home'.

'I see. Then perhaps we can have a word with her?' The little one gives a start, but the other one puts a hand on her arm and says, 'No time like the present, dear thing.'

Doria draws another breath. 'Signora Elvira is resting and is not to be disturbed.'

'I trust she isn't ill,' the little one says.

'Oh, no!' Doria blurts out, lost in a tangle of her own making. 'It's on account of the baby.'

'The baby?' the two of them chorus.

'Yes. It's only a few days old ...'

'Christ!' Flamehead says.

Doria crosses herself.

The small one clutches the other's arm, her almond eyes suddenly dull and flat.

'Come on, Corinna,' the tall one says. 'Let's get out of here!'

And with that, they turn and hurry down to the gate.

CHAPTER 37
PUCCINI SITS BY THE LAKE

A week has gone by since the two young women came to the villa, and Puccini, knowing nothing of their visit, is sitting by the water with Don Zeno, catching a little mid-morning sunshine.

'Did you know there was a patron saint of haemorrhoids?' the priest says.

Puccini raises his head, which feels heavy and sluggish, as if molten lead has been infused into his brain. 'What did you say?'

'Haemorrhoids,' Don Zeno repeats. 'I'm surprised you haven't got them, sitting in that wheelchair.'

The composer stares morosely at the water. 'It's the only damned thing I haven't got.'

'Saint Gonçalo,' the older man continues, 'Portuguese … thirteenth century.'

'We had a Portuguese cook once,' Puccini mutters, 'in my grandparents' house in Celle. She had a moustache …'

Don Zeno continues as if he hadn't heard. 'I pray to him every day, but it doesn't make a blind bit of difference.'

There is a pause while Puccini takes this in, then he says, 'Perhaps you should consult Poldo. He's not a saint, but he does seem to have a cure for just about everything.'

'Yes,' the priest agrees, 'he's good with the body, but what about the soul?'

'The soul?'

'Yes, Giacomo, the soul. A guilty conscience is like poison running through your veins, numbing your sensibilities and blinding you to the infinite wisdom of the Holy Spirit. The wages of sin and all that …' The comments are aimed at him, but Puccini is

252

neither offended nor annoyed. He is merely lost, stunned, incapable of responding. Don Zeno rises slowly to his feet. 'I must go,' he says. 'It's time for confession.'

'It probably is,' the composer replies. He watches the priest climb awkwardly onto his bicycle and pedal off along the path, then turns his head and stares at the mountains, the shoreline, and the thick curtain of reed hiding a honking quacking chorus of waterfowl waiting in the wings of their watery theatre. It is a landscape as familiar to him as his own body, one that in the past has overwhelmed him with its scale and beauty, with the drama of its subtly changing shades. Now it seems as bland and lifeless as a desert littered with dead animals' bones bleached by an unforgiving sun. Not only has his world lost its colour, but its tempo has changed, slowing to the beat of a failing heart; his music, the one thing that could save him, silenced by thoughts of Corinna, and the vilifying words of Giulio Ricordi's letter, tucked under his rug.

You have offended me by not keeping your word, your promises ... Puccini closes his eyes, but the words are still there, grinding out their grim accusations. *You have never understood the difference between love and a filthy obscenity which destroys the moral perception and the physical vigour of a man. Is it possible to think that sadistic lust has more of a grip on you than does your pride as an artist and as a man, than the insistent pleas of your family and friends? Oh! By God! This is too much. Come on, Puccini. Come on, dear Giacomo – as painful as it might seem at this moment, break this chain of lewd excitement, and rise up to nobler and higher ideas* ...

'Good day, Maestro ...'

Puccini opens his eyes and sees the matchstick figure of Mingo, the postman. 'What do you want?' he growls.

'Sorry to disturb you, Maestro, but I need a signature.'

'What for?'

Mingo holds up a small square parcel. 'It's from Turin ...'

'Turin? Turin!'

'There's a fee to pay,' the postman adds slyly, 'but I can always come back another day, when Signora Elvira is at home.'

'How much?' Puccini asks, trying to disguise the excitement in his voice.

'Signora Elvira usually gives me three … I mean five lire …'
'Five? That's direct robbery! Oh, never mind! Here you are,' he tosses a coin to the ground. 'Now go away and leave me in peace!' Doria looks up from her dusting, and through the French windows sees Mingo trotting along the path, waving his fist in a victory salute. Thinking to spare him the bother of coming to the front door, she steps out under the awning, which is when she hears a loud splash, as if something heavy, like a log, has fallen into the lake.

'Aiuto! Help! Help!' Dropping her duster, she tears along the path and through the back gate to where Dario, Bruno the wife-beater, and another burly reed-cutter are hauling a body from the water.

'Quick, girl!' Dario shouts, 'Go and get a blanket!'

'O Santa Zita!'

The sodden load groans and chokes out a mouthful of water. 'Christ alive!' it gasps. 'It's bloody freezing in there!' It was an accident. Everyone says so, even Signora Elvira, who rushes back from Milan as soon as she hears the news. The wheelchair brakes had failed, and being so close to the water, Puccini could do nothing when it started to roll down the bank. The composer, on the other hand, gives no explanation. His tumble into the lake had chilled him to the bone, and by evening he is shivering hot and cold with a fever, his throat ragged, a toneless bark the only sound to emerge from his mouth.

Doria has no time to listen to all the hubbub that surrounds the accident because she is run off her feet filling the bedwarmer with hot coals and preparing throat compresses and infusions of borage for the Maestro. But at the end of the day, when she retires to her room more exhausted than usual, she takes a moment to lift the corner of her mattress and gaze at what is hidden there; the coin that the Maestro had given her for taking his letter to the post office (which she'll use on Sunday to buy pastries for Lucia and Eva), and a funny sort of glass jar with an old lid, blue inside, that she picked up from the mud near the overturned wheelchair. In it is a scrap of paper with two words – one too terrible to say! – and a pair of earrings like the ones the gypsies sell, which she'll give to Alice on her wedding day.

Chapter 38
A FIGURE APPEARS

It is November, five weeks after Puccini's tumble into the lake, and the composer is standing at the French windows watching dark clouds roll across the sky, tipping their drenching load onto hapless villagers as they trudge through the thick sludgy earth. The rain will not let up. It has been pouring for days and days, the sky blurred and swollen, the field's drains and ditches gurgling away, the brook overflowing near Bernardo's beehives, leaving them stranded under the dripping branches of the acacia trees. Everywhere water is standing in puddles and ponds, while fast moving streams and tributaries gush into the lake, raising the level perilously close to its margins, and swamping the jetty where Puccini's new motorboat is moored. Poldo, who is leaning out of the studio window trying to fix a faulty catch, looks up, wipes the raindrops from his eyes, and mutters through clenched teeth, 'The Almighty is emptying his bladder on us!'

Puccini cannot think back to that day he fell into the lake without shaking his head in bafflement. Did he dream it, or had Mingo's parcel really contained his mother's pearl earrings, those that had gone missing from the chalet all those years ago? And the scrap of paper, no bigger than a postage stamp, with *You bastard!* written on it in Corinna's hand – had that also been a figment of his imagination? How could it be so? He still remembers the weight of the tiny crystal jar in his hand, the tarnished silver lid, the shock when he opened it and saw what was inside, a shock so immense he had jumped to his feet (more of a lurch, given the leg brace), setting the wheelchair in motion and pole-axing him into the water. Yet afterwards, when he sent Poldo to retrieve the jar and its contents, the gardener could find nothing but Giulio Ricordi's letter, transformed into an ink-streaked sodden lump of papier-mâché. Even Mingo, when questioned, denied all knowledge of the parcel, and had certainly never asked for any fee.

Puccini will never know the truth, but in the weeks that follow, he finds himself buried under the weight of an intense nothingness, as if he and time itself have both been suspended. His days are drifting nowhere, the ebb and flow of his thoughts too painful to bear. Even now, after all these months, when he remembers Corinna and the love he has lost, tears run down his cheeks, as real as the raindrops pelting the saturated earth. One weekday after lunch, Puccini shuts himself away in his studio, giving strict instructions that he is not to be disturbed. Taking a glass of whisky over to the piano, he settles down and begins to play, his fingers finding the pentatonic scale that evokes both Butterfly and the Corinna he once knew. And as he picks out the notes, a figure appears to him, a slender woman lit up by a shaft of light coming from an immense darkness. And she is not alone. Standing near her, her head bowed, is another woman who so resembles her that the pair could be twins, an impression enhanced by the fact that they are both wearing silk gowns and have blossom pinned in their sleek black hair. Between them, clutching their hands, is a small boy with oriental eyes, a son about to meet his father for the first time.

A tune is taking shape in Puccini's head, a long, overarching melody that calls forth the breeze of the night air, the heady fragrance of exotic blooms, the pulse of the unknown. He starts to sing along – *good grief, what am I doing?* – loudly at first, his head thrown back, then easing off, the notes becoming softer, more muted, until all that can be heard coming from his mouth is little more than a gentle hum.

Elvira is standing at the drawing room window watching the rain splash onto the window ledge, forming glistening pools that swell then burst over the edge and trickle to the ground. Like tears, she thinks, being squeezed from a vast implacable sky. Like the tears she has shed for Renato, her lost son, and for

Giacomo. But not anymore. She reaches out to straighten one of the long-stemmed roses (yellow and without perfume) that have replaced the lilies, and as her fingers tug at the offending bloom, her mind wanders back over the events of the past few weeks.

When Elvira heard of Giacomo's fall into the lake, she immediately rushed back to be by his side. Of course she had, for who else would care for him as she did? And this time, he was appreciative of her efforts, holding her hand as if he never meant to let it go, and moaning in his fever. 'I need you, Elvira … Don't leave me here alone, I beg you!' And so she had abandoned her plan of transferring to Milan, and instead invited Fosca to bring the baby to the lake for the summer, where the air was fresher and there was Doria to help.

She had accompanied Giacomo to the premiere of *Tosca* in Paris, a trip that proved a great success. The French capital, an elegant city at the best of times, was sliding gracefully into autumn, the trees in the Bois de Boulogne a magnificent mosaic of golds, yellows and fiery reds. Inspired by the beauty of the setting and buoyed by the excellent efforts of the Opéra Comique, Giacomo tried walking without his stick for the first time and managed rather well. Then, at the opening, he insisted that she be given pride of place in the box, and the next day took her to the Galeries Lafayette, where she bought a set of cake forks for Ida, and silver dishes for herself.

Elvira gives the rose a final tweak and turns to face the mantelpiece, where the photograph of Fosca and Renato as young children is now proudly displayed next to the image of her mother. She has been on a journey, she realises, as she gazes at the angelic infant with the dark eyes, not just to another country, but to another part of herself – the part that harboured lost love and hope, the part that from time to time would reveal itself obliquely in outbursts that cut her, and others, like shards of painful glass.

Now her journey has come to an end. It happened when, spurred on by the heightened sense of love and joy that Fosca's baby brought her, she wrote to Renato, telling him of his new niece, and assuring him that he had a family waiting to welcome him with open arms. To her surprise, he wrote back that his grandmother was ailing and he had taken over the running of the shop. The missive was not much, yet it was everything. As Elvira stands listening to the rain dripping onto the window ledge behind her, finally she feels at peace.

Chapter 39
EARLY IN THE NEW YEAR

At five minutes to ten on a bitterly cold moonless night in early January 1904, Don Zeno limps across the *piazza* and arrives at his church, pulls the large iron key from under his cape, turns it in the lock and pushes open the door. Making his way down the aisle, he stops every few yards to light a candle at the end of one of the pews, grateful, just this once, for the verger's drinking habits, which ensure that by now he will be safely snoring in his bed, or slumped in front of a fire that has long since gone out, dozing off his daily intake. The last thing the priest wants is for the verger to discover the church unlocked and candles flickering at the windows, a circumstance that would panic him into puffing around the village, banging on doors and shrieking at the top of his voice that the devil had come to take them all. A carriage, quieter than the motorcar, draws up as a bell sounds out the hour, a signal for the horse to stamp its hoofs and let out a series of whinnying snorts. Ida's husband, Giuseppe, is the first to step down, and when he has straightened his coat and realigned his hat, he walks around and opens the nearside door, reaching in to help Elvira climb safely down onto the flagstones. Illuminated by starlight, and with only a handful of people to see her, she looks quite lovely in a soft wool coat and matching hat with a fashionable wisp of netting arranged on her brow.

Don Zeno is waiting by the altar rail, and as he watches Elvira coming down the aisle on the arm of her brother-in-law, he is struck by her pace, which is slow and leisurely, as if she is savouring each moment of the short journey. Then, as she passes a candle, he notices the colour of her outfit, which is the same green as the letters he had collected from Andrea's bar week in, week out, and taken back to his presbytery to burn. He steps forward to greet her, his face glowing from the satisfaction of knowing that he has done his Lord's will.

'Welcome, my dear,' he says, taking her hand, which trembles in his own like a small bird.

The ceremony is over in a matter of minutes, the facts noted meticulously in the parish records:

Maestro Giacomo Puccini, son of Michele and Albina Magi, and Elvira Bonturi, widow of Narciso Gemignani, born in Lucca and resident in this village, having obtained the dispensation of the three canonical banns, being free of the impediment of crime and with no impediment now existing against the valid and lawful celebration of their marriage, were by me here, subscribed the third of January 1904, united in the holy bonds of Matrimony in the presence of the two witnesses, Signor Giuseppe Razzi and Signora Ida Razzi.

Neither Fosca nor Antonio attend, and the occasion goes unmarked in the villa.

The next day, Puccini leaves for Milan to begin rehearsals of *Madama Butterfly*, his only comment recorded in a brief note to his wife.

'Now are you happy?'